BIG SHOULDERS

William Jamerson

Pine Stump Publishing
Escanaba, Michigan

www.williamjamerson.com

Cover Design: Ingrid Blixt
Woerpel Images, Escanaba, MI

Cover CCC Photo provided by: The Delta County Historical Society

PUBLISHER'S CATALOGING-IN-PUBLICATION DATA

Jamerson, William Brian.

Big shoulders : looking for his dad, a boy finds a father / William Jamerson.

p. cm.

ISBN 978-1-882882-12-0

1. Coming of age—Fiction. 2. Michigan—Fiction.

PS3610.A44 B54 2007
813`.6—dc21 2007934159

To Michael,

Who got so much from the CCC

And who gave back so much more.

Acknowledgments

When I came to understand the tremendous impact the Civilian Conservation Corps made in the state of Michigan, I resolved to tell their story. My interest began in 1991, when as a documentary filmmaker, I discovered a roll of 8mm film depicting CCC enrollees harvesting trees at Chittendon Nursery and planting them in the Manistee National forest. From Chuck Symons' excellent book, *We Can Do It!* I learned the CCC planted 480 million trees, more than any other state in the country. The CCC also constructed 7,000 miles of truck trails, built over 500 bridges, planted over 150 million fish and spent 140,000 man-days fighting forest fires. Over its nine-year run from 1933 to 1942, over a hundred thousand young men enlisted in the corps and occupied an average of fifty-seven camps annually.

In June of 1992, I attended a Civilian Conservation Crops reunion at North Higgins Lake State Park where I met many former enrollees eager to tell their stories. The Civilian Conservation Corps Museum across from the park is a must-see for anyone interested in learning about the corps. It includes a barracks, lookout tower, a nursery and a bronze statue of a CCC boy. I subsequently used those interviews in a PBS program I produced, *CAMP FORGOTTEN – The Civilian Conservation Corps in Michigan.* The hour-long program aired on over sixty PBS stations nationwide.

The legacy of the CCC goes beyond the improvements they made to our natural resources. The CCC transformed the lives of young men who needed work and lacked self-discipline and confidence. They came from families on relief who struggled through The Great Depression. The work camps not only provided food, shelter and work, but offered evening classes, chapel services and sports opportunities. Almost every man I spoke with at the reunion said the CCC was a life-changing experience.

Over the years, I developed many wonderful friendships with these men while attending their reunions. I also participated in the ad-hoc *Bring Back the CCC Committee* that was successful in reinstating two CCC camps in Michigan in the late 1990s, Camp Vanderbilt and Camp Alberta. Much of the credit for our success goes to the Rev. Bill Fraser, our inspiring leader and a former CCC enrollee, and Dale M. Herder, Ph.D., our long-time chairman. Some of the active committee members included Richard Laing, John Roundtree, Frank Munger and John Selesky. Many more contributed their time and energy.

Special thanks for this book go to the members N.A.C.C.C.A. Chapter #129 in Grayling, Michigan, of which I am a proud member. They have devoted themselves to preserving the legacy of the CCC by identifying abandoned camps with signage, hosting CCC reunions and promoting the sale of bronze statues of a CCC boy to state parks and forests across the country.

Many of the stories in the book I gained from first-hand interviews from the many reunions I attended over the years. Any resemblance between real and fictional persons is purely coincidence.

I am grateful to the readers of my manuscripts who provided valuable feedback. Mary Cole, Pat Fittante and Peter Gianakura each brought a different perspective in their critical analysis. Sandy Vincent from the Newaygo Historical Society provided wonderful source materials. A special thanks to my CCC friends Mike Rataj, John Selesky and Stan Ward who read my drafts and made helpful comments and suggestions.

Marsha Garvin, my line editor, is proof positive, that "to write is human, to edit is divine." Janet Flickinger-Bonarski, my story editor, reviewed my manuscripts with a trained eye. Her wise comments and suggestions were invaluable and helped make this a better book.

Foreword

It was in the height of The Great Depression in 1933, that President Franklin Roosevelt created the Civilian Conservation Corps. The federal program put unemployed young men to work restoring our nation's damaged natural resources. The seventeen to twenty-five year-old young men came from families on relief. Over three million enrollees enlisted nationally during the nine-year duration of the program.

Non-commissioned army officers administered the camps while forest service officers, conservation officers and local experienced men led the enrollees in resource conservation and building projects. CCC boys fought forest fires, built state parks and planted hundreds of millions of trees. They also created truck trails, restored riverbanks, built fish hatcheries and eradicated plant diseases.

Educational advisors taught evening classes on engine repair, woodworking, typing and other trades. Many boys earned their eighth-grade diplomas while chaplains provided spiritual guidance on Sundays. The young men went into nearby towns on weekends for recreation.

The enrollees earned thirty dollars a month, with twenty-five dollars sent directly to their families and the balance given to the boys. Their income not only supported their families back home, but also provided much needed revenue to surrounding communities. The CCC did more than restore America's wilderness; it transformed the lives of young men, many who never had a job before.

Characters
Alphabetical Order

Agnes	camp mascot - beagle
Arky	enrollee; Arkansas hillbilly
Betty	Nick's girlfriend
Bricks	enrollee; assistant leader
Captain Bullock	company leader
Curly	camp baker
Czeslaw	Nick's older brother
Doris	Frank's girlfriend
Farmer	enrollee; camp bully
Frank	enrollee; Nick's best friend
Gabe	Nick's younger brother
Isaac	Local Experienced Man
José	enrollee; dynamite expert
Lefty	neighborhood beat cop
Luke	enrollee; troublemaker
Mario	enrollee; Bobby's best friend
Mr. Kiefer	head cook
Mr. Koski	stone mason
Mr. Mulligan	First Sergeant (Senior Leader)
Mr. Thacker	Supply Sergeant
Mr. Wells	Native American educational advisor
Nick	enrollee; on probation
Ollie	enrollee; practical joker
Rosie	cobbler's daughter
Scruggs	enrollee; barracks leader
Squirt	enrollee; truck driver
Sweet Bobby	enrollee; orphan
Thelma/Rusty	lumber camp owners
Turk	enrollee with bad temper

We Can Do It!

—CCC Motto

No, you can't!

—Sgt. Mulligan

Chapter 1

Born at the Wrong Time

I was always a lousy crook—they either caught me or someone squealed on me. In 1937, during The Great Depression, I stole a pair of shoes during my junior year in high school. What I did was wrong, but I was desperate *and* impatient, two things that will turn a good boy into a thief. Who told me I was a good boy? Our neighborhood beat cop. He should know, because he busted me for stealing those shoes. Today, I think of them as my *lucky* shoes, but back then, they only brought humiliation.

If my high school had sponsored an ugly shoe contest, they would have paid me *not* to enter. It wouldn't have been fair to the others—my shoes were *that* awful. People cringed or looked away when I came down the hall. Students often snickered or laughed, and who could blame them? The shoes *flapped* when I walked because the soles had separated from the leather uppers. I kept my feet close to the floor when I shuffled down the hallway.

Those shoes were a big deal to me because they were the only pair I owned. God knows how many times I tried to fix them. I wrapped tape around them, but it wore off. I tried glue, but it still came apart, *and* it burned my feet. The cobbler offered to repair them for only twenty cents, but I couldn't afford it. Twenty cents bought three or four dozen eggs in those days, and in our family, food came before feet. The only way to get new shoes was from a relief agency.

I avoided going to the agency as long as possible because I felt ashamed when people recognized me there. After a few weeks of putting up with the shoes, I gave in and went to the agency. A tired-looking woman in line ahead of me held a cranky baby in her arms. When she gave me a hopeful smile, I looked away. Her three scruffy children played jacks on the floor with *stones* instead of jacks. A stubble-faced man who stood behind me wore a threadbare suit and reeked of alcohol. After an hour or so, I stood in front of a frumpy, gray-haired woman seated behind a big wooden table.

"Name?" she asked without looking up.

"Radzinski, Nick," I answered.

"Been here before?"

"Yes, ma'am." She flipped though an index card box.

"What do you need?" She asked with her eyes down.

"Shoes."

"What size?"

"Nine." She scribbled down the information.

"Come back in two weeks...next." She never looked up the entire time! I wanted to crawl into a hole. Maybe she thought I was ugly. I got sucker-punched my freshman year when I was standing at my locker and my nose grew back slightly bent. My bushy brown hair looked like a mop, and my shoulders stood out. I was an average-sized guy, but I had the shoulders of a tackle with the Detroit Lions. In fact, my friends even called me *Shoulders*. It was a good thing my shoulders were big, because I carried an eight-hundred-pound chip on them.

I walked out the door of the relief agency straight into a chilly March wind—Detroit was like that in the spring. I buttoned up my coat and hurried down the sidewalk. On my right, I passed an intelligent-looking man in a heavy overcoat selling apples out of a bushel basket. The neatly written sign read *Apples—Five Cents.* The man glanced down, just like the relief woman.

It dawned on me that he looked away because it helped him sell more apples. Maybe the relief woman looked away so not to embarrass anyone. I felt lousy. The crummy economy caused all the trouble. From the time I was ten years old, The Great Depression was all I knew. There was no money, no jobs, no food and nothing to do. I was *born at the wrong time.* My parents had never lived through a great depression—why should I? My grandparents never knew a great depression—why me? Every generation went through bad times, but *nothing* like The Great Depression.

One out of three dads stood in unemployment lines. Soup kitchens kept open around the clock feeding the hungry. People lost their homes, and fathers abandoned their families. The few jobs went to men with families to support, so teenagers had no chance to work. I hung out on street corners or played baseball with my friends. Sometimes, I got into trouble.

I passed by a shoe store and looked into the window. Shiny leather shoes of all shapes and sizes dazzled my eyes. All I needed was a couple bucks and I could have walked out in a new pair. *Two weeks is too long a wait!* I continued walking. Krzymowski and Sons put a table outside their shoe store with markdowns so I decided to check them out. I got on a streetcar at Joseph Campau Avenue and rode it near the store. When I stepped out, I pulled my hat down and flipped my collar up.

I spotted the table of shoes in the distance and quickly cased out the scene. Only a few people were near the store, so I acted quickly. I made a beeline to the table and quickly picked out a pair of shoes my size. The soft leather felt good in my hands, they would feel better on my feet. A police siren in the distance made my head jerk—it was a bad omen.

I hesitated. Part of me wanted to put the shoes down and

walk. A cop busted me a few weeks earlier for stealing a canned ham, and I dreaded another run-in with the judge. I shook off my doubts—three years on the track team gave me confidence. After a quick peek in the window, I stuck the shoes inside my coat and walked away

A few seconds later, a man yelled, "Stop, thief!" *Oh, boy, here I go again!* I took off as if someone had shot a starting pistol. I sprinted down the street with my shoes flapping. After a few blocks, I ducked into an alley—a big mistake. Seated on a crate with a cigarette in his hand, was our neighborhood beat cop. My heart sank—this was serious.

The lieutenant smiled dryly. "What do you got under your coat, Nick?"

"Ah…nothing," I stammered. "Sure is cold."

"Yep, it's cold all right." he muttered, took a drag and tossed his smoke. Lefty Lefowicz was a tall, thin cop with a beak of a nose that smelled trouble a mile away. "C'mon," he snapped, "open it up."

I unbuttoned my coat and handed him the shoes. He studied them for a moment and twisted his mouth into a brief sneer. "So…you've been doing some shopping, eh?" He grabbed my arm firmly. "Let's go," he muttered.

That was the story of my life—busted for doing the wrong thing for the right reason. I *needed* those damn shoes! While we walked to the station, I flicked my toes up to make a louder slapping noise. Lefty gave me a sideways glance and smirked; he knew what I was doing.

I thought about what my mother would do to me when I got home. When she knew I was in trouble, she hid an ironing cord under her apron. As I walked by her in the kitchen, she took it out, and whipped me on the butt. It hurt just thinking about it.

Two weeks later, I slouched in a chair in Judge Jenning's office with half a dozen other boys. Lieutenant Lefowicz had recommended us for the CCC. Lefty sat in the corner of the room with his arms folded, eyeing us. Thick law books filled the shelves behind the judge's desk. The judge looked distinguished in his gray suit, but his curly, gray hair hung messily over his collar. He needed a haircut.

"You're all on probation for one year," the judge said in a deep voice. "You *can* go home, but I *strongly* suggest you join the CCC. If you stick around here, you'll just get into more trouble."

Then he gave us a short lecture on choosing friends. "You have to get away from this environment and your so-called friends. They're really not your friends...they're just guys you get in trouble with." Then he took questions.

"Is the CCC like a juvenile home?" a boy asked.

The judge tamped tobacco in his pipe. "No," he said. "Maybe one in twenty has a police record. The CCC is for good boys from families on relief."

"Then why should *we* go?" a skinny kid asked.

The judge struck a match and lit his pipe. "Well...all of you come from families on relief and the lieutenant sees something good in you."

A boy with a whiney voice asked, "So why do we have to be on probation for *a whole year*? It's not fair."

The judge rubbed his chin thoughtfully. "You don't think that's fair? Okay, I'll tell you what...I'll make it *two years*." The boy's jaw dropped.

After his pitch, the judge asked for our decision. We all said yes. He leaned forward. "You made the right choice. I don't want trouble out of any of you...and *no fighting*."

When I walked out of his office, I realized what I had agreed to. *I'm going to a work camp for stealing a pair of shoes. I must be crazy!*

My mother waited in the lobby. She looked ten years older than her age, with a head of gray hair and face full of deep wrinkles. "I'm so proud of you," she said when I told her the news. She gave me a big hug.

"Geez, Mom, it's like going to Sing-Sing."

"Don't say that," she said. "You saw what it did for Alfonse and Fabian."

"Yeah, I know." They were a couple of toughies who came back from the CCC saying "yes, sir," and "no, sir."

Lefty caught up with us in the cloakroom and helped my mother with her coat. "Nick," he said, "you're a good kid, you just got to get away."

I said nothing.

"C'mon, put a smile on your mug—you're getting three meals a day and some dough in your pocket."

For the last few years, Lefty had caught me skipping school, stealing, and destroying property. When he brought me home, he would slap my face right in front of my mother. Mom always took his side. "Slap him a few more times for me," she said when he finished. I wondered if they slapped boys in the CCC.

On the streetcar ride home, my mother mentioned some guys I knew who were in jail. "You made the right choice—you're not going behind bars."

"Oh, yeah?" I said. "There's better food there than home." She slapped my arm. As we walked home, the air smelled of furnace smoke from the rundown rental houses in our neighborhood.

"When you come back in a year, things will be different," my mother said.

"How's that?"

"Because *you* will be different, you won't want to be part of that street life anymore."

"Sure Ma." Unless I found a job, I knew where I would be.

That night, I struggled with where I wanted to live. On one hand, I hated the cheap apartment we lived in, with all the noisy neighbors, creaky pipes and musty smell. On the other hand, I worried about living in a work camp run by a bunch of ex-army officers.

Then, there was my dog. Somebody in the apartment house left the yard gate open so Queenie got out. A car hit her. I had a hunch a certain person left the gate open on purpose, because Queenie barked a lot. That was what dogs did, they barked. So they killed her. From a table drawer, I took out a photo album with a cracked leather binding. It told the story of a family marred by tragedy. I put my feet up on the sofa and edged closer to the lamp.

The first seven years of my life, I lived on a dairy farm in Bay City, Michigan. I was born in 1920, at a time when horse-drawn wagons were common, phones were hand-cranked and children still walked to one-room schoolhouses. The simplicity of those days still gives me a feeling of nostalgia. The aroma of bread baking in the oven, the sight of cows coming in from pasture and the sound of the dinner bell, even now brings a smile to my face. There was a natural rhythm and order to each day, as predictable as the rising and setting of the sun.

But behind the tranquil scene, hidden forces were at work. I was ignorant of most of those things, but sometimes at the dinner table, I heard talk about the lack of rain or the low price of milk. In spite of hardships, our family endured. Money was tough to come by, but we always had food on the table. My dad bartered with other farmers, trading milk for produce. This was important because there were six children to feed. Although it happened almost eighty years ago, the events of one cold winter day in February of 1927 are still vivid in my mind.

My ten-year-old brother had fallen through the ice on a river as he walked home from school. Our two older sisters jumped in to save him, but were unable to lift him out of the water. The girls managed to climb out, but as they walked home, they collapsed and froze to death. That left Czeslaw, my older brother, my younger brother Gabe and me, as the only children left in the family.

The flowers brought by family and friends did little to

ease the sadness in our home. People came from near and far to pay respects. I can recall images of people huddled in the doorway, whispers in the hall, the scuffling of boots on our wood floor. Two somber men in uniform came in with big round hats in their hands. I later found out they were the state police. My folks shooed my younger brother and me away to our room while the men asked my parents questions. Gabe cried and cried—it drove me crazy. I wanted the men to go away.

The warmth and happiness in our little house disappeared that winter. How I missed my mother's laugh. I remember the far-away look in her eyes, it seemed like the light went right out of her life. My father rarely spoke and retreated to his whittling.

"Your brother and sisters have gone to heaven," my mother told me every time I asked where they went. I had no idea where heaven was, but I knew people never returned from there. It bothered me that I had no sisters to grow up with anymore. A few days before their death, I wrestled for fun with one of them in our living room. She pinned me down and tickled me until I thought I would die. Then she died.

My siblings' deaths had a profound effect on me. Death was no longer something far away, but a thing that could happen in a moment. For the first time in my life, I feared being alone and separated from my family. I shuddered when I looked at my departed brother's empty bed.

In time, winter faded away. Fields of snow gave way to pastures of green oats and barley. The cows produced a lot of milk that summer, but so did the cows on other farms. A milk surplus made prices fall so low, that it cost more to produce it than to buy it. Without an income, Dad could not pay his taxes.

One day, I walked out of the barn to see my dad and older brother stacking furniture in our rusty Model A truck.

I knew right then we had lost the farm and ran crying to my mother. Even the candy she gave me did little to cheer me up. When it came time to leave, my younger brother and I squeezed between my parents. As we drove by a sugar beet field, we saw Mexicans stooped over as they weeded crops with short, three-foot-long hoes. My mother said it was cruel to give a person a short hoe. "I never saw a white man with a short hoe in my life," she said. It seemed to me everyone who tried to make a living off the land got a bum deal.

We moved to the city of Hamtramck near Detroit, because my dad had relatives there. Dad rented a house with fake brick exterior and pipes that rattled. My father found a job as a millwright at the nearby Dodge plant, and he rode the streetcar to work each morning with a lunch pail in his hand.

Our family had grown with the addition of my new baby sister Anya. Her cheerful smile brought sunshine into our home. The move to Hamtramck and the arrival of the baby seemed to give us a fresh start. To a boy of eight, everything seemed new and exciting. A neighbor boy took me to visit the school I would attend in the fall. The three-story brick building looked huge.

"I can't go to that school," I said. "I'll get lost in it."

"You'll get used to it," he said. "It's easy to find the rooms."

I was confused. "You mean we go to more than *one room*?"

A bowling alley stood a few blocks away from our house and a candy store was nearby, too. Cars came and went at all hours of the day. We heard the clang of the streetcar from one street over and the occasional wail of a fire engine. The sounds of the city thrilled me and kept me awake at night wondering what was happening.

During our first winter in the city, my baby sister got sick. She caught cold after my older brother gave her a bath. My father should have repaired a hole in the window above the tub, but instead, he stuck a rag in it. When the rag fell out, the frigid air blew in. My sister's cold turned into pneumonia and Anya died a few weeks later. She was only six months old. It happened a year after the loss of my other siblings and again plunged our home into gloom and despair.

The number of children my mother had lost was shocking. It haunts me even now to think of it. With the death of Anya, my mother had lost three children to natural death, three to miscarriage, and three more to accidental death. The number *three* was sacred in the Christian religion, but not in my family.

When my sister passed on, my father grew sullen and blamed himself for her death. He spent his free hours at the workbench working quietly on his carvings. When I came to cheer him up, he spoke little. Dad slid into a depression and within a couple weeks lost his job. My mom supported the family with her job as a waitress, but money was tight. We soon found a cheaper home to rent. My family's money problems led to arguments between my parents. It seemed like they fought every night with yelling and furniture banging around. I wanted to run upstairs and protect her, but I was too afraid so I stuck my head under the pillow.

One morning, my mother came down the stairs with bruises on her arms. When my older brother Czeslaw saw the marks, he confronted my dad and threatened to kill him if he ever laid a hand on Mom again. My brother could do it too—he was twenty-three years old and stood six inches taller than Dad.

A month later, my folks quarreled in the kitchen while my mother cooked potato pancakes. Dad took the spatula from her hand and smacked her on the face, making a big red mark. He skipped town before Czeslaw found out and never returned.

The day my father left, I came home from school and found his dark-stained baseball glove on my bed. It had a big thumb and three fat fingers, and was much too large for my hand. Dad had promised me a new mitt for my birthday, but it was still months away. When I showed the glove to my mother, she forced a smile and gave me a big hug.

"You'll be a great ball player someday," she said.

Confused more than unhappy, I sulked over Dad's leaving. In one way, I was glad he left, because he had hurt Mom. But, I still loved him and hoped he came home and would be nice to her. It took months before it sank in that he was gone for good.

I wondered if *I was the reason* Dad ran away. When things went wrong, children blame themselves. After my father lost his job, he spent more time at home and had to put up with Gabe and me fighting all the time. Dad lost his temper easily and yelled at us for little things like coming in the house with dirty shoes. As I grew older, I realized I was not the reason he left.

The first months after my dad left were scary for my brother and me, because we were afraid the relief lady might take us away. She checked to see if my mother had enough food to feed us and that we were properly clothed. Mom's job at the restaurant kept her busy twelve hours a day. She scraped enough money together to pay the six-dollar-a-month rent and keep food on the table. I remember how Mom reacted the day she found a bag with cans of food on our back stoop. She sat on a kitchen stool, holding her apron up to her face sobbing.

At first, Mom was irate that Dad deserted us, but after a few years, she softened up. "A man can only take so much sorrow in his life," she used to say. I took the opposite position. The more she struggled, the more I resented my father. I thought he was heartless and self-centered and should have returned home. If he had walked in the door, I would have kicked him in the shin. I hated him for what he did.

Gabe and I quickly made friends in our new neighborhood. We attended a Catholic school where most of the kids spoke Polish in the schoolyard. I studied hard and behaved in class, but as I got older, I challenged the teachers. In those days, teachers did not like us to have our own opinions, so I often got in trouble. One day I asked a nun in catechism if Jesus ever got married. She called me up, wrapped my knuckles with a ruler, and sent me to the priest, where I got a stern lecture.

One day I had to report to the priest's office where Gabe was already waiting with Mother Superior. My brother had asked a girl if her breasts gave out milk. When the girl reported him to the nun, her teacher threw a fit. The priest told Gabe he was not welcome in school anymore. Mother Superior gave me a stern look and said, "You better let Nick go too."

"Huh?" I said, bewildered.

The priest looked nervously at me and then back to the nun. I knew who wore the pants in that room. "You better go, too," he mumbled.

I cried afterwards, because I really liked two of my teachers, Sisters Erika and Angelika. Sister Erika later came to our house and spoke to my mother. She said Mother Superior should not have kicked me out. I loved Sister Erika and felt a special bond with her even though I was only ten. It was a shame Erika was a nun, because she was beautiful and deserved a husband. In fact, I wanted to marry her.

My mother continued to take Gabe and me to church. I never liked confession and long prayers; they seemed like something from the old country. I rebelled against the church teachings. How could it be the will of God to let my brother and sisters drown? And if God was watching over me, why did he let my dad run away? The Bible said everything God made was good, so why did we have The Great Depression?

My mother made me attend catechism. The only thing

I liked about Holy Communion was looking at the pretty girls when they walked down the aisle in their white dresses, with flowers in their hair. It looked like a wedding, a marriage between the children and the church. But, it was not my wedding—I wanted nothing to do with church.

While the realm of the church was stern and cold, I found life on the street exciting and fun. You could hear Polish spoken around every corner. In fact, you could live your whole life in Hamtramck without speaking a word of English. My town looked like someone had carved a city out of Poland and dropped it into the middle of Detroit. People spoke Polish at the flower stand, in restaurants and on the streetcar. You heard the language spoken by everyone, from the butcher to shoeshine boys. We even had local newspapers written in Polish. Polka music streamed out of radios in barbershops and vegetable markets.

The town came alive on Saturday night, when it seemed like everyone went out dancing. I sneaked into dance halls with my buddies to watch people do the polka and jitterbug. Women with flushed cheeks smiled and laughed as men swung them around to the exciting music. When the songs turned naughty, the adults chased us out.

Before I went out on Saturday nights, Mom always cooked my favorite Polish dish, a potato and cheese dumpling called pirogi. My mother, my brother and I made an assembly line at the kitchen counter. Using a drinking glass, my mom cut a round circle in the dough and then slid it over to me. I put cheese and potatoes on it and passed it to Gabe, who folded the dough over into a half-moon shape and crimped the edges. His little fingers were the perfect size for the job.

Mom boiled the dumplings in water, dried them off, and then fried them in grease where she had just cooked onions. The frying dumplings made the best smell in the world. The taste of the melted cheese and potatoes was mouth-watering and put a smile on my face every time.

Other nights, I often lay awake in bed on an empty stomach. The kitchen shelves in our house rarely had more than a few cans of soup or beans. The day-old bread Mom bought at the store was really a week old and hard as a rock. She paid ten cents for two loaves. If there was no meat or cheese in the icebox, we ate the bread plain with margarine. I turned ornery when I was hungry.

During my early teenage years, I became jealous of other families who had more things than I did. It bothered me that other people owned cars and their children wore nice clothes. I hated going out to the garage to use the bathroom when other families had indoor plumbing. The jealousy made me grouchy. If I passed a neighbor on the sidewalk, I looked the other way. A couple of times I walked past some nuns and didn't even take off my hat!

I think I was thirteen or fourteen when I began to steal, but I never had the *heart* of a crook. Once, I stole a bicycle from a neighbor, but when I saw him delivering newspapers on foot the next day, I felt sorry for him. That night, I put the bike on his porch, rang the bell, and ran away.

Breaking into a building was a no-no. In fact, I never lifted anything *inside* of a store, only *outside* where they put stuff on tables out on the sidewalk. Stealing did not seem quite so bad when it happened outside. After I stole something, I knew all the shortcuts and alleyways to outrun adults.

My favorite get-away was around the corner of the Ferry Market on Chene Street. I ran down an alley, climbed a fence, cut across a backyard and scaled another fence. A big German shepherd waited in the backyard. There was time to cross the yard, because the dog sat up on the porch next to the house. It gave me about five seconds before he could catch me. But, when the person chasing me climbed over the fence, the dog was waiting. Our beat cop was wise to the trick, but others fell for it. I will never forget the sound of that dog barking with a man screaming, "Get away...get away from me!"

My friends and I were selective from whom we stole. Most sweet shops sold ice cream for two cents a scoop or four cents for two scoops, but one store sold two scoops for only *three cents*. We never stole from that store because we wanted to return to buy ice cream. At another store, the shopkeeper often gave us two pieces of penny candy for one cent. We never stole from him, either. I think he did it to keep us from stealing.

If any of my friends stole *inside* a store, he was not a friend anymore. We knew who was pinching what and we knew the penalty if we were caught. When we spent a night in a juvenile home, it was not a big deal, because we got a warm bed and a couple of good meals, but we knew better than to make it our home.

Sometimes I teamed up with my brother to steal. I worked as a stock boy in a grocery store and one day the grocer told me to put the cases of empty bottles in the backyard. I tipped off my brother who loosened a board in the fence next to the spot the bottles were stacked. Then he reached inside the fence and grabbed them. Czeslaw took the bottles back into the store for the deposit money. I got a handful of pennies and a few nickels for my share of the loot. Feeling good, I stood and waited at a street corner until people showed up. Then, I reached into my pocket and jingled the coins. I wanted the whole world to know I had a pocketful of money.

Sometimes things went wrong and boys squealed on me if I did not share my booty with them. Once I stole a handful of bottle openers and a boy pestered me to give him a couple, but I refused. The next day the shopkeeper knocked at my door looking for those bottle openers. News traveled fast around my neighborhood, especially *bad* news. If a boy got in trouble, his mother often found out about it *before* he got home. Mom lost her temper when the cops brought me home. Sometimes she threw dishes at me in the kitchen. They smashed against the wall into a hundred pieces.

"When will you ever grow up?" she screamed.

One year, Gabe and I gave her some enameled teacups for her Christmas present because they were unbreakable. My mother thought it was mean of us, so we returned them.

I closed the photo album, reached over and pulled the chain on the lamp. The room went dark and I slowly stood up to go to my room. It felt like a chapter in my life was ending. In spite of the bad things that happened to my family, I was still afraid to leave home for a work camp.

In the weeks leading up to my CCC enlistment, I spent a lot of time second-guessing myself about my decision to enroll. Many questions filled my head, so I was relieved when Lefty finally called a meeting of the new recruits at the YMCA. A few of the boys walked in laughing and joking after shooting baskets. We sat around a big wooden table in a meeting room. Basketball and boxing trophies packed the glass case.

The lieutenant reached for the ashtray and took a pack of Camels from his front pocket. "For most of you boys, it'll be the first time in your life you ever worked." He scratched a match under the tabletop. "It's *not* going to be easy, but you can do it." I noticed some anxious looks around the table.

"There will be night classes for things like engine repair and woodworking...don't pass them up. I want each of you to come back here with some skills." Lefty got up and paced around the table. "After a week or two, some of you will get homesick, but whatever you do, *don't leave camp.* If you try to hitch a ride on a train, you might take the wrong one and end up in some rail yards. Any of you know what it's like getting stuck in a rail yard?" Most of us shook our heads.

He took a short drag. "You don't want to know. If you run away...you'll wish you'd stayed. You'll spend your *whole life* wondering what might have happened if you'd stuck it out." Then the lieutenant took questions.

A red-haired boy asked, "How much army stuff goes on?"

"It's *not* an army camp," Lefty replied. "No one's going to put a rifle in your hand and make you march."

"But why the uniforms?" the boy persisted.

"CCC camps are run like an army camp...but you're *not* training to be soldiers," he said, irritated.

"Can we leave camp on weekends?" a wiry kid asked.

Lefty grinned. "Are you kidding? They drive you into town on the weekends. Some of you will meet your next sweetheart up there." A few of us smiled, it sounded better all the time.

The lieutenant sat back down in his chair. "Most of you never got the whippings you deserved when you were kids...so you never learned to follow orders. *If* you want to make it in the CCC, do what they tell you and do it *the first time*. I don't want to see bad probation reports coming across my desk."

"Yes, sir," we muttered.

I felt better after the talk, still scared, but not as much as before. I wondered if I could live with so many rules. Lefty said the CCC punished boys by making them by do things like cut the grass or shovel the snow, but I suspected there was more he didn't tell us.

The toughest part of leaving was saying good-bye to my friends around town. Some of them I had known since I was a little kid, like Stash the iceman. His name was Stanley but most people called him by the Polish version. Stash was the only black man I knew who spoke Polish. He wasn't fluent, but he knew enough to get by.

"Lud, lud," he yelled as he drove down the street on his horse-drawn wagon. Women stuck their heads out the door and yelled how many pounds of ice they wanted. Stash opened the back hatch of the wagon and took out a block of ice with a pair of tongs. His biceps flexed as big as hams. As he carried the block of ice to the kitchen, his horse pulled the wagon up to the next house with no driver.

Stash built the wagon by himself and was very proud of it. When I asked him why there were no joints in the wood, he patted the side and said, "Dat's what dey call plaaa-wood...it's new."

"That's not real wood?"

He laughed. "Dat's real wood all right, but dey make it from little pieces glued together."

I ran my hand over it. "It's so smooth."

"Dey say it lasts longer den real wood."

I let out a low whistle. "What will you do if people trade their ice boxes in for refrigerators?"

He latched the door shut. "Don't worry 'bout ole Stash. If dey don't need ice, I'll deliver somethin' else."

"Like what?"

He thought a moment, and then grinned. "Maybe ice cream."

"That'd be great," I said. But, I still worried about him. Cars put horses out of business, so I figured refrigerators might do the same to the icebox.

Another friend of mine was Skip, the waffle man. Short and powerfully built, he wore bangs over his forehead like Moe in the Three Stooges. He did business out of a white truck with side panels that opened up into a counter top. The sweet aroma of his waffles was all the advertising he needed to attract a line of people. He charged a nickel for a waffle that was about twice the size of a hamburger bun and topped with powdered sugar.

Skip served up the food lightning fast as he poured batter on one set of irons and pulled hot waffles off another. He shuffled waffles out to the customers as if he was dealing cards. His forearms turned snowy white from the sugar. Skip gave boxing lessons to boys at the gym. I never boxed, but he gave me advice on staying out of trouble. "You talk too much, Nick," he would say. "Keep your mouth shut and eyes open."

I took his advice and kept quiet about the things I saw

on the street. As I became older, boys in the gangs noticed me and became friendly. They sent me to the store to buy pop or cigarettes. In time, they trusted me to deliver packages. One day, I peeked inside the paper wrapping of a package and saw a pistol! My eyes almost popped out. I delivered the gun, but I never collected my pay. It was the last package I ever delivered.

I found Skip cleaning his waffle irons. “Don’t let those bears get you,” he joked.

I leaned on his counter. “I’m going to miss it around here.”

He dipped his rag in soapy water. “They’re gonna pay you a buck a day...what are you moaning about?”

“Yeah, I know,” I said.

Later, he took a waffle out of the warmer. “It’s on me, kid. You be sure to come back in one piece.”

“Thanks,” I said and took a big bite. “I’ll be back.”

I hiked to Ferry Market to say good-bye to some of the people who sold produce. My favorite vender was Mrs. Rosenberg, a short, buxom Jewish woman who carried the best fruit in the market. The apples and pears she handled came wrapped in tissue paper and were spotless. She saved the tissues and flattened them on the counter. After she collected a neat pile, she put them into the garbage.

Gabe and I stopped by on our way home from school as little kids and picked through her garbage to find those tissues. We gave them to my mother who hung them on a nail for toilet paper. The toilet paper in our home was only for guests. When I stopped by the market, Mrs. Rosenberg was sorting through fruit. She wore the same green apron every day, with her dark hair pulled back behind her head.

“Nick,” she said with a warm smile. “I’m going to miss you...take a couple of these for your trip.” She picked up two apples.

“You don’t need to do that.” I said. “I just came to say good-bye.”

She leaned across the table and pressed the fruit into my hands. "You'll need them on the train," she said. I thanked her.

We chatted a few minutes about the CCC and then I said good-bye. After a few steps, I turned around. "Mrs. Rosenberg, there was something I always wanted to ask you."

She looked up. "What's that?"

I walked back to her table. "When I was a little kid, I used to go through your garbage."

"I know."

"Sometimes, when I was going through the garbage, you threw out fruit that was still good. What'd you do that for?"

She smiled gently. "I put it there for you and Gabe."

"I know, but why?"

She sighed. "Because you never begged like the other boys...you never *begged.*"

I bit my lower lip, stumped for something to say.

She came around the table and cupped my face with both her hands. "Take care of yourself, Nick...come see me when you get back." Her loving eyes were like dark pools of pond water.

"Sure, Mrs. Rosenberg...I'll come back someday."

I would miss Mrs. Rosenberg, but not my older brother. After my dad ran away, Czeslaw moved back into our house and brewed moonshine in an old barn in the backyard. Prohibition raged on and people wanted their booze. My brother made me deliver it around the neighborhood in a little wagon I called a "gig." I did what he told me because he was fourteen years older than I was.

He even made me deliver booze in the rain. Imagine, an eleven-year-old kid with a floppy hat, soaked to the bones, pulling a wagon loaded with mason jars of hooch. I delivered to all kinds of customers, from the fireman across the street to our dentist, who took liquor instead of money for my family's bills.

When the customers lived too far away, we rode in my brother's jalopy. Czeslaw cut a hole in the floor behind the front seat and covered it with a piece of carpet. He told me to empty the jars in the hole if cops chased us. One night when we were making a delivery, a police car followed us out of an alley. Czeslaw told me to get ready to pour out the booze. I got so scared I peed in my pants. Luckily, the cops turned away.

My brother belonged to the communist party. He blamed the rich for all the troubles in the world. Unfortunately, most people hated communists, so he often came home from political rallies bruised and bloodied. He moved to Kalamazoo where he worked at a talent agency representing novelty acts. Some of his clients included a one-arm juggler and a woman sword swallower. He booked them on a circuit from Chicago to Detroit, so he stayed at our house when he was in town.

A week before my CCC initiation, Czeslaw pulled up in his beat-up Dodge sedan to say good-bye. We sat on the porch steps of the apartment house. "If you change your mind about going, one of my acts needs someone to saw in half," he joked.

"No thanks, I'll do the sawing where I'm going."

"You ought to send an extra dollar or two to Mom..."

"Oh, so you're giving me advice?" I said, my junkyard dog attitude flared up. "Why? So you can mooch more off of Mom?"

My brother scowled. "Don't forget the bills I paid around here with the booze I made."

I slapped a baseball into my mitt. "How *can* I forget, I was the guy who delivered it...remember? And you never even paid me."

"What are you a wise guy?" my brother said and stood up. "I remember when you were still in diapers."

I got up and stuck out my jaw. "In case you haven't noticed, I'm seventeen now."

He smirked and walked over to his car. "Aw, dry up. You're still a shrimp." He climbed in and slammed the door. "I stop by to be a nice guy and say good-bye and you'd think I just shot your dog." He flicked his cigarette butt at me and drove off. I kicked an old beer can off the sidewalk. My brother made me do his dirty work when I was a kid and I learned my lesson. No one was going to push me around like he did.

On April 1, on a cold and dreary morning, I boarded a train to Battle Creek for my two-week CCC initiation at Camp Custer. I remember very little about those two weeks except that I spent most of the time standing in line for things like physicals, shots and getting supplies. The aptitude tests asked stupid questions, like does 2 x 2 = 5. Some of the fellas thought it was a trick question and answered it true. We endured endless jumping jacks, push-ups and long walks. My stiff boots gave me blisters and the uniforms itched like the devil. I came home with fresh needle marks on my arms and a bunch of sore muscles.

Three days after I returned home, I headed back to the train station for my trip north to the CCC camp. A terrible foreboding came over me as I rode on the streetcar with my mother and brother to the station. I stared out the window at sad-faced men standing on the sidewalks; they might be out of work, but at least they had their freedom. The minute I walked into the CCC camp my personal life was over, someone else owned me.

No one said much as we walked on the train platform. Short bursts of steam hissed out from the train cars. My stomach felt unsettled. "Don't be surprised if I come home early," I said to my mother. "It might not work out."

She turned to me with raised eyebrows and fire in her eyes. "Don't even *think* about coming home early," she said. "Radzinskis *never* give up."

"Yeah...sure," I said, well-knowing my dad gave up on fatherhood a long time ago.

"You're just as tough as any other boy," Mom said.

Gabe trailed behind quietly. He seemed sad that I was going, but did not admit it.

"You'll be seventeen in a year," I told him. "Maybe you can enlist someday."

"Someone's got to stay with Mom," he said and patted her back.

She frowned. "Don't worry about me," she said. "You can go too if you want to."

Mom's overcoat looked as faded as a weathered barn. "When you get that first pay check from Uncle Sam, use it to buy a new coat for yourself," I told her.

She said nothing.

"I mean it," I said.

"Okay," she said. "But first, I have to pay some bills."

When we got to the train car, she slipped some coins into my hand. "You look mighty handsome," she said and fixed my tie. "I bet some gal up there is going to fall for you."

"There's only one gal for me and I'm looking at her." She forced a smile. There was sadness in her gray eyes; as if all the color had faded away. The heavy worry lines on her face told of the sorrow in her life. I hoped the money she got from the CCC made her happier.

"You know we're not the kissing kind," she said before she leaned up and gave me a peck on the cheek. "Make me proud." She took a handkerchief from her purse and wiped away some tears.

"Don't forget to buy that new coat," I said.

"I won't." She sniffled.

I shook hands with my brother. "Let me know if the food's any good...I might sign up," he said.

"Sure, I'll let you know," I said and slapped him on the shoulder. "Take care of Mom...I'm counting on you."

"All aboard!" the conductor yelled further down the platform.

I stepped into the train with a gunnysack over my shoulder and turned to give them a quick wave.

A moment later, the conductor closed the door. The train jerked and slowly rolled out of the station. I walked down the aisle, found a seat and slid down the window. With my head sticking out, I waved to Mom and Gabe until they disappeared from view. I felt very alone.

Chapter 2

Rookie

The train wound its way slowly out of Detroit, past apartment buildings, junkyards and abandoned factories. The gentle rocking motion felt soothing. I leaned near the window and watched for people. Hobos warmed themselves around a fire that burned in an oil drum. Small children with pails in hand ran along the tracks looking for pieces of coal that engineers tossed out for them. They took it back home to grateful parents.

I bunched up my sweater to cushion my head and closed my eyes. My thoughts turned back to the early days of the depression and the reason why I was going to the CCC in the first place. It took a couple years after the stock market crash of 1929 before the economy turned sour.

A neighbor lost his job at the Dodge plant around that time and sold firewood door to door to earn money. I followed him along the sidewalk as he pushed his wheelbarrow of logs. I would run up to ring the doorbells to save him the trip. He gave me his gum wrappers so I could lick off the powdered sugar. The man had moved out of his home into a rooming house so his wife qualified for relief.

People who kept their jobs were not much better off than those who lost them. Many worked fewer hours with less pay. Before the depression, my mother earned a couple dollars a day as a waitress. When the bad times hit, her income dropped in half. Mom's tips went from nickels to pennies. She counted her earnings at the kitchen table after work, sliding two pennies at a time into the palm of her hand. The image of my mother sitting under the light bulb made me sleepy.

A hard jolt woke me up. The train had shifted tracks as it entered the Saginaw train yards. A railroad policeman walked through the rain wearing a dark wide-brim hat and oilskin raincoat that hung to his knees. He carried a lantern in one hand and a nightstick in the other as he looked for hobos trying to hitch rides on passing trains.

An old tramp once told me there were good train dicks and bad ones. He said that the dicks had to hit you with their sticks to teach you a lesson, but the good ones held their swing back just before they connected because they felt sorry for you. The bad dicks who really laid into you were cold-hearted. He said they had to be, because when you hurt people for a living, you could not show any feelings.

I turned away from the window and looked across the aisle. A couple with two small boys ate cold chicken with their hands. It reminded me of the time I stole a goose off a farmer's truck a month earlier. As I ran away with the big bird in my arms, it flapped its wings so hard it almost broke my neck. The farmer did not chase me because my buddies were ready to grab his other birds if he left his truck. Mom scolded me when I walked in the house with it. "You should have taken it back," she said.

I lied. "Geez, Mom...I couldn't catch up to him."

She knew I stole it. "It still doesn't make it right."

We cleaned and gutted the goose in our backyard. My mother did most of the work, since I had a weak stomach when it came to blood and guts. When I was a boy on the farm, my dad made me carry away the intestines after he gutted a pig. It made me sick to my stomach. I never got used to it.

My mother roasted the goose to perfection in our oven and made rich gravy that we poured on the meat and boiled potatoes. It felt like Christmas in our house that night. The best part of the meal was watching my mother. She always ate quickly, hardly speaking a word. When she laid her knife and fork on her dish she smiled with contentment.

"Good, yes?" she said in Polish. My brother and I happily nodded as we chewed away. As I reminisced about that delicious meal, the gentle rocking of the train lulled me back to sleep.

Several hours later the train arrived in Mackinaw City, the northernmost town in Lower Michigan. They disconnected our car from the engine and loaded us onto a big dark train ferry called the *Chief Wawatum* for the trip across Lake Michigan.

I stepped outside the train during the crossing and climbed up the narrow metal steps to the deck. The cold damp air felt like the inside of an icebox and gave me the shivers. The wake from the boat trailed off over the smooth lake surface. I took a deep breath of the moist lake air and gripped the cold handrails. I felt like a sailor at sea. After a few minutes, I went back inside to warm up.

The ferry ride lasted less than an hour, but when we came ashore, it felt like we had arrived in a different country. The horizon was barren except for a few lights in the town. I wondered why people lived up here and what they did for a living. They re-connected the train cars and we were on our way. I wrapped myself in my blanket and closed my eyes. Sunrise was only an hour or so away.

"Coffee, fresh hot coffee," a black porter in a neat gray uniform said in a hushed voice as he made his way along the aisle. I opened my eyes and dug a nickel out of my pocket. He poured me some coffee and with the warm cup cradled in my hands, I watched the sun come up over the barren landscape.

During the night, an attractive woman had sat next to me who looked to be in her early twenties. She was pretty enough to be in a Sears-Roebuck catalogue, with a head of auburn hair and a wide smile. She worked as a nurse at Fort Brady, the CCC district headquarters in Sault Ste. Marie.

"Small world," I said when she told me. "What do you treat the boys for?" I noticed the ring on her finger and envied the lucky guy who snared her.

She sipped her coffee. "Spider bites, the flu, broken noses."

"Are there a lot of fights?" That worried me.

She pursed her lips and shook her head. "I don't think so, but they have boxing teams...and they box to settle arguments."

I almost spilled my coffee. "What?"

The nurse smiled at my reaction. "They're called grudge matches." She offered me a piece of her donut.

"Nuts..." I said, and took it. "I should've taken boxing lessons when I had the chance."

"Don't worry," she said. "I think you can take care of yourself with those big shoulders." I blushed.

"If my nose gets busted maybe you can set it straight." Conversing with women was not my strong suit.

She looked amused. "I don't think that'll happen, but if it does, we'll fix you up."

We rode through an area covered with blackened tree stumps. Spindly roots that resembled spider legs held the stumps several feet off the ground. It looked like hell after the fire went out. The nurse said the soil under the stumps washed away after the fires. "That's the strangest sight I've ever seen," I said. "Those lumberjacks sure left a mess."

"That's why *you're* here...to reforest the land."

"But, I never planted a tree in my life."

"Don't worry, the foresters will teach you."

I stared out the window. The logged-over land looked ominous and gave me a funny feeling in my stomach. "I wish I had some friends going with me." I said.

She patted the top of my hand. "You'll make new friends in no time."

We passed a sign that read TROUT LAKE and the train began slowing down. "Hey, this is it," I said and looked side to side. "It was swell talking with you." I stood and grabbed my gunnysack.

"Good luck," she said. "Don't let bed bugs bite you."

I grinned. "I won't." Then I turned and hurried down the aisle.

I stepped off the train onto the platform and saw a dozen CCC'ers clustered around a baggage cart off to the left. I was in no hurry to meet anyone so I walked to the back of the depot. The air smelled like wet leaves with a tang that I later would recognize as pine trees. The town of Trout Lake was no more than a dozen weather-beaten buildings. Five recruits hurriedly walked by, led by a skinny fella with greasy hair. He waved for me to join them. "You hungry?" he asked.

"Sure," I said and tossed my gunnysack on top of the others and ran to catch up with them. I joined them across the street at Johansson's General Store. Inside, the store smelled of new goods with shelves of overalls, wool sweaters and blankets. From cans of beans to sacks of flour, the store was a woodsman's dream. The head of a black bear glared down from above the cash register. Detroit seemed like a million miles away.

The aroma of smoked fish from the back of the store caught my attention. I went back and found tubs of trout, salmon, and chubs along with wheels of cheese in the glass deli case. I ordered a small piece of cheddar cheese and a hard roll for a snack. The grandfatherly shopkeeper glanced nervously at the other boys as he wrapped up my roll.

On my way out, I inspected the furs that hung on a wall. Pelts of raccoon, red fox, weasel, and beaver cost fifty cents to three dollars. I figured the skunk pelt would make a great present for my older brother. Back at the depot, I found a bench and ate my snack. The fella who invited me to the store, walked by and tossed me a Baby Ruth. "It's on me," he said.

I stuck it in my pocket. "Hey, thanks," I said. The boys seemed friendly. *I might like it up here!*

I chewed my roll and watched an occasional car pass by. After a few minutes, a forest green convoy truck pulled up with the words *Camp Raco 667th Company* painted on the door. I dusted the crumbs off my pants and hurried to get my bag. The door opened and a man in uniform stepped out with a clipboard in his hand and a hat that sat cockeyed on his head. A stout, fleshy man with a full face and thick lips—he *looked* like a sergeant. A few dozen of us bunched around him. He gave us the once over and made a sneer that looked like it went back three generations.

"Men, and I use that term loosely...welcome to the CCC. I'm your senior leader, my title is First Sergeant. Since I'm a non-commissioned officer, you can call me Mr. Mulligan. Or, you can call me sergeant. Or, you can call me sir. But, the first time one of you calls me *sarge*, you'll be on your hands and knees looking for that missing a-n-t until hell freezes over!" I felt my jaw drop. "The only people who call me *sarge* are my friends and I have NO FRIENDS!" We shuffled back a step.

He took out a handkerchief from his back pocket and noisily blew his nose. "I don't like surprises, so don't try to put anything over on me. I know *everything* that goes on in camp," he growled. "If you're sent to me for punishment, may God have mercy on you, because I WON'T!" I felt queasy. *What did I get myself into!*

Suddenly, the white haired shopkeeper from the general store appeared. I tensed up while he spoke to Mr. Mulligan. Something was wrong. A minute later, the sergeant turned around with a gnarled up face. "Which one of your knuckleheads stole those candy bars?" My knees buckled. *I still have the candy bar!*

No one said a word, so the shopkeeper pointed to all of

us that came into his store. We stepped to the front. "Empty your pockets," the sergeant barked. I took out my candy bar, the only one who did. Mr. Mulligan stuck his nose an inch from my face—his breath stank like rotten meat. "Did you steal that?"

My insides churned, I said nothing.

"Well...did you?" he snapped.

I took a deep breath. "Yes, sir."

The sergeant showed no reaction and moved to the next boy. "And you?"

"No sir." All the others denied it too.

"About ten candy bars were stolen, and I don't think he ate them all by himself," the sergeant said, pointing at me. "Some of you guys are lying." He ordered each of us to give Mr. Straub a dime to cover the cost of the candy. Then he told us to report to his office when we got to camp. After a quick roll call, we boarded the truck and sat on two long benches that faced each other.

The ride to camp seemed to take forever. A canvas top over our heads protected us from the wind. I watched the dreary landscape though the opening in the back. While the other boys laughed and joked, I gritted my teeth. I felt dumber than a box of rocks. The boy next to me tried to cheer me up. "Hey, at least you didn't squeal."

"Oh yeah? Well, I should've," I muttered. Luke, the boy who gave me the candy bar, sat at the other end of the truck. He knew I was furious. *How can I be so stupid!*

I rubbed my arms to warm up from the chilly draft that blew in from the rear. It felt cold for the middle of April, too cold. In time, the boys quieted down until the only sound we heard was stones hitting the underbelly of the truck. The skies darkened and a gentle rain began to fall. After an hour's drive, the truck pulled into camp. We passed by two stone pillars at the entrance, and soon came to a stop in a large muddy parking lot.

We stepped outside into a cold drizzle. A dozen or so

army-type buildings laid out in a large square made up the camp. They called the grass area between the buildings "the quad." The flagpole and library stood in the center of the quad and a water tower rose up from behind the barracks near the woods. All the camp needed was a high wire fence to make it look like a prison. I hoisted my gunnysack over my shoulder and trudged up to my new home.

"It's a real toad choker," one of the boys joked about the rain. A few fellas laughed, but not me. At the barracks steps, I wiped the mud off my feet and stepped inside. The building felt toasty warm from the wood burning stoves at each end. Cots ran along the walls on both sides with green footlockers at the base of each bed. Our barracks leader was a rugged-looking, sandy-haired fella who made the rest of us look like high school freshmen. Johnny "Golden Boy" Scruggs was a lighthouse among lampposts—he stood at least six-and-half-feet tall. The twenty-one-year-old picked up his nickname from his seventeen Golden Glove wins in the boxing ring. One by one, he assigned us a cot, putting us in between the veterans.

"Now listen up," Scruggs said. I noticed a scar just below his cheekbone. "Fifty cents a month will be deducted from your paychecks for the next six months to pay for your footlocker. No food in the barracks...it brings in the ants." Then he went over the schedule, from reveille to curfew.

After unpacking, I reported to the First Sergeant with the other boys charged with the stolen candy. I felt nauseous, and anxious to find out what kind of punishment he planned for us. Few spoke as we walked along the concrete path. The six of us slowly made our way into his small office and stood shoulder to shoulder facing his desk. Large camp maps covered the wall behind him, and a single portrait of President Roosevelt stared out at us. Mr. Mulligan looked up from his desk—he puckered his lips as if he just bit into a lemon.

"Okay, fess up," he said. "Who stole those candy bars?" He waited for what seemed a minute. No one spoke. "If that's the way you want it, you're all getting the same punishment." He wrung his hands and glared at us. "You need to understand, *stealing* is a major offence. I don't care if it's a candy bar or a sack of potatoes, I WON'T STAND FOR IT!" We shifted uneasily.

He spoke in short, chopped sentences. "You embarrassed me today...you disgraced your camp...you jeopardized your future. For what...a stinking candy bar?" He shook his head in disgust.

"You better smarten up fellas, or you're not going to last." He confined us to camp for a month and ordered us to clear farmland each night after supper for the next two weeks. A nearby farmer had agreed to grow potatoes if the camp sent workers to pull weeds from his overgrown field.

The sergeant looked at the rain dripping down the windowpane and gave a cynical smile. "Since the weather is so lovely, you can begin work today." He dismissed us and we filed out.

"Radzinski, stay," he said. I held my breath as he opened a folder on his desk. "Do you know you're on probation?"

"Yes, sir."

He shuffled some papers and then glanced up. "You have a history of stealing...I want it to *remain* a history."

"Yes, sir."

"We have a dozen men on probation and I watch them *very carefully*. Understand?"

"Yes, sir." I breathed a sigh of relief when he dismissed me. *At least he didn't slap my face!*

I went straight to lunch. The sign above the mess hall door read TAKE ALL YOU WANT, BUT EAT ALL YOU TAKE. Three rows of picnic-style tables ran side by side with long open walkways in between. It looked like two hundred boys could fit in the room. Orderlies dressed in white uniforms, seated each person to make sure there were no empty spaces.

They brought out bowls of lamb stew, plates of dinner rolls and butter...real butter! The stew contained big chunks of meat, it was the kind of food that stuck to your ribs. I knocked off a couple bowls and ate several rolls.

"Was the sergeant tough on ya?" A redheaded boy asked from across the table. He spoke with a southern accent.

"Nah, just some weed pulling in a farmer's field," I said and chewed my food.

"Ya ever pull weeds before?" the boy asked. I noticed freckles covered most of his face.

"I've pulled a few dandelions," I joked.

He smiled, his buckteeth were big enough to eat corn through a picket fence. "Yer a city boy aren't cha?"

I took a swig of milk and nodded. "Where are *you* from?"

"Arkansas." He went by the name *Arky* and said he lived with his aunt in Michigan before he enlisted.

"How'd you end up in Michigan?" I asked.

"Had to get outta town," he said.

"I've heard that before," I said.

After our meal, we walked to the flagpole together for an orientation meeting. Arky grew up in the hill country with no electricity. His family hunted year-round to put food on the table. He told me about the strange food they ate.

"Squirrel stew?" I said. "Yuck."

"It's gooood," Arky said. "Ya add corn, taters, bacon and tomatoes...mmm, mmm."

My belly hurt from eating too much food. "Don't say any more, or I'll throw up."

We milled around the flagpole and waited for the First Sergeant while a misty rain drizzled down. Finally, Mr. Mulligan strode up wearing a long green raincoat and a wide brimmed hat. "Any complaints about the food?"

A chorus of "no, sir!" came back.

I hiccupped loudly. The sergeant peered around the boys to see who did it. "Was that *you*, Radzinski?" he asked. I nodded and hiccupped again. He shook his head. "Four o'clock is quitting time around here, not three-thirty. And don't go exploring in the woods—I don't want anyone getting lost."

The sergeant went over some rules and then introduced us to Captain Bullock, a small compact man with a high forehead and large white mustache. He looked like he just returned from the last war. His laced-up boots came to his knees and brown army pants flared out at the thighs. "There is a right way and wrong way to do everything in this camp," he said in a thin, piping voice, "from making your cot to chopping a tree." Follow instructions and don't cut corners." He spoke in clipped sentences like the sergeant.

"I heard about this candy stealing incident in Trout Lake...*it's unacceptable!* We don't need our name rubbed in the mud because some of you don't use your brains." He spoke about work projects. "Your number one job is planting trees. You're not doing it for your children. You're not doing it for your grandchildren. You're doing it for your *great*-grandchildren."

Then he talked about getting along. "We care about you, don't *ever* forget that. Once in a while, we're going to punish you, but all you have to remember is...we *care for you.* The best memories you'll take from camp will be the friendships you make. I hope we can all be friends."

After the captain's speech, the First Sergeant introduced us to the six barracks leaders and their assistants. "If you don't *listen* to your assistant leader, you have to *answer* to your leader. If you don't *listen* to your leader, you have to *answer* to me. Take my advice...do what your leader tells you."

A couple older boys walked behind Mr. Mulligan as he spoke. They carried a long pole with a hook attached. The sergeant turned. "Where the heck are you going with that sky hook?"

"We're taking it to the equipment room," one of them said.

"Make sure it gets there," the sergeant muttered.

When he finished his talk, our leaders took us on a tour of the camp. Scruggs led a dozen of us to the bathhouse and latrine. Toilets ran along one side with showers on the other and a long sink basin down the middle. "Keep this place clean—if you get latrine duty, you'll be the one to clean it up," he said.

Next stop was the supply building for blankets and clothes. Mr. Thacker, the supply sergeant, was a Local Experienced Man or L.E.M. for short. A former lumberjack, he ran a lumber camp store many years. Scruggs told us his nickname was "Nine Lives Ned." We got a chuckle out of that. "He picked up the nickname in his lumberjack days," Scruggs said. "But, don't ever call him that. He's Mr. Thacker to you guys."

The supply room smelled of freshly laundered clothes. Tall shelves behind the counter contained neatly folded shirts, pants and blankets. We formed a line and inched along as a tall, bland-faced, gray-haired man picked out clothing for us. He moved methodically and spoke with a gravely voice.

"Take care of yer clothes," he said. "Don't get 'em torn up fer no reason." He quickly sized up each boy. When my turn came, he looked me over and laid out two shirts and pairs of pants. The shirts were medium-sized.

"Mr. Thacker, can I please have a large? This'll be too tight for my shoulders."

He furrowed his brow. "That'll fit...now git movin'."

I protested. "I got *big shoulders*...this shirt's too small."

His eyes narrowed. "I said...keep movin'." He began picking out clothes for the next boy.

I looked for Scruggs, but he was gone. Without a second thought, I unbuttoned my shirt and tried on the one he gave me. The other boys watched with wide eyes. Thacker didn't scare me—I wanted a shirt that fit.

Thacker made short sideways glances at me while I dressed. I noticed his face twitch as if he had a tick. With the shirt buttoned up, I moved my arms around like crab claws. The shirt clung tight around the shoulders and held back my arms. The other boys laughed. "Look, I can't touch my hands." Mr. Thacker glanced over at me and went back to work.

Scruggs walked in. "What's going on?"

"He thinks he's a smarter than me," Thacker said.

"This shirt's *too small*," I said. I removed it roughly.

"So, what?" Scruggs said with a smile. "There's only two sizes around here, too big and too small. Right, Mr. Thacker?" The supply sergeant scowled.

Scruggs leaned over the counter. "What do you say...can we give this rookie a break?"

Thacker sniffed, went to the shelf, and picked out two large shirts. He tossed them on the counter. "Thanks," I said and took them.

As we walked back to the barracks, our arms loaded with clothes and blankets, Scruggs came up to me. "Be careful around Thacker. He's *king* in the supply room...you don't want to embarrass him."

"For chrissakes. All I wanted was a bigger shirt."

"Don't tangle with him...he can be grumpy. All those years working in the woods gave him arthritis and rheumatism."

"Yeah, right," I replied. I was already getting a taste of life in the CCC. If asking for a bigger shirt was a big deal, I was in for plenty of trouble.

"How'd he get the name Nine Lives anyway?"

"One story goes that he and a couple pals drank some wood alcohol by mistake."

"Yeah?"

"They died, Ned only got sick."

"Geez, he must have a rock gut...know any others?"

Scruggs nodded. "Another time he was sawing a tree and a widow maker came down..."

"Widow maker?"

"Yeah, that's when a branch hung up in a tree falls on the men sawing underneath."

"What happened?"

"It killed his partner..."

"Oh my God..."

Scruggs shot me a wry grin. "He knows how to cheat death."

When we returned to the barracks, they gave us time to

put away our clothes and make up our cots. I squared the corners of my cot just right and tucked the blanket extra tight. A few cots away from mine, a rookie struggled to pass inspection. "I can't do it!" he yelled. The dark hair rookie thumped his cot on the floor. "Turk" Truszewski was six feet of bone, muscle and grit. Built thick like a boxer, he moved around in tight, jerky movements.

"Try again," Scruggs, said.

Turk picked up the cot and flipped it over. "*Now*, I'll start over." His nostrils flared. "Mind your potatoes," he snarled at the rest of us. Scruggs quickly took charge. "Follow me," he said and led Turk outside on the steps. They returned a few minutes later and Turk went back to his cot. After a few more attempts, he finally passed inspection.

Then Scruggs led us out for the rest of the tour. It had stopped raining and a mild breeze blew as we cut across the quad. The air smelled musky, like damp leaves. Big, barn-like doors at the equipment building slid open and revealed a large room that held enough tools to fill a hardware store. Dozens of picks, axes, and shovels stood neatly racked in long rows. Two orderlies explained Standard Operating Procedure, or S.O.P., for checking out things. Sports equipment like tennis rackets and croquet mallets also were available to use.

From there, we walked down a cinder trail to the garage, set back about seventy yards from the camp in case of fire. The odor of motor oil and engine exhaust greeted us when we walked into the chilly building. Half a dozen trucks and other vehicles were in for maintenance. A couple L.E.M.s worked under the hood of a truck while another squatted by a car, replacing a tire.

"In case you haven't figured it out, this is where engine repair class is taught," Scruggs said. "It's also where you'll meet for truck driving class." While he talked about the classes, I noticed a pair of needle nose pliers on a workbench. I slinked over and quietly slipped them into my pocket. I needed them to tighten up the lacings of my baseball glove.

From the garage, we headed to the dispensary. We were halfway there when we noticed Turk missing. "He must've ditched us," someone piped up. A frown came over Scruggs' face. We turned around and headed back to the garage.

"Doggone it," Scruggs said as we walked in the door. "Turk, get over here!" The rookie pulled his head from under a hood.

"I'm coming," he said and picked up a rag to wipe his hands.

"Thanks for sharing him with us," a L.E.M. called out. Turk strode up wearing a sheepish grin.

Scruggs clenched his jaw. "What's going on?" he snapped.

Turk shrugged. "A little carburetor trouble."

"Oh, a wise guy, eh?" He grabbed Turk's arm roughly and led him ahead of us.

Next, we visited the camp surgeon at the dispensary and then watched the blacksmith repair a chain. Scruggs then took us to the transportation office followed by a visit to the powerhouse. The camp was like a self-contained village and even included its own generator and water supply.

When the tour ended, most of the boys took off for the rec hall for some fun. I reported to weed-pulling duty. With shovels over our shoulders, six of us walked to the farmer's field led by an assistant leader. I wondered why they gave us shovels until I saw the waist-high weeds. Soon, I was digging in the sandy soil. Luke kept his distance from me until we passed each other on the way to the burn pile. "Why'd you leave me holding the bag?" I asked.

He sneered. "It's not my fault you didn't eat it."

"That's a bunch of baloney. You set me up...you set *everybody* up."

"Oh, yeah? No one else is complaining."

"Well, I am." I glanced over and saw the assistant leader walking in our direction. "Don't let me catch you alone," I said.

"Oh, I'm really scared," he scoffed and we moved on. I wanted to smack him with my shovel. Where I came from, you never left your buddy to hang out to dry.

The next morning my back throbbed with pain. I dragged myself off the cot, made my way to the bathhouse and splashed cold water on my face. Only two hours of pulling weeds and I ached all over. *Am I a softie?*

At breakfast, I loaded up on pancakes and sausage. Most of us ate in silence. "This coffee tastes like paint," Turk said loudly at the next table. The head cook came up behind him.

"Vat did you say?" Mr. Kiefer spoke with an accent.

Turk looked up in surprise. "Oh, I said the coffee tastes like paint...and that's *just the way* I like it."

"Oh...is zat so? You vant more?"

Turk shook his head no.

Mr. Kiefter chuckled and walked away. I heard he ran the kitchen like a drill sergeant.

After breakfast, I saw Turk outside the mess hall, smoking a cigarette. The guys called him "Tornado Turk," because of his temper. "Hey," I said and sat down on the bench next to him.

"Yeah?" his heavy eyelids made him look tired.

"Someday, let's buy a can of Maxwell House and make some real coffee."

He smiled wistfully. "That's what my mom drank."

"Where's home?"

"Saginaw. I live with my dad...my mom's in Milwaukee."

"Why?"

"That's where she's from...she dumped my dad."

"What happened?"

"He couldn't pay the bills, so she hit the road."

"What's he doing?"

"He slings hash and plays clarinet at night...he thinks he's the next Artie Shaw."

"I like Artie Shaw..."

"Yeah, but I miss my mom."

"Milwaukee's not so far away."

He took a draw on his cigarette. "It's far enough...I haven't seen her for a year."

"Save your money. Go there when you get out of camp."

Turk nodded and flicked his butt. "Speaking of money, can I borrow a dime for some smokes? I'll give it back on payday."

I winced and reached into my pocket. "Here's a nickel, keep it." I knew better than to loan money.

Turk grinned and slapped my shoulder. "You're all right, kid." We headed off to the equipment building to join the other rookies to get some tools. As we cut across the quad, a few chirping birds reminded me it was spring, but the trees were still bare. The boys clustered around Isaac, a L.E.M. who had worked as a lumberjack. A short, wiry fella, with a big, droopy mustache that covered his mouth, he wore a gray wool cap, red neckerchief, suspenders and socks pulled up over his pant legs.

He spoke with an accent I found out was Norwegian. "Pickin' der right size axe is like gettin' der right size baseball bat." Isaac asked a rookie to grip an axe handle and to let it swing by his side. The enrollee tried different sizes until he found one that gently scuffed the ground.

Isaac then put on a chopping show by squaring off a log. He straddled a foot-wide log and swung with short accurate strokes—the chips flew like popcorn out of a pan. He chopped two sides of the log flat, turned it over and did the other two sides until it was square. He taught us some safety rules before everyone picked out an axe and boarded a truck.

We drove twenty minutes to a work site where we cleared poplar trees for a new road. I teamed up with a Mexican boy about my size. With light skin and a head of dark curly hair, he looked more Italian than Mexican. We talked as we dragged trees to the log pile. José grew up in Detroit in a house with fourteen family members. Three children slept in each bed.

"With the little one sideways at your feet?" I asked.

"Yep," he said. "You've done it?"

"Yeah, for a while."

José said he ate more food in his first day at camp then he did in a whole week at home.

We worked about fifty feet from each other, chopping trees. I wrapped my hand in a handkerchief because of blisters. When the lunch truck rolled in, I yelled out, "José, chowtime!"

When José looked up, his axe bounced off the tree and hit his ankle. He fell down moaning. "I'm coming," I said as I ran over. The blade sliced through the leather with blood oozing out over his ankle. I felt sick and took a deep breath.

"You okay, Nick?" José asked.

I knelt to my knee. "Yeah, I'm all right." I looked over my shoulder at the other boys running our way. "Don't tell anyone I distracted you, okay?" The last thing I needed was the sergeant breathing down my neck again.

He grimaced, "I won't, the axe just slipped."

"Atta boy." Three other boys came over. We pulled José's boot off and wrapped a handkerchief around his injured ankle.

José put his arms over our shoulders and we walked him to the lunch site. After we ate, we set him in the truck with his leg propped up. "Hang in there buddy," I said.

He looked discouraged lying on the floor of the truck. "My first day of work and I get hurt."

"Cheer up, you'll be back in no time," I said.

He grinned—his dimples made him look about fifteen.

After the truck pulled away, Isaac came up to me. He took his pipe out of his mouth and gave me a skeptical look. "What really happened out dere?"

I shrugged. "I dunno, I wasn't even close to him," I said.

Isaac studied me for a moment, and twitched his big

mustache. "I hope dat's de truth, I don't want any funny business goin' on."

When we arrived back at camp after work detail, I could hardly pick up my axe; my arms hung limp like noodles. Later, at supper, I learned that Luke pulled a knife on a boy during an argument. Mr. Mulligan drove him straight to the train station. *That little creep slipped through my hands!*

When I finished eating, I stopped by the infirmary to visit José and found him lying in bed flipping through a book. "How's my partner doing?" I said and patted his shoulder.

He handed me the booklet "Take a look."

"Dynamite Safety? Why're you reading this?" I asked.

"I'm going to be a dynamite man. I just got to pass a test."

"Hmmm, interesting stuff," I said as I leafed thorough the pages. "Beats swinging an axe."

"I always liked firecrackers...one time I blew up a dead cat." His eyes beamed with excitement.

"Tell me about it another time," I said. He nodded. We talked a while about some of the things he learned in the book.

I got up to leave. "Good luck on the test."

"Yeah...I can't wait," he said with a grin.

I was glad for José. Something good came out of something bad. I also had dodged a bullet.

After supper, I was back in the farmer's field. The temperature dropped into the thirties and the dampness made it seem colder. I took out a handkerchief, and blew my nose. For the past hour, I had pulled weed after weed. While I tugged at the plants, my anger grew for confessing to a crime I didn't do. The crew leader leaned against a stump and watched us as if we were slaves. I felt like a caged wolf, penned in against my will. A train whistle went off in the distance and a boy yelled. "I bet that's Luke!"

"Yeah," another called out, "he's probably sipping a cup of coffee right now."

"Yeah? I hope he spills it in his lap," I shouted. I got a few strange looks.

Later that night before curfew, I took out a piece of stationery and scratched out my first letter home.

Dear Mom,

I got to camp OK. It's cold up here. We cleared trees to make roads. I'm pretty good with an axe—you wouldn't believe how sharp they are.

The work is hard, the cots are hard and the leaders are hard—I can hardly write because of my sore hands. On the first day, I was blamed for something I didn't do. Now, they make me pull weeds for punishment.

Tell Gabe the food is good and we get to eat all we want. The only thing I didn't like was the pickled pigs' feet. Today a boy found a bandage in his stew. We think it came off someone's finger.

That's all for now. Tell Gabe to sign up, because he deserves it.

Love,
Nick

During the night, I woke up to the sound of rain pounding on the roof. I heard someone sniffle, probably a rookie who missed his mom. I fluffed my pillow and pulled my blanket up under my chin. I missed my mom too, but not enough to cry about.

Camp was like a little Ellis Island with boys from different nationalities. Many of them spoke their immigrant parents' native tongue. By the end of the first week, I met boys from Swedish, Irish, Lithuanian, Finn and Italian families. There were lots of Poles, maybe twenty from Hamtramck alone.

Mario was an Italian boy from Detroit with olive-colored skin, wavy brown hair and movie-star looks. He talked to people as if he never found anything as fascinating as what that person had to say. Almost every night he sang Italian songs just before lights out. Most of the fellas quieted down and listened as Mario sat on his cot with his back against the wall, singing with a beautiful tenor voice.

Mario's best friend was an orphan we called "Sweet Bobby." While Mario was outgoing, Bobby was quiet and shy. I often saw him with a distant look in his eye as if he was deep in thought. Mario played sports while Bobby liked to read. Mario argued with anybody, but I never heard Bobby raise his voice. Although they had many differences, the two were inseparable.

One night after supper, the sergeant called a meeting in our barracks. Bobby and Mario were playing cribbage on Mario's cot when the sergeant came in. With a haggard face, he looked like he was ready to go home to his wife and kids. He waited with his hands on his hips for everyone to quiet down. "Men, Mother's Day is coming up in three weeks," he said. "Last year not many of you sent gifts to your mothers, so this year, we bought a gift *for you.*"

He held up a red pillowcase with a Mother's Day poem stitched on it. Some of the boys quietly nodded with approval. "I need twenty-five cents from each of you to pay for these things—the camp will ship them direct to your homes." The guys groaned.

Mr. Mulligan glared at us. "Button it! And I need a letter to your mother. Not a paragraph, a *real letter*...any questions?"

A hand shot up. "Sir, can I buy my own present?"

"No, everyone has to do it."

"I don't have a quarter," another said.

"Borrow one. Anyone else?"

Bobby raised his hand. "Sir, I don't have a mother...I'm an orphan." All eyes turned to the sergeant.

The sergeant rubbed his jaw for a moment. "Ah, geez... borrow one, Bobby," he said gruffly. "Just borrow one." He turned and walked out the door.

Bobby turned to his best friend. "Can I borrow your mother?"

"Sure," Mario said. "I got a great mom." Bobby grinned from ear to ear. Bobby wrote a letter that night and read it to us. It began, *Dear Borrowed Mom.* He told her about himself and his friendship with Mario, ending it by wishing her a Happy Mother's Day. He signed the letter, *Love, Your Borrowed Son.* After he read it to us, our faces went from silly to serious.

Bobby's letter made us appreciate our moms. I know I took my mother for granted. The problems I caused her made me sick just to think about it. I took out a piece of stationery and wrote a letter. I included the one thing she wanted to hear. *I'm not giving up!*

A veteran in camp loved to bully rookies. William Clarence Fields was a big, strong farm boy we called "Farmer." We crossed paths often because his cot was in my barracks. He disgusted me with his pockmarked face and big, bulbous nose. Something was not quite right about him, especially when he made his leering grins and got in your face.

Farmer stuck nicknames on the rookies. My red-haired friend Arky was "Hillbilly," José, "Baby face," and I was "Rat-Eye." He thought it went well with my last name Radzinski. No one thought the nicknames were funny except Farmer, who broke out in a guttural laugh each time he used them.

Farmer loved to argue. God help the boy whose father drove the wrong kind of tractor, because Farmer showed no mercy. One night after supper, with the mess hall half empty, Farmer tore into a rookie about his father's McCormick tractor.

"McCormicks stink," Farmer said with a sneer. "John Deere makes the best tractor...you gotta set your old man straight."

My blood boiled as I listened. "Why don't you lay off, you big lout," I said.

Farmer slowly turned around with mouth wide open. "Excuse me," he said to the boy. Then he walked over and sat down at the table across from me. He set down his tin cup—the one he used to spit his tobacco juice.

"Has it ever occurred to you that maybe his dad can't afford a John Deere?" I asked.

He gawked. "You know nothing...*nothing* about tractors."

"Oh, yeah? My dad drove a Ford when we had a dairy farm."

His wrinkled his nose and sneered. "Your old man drove a Ford? Ford tractors are crap."

He got me fired up. "Who *cares* what you think?"

Farmer made a leering grin, snaked his arm across the table and grabbed my plate of apple pie. "Give it back," I said and reached to get it.

He pulled back and flashed his tobacco-stained teeth. "I'm a magician, see...I'm going to make this disappear." He picked the pie off the plate and took a big bite. "Oh...that's goooood," he said in between chews.

I pretended to ignore him and casually took a bite of my roll. Just as he was about to take a second bite, I reached over and pushed the pie into his face. Apple filling smeared on his nose.

He wiped his mouth with the back of his hand and contorted his face into a glare that would make Boris Karloff proud.

"You're a dead man, Rat Eye," he snarled. Then he lunged across the table at me. Turk, who watched the whole scene unfold, grabbed Farmer from behind and wrapped his arms around him. Two or three other boys jumped in and helped Turk restrain him. There was a rule that if someone saw a fight he had to break it up, or he got into trouble.

A couple minutes later, Scruggs rushed in the door. "What in blazes is going on?"

"Farmer stole my..." I said.

Farmer cut me off. "That futz pushed pie in my face..."

"Yeah, it was *my* pie."

"Hold it, hold it," Scruggs said raising his arms. He went off to the side and huddled with a few of the boys who witnessed the incident. A couple minutes later, he returned. "We're going to settle this thing right now." He turned to the others.

"Get the boxing gloves." *I never wore boxing gloves in my life!*

Farmer grinned at me, and who could blame him? He stood about six inches taller and weighed about fifty pounds more than I did. Scruggs led us behind the barracks to a grassy area where a few dozen enrollees formed a circle. I thought of the nurse who I met on the train. She might get see me again soon!

The boy who laced up my gloves gave me some tips. "Keep the gloves up," he said. Then he showed me how to tuck my elbows in. "Protect your face if he starts pounding you."

"Are you crazy?" I said. "I'm not going to be his punching bag. I'll go down swinging."

The boy shook his head. "You rookies never listen."

I felt panicky and tried to think of a fight strategy. Maybe I could knee him in the crotch if he got too close or hit him below the belt. What I really needed was luck. I looked up at the sky, no rain in sight. If I could stall for fifteen minutes, maybe they would call the fight for darkness.

Scruggs waved us into the circle. I walked hesitantly, while Farmer bounced on his feet and smacked his gloves together with delight. With flushed cheeks and a sick smile on his face, he looked ready to beat me to a pulp. *Why didn't I take boxing lessons?*

The gloves felt heavy and awkward. My hands sweated from the wrapping they put on before they slipped the gloves on. I looked nervously around at the boys surrounding us and saw Arky sitting at the edge of the ring with a slingshot in his hand. The other boys crowded around him, giving him cover. Then I realized, Arky was there to help me!

When the ref blew the whistle, the boys in the crowd hollered like crazy. I was distracted for a moment, but got my wits back and shuffled to my right. Farmer walked right up to me and easily knocked me down with a hook, his fist felt like a sledgehammer.

I got up, charged him like a pit bull and ran headfirst into his chest. I wrapped my arms around and gave him some kidney punches. He tried to push me away but I held on like an octopus.

"Get him off of me ref," Farmer complained. Scruggs stuck his arms between our bodies and separated us.

Farmer and I circled each other warily until I got him to move in front of Arky. The big gorilla was about to come at me when I saw a pebble fly off his backside. "OW!" he shouted and turned his head. When he did, he dropped his gloves. I moved in and gave him two hard punches in the gut. "Uhhh," he groaned and doubled over. The boys cheered like mad.

Before I could finish him off, Scruggs rushed in between us. "Break it up!" he shouted and pushed me away with his long arms. While Farmer caught his breath, Scruggs steered me to the other side of the circle and told me to stay put.

He turned back to the boys. "Which one of you fellas threw that stone?" he barked. They shook their heads and shrugged. Arky had slipped away.

Scruggs shook his head. "That's it, fight's over," he said and waved Farmer and me to the center of the ring. "Shake hands." He put our gloves together.

"That fight wasn't on the level," Farmer complained.

"Forget it...it's over." Scruggs said. "I don't want you guys arguing again or you're going back in the ring."

Farmer smirked, "Sure, ref."

Scruggs caught on. "Oh, a smart ass, eh? You start something with Nick, and you come into the ring with *me*." Farmer pouted. He knew better than to argue with the camp boxing champion. "Get those gloves off and beat it," Scruggs said.

The freckle-faced kid from Arkansas saved the day. It helped to have friends in low places. Sure, the fight wasn't fair, but who ever said life was fair? Farmer got what he deserved. After a boy untied my gloves, I held my hands to my face. *My nose is still in one piece!* I wondered what Mr. Mulligan thought about the match. I noticed he watched from the steps of the barracks.

A few days after the boxing match, I made a new friend, Frank Franczewski. He was one of the guys who grabbed Farmer in the mess hall ruckus with Turk. A square-jawed Polish fella from Chicago with big biceps and a barrel chest, Frank studied books by Charles Atlas the body builder. Whenever he saw a low tree branch, he grabbed it and did chin-ups. Frank envied my shoulders and bugged me on how I made them so big. He didn't believe they grew by themselves. One day, I was leaning against the wall on my cot reading a book.

"Stay right there, Nick," he said. Then he took a pencil and scratched little marks on the wall to measure the width of my shoulders.

"Now get up and do me." He sat in my place and I marked his shoulders, he was about an inch less on each side. That bugged him because he was taller than I was and bigger all over. He pestered me again. "C'mon...how'd you make 'em so big?"

"I told you already, I got them from my dad."

"Aw, you're holding out on me..."

"You're screwy."

Anyone not from the Windy City was small potatoes to Frank. He bragged about the tall buildings, the baseball teams and the dance halls. *Everything* was bigger and better in Chicago. When I told him about Woodward Avenue in Detroit, he cut me off and crowed about Michigan Avenue.

One thing Frank didn't boast about was his dancing. He didn't have to. Frank jitterbugged better than anyone in camp and earned the nickname, "Slip and Slide." Frank told me his dad refused to dance with Frank's mom. She turned to Frank for her partner and taught him to dance when he was little.

"She made me stand on her feet when I was five years old and taught me the polka, fox trot and waltz."

I jumped him in checkers. "No kidding?"

"Yeah. Every night after supper, she'd put a record on the gramophone and we'd dance in the living room. By the time I was eight, I could dance to anything."

"I wish I could dance good."

"I'll teach you. I might even send a dame your way when I get too many." He toyed with a checker. "Girls love good dancers."

I looked up. "So you think I'm hard up?"

He made a move on the board. "Don't work yourself into a lather. I'm just offering." Frank irritated me at times. His big ego got under my skin, but we had things in common. We both spoke Polish, we came from a big city, and our dads left home when we were kids.

"Let's find our dads when we get out," Frank said one night.

"Yeah," I said. "We'll save some money and track them down." We made a pact to find our dads and then spit on our hands and shook on it. For the first time, I thought there was a chance of seeing him again. Even though Dad deserted us, he was still my dad. Plus, I wanted to find out the *real reason* he left.

Later that week, Frank and I explored a swamp near camp and found some climbing trees. I took some rope from the equipment room when no one was looking. We tied it between two trees, hung a pulley on it and slid from tree to tree like a couple of monkeys. Frank and I played on those ropes almost every night before supper—it was our own private playground. We played like children, and whooped it up in the treetops.

We always ran back to camp in time for supper. The meals began with a bowl of soup followed by a hot meat dish, like corned beef, pork chops, or ham. Bowls of boiled potatoes and baskets of fresh-baked rolls helped fill us up. Pitchers of cold milk quenched our thirst, and they served coffee at the end of meal for the few boys who wanted it. For dessert, Curly the baker whipped up treats like pineapple upside-down cake, banana pudding, and cherry pie. Curly ate well and showed it. I got a kick out of his name because he had a round bald head with a narrow ring of hair. If there were a vote for the favorite person in camp, Curly would have won easily.

After a couple weeks in camp, the thought of hunger faded from my mind. It was hard to imagine that I used to eat bread and margarine for a meal. One day in the bathhouse when I looked in the mirror, I noticed my ribs didn't stick out anymore. The extra weight would help me out the next time I tangled with Farmer.

It was the first week of May and I wondered when spring would arrive. Everything seemed colder when you lived in the woods. The thin, tarpapered walls of the barracks did little to hold back the damp chill. The drying racks above the stoves filled up quickly with wet socks and soggy clothes after a rainy day of work in the woods. The barracks sometimes smelled worse than a locker room.

After two weeks, the weed-pulling punishment finally ended, so I relaxed after supper instead of work. Unfortunately, the free time meant more chances of running into Farmer. "What are *you* doing here?" Farmer asked one night in the library. I looked up from my copy of *Life* magazine and saw his pimpled face glaring at me.

"I'm taking a shower...what do you think I'm doing?"

"Did your time in the weed field, eh?"

"Yeah, what of it?"

He lowered his voice. "I hear there's candy in the canteen. Maybe you can steal some."

I covered my face with the magazine, "Go away."

Farmer leaned over and in a hushed voice said, "I'm going to tie you up like a pretzel someday. They might even take your picture and put it in that magazine."

I put the magazine down and sniffed. "Hey, what's that? It smells like cow manure."

Farmer raised his lip into a sneer. "I'm going to rub your face in manure someday."

The more I talked to Farmer, the more he seemed like a

big windbag. The tough guys in camp boxed on the team, but not Farmer. He got his kicks from taunting rookies half his size. I still needed to be careful around him. The crazed look in his eyes made me uneasy; he could snap and start pounding me. I only felt secure when other people were around.

Saturday was inspection day with clean-up all morning long. Some boys scrubbed the latrine while others washed windows. There were floors to sweep, leaves to rake and wood to chop. I picked up cigarette butts along the sidewalk. When eleven o'clock rolled around I heaved a sigh of relief—another week was over. A day and a half of freedom!

After lunch, Frank invited me to explore the woods. "Don't worry, we won't get caught," he said. With six months under his belt, I figured he knew the ropes. We sneaked behind the equipment building and waited until no one was in sight. "Let's go," he said. Then we walked quickly across the clearing into the woods. Ferns and other plants poked green tips out of the dead leaves on the forest floor. After a few minutes, we stumbled onto a patch of flowers Frank identified as trilliums. They had three petals like a lily. I knelt and picked one.

"For your girlfriend?" Frank teased.

I put it in my wallet. "Nah, for my mom."

We began walking again. "You got a girlfriend?" he asked.

"Nope. There was a girl I liked but I never asked her out—I was too broke."

"Too bad."

"Yeah, I was stupid. Before I left to come here, she told me I should've asked her out."

"Oh geez..."

"She said it didn't matter if I was broke."

"You dimwit."

"Don't rub it in."

Ten minutes later, we came to a simple lean-to made of boards nailed to a tree. I ran over, peeked under it and saw a motorcycle. "Yours?" I asked.

"What do you think?" Frank said. "We didn't come here to pick flowers." He wheeled the beat-up bike out of the shelter. I rubbed my hand on the rusty gas tank, which had an Indian with a feather headdress painted on the side. "I thought bikes were illegal," I said.

Frank smiled. "You don't *break* the rules, but it's okay to *bend* them." He said enrollees hid cars and bikes in the woods or in farmers' barns. "The trick is to keep 'em out of sight...and don't talk about them." A lot more things went on in camp than met the eye. I liked that.

Frank threw his leg over the seat and gave it a couple kick-starts until it turned over. RMMM, RMMM! He gunned the engine. It disturbed the peace and quiet of the woods with loud noise. He pulled his cap tight over his head and waved. "See ya, moron...watch out for the wolves!" He put the cycle in gear and kicked up dirt and leaves with his tire. "Yeee-haaw!" He yelled and shot off through the woods.

After he went out of sight, I dusted off a tree stump and sat down. The drone of the motorcycle faded out after a minute or two. It became eerily quiet except for the distant sound of a woodpecker, which echoed through the woods. For the first time since I was a child on our farm, I was alone in nature. Not a soul in sight.

I breathed deeply and closed my eyes—the tangy, pungent smell of pine trees filled the air. The grimy concrete jungle of the city seemed far away. The thought came to me that I had made a full circle in my life. I began my life on a dairy farm and then moved to a crowded city. Now I was back in nature. I felt a wonderful sense of peace.

The people, places, and things in my life seemed unimportant compared to the serenity I felt in the woods. Life in the big city offered the promise of happiness, but here I felt *fulfilled.* In the city it was all about getting things—here it was *experiencing* things. That angry teenager back in Hamtramck who cheated and stole seemed like a different person. If I could just hold onto the good feeling and take it back to camp, maybe I could last the full term of my enlistment.

I felt a shiver of excitement run through me when I heard Frank's motorcycle in the distance. My hands yearned to grip the throttle and let it rip. Frank stormed in, sliding to a stop over the loose leaves. "Your turn," he said. I straddled the bike and Frank gave me some pointers on changing gears.

V-ROOM! Away I went down the path with a cool breeze in my face. I smiled to myself—free at last. After five minutes or so, the trail led up to a small hill. I saw the skid marks where Frank stopped so I slowed down and turned off the engine. I walked up the hill and noticed a small waterfall that trickled about fifteen feet down over large, moss-covered boulders. I knelt on some slippery rocks over a little pool and splashed water into my mouth like an animal. It was ice cold. I never knew water could taste so good.

My thirst quenched, I drove back to Frank. We put the bike under the lean-to and then hiked to an abandoned lumber camp. Most of the log buildings had caved in beyond repair. In a small hut, someone had nailed can lids to the walls, from the floor to the ceiling. I ran my hand over them. "What do you think they put these here for?" I asked.

"To keep the heat in," Frank said. "Isaac told me."

"Geez, it must have been cold out here."

"Yeah, and no hot showers." Frank said.

"Thacker probably worked in a camp like this."

Frank gave the rotten wood a little kick—a piece broke off. "That's probably how the poor guy got so cranky."

"He's not a poor guy. He's a creep."

Frank picked up a rusty axe head. "Most of the fellas in camp like him."

"Why's that?"

"If you get supply duty...you'll find out."

"What goes on?"

"He gets a few boys each week to help him refold the clothes, army-neat."

"So?"

"He's as slow as molasses, so no one works hard."

"Oh, yeah?"

"And Curly keeps him supplied with cookies..."

"Just my luck," I said. "I pick a fight with a guy who gives out cookies."

"Aw, he'll get over it."

We walked back to camp tired, but refreshed. Even wet boots and cold feet did little to dampen my spirits. I was on my cot pulling my socks off when Scruggs called for a locker inspection. They usually called surprise inspections when things were missing. Our barracks leader walked slowly from locker to locker with a clipboard in hand.

When he got to me, Scruggs knelt on the floor. "Take off the top layer," he said. I removed my baseball glove and some shirts. "Give me the glove." He took it and stuck his hand inside. "What's this?" He pulled out the pliers. I gulped.

Scruggs shot me a cross look. "Where'd you get these?"

"The garage."

"Why'd you take 'em?"

"To tighten the strings on the glove."

Scruggs shook his head. "C'mon." We grabbed our coats and went outside. He sat me down on a bench. "*This* is on my list of stolen items," he said, holding the pliers in front of my face. "You can't take things that don't belong to you."

I said nothing.

"There're two hundred guys in this camp—if everyone took stuff without permission we couldn't operate."

"I was going to return it..."

He cut me off. "That's a bunch of baloney—you could have signed it out." He lectured me on stealing and said that next to fighting, stealing was the fastest way to get kicked out of camp. "I'm not going to report you this time, but don't do it again."

"Thank you." I breathed easier. For once, I caught a break.

I repacked my trunk, and carefully replaced each item in its proper place. On the cot next to mine, a veteran played a Gene Autry song on his guitar. Ollie appeared older than his nineteen years because of his heavy five o'clock shadow. He was a loner, but when he opened up and talked, he was probably the most interesting person in camp. At fourteen, his mother packed his bag and let him leave home. He hitched a train from Michigan to California, riding with the hobos.

He witnessed muggings, rapes and murders during the three years he spent on the road. He worked on a fishing boat off Catalina Island and an avocado farm in the valley, but mostly he bummed around. Ollie rarely spoke about his travels, but when he did, the boys stopped and listened.

Ollie also pulled off some of the best pranks in camp. He never seemed to worry about getting in trouble. "Baby, I don't care," he would often say with his deep voice. Some of the boys thought Ollie put the live possum in the company clerk's filing cabinet and that he was the one who ran a pirate's skull and bones up the camp flagpole.

As I repacked my trunk, I asked, "Why does it matter how trunks look on the inside?"

Ollie looked up with a roguish grin. "It doesn't. They just want you to obey the rules."

"Yeah? Well, it's a dumb rule," I muttered. The two last things I put in the trunk were my baseball mitt and a woodcarving my dad made. It was an Indian chief with a feather headdress carved out of a log-end. It looked like the Indian on a buffalo nickel. When we lived on the farm, my dad sat on a stool in our living room on long winter nights and whittled. I swept up the wood chips on the floor, threw them in the stove and watched them burst into flames. Those were happy memories.

When I held the carving in my hands, it reminded me of the good memories of my dad, the time *before* I lost my three siblings to the river. I fingered the outline of the headdress, and imagined how my father's hands once touched the very same piece of wood. I often wondered what my life would have been like if that terrible accident on the ice didn't happen and if my dad could have kept the farm.

I never appreciated the warmth of the sun until I joined the CCC. The cold sogginess from working in the woods seemed to cut to the bone. When the sun came out, I liked to lounge on the barracks steps like a turtle on a log. My favorite time of day was just before supper when I could soak up the late afternoon sun and practice my new hobby, whittling. When I saw Isaac chiseling one day, I ran and showed him my dad's carving.

"Dat's one nice piece of work," he said, turning it over slowly in his hands. The next thing I knew, Isaac put a knife in my hand, a piece of pine in the other and began teaching me to whittle. I started with something simple, a little baseball bat.

One warm Saturday afternoon as I whittled on the steps, Arky walked up with a slingshot in his hand.

"Put that away," he said, "we're goin' a' huntin'."

"For what?" I asked.

He put foot on the step. "Anything with four legs."

"Oh, yeah?" I glanced at his slingshot—the strap looked like it came from an old inner tube. "You'd shoot a bear with that?"

Arky blew a bubble. "You know what I mean..."

"Got permission?"

"Why bother?" Arky picked up a pebble. "They don't let rookies go into the woods."

"I know," I said and continued slicing.

Arky pulled a compass out of his pocket. "We won't get lost...look at this."

I fingered the silver colored compass he handed me. "I can't go...the sarge'll kill me, if he finds out."

Arky waved the slingshot under my nose. "Don't be chicken, I'll even let you shoot." He put the slingshot in my hand.

I stretched the rubber and thought about it. My trip with Frank was fun, so I agreed to go. "Okay, but just a couple hours."

Arky smiled. "Attaboy...we'll be home by supper."

A cherub-faced boy with round glasses walked up with a paper bag in his hand. I recognized Elliot from the mess hall, where he served food as an orderly. He kept every hair on his head in place and dressed impeccably neat. The boys teased him for keeping his shoes in a perfect line under his cot when most of us were sloppy. Elliot spluttered when he got excited, his thoughts often spewed out faster than his words.

Elliot grinned when he saw me. “Are you going, too?”

I tried not to show my displeasure. Elliot could only slow us down with his extra weight. “Yep,” I said.

He held up the bag. “Arky said I can bring the food.”

Arky was smarter than I thought. “Good idea,” I said and peeked in the bag and saw some sandwiches wrapped in waxed paper. “Peanut butter?” I asked.

Elliot grinned and nodded excitedly.

“Let’s get goin’,” Arky said. I stuck my carving under the steps and followed him behind the barracks.

With our backs against the equipment building, we waited until the coast was clear. “Oh, boy. I’ve never done this before,” Elliot gushed.

“Never killed an animal?” Arky asked.

Elliot’s eyes widened. “You’re not *really* going to kill anything are you?”

“You’re greener than gourd guts...of course we’re gonna kill.” Suddenly, he slipped his big buck knife from his sheath and held it under Elliot’s nose. “Why d’ya think I brought this fer?”

Elliot’s stuttered. “Geez...ah...maybe I shouldn’t...”

Arky cut him off. “Run for it,” he said. We took off and cut across the clearing for the woods. A hundred yards into the woods, Arky raised his hand for us to stop and pointed to a squirrel hopping around.

“Don’t hurt the little critter,” Elliot whispered.

“He won’t feel a thing,” Arky said under his breath. He picked a stone off the ground and threw it to the other side of the animal. The squirrel ran in our direction and stopped on a tree stump about fifty feet away. It stood up on its hind legs and looked around while Arky pulled a pebble from his pocket and carefully put it in the slingshot. He slowly pulled the rubber band back, aimed and released.

WAP! The stone hit the stump just below the squirrel and knocked off a chunk of bark—the squirrel jumped a mile high.

"What a shot," I said. "You almost hit him!"

"Close don't count." Arky said, disgusted.

Elliot grimaced. "Geez, don't shoot so hard next time." Arky shot me a sideways glance and smirked.

We hiked through a sparsely wooded forest and saw no animals until Elliot let out a yelp. "Look!" He pointed to a furry carcass that lay by a clump of cedar bushes.

We checked it out. "It's a moose, probably a few weeks old," Arky said and knelt beside the awkward looking creature, which had a long snout and bony legs. "It's only been dead a few days. We better be careful...the mother might still be around."

"Ah...ah, fellas, I think that's the mother," Elliot spluttered. He pointed down a small ravine where a big brown creature headed in our direction.

Arky sprang up. "Let's go," he said in a hushed voice. We sprinted off toward some big trees. Arky and I covered about fifty yards when I heard Elliot cry for help. I turned and saw him on his knees.

"Oh, for chrissakes," I muttered and ran back. By the time Elliot got back up on his feet, the moose was closing in! I picked up a long tree branch off the ground and stood between Elliot and the moose. "Scram!" I yelled.

I held the branch out to protect myself. My jaw dropped when the moose approached me. It was as big as a horse with an ugly hump on its back. The beast pulled back when I stuck the branch in its face. I shifted from side to side like a bullfighter and kept the animal at bay. The moose snorted and stomped its feet, irritated with the branch pricking its long snout. It lunged at me a couple times, but I fended it off while Elliot ran away. My arms were about to give out from the weight of the branch when suddenly the moose reared up. EEEAAAW! It bellowed.

"Run for it!" Arky shouted. He had shot a stone at the moose's backside! I dropped the branch and ran for the nearest tree. As I climbed up the scratchy branches, I heard another EEEAAAW! I turned and watched the animal trot off.

Arky smiled, showing off his buckteeth. "Are you nuts?"

I climbed down and dusted myself off. "I must be."

We heard a thud, turned, and saw Elliot on his rump next to a tree. "Let's get out of here!" he yelled.

"She's not coming back," Arky said. He sized up a scruffy looking Elliot. "You look like you were drug through a knothole backward."

Elliot looked down at the pinesap stains on his clothes. "Oh, geez...I'm a mess."

"A little Fels Naptha will clean you up," I said.

A smile came to his chubby face. "Hey, thanks for saving me, Nick...you were *really* brave."

"More like *really stupid*," I said.

Elliot raised his arms in frustration. "Oh geez, I lost the sandwiches." He began retracing his steps.

Arky patted his pockets and rolled his eyes. "Dang it, I lost my compass."

"Oh, great," I said to myself.

We all backtracked. A few minutes later, Elliot returned with his bag of sandwiches *and* Arky's compass. "I think the moose stepped on it," he said and handed it to Arky.

Arky inspected the shattered glass. "We're lost aren't we?" Elliot asked.

The freckle-faced boy gave Elliot a long look. "Better save them sandwiches, we may need 'em."

Elliot looked distraught. "Oh, noooo," he moaned.

"C'mon," Arky said and stomped off. "We'll head north 'til we come to the train tracks."

I said nothing. After tangling with the moose, I was happy just to be alive.

We tramped through the woods in silence. The afternoon warmth disappeared as the sun dipped lower in the trees. I felt my toes getting damp from the wet leaves we trudged through. Elliot looked crestfallen, "I'm so stupid, I should never have come."

"You're not stupid," I said. "Dumb, but not stupid."

"Huh?" he said with a puzzled look.

"Stupid is when you do a dumb thing twice."

Elliot smiled. "Gee, so I'm just dumb?"

"Yeah." I said. "Just, dumb." I winked at Arky.

We plodded through a cedar swamp. The woods all looked the same to me—we could have been walking in a circle for all I knew. I decided to pop a question that had been on my mind. "Elliot, what's the trick to getting a job as a mess orderly?"

"It helps if the mess sergeant likes you," he said.

"What do I have to do?"

"Volunteer for meat patrol."

"What's that?"

"Sometimes, we need an extra hand when we make meat runs. Arky does it."

Arky looked back. "Yeah, I love it...and it pays."

"Tell the mess sergeant I want to go." I said.

"Sure," Elliot said.

A cool breeze kicked up; I shivered and rubbed my arms. The thought of a night in the woods gave me goose bumps. In the distance, a train whistle blew. Arky put a finger to his lips.

After it faded away, Elliot asked. "The tracks are near, right?"

Arky deadpanned. "You make a scarecrow look like a genius."

"Really?" Elliot looked baffled, but pleased with himself.

Fifteen minutes later, we arrived at the railroad tracks, but we had no idea which way to turn. Arky squatted on a rail and pondered the decision. He tossed a few pieces of grass in the air and watched which way the wind blew them. Finally, he stood and walked east. "I think the whistle went off at the camp road," he said. "We'll find out soon."

Elliot, his appetite back, snuck quick bites of a peanut butter sandwich. I gave him a dirty look. "We're going to make it," he said. "I just know it." Half an hour later, we came to the gravel road that led back to camp. "I knew it...I knew we'd make it!" Elliot shouted.

"Calm down," I said. "Don't draw any attention."

We entered the front gate just before suppertime. As we approached the barracks, Mr. Mulligan suddenly came around the corner of the mess hall. "Hold it right there," he shouted. My stomach dropped. He eyed our filthy clothes. "Where have you fellas been?" he asked.

His jaw tightened as he listened to our story. "You know better than to leave camp without permission. Come to my office after breakfast." Then he dismissed Arky and Elliot.

"Radzinski, have you forgotten you're on probation?"

I shook my head and looked down at the ground. Then, I felt his hand bump under my chin, which jerked my head up. "You look at me when I'm talking to you," he barked. "I want a letter from you that tells me why you should stay in camp. Bring it with you in the morning."

"Yes, sir." I dragged myself wearily back to the barracks, too tired to be angry, too discouraged to care. I slammed the door and looked around the empty building. *I've had it with this damn camp!* I threw my hat on my cot. If I packed right away, I could be back at the tracks and catch a freight train by nightfall. The growling sound in my stomach reminded me there was other business to take care of. I ran to the bathhouse, showered, and dressed for supper.

Later that night, I wrote a letter to the sergeant. I said the money was important for my mother to pay the rent and buy food. Then, I wrote about the job skills I learned and the friendships I made. I left out that I hated the stupid rules and the sergeant.

The next morning Arky, Elliot and I reported to Mr. Mulligan's office after breakfast. We stood shoulder to shoulder at parade rest with our hands behind our backs. I noticed beads of sweat on Elliot's forehead while Arky studied the maps on the walls.

Suddenly, Mr. Mulligan burped, messily. Elliot broke out in giggles—his flab shook like Jell-o. The sergeant gave him a dirty look. "Clam up," he said. Elliot froze.

The sergeant toyed with my letter and spoke slowly. "You fellas risked your lives *and* your place in camp for a romp in the woods. The last time someone got lost, I pulled everyone off work duty for a search. It took us all day to find those guys."

He ran his thick, sausage-like fingers through his thinning hair. "Don't do this to me again...I got enough problems without losing my men in the woods." We nodded. He assigned us to night patrol for two weekends, which meant we stayed up all night keeping the stoves burning.

He dismissed us. "I knew we'd get caught," Elliot whined when we were a safe distance from his office.

"Unlucky," I said.

"We weren't unlucky," Arky snapped. "We walked in the front gate."

"You're right," I said.

"The next time, we sneak in," Arky said with a devious grin.

I nodded. "Yeah...we sneak in."

Arky and I stared at Elliot and waited for him to agree. He glanced nervously back and forth at us. "Ah...ah, I gotta go back to the mess hall," he stammered and scurried off.

"EEEAAAW!" Arky mimicked the moose.

Elliot stopped in his tracks and jerked around in surprise. Arky and I chuckled and headed to the truck for work duty. I learned a valuable lesson. If you break the rules, you had to be smart about it. We dropped our guard and paid the price.

Chapter 3

The Search Begins

A week later, I lounged on the bench outside the barracks and read a letter from home during mail call. The early evening sun cast a soft golden glow around camp. I gasped when I got halfway through the letter, then I passed it to Frank. He put down his own letter and read mine. A big smile came to his face. "If that don't beat all," he said softly, "a thousand bucks."

My mother wrote that my uncle died after a night of heavy drinking. He walked onto the path of a train. Uncle Tobias was the reason I didn't smoke or drink. At family parties, he got drunk and started big arguments with everyone. I never wanted to end up like him. Since he never married, his insurance policy went to his brothers and sisters. My dad was entitled to a thousand dollars, but there was a hitch—he had to claim it in a year.

Frank and I got up and walked across the quad to get away from the other boys. "I got to find my dad, that's a lot of dough," I said.

"Pick three towns he might be living in," Frank said.

I thought for a moment. "Well, Detroit...for one."

"Okay, another."

"Maybe, Duluth, because he worked at a sawmill there when he first came to America."

"Okay, one more." He said. Some boys passed us with baseball mitts and bats.

I really tried, but I couldn't come up with a third. "It's a big country out there; he could be anywhere."

"We'll, at least you got a start," Frank said. "Make a list of his friends, buddies at work, relatives—you need to write *every one* of them."

"My mom can help..."

"Of course," Frank said. "What are you going to do if you find him?"

"Hey, it's not *my* money," I said.

"But, he might give you some..."

"He better give some to my mom..."

"C'mon, you deserve some, especially if you find him."

I thought for a moment. "Yeah, maybe you're right." I felt Frank's hand on my shoulder.

"If you get some, would you buy anything for your ol' pal, Frank?" He flashed me a big grin.

I looked at his burly arms. "Yeah, I'd buy you a set of dumbbells, *big* dumbbells."

He punched my shoulder. "Good for nothing."

I laughed. "Okay, you can be my chauffeur, but you got to wear a Tigers cap when you drive."

"Funny." Frank muttered. As we walked back to the barracks, I came up with ideas for spending the money. Number one was a house for my mom, followed by new furniture. It seemed like we moved about every two years into a smaller, cheaper apartment and each time, we gave up some furniture.

The next night, I wrote a missing-persons ad for the Duluth Tribune. I got the name of the paper from a boy who came from that city. I figured my dad might have been in contact with old friends there. I put two quarters in the envelope and asked the paper to run the ad as many times as possible. The ad was a long shot, but I had to start somewhere.

Searching for: Marek (Lew) Radzinski of Hamtramck, Michigan. Five foot nine inches, 55 years old, gray hair, and big shoulders. Millwright and woodcarver, speaks Polish. Plays ukulele. Contact son, Nick Radzinski at CCC Company 667. Raco, Michigan.

A few days later, I relaxed on the barracks steps after supper. A gentle warm breeze came out of the south and I noticed small green leaves sprouting on the trees. In the distance, I heard the crack of baseball bats as boys tried out for the baseball team.

I hemmed a boy's pants to earn some extra money. My mom never had time to mend my clothes, so she taught me how to use a needle and thread. Other boys also had sidelines to make money. Elliot sold sandwiches, Arky stuffed animals and Frank cut hair.

"Mind if I join you?" I heard someone say.

I turned and saw Turk. He was likeable, but peculiar. Some boys thought he was crazy because of his temper. "Sit down," I said. His thick, dark hair looked more like a beaver pelt than human hair.

He laid a pouch of Bull Durham tobacco by his side and began rolling cigarettes. He used a *Colliers* magazine in his lap to catch loose tobacco. "What do you get paid for that?" I asked.

He slid a paper along his tongue. "Dime a hundred."

"Not bad." I noticed his big arms were in the same league as Frank and Farmer's. Turk did voice imitations of movie stars. "Hey, give me a Cagney," I asked.

He scowled, "All right, you dirty rat...you can't talk to me that way." The accent was dead-on. He did a Clark Gable and later a John Wayne.

"You ought to go into radio," I said.

"Funny you should say that...I never got to listen to radio shows the other kids listened to."

"Huh?"

"My folks said *The Shadow* was too scary for me."

I dropped my thimble. "I don't believe it."

"Yeah...they were strict." His voice tensed up. "They made me wear ties to school...*none* of the other kids did." His hands shook as he fumbled with the rolling paper.

"Relax...calm down," I said. *Do I sound like that when I whine?*

Just then, our assistant barracks leader walked around the corner. "Bricks," was a lean, clean cut, by-the-books kind of guy who I tried to avoid.

"Hey, I need you fellas to find the skyhook."

I laid the pants down. "You're joking, right?"

"Sarge wants it done." Bricks scribbled something on his clipboard.

Turk curled his lip in disgust. "Where do we look?"

"Check with the mess sergeant and the garage," Bricks said.

"So, where do we put it when we find it?" I asked.

"The equipment room...any other questions?" he asked.

We shook our heads.

"Thanks, guys." He hopped up the steps and went inside.

Turk gathered up his cigarettes. "Son of a bitch!" he said. "This is *my* free time, why do I have to look for a damn skyhook?" He lit up a cigarette and took a short drag.

"Something that big can't be hard to find," I said.

For the next hour, we searched all over camp, the barracks, kitchen, garage, even the icehouse. Nobody knew where it was. We even stopped in the canteen and asked around. Ollie waved me over to the pool table. He spoke just above a whisper as he racked up the balls. "Don't tell anyone I told you this, but there's *no such thing* as a sky hook."

"But, I saw it with my *own eyes*," I said.

Ollie smirked. "You *thought* you saw it...but it was fake, a set-up. The sarge was in on it, too."

"The sarge? That crummy rat." I picked up a ball and zinged it into a corner pocket with a loud crack.

"Easy does it," Ollie said.

I stepped outside and told Turk. He gave me a look that would turn water into ice. Then he stormed down the steps and headed straight for the woods cussing his head off.

"Hey, come back!" I yelled.

"Leave me alone!" he shouted.

I sat down on the rec hall steps, watched him pick up a dead branch, and begin smacking it against a tree. I shook my head. "That guy does have a temper," I said to myself.

Later that night, I heard stories of boys looking for shorelines, cans of striped paint, and left-handed monkey wrenches. It was open season on rookies. I vowed never to let anyone dupe me again.

The next day before supper, Turk and I found the barracks empty and nailed Bricks' boots to the floor. The sergeant called us into his office the following day.

"'Fess up, Radzinski," he said with his face inches from mine, "You nailed those boots to the floor, didn't you?" As he spoke, he squeezed my shoulder so hard that I scrunched in pain.

"Okay, I did it," I croaked, "But, he deserved it...we wasted a lot of time looking for that thing."

Mr. Mulligan returned to his desk and picked up a pen. Turk glowered. "I don't like doing this," the sergeant said scribbling out a note. "But, you give me no choice." He handed the paper to Turk. "Give this to Mr. Kiefer, and next time—you guys think twice before you do something stupid."

Outside on the steps, Turk handed me the note. "I don't want that piece of crap."

I read it as we walked to the rec hall. "Eegghyuck," I said and smacked my forehead with the palm of my hand. "He gave us grease pit duty!"

"SON OF A BITCH!" Turk yelled and waved his fists in the air.

Grease pit duty was the worst punishment in camp. The cooks put their dirty grease into a giant tub behind the kitchen. A couple times a month someone emptied it by leaning over the tank with a bucket attached to a pole, and scooping it out. Then, they carried it to the dump. The shorter the handle you used, the worse the punishment, because it forced you to lean directly over the pool of scum. The grease reeked—it made a diaper pail smell like a bed of roses. When anyone made a shortcut behind the kitchen, he could smell the grease pit from twenty feet away, and that was with the lid on. The sergeant assigned us a four-foot pole, one-step above the dreaded two-footer.

I figured Mr. Mulligan was trying to make me quit camp, because the punishment didn't fit the crime. It was fine for someone to play a joke on us, but not the other way around. Nailing shoes to the floor was a harmless prank, a step above short-sheeting a bed.

The punishment put me in a sour mood the rest of the day. After supper, I busied myself with my latest carving, a canoe. Turk split logs at the woodpile to let off steam. While I chipped away at the wood, the thought came to me that I should transfer to another camp. I could get away from Mr. Mulligan, *and* my mother would still receive her monthly paycheck. Ever since the stolen candy incident, things had gone downhill between the sergeant and me.

That night I wrote a letter to Captain Bullock and requested a transfer to a camp closer to Detroit. I wrote that my brother was in trouble and my mom needed me home on weekends. There was enough truth to it so my mom could back me up if they questioned her. I hoped the captain was in a good mood when he got it.

The next day a bunch of enrollees huddled over a table in the rec hall. The *Soo Evening News* headline read, NEXT WAR MOVE UP TO HITLER. The article said Hitler visited the Italian dictator Mussolini to work out a new treaty. Mario leaned on the table with both hands. "I hope those two idiots choke on their meatballs."

"That's too good for them," I said from an easy chair. "We need to send Al Capone to put some holes in their uniforms."

Ollie chalked up his pool cue. "The only guys going over there with guns are saps like us."

"You're crazy," said Mario. "No politician is going to push for war."

Ollie calmly shot a ball into the side pocket. "So, who's going to stop Hitler? The Czechs? Poland?"

That started an argument about which country could stand up to Germany. The worried looks on the boys' faces told me they took it seriously. Most of us had uncles who died in the last war.

"Unless Hitler invades us, there's no way America is going to fight." I said.

"The Krauts didn't invade us last time," Arky said.

"Yeah, but they sank our boats," I shot back.

"We're in, if England's in," Mario said.

"We're in, if the Germans attack France," Ollie said.

José took a bite of his Mars Bar. "Don't forget that France built the Maginot Line."

Ollie cued up a shot. "The only thing the French army is good for...is military parades," he quipped.

That got a few laughs. I went back to my magazine and waited for my turn to play ping-pong. News from the outside world depressed me. I hoped they approved my transfer, because I was in no hurry to return to the streets.

On a cold, clammy morning a few days later, Turk threw a fit. Still surly from grease pit duty the day before, he refused to get on the truck for work duty. He paced fretfully around the loading dock as a crew leader fetched the sergeant.

Mr. Mulligan marched directly up to the brawny rookie. "What's the problem?" he snapped.

Turk avoided the sergeant's eyes. "I don't *have to work* and no one can make me."

The sergeant shuffled to his right to get in Turk's line of vision. "Oh, yeah? What are you going to do?"

"I want to go home."

"Go right ahead, but first, turn in your clothes."

Turk pouted, probably because he had no civilian clothes. "Aw...I'm going back to bed," he said and walked away.

"No one goes back to bed once his cot is made."

Turk stopped and turned. "Okay, I'll just wait in the mess hall."

The sergeant held his ground. "No one's allowed in the mess hall until supper."

"Damn it! I won't go!" Turk yelled and crossed his arms defiantly.

Mr. Mulligan walked over to him and spoke quietly. "We need good workers like you. You're big...you're strong... and you're smarter than most of the morons around here. C'mon, shake a leg." Without another word, the sergeant headed back to his office.

Turk glanced up at some of the guys in the truck staring down at him. "What are you *morons* looking at?" Then he climbed into the truck. Turk never had a chance—we all knew that.

About twenty minutes later as we rolled down a two-track far out in the woods, the truck slammed on its brakes. POW! We hit a moose that walked right in front of us! I recognized the animal with its long face and the hump on its back. We emptied out of the truck to check out the animal and truck damage. The beast was huge and dented our hood five feet off the ground. A handful of us dragged the carcass off the road. Out of the blue, a baby moose ambled up, gimpy-legged, and nuzzled its mother.

Arky slowly approached the animal and petted its neck. He turned to our work superintendent. "Can I take it to a new mother? I know another moose that lost her baby."

The super puffed on his cigar. "You know animals don't take each others' young," he said.

"I know," Arky said, as he stroked the baby. "But I'll skin the dead one and put the hide on the live one. The scent will trick her."

The officer smiled and pushed back his cap. "Son, that might work with a calf, but do you think it'll work with a moose?"

"I can't guarantee it...but I'd *sure* like to try."

The super nodded. "Okay, give it your best shot. Good luck."

Arky's face lit up. "Thank you, sir." He stroked the side of the animal's neck as it lay next to its dead mother. What a strange coincidence that Arky knew the whereabouts of a mother and baby moose that needed each other. It gave me a good feeling knowing the baby moose had a chance for a new mother.

I found a note on my cot later that day when I returned from work detail. The captain turned down my transfer request. Mr. Mulligan probably advised against it. I walked out to the edge of camp, picked up some rocks and made target practice out of every bird I saw. I would have flown right out camp that night if I had wings. The thought of facing the sergeant every day made me want to slam my head into a wall.

My predicament offered no easy answer. If I went home early, my mother would be out twenty-five bucks a month and she would use the ironing cord on my backside. If I stayed, the sergeant and his staff would make my life unbearable. With six barracks leaders and a dozen officers, I stood no a chance of getting a fair shake. The leaders planned to nail me the first chance they got, just like the cops back home. If the sergeant thought he could break me, he was in for a surprise.

During my scuffle with Farmer in the mess hall a couple weeks earlier, I bumped his can of tobacco juice and spilled it on the sleeve of my uniform shirt. I neglected to wash it right away, so a rusty colored stain set in. I hoped the leaders wouldn't notice it, but Scruggs detected it at supper and told me to replace the shirt as soon as possible. I hated the thought of seeing Thacker again.

After work duty, I brought the shirt to the supply room. I adjusted my eyes and blinked in the murky interior. Rays of light shone through a window and illuminated dust particles suspended in the air. The radio crackled in the background with the sound of an orchestra playing. I plodded up to the counter. Thacker sat hunched on a stool, knitting a wool cap. He looked up and frowned.

I laid the shirt on the counter. "I need to replace this," I said. He set the cap down and inspected the shirt. "You owe me a dollar."

I recoiled. "I shouldn't have to pay—another boy put his tobacco can on the table."

He flashed a wry smile. "Make *him* pay."

I protested. "He's not going to pay..."

Thacker cut me off. "Too late now." He set a new shirt on the counter. "I'll take it from your next paycheck."

I said nothing and walked out. Something about Thacker struck me as odd. *Is he pocketing some of* the *money?*

The next morning, I stopped by the sergeant's office after breakfast. "Got a minute, sir?" I asked through the screen door. It was a warm morning and I hoped the sergeant was in a good mood.

"C'mon in," he said. He dug into his teeth with a toothpick as he listened to my story about the stained shirt. "I'll see what I can do," he grunted.

"Thank you sir," I said and turned to leave.

"By the way," he said. "I'm looking for ways to improve the camp...got any suggestions?"

I wanted to tell him to scrub half the rules. "No, sir, things run pretty smooth around here."

"C'mon, there *must be something* you'd change."

I scratched my head and thought a moment. "Well...I like to sit on the barracks steps."

"Yeah?" he leaned forward with pencil in hand. "I wish the boys stomped their boots on the lower step instead of the top one, because I always have to sweep it off before I sit down."

"Good suggestion," the sergeant said and scrawled on a note pad. "How about another?"

"Oh, no, I can't think..."

"Just one more."

I looked out the door. "Well, it would be nice if the guys didn't slam the doors around here."

"Good point." I walked away from his office with a bounce in my step. *Maybe he's ready to show me some respect!*

The next day after supper, boys headed out to the baseball field with bats and gloves in their hands. Others carried books on their way to classes. Mario and I tossed a baseball by the flagpole. Suddenly, a voice came over the loudspeaker. "A woman is coming into camp, please be on your best behavior."

All eyes turned to the entrance where a dark gray delivery truck from Rossello's Shoe Repair drove in and pulled up next to the supply room. We stopped and watched a tall brunette step out of the driver's seat. Her knee-length dress showed off a fine pair of calves. I felt my pulse quicken. While she walked to the rear of the truck, three enrollees ran up to offer help. She opened the back gate, and they gave her a hand unloading boxes.

"Mama mia. Now that's a woman," Mario said and thumped the ball into his mitt.

"Who is she?" I asked, thrilled to see my first gal in a month.

"Rosie, the cobbler's daughter. She's dropping off shoes."

"She's one hot tomato." I said. Mario laughed and pulled my cap down over my eyes.

"Don't get too excited, rookie. She plays hard to get. A lot of us have tried."

"Even you?" I asked.

"Yep, even me," he said with a grin. "I'm Italian and I *still* couldn't get a date."

"Hey, Nick, heads up!" I turned around and saw Ollie throw a ball over my head.

"I got it," he said and ran after it.

"I have to see this," I said and followed Ollie. I felt a twinge of excitement as I got near her. Rosie held a crate in her arms and turned towards Ollie. Her red lips turned up into a tantalizing smile. Long brown wavy hair fell loosely to her shoulders.

"Hiya, cupcake," Ollie said and picked up the ball. "I've got an extra ticket to the movies Saturday night. Wanna come?" She smiled slightly and shook her head no.

Ollie slapped the ball in the mitt. "They got a drawing for some free waffle irons...you don't wanna miss that."

"I bet you want me to cook your breakfast," she mocked.

"Yeah...that'd be sweet."

Her smile turned to a scowl. "I wouldn't fall for a lug like you in a million years."

"You don't have to wait that long. We can go dancing this weekend...what do you say?" He flashed an impish grin. "Let's meet at Gould's."

Rosie handed a box to a helper. "Don't you *ever* give up?"

Ollie held his glove hand up and put his right hand on his stomach. Then he began swiveling his hips. "C'mon Rosie darling...dance with me." He looked ridiculous. Rosie giggled. Ollie began singing. "Come, get together...let the dance floor feel your leather...step lightly as a feather..."

"Stop...enough already!" Rosie said cracking up. "Okay... I'll meet you at Gould's, but I'm bringing a friend."

"Great," Ollie said and put his arm over my shoulders. "Does she need a date? Nick here can cut a rug."

Rosie looked at me and I blushed. "Sorry, she's taken," Rosie said. She slammed the truck gate. "You better be nice to me."

Ollie held up his hands. "I gotta be nice, there's two hundred guys in here who'll clobber me if I'm not."

After she drove off, we walked back to the quad. "Hey, thanks for trying," I said.

"Aw, it was nothing," he said.

"How'd you get her to say yes?"

Ollie tossed the ball to me. "Two things. First you got to be persistent. That was the fifth time I asked her out, most guys give up after the third."

"What's the other?"

"Make 'em laugh," he said. "Even if you look stupid, you gotta make 'em laugh." He swiveled his hips and spun around on his toes. I chuckled. Watching Ollie in action fired me up to meet some girls.

A couple days later, the sergeant called a meeting just before supper. Dressed in uniform and ready to eat, we hoped he kept the remarks brief. He talked about an upcoming inspection and then he surprised me when he brought up my name. "As you know, I like to find ways to improve things in camp. Can Nick Radzinski please step forward?"

My heart stopped for a second. I took a deep breath and hustled up front. "Nick has made a couple suggestions I want to share with you. Most of you know he likes to sit on the steps while he whittles." I heard some giggling from the boys. "He says a lot of you stomp your dirty feet on the *top step* before you go in the barracks." The sergeant turned to me. "Nick thinks you should stomp your feet on the *lower step*. That way he won't have to sweep off the dirt when he sits down." I heard snickering in the crowd. I felt myself heating up inside.

"And...Nick thinks there is too much door slamming going on. Can you guys try to be a little more thoughtful and close the doors gently?" The snickers turned into laughs. I kept my eyes glued to the ground and bit my lower lip. "Thanks Nick, you can go," the sergeant said.

I shouldered my way back into the group, red-faced. "Don't let him bother you." Frank whispered to me.

"Shake it off," Arky said from behind and patted my shoulder.

At supper, a lot of guys told me to brush it off, but it did little to help.

"Don't get worked up over it," Turk said from across the table.

"Yeah," José added. "He just wants you to get mad."

After eating, I found some privacy on my cot and hemmed a pair of pants. I poked myself with a needle three times, as I tried to figure out why the sergeant humiliated me. On one hand, he wanted me to buck up, and then he embarrassed me in front of everyone! I felt like a lumberjack balancing on a log in the river, and the spinning log under my feet was the sarge. He wanted me to go down...but why? *Does he want me to go over-the-hill?*

The next day we cleared trees and brush under a power line. As I passed other boys on the way to the burn piles, they told me the sergeant was mean for what he did to me the day before. Their words took away some of the sting.

At lunchtime, I searched for a place to eat alone. I found a log in a clearing to sit on and laid out my food beside me. I bit into a ham sandwich and watched a chipmunk pop in and out of a hole in an old stump. Its yellow stripes helped it blend into the forest floor. If only I could blend into the background like he could. I heard my name and saw Frank walking up.

"What's eating you," he said and sat next to me. "You hiding from somebody?"

"What do *you* think?" I said.

"You're not letting Mulligan get to you?"

"He shamed me in front of the *whole camp.*"

Frank took a swig of milk. "So what? You're not the first. I've seen him do it to other guys."

The chipmunk darted back into its hole. "I don't care who he does it to, it still doesn't make it right."

"There's a method to his madness," Frank said.

"That's hard to believe."

"He's just testing you...to see what you're made of."

"That's a bunch of hooey." I scooped up a forkful of potato salad.

"The longer you're here, the better he treats you."

I stopped chewing. "I'm on probation...my name is mud."

"That's funny," he said. "I thought it was Nick."

"Aw, shaddup..."

"Stop your belly-aching. I've seen other guys on probation make it through." He bit into his sandwich.

The chipmunk climbed on top of the stump. "I don't want to hear about other guys," I said.

We ate the rest of the meal in silence. When he finished, Frank stood up and gave me a silly smile. "Look at the bright side—the guys might stop wiping their boots off on your step."

"Get out of here." I picked up a stick and threw it at him. Frank tried to convince me I was like any other guy, but he was wrong. The officers treated me like a second-class citizen because I came on probation. They weren't going to let me forget it either.

After work, I found a note on my cot from the First Sergeant. He wrote that Thacker reduced the fine for the stained shirt to fifty cents. I crumpled up the note. "That's a bunch of baloney," I said. "I shouldn't have to pay a dime."

Frank pulled off his socks, as he got ready to shower. "It's better than paying a buck."

"Whose side are you on?" I said and undid my boots.

"Hey, Nick," I turned. Scruggs pointed at my footlocker. "Open it, please."

"What's up?" I said as I knelt beside it.

"Some knives were stolen from the kitchen."

"Why would I take them?" I flipped the lid open and removed my baseball mitt and Dad's carving from the top.

Scruggs frowned. "You've been doing a lot of carving lately."

I let out a groan. "Oh geez, you *know* I use Isaac's knives."

"Yeah...but I got to check anyway."

Piece by piece I emptied the trunk.

Scruggs poked around until he was satisfied. "That's all. Sorry for the trouble," he said.

I said nothing and repacked.

Frank scooted down on the floor and helped me pick up. "Don't let it bother you," he said.

My hands were on fire as I organized the locker. "Didn't you tell me things will get better with the sarge?" I snapped. Some fellas overheard me and turned their heads our way.

"Don't blow your top," Frank said under his breath.

"Easy for you to say," I slammed the locker shut. I finished undressing, wrapped a towel around my waist, and stomped out the door. Stolen candy bars, nailed shoes to the floor, a hike in the woods and now they accused me of stealing a knife? None of it added up to a hill of beans! Back home, guys my age stole cars and mugged people.

After supper, I took a Doc Savage book out of my locker. Doc was a fantasy hero who searched for missing people, killed strange creatures, and saved the world from the bad guys. This latest book told the story of a five-man army he took to the South Pole in search of a missing ocean liner and treasure. Their only clue was a map tattooed on the back of a blind violinist.

I lay on my cot with the book propped on my pillow and tried to focus on the story. Suddenly, Arky barged into the barracks. "Hey guys," he yelled, "The mother moose took the baby—*she took the baby!*" Everyone turned around. "I saw them walkin' through the swamp by Paradise Lake... dang, you should've seen it!" Some of the boys clapped, others shouted "Atta boy, Arky!"

"Hey Arky, there's a baby skunk wandering around camp, think you can find it a mother?" a boy teased.

"That joke stinks," Arky shot back.

Another piped up, "Can you find *me* a girlfriend?"

"Sure," Arky said, "but she might have four legs and a hard bite." He kept us in stitches. When the barracks quieted down, I went back to my book, but I found it hard to concentrate. The pages could have been blank, the way my mind wandered. The locker search still bothered me. I hated living under a cloud of suspicion and felt like I didn't belong in camp.

Saturday arrived a couple days later. After lunch, some veterans took a rookie out into the woods for a snipe hunt. A snipe was a bird that looked like a morning dove and like most birds, was almost impossible to catch by hand. They gave the guy a burlap sack to catch it with and left him alone in the woods. The sandy-haired rookie went along with the joke. "Squirt'" stood barely five-and-a-half feet tall and probably weighed no more than a hundred pounds soaking wet.

The pint-size enrollee shocked everyone when he strutted into camp a couple hours later with a snipe in his hand. I jumped off the barber seat where Frank was cutting my hair and we both ran out to see the bird. Squirt had tied its legs to a string, and hung it on a tree branch for everyone to see. Brown and white markings covered the bird and a long slender bill protruded from its head. It seemed like half the camp came to see it, even a few officers stopped by.

Squirt told us he saw the snipe floating in a pond so he threw a stick at it and killed it. A bunch of fellas put Squirt on a blanket and heaved him high up into the air like a bird. He yelled and flapped his arms around like a wounded duck.

While I watched the action, someone whispered in my ear. "That's how you're gonna fly when I sock ya, Rat Eye." I turned and saw Farmer with his trademark leering grin. A fresh batch of ugly red pimples covered his face.

"Aw, take a hike," I said and turned away from him.

"Don't turn your back on me, city boy," he said and gave me a shove.

I stumbled forward to my knees and looked up to see

Bricks coming our way. “Do we have a problem here?” The assistant leader asked.

“No problem,” Farmer said, patting me on the shoulder. “We was just conversing.”

“Yeah, just conversing,” I said as I dusted myself off.

Bricks looked at us suspiciously. “You guys stay away from each other.” We both nodded.

“You really want that match with Scruggs don’t you?” I said after Bricks left.

Farmer spat tobacco juice by my feet. “It’s *you* I want.”

“Be careful what you wish for,” I said as he walked away.

He made his hand tremble. “”Yeah, I’m scared, see me shaking.”

I went back to my haircut with Frank. I enjoyed taunting Farmer; maybe it was a death wish. One swing with his big paw would put me in a hospital. *Maybe he’s my ticket out of here!*

The following week, I began an arts and crafts class that met twice a week after supper. A Cherokee Indian taught the class. Mr. Wells was one of the most respected men in camp and well-liked by the boys. He originally enlisted at Camp Marquette, an Indian CCC camp when he was thirty-six. When the captain of the camp discovered Mr. Wells had a teaching degree, he transferred him to our camp to be an educational advisor. He attended a Lutheran teachers college, but I heard he had some books on Eastern religions.

My jaw dropped when Mr. Wells walked into the classroom. He stood about six-and-a-half feet tall with broad shoulders and dark braided hair that hung halfway down his back. A handsome man with a long straight nose and high cheekbones, he walked with a commanding presence. He dressed in a white shirt like other educational advisors, but wore a leather vest instead of a jacket. His string tie held an oval silver piece with a blue stone set in it.

On our first night of class, Mr. Wells led us into the woods to search for birch and cherry wood to make bows and arrows. He wore moccasins and walked noiselessly with long graceful strides. It seemed like he could walk on eggshells without breaking them. The rest of us made a ruckus as we stomped through the brush, cracking twigs and snapping branches as we tried to keep up.

Mr. Wells told us stories along the way. He said Sitting Bull was not just a chief, but also a shaman, which was a wise man. He described Sitting Bull's victory at Little Big Horn and how in later years, the chief became so popular that the army tried to arrest him, but during an ambush, a bullet in the head killed him.

It surprised me to learn that Indians did not have a word for *lie* in their language. Mr. Wells said the white man came with the hand of peace, but made war. I listened closely because it was the first time I ever heard the Indian side of their story—it was far different from what I learned in school or saw in the movies.

On our walk in the woods, we discovered a patch of pink, white and yellow flowers growing out of the leaves. "Those are Moccasin Flowers or what the white man calls Lady Slippers," Mr. Wells said. I knelt next to one.

"How did they get their name?" someone asked.

"An Indian maiden met a handsome young brave from another tribe at a clan meeting and the two fell in love." Mr. Wells spoke slowly and used his hands in a graceful manner as he told the story. "One day the two tribes had a dispute over hunting lands, and the tribal meetings ended. The young lovers were forbidden to see each other again." The fellas moved in closer to hear well.

He continued. "The young maiden became distraught and suffered in sadness all winter long. In the spring, just as the snow was melting, she ran through the woods to the lake. Standing high atop a cliff, she leaped to her death. All she left behind was a single moccasin which had fallen off her foot as she ran through the snow." We listened spellbound. "When the snow melted, little flowers came up where she made footprints in the snow. The flowers looked like a moccasin or a slipper." He paused. "That's how they got the name Lady Slipper."

Mr. Wells told the story with more suspense than a radio show. We then peppered him with questions about growing up on a reservation. Everything he said was new and interesting to me. I understood why he commanded such respect in camp.

A few days later, Elliot invited me to join him and Arky for meat patrol. He said the mess sergeant approved my going along. "Hot dawg," I said when I heard the news. Soon we barreled down the road in a Dodge pickup with Elliot at the wheel. I sat by the door, elbow out the window, with Arky squeezed between us. The cool morning air rushed into the truck and I watched the wildflowers fly by as we drove down the dirt road. It felt great to get away from camp.

"So...what are we picking up?" I asked.

"Lamb," Elliot said and giggled.

They were up to something. "Okay, what's going on?" I asked.

Arky explained that a rancher called the camp and offered to sell us some sheep killed by a predator.

"We're going out for dead animals?"

"I'm doin' the dirty work," Arky said.

I slapped my hand on the door. "That's just great." I said. "I HATE animal guts!"

Half an hour later, we drove up a long, narrow two-track to the ranch. Recent rains turned the grass fields to a rich green color. A dozen sheep carcasses lay scattered across the pasture. We saw the rancher sitting on a little stool shearing one of the carcasses. The man wore a faded hat and leather chaps. He sheared thick matted hair off the sheep with a hand clipper.

"How you fellas doin'?" he asked when he saw us approach. The belly of the sheep was sliced open with its guts hanging out. After one look, I felt ill and walked over to a clump of bushes where I upchucked. I heard laughing behind my back.

"Don't mind him," I heard Arky tell the man.

When I returned, I overheard the rancher explain what had happened. "I think some bear cubs got separated from their mother. When they couldn't suckle the sheep, they tore into their bellies with their claws."

"Those were *mean* cubs," Elliot said.

"Better get to work before the meat spoils," the man said. He pointed to a spot behind us. "Just over that ridge is a creek where you can rinse them." He identified the two sheep he still had to shear.

We grabbed our buckets of supplies and headed toward a sheep. Arky worked quickly with his buck knife. He removed and emptied the intestines for use as sausage casings. The rest of the organs he dumped into a bucket.

Elliot and I carried the rendered carcasses to the stream, gripping them by the legs. We waded into the shallow water and dragged them back and forth, washing off most of the blood and loose matter.

Arky worked quickly and cleaned a dozen sheep in a couple hours. "I've been doin' this since I was six," he said proudly.

"When I was six I was feeding calves," I said.

"When I was six, I washed my dog," Elliot bragged.

"Dang...maybe you guys are ready fer my job," Arky joked.

"No thanks," we said.

We loaded the carcasses onto the truck and covered them with damp tarps to keep them cool. Eliot paid the rancher $1.50 for each animal and then we drove back to camp with Arky at the wheel.

"That wasn't so bad, was it?" Arky said to me.

I looked out the window at cows in pasture. “I can handle it,” I said softly. I wanted that job in the kitchen. Working in the woods in the winter sounded awful to me. I turned to Arky. “So how’d you get into trouble back home?

“I shot at a man,” he said calmly.

“WHAT?” squawked Elliot. He squirmed next to me.

“My brother and I were drivin’ one day and a big ol’ truck wouldn’t let us pass.”

“So?” Elliot said.

“So...I grabbed my 30-30, leaned out the window and took a couple shots at him.”

Elliot’s jaw dropped. “What happened?”

Arky smiled smugly. “He pulled over right away and let us pass.”

“How’d they catch you?” I asked.

Arky shook his head. “He must’ve wrote down our license plate, cuz a cop came to my house the next day.”

“What’d the judge say?” I asked.

“He said I was lucky to be only fifteen and told me to get out of town...that’s why my folks sent me to live with my aunt.”

I noticed a woodchuck amble off into a ditch on the side of the road. “Funny thing about judges,” I said. “If you’re under eighteen they want you out of town.”

“You got that right,” he said. Arky impressed me with his knowledge of the wilds. I asked him what he would do if a bear attacked him.

“And I got no gun, no knife?” he asked.

“Nothing,” I said.

“I’d jam my arm down its throat...choke it to death.”

“HUH?” Elliot jerked next to me.

The truck veered a little. “I’d lose an arm, but save my life.”

“Never thought of that,” I said. I liked this kid. We turned onto the camp road and soon drove through the entrance. After we dropped off the meat at the kitchen, we showered. Then we scrubbed our clothes outside, using a washboard and wringer.

While we washed, Thacker walked by with an armful of blankets. He gave me a cold stare. "Heard you talked to the sergeant about your shirt," he said.

"Yeah...I did," I said and slowly turned the wringer handle.

"You got a big mouth," he said as he sauntered by. I looked away.

After he left, I turned to Arky who was hanging clothes on the line. "Something's not quite right about that man."

Arky nodded. "Back in Arkansas, we'd say he's one fish shy of a full string."

I chuckled, but deep down Thacker worried me. The supply sergeant was just a few notches down from the First Sergeant in pecking order, and he could make trouble for me.

That night after supper, I went into the barracks to get my baseball mitt. José sat hunched over on his cot reading a letter. I was almost out the door when I heard him sniffle. I turned and saw him rubbing his eyes.

"Bad news?" I asked.

José motioned his head to the letter that lay next to him. I pointed to my chest. "You want me to read it?" He nodded so I picked it up. His sister wrote the letter in English.

> *Dear José,*
>
> *We are all very proud of you and the fine job you are doing. Your last paycheck helped us buy lots of food like beans, corn meal, rice and sugar. The pantry is so full you wouldn't recognize it. Mama spends a lot more time in the kitchen because of you. She is always singing.*
>
> *There was enough money left over from your last check to buy Josephina a new Easter dress, a pair of shoes and an Easter bonnet! I wish you could have seen how pretty she looked at church. We thought of you that day.*

Papa thinks he may get a job at the River Rouge plant. They are hiring new workers next week, and he is friends with one of the foremen.

Thanks again for your hard work. The money you earn has really helped us. We think of you often. Keep up the good work and be careful.

Love,
Olivia

I rested my foot on his trunk and thought for a moment. "I bet you're unhappy because you miss your family." José shook his head no.

I thought some more. "I got it...you're sad because there wasn't enough money for your parents to buy anything nice for *themselves.*" He bit his lower lip and nodded.

"Jeepers creepers don't feel sorry for them. It made them happy to buy all those things, right?"

He looked up with wet eyes. "Yeah, I guess so," he sniffled.

"You shouldn't be unhappy. How old is Josephina?"

"Nine," he said.

"I lost my three sisters...Anya would be eight right now, but she died as a baby." I felt my own eyes become misty. "I'd give my eye teeth to see her in an Easter dress."

"Aw, shucks," José said. "I'm sorry."

My voice cracked. "Don't worry how your family spends the money...just be grateful you still *have* a family."

He wiped his nose with his hand. "You're right."

"You're damn right, I'm right." I slapped his shoulder lightly. "C'mon, grab your mitt," I said.

"Okay," he said, and moved slowly to his trunk.

"I'll wait outside." I needed some fresh air to clear my head. A wave of disappointment hit me whenever I thought about my sisters. I sat on the steps and looked out over the quad. *What I would do to see my brother and sisters again for just a day.*

"You ready?" I looked up. José stood on the steps with a pensive look on his face.

"You bet," I said and tossed him the ball. We cut across the quad to the baseball diamond and looked for a pickup game.

The following Monday I reported to K.P. duty. It was not a punishment but a job everyone was required to do. They assigned me pot-washing duty, the toughest job in the kitchen. As I scrubbed, I wondered if the sergeant handpicked my job. I looked over my shoulder at the other boys who laughed and joked around while they peeled potatoes and mopped floors.

No one bothered to talk with me. I couldn't hear them if they did because the pots banged so loud. At least it gave me time to think about my dad. I had written quite a few letters to people who knew him and asked our postman to check for forwarding addresses. I also wrote to the last two companies he worked for in Detroit to see if he had been in touch. My mother wrote to his cousins, nephews and nieces.

Mom said my uncle's insurance money went to his brothers and sisters if we did not find Dad. She sent me my uncle's rabbit foot and hoped it brought me luck. I tied it to my belt loop and wore it every day. I wondered if he wore it the night he stepped in front of the train.

I needed more than a rabbit foot to bring me luck—it would take a small miracle to find my dad. Even if I found him, there was no guarantee he would share a dollar with Mom. She deserved at least half of it so she could move into a new house, but Dad could have remarried and a new wife might have other ideas on how to spend the money. I needed to find my dad first and worry about the money later.

By the end of the day, my hands were as wrinkled as prunes, but at least I got to work in the kitchen. I loved the smell of roasts in the oven, soups simmering, and hash browns frying. Someday, if I played my cards right, I would be a mess orderly.

When Saturday finally rolled around, Frank and I climbed on the afternoon truck for "the Soo." I looked sharp in my uniform and money in my pocket put a smile on my face. Frank wanted to go in civilian clothes, but I didn't have any nice clothes to wear, so he wore his uniform, too. A few dozen of us squeezed onto the benches in the '36 Chevy truck for the hour-long ride.

We sped down dusty roads past newly green forests, fields blooming with wild flowers, and weather-beaten barns. With June only a few days away and temperatures in the seventies, it felt like summer. I sat in the rear of the truck and waved at everyone we passed—farmers on tractors, mothers hanging laundry, and boys feeding cows. Every new face was a welcome sight.

Main Street in Sault Ste. Marie bustled with people, including women carrying shopping bags and children on skates. It seemed strange to be in a city again after living six weeks in the woods. The truck dropped us off by a movie theatre where we unloaded and headed off in different directions. Frank and I crossed the street and walked toward the locks. I could hardly wait to see some girls.

"We're in luck," Frank said. Two fresh-faced women in overalls walked toward us. They looked to be in their early twenties and each wore a cocky smile. This could be fun!

We stopped. "Hi girls," Frank said, "Know any good bakeries around here?"

They separated and walked on either side of us. As they passed by, they bumped us with their shoulders. I stumbled and almost fell. They snickered as they continued walking.

"What the hell was *that* all about?" I asked.

Frank brushed it off. "That doesn't happen too much, don't let it bother you."

"She almost knocked me off my feet and you're telling me to forget about it?"

"Relax, there're plenty of girls who like guys in uniform, we just ran into the wrong ones."

We started up the sidewalk again. "I'm shopping for new clothes *today*," I said. "This is for the birds."

We hiked to Brady Pier where the blooming gardens and manicured shrubbery created a beautiful park-like setting. Dark plumes of smoke drifted from the paper mills on the other side of the river. The locks were a narrow channel of water no more than a hundred feet wide. Ore freighters from Duluth passed through the waterway on their way to Lake Huron. We walked along the concrete walk and watched a long rust-colored freighter slowly rise while water filled the lock. Sailors waved down to us from the deck. “What a life,” I said.

Frank grinned. “Yep...a girl in every port.”

“You’re all wet,” I said.

“Hey...that’s the life of a sailor.”

“Fooling around gets you in trouble.”

“Oh, yeah? Since when are *you* an expert on women?”

“I’m not, but I had a buddy who got gonorrhea messing around with the wrong kind of women.”

Frank held up his hands. “Spare me...”

“It’s no joke...I drove him to the doc for his shots.” Frank shut up for a while.

From the locks, we walked down Portage Street and came to some tourist shops. Out on the sidewalk a gray-haired Indian woman sold hand-woven baskets, birch bark canoes and teepees. I paid thirty cents for a small canoe. As she took my money, I noticed that her faded, shapeless dress looked like it came from a relief agency. After we left, I asked Frank, “Did you see her clothes?”

“Yeah, pretty shabby,” he said.

“Why doesn’t she wear Indian clothes?”

“Beats me, maybe she’s too poor.”

“Doesn’t seem right, maybe it’s the depression.”

I stopped and watched through a store window while a man made fudge. He poured thick creamy chocolate out of a brass mixing bowl onto a marble table and used a trowel to form it in a large rectangular shape. I was absorbed in his work when I heard Frank yell, “Hurry up, the streetcar’s coming!”

I ran to catch up and we both climbed on. A staid looking man in a suit gave us a critical look when he saw us. Later, I asked Frank about it. "Some of the locals think we're troublemakers from the city," he said.

I grinned. "Who can blame 'em?"

Walking down Main Street I noticed that people wore nicer clothes than they did in Detroit. I also saw that there were no bums on the park benches. "Don't they know there's a depression going on?" I asked. "Where're the empty stores?"

"Government jobs keep this town running," Frank said. "Fort Brady, the locks...lot of work around here."

We turned down a side street and explored a neighborhood of white cottage-type homes. Yellow daffodils brightened up of the gardens, and the yards looked neatly mowed.

Two young boys roller-skated by us. "Did you see that?" I said. "No patches on their pants."

Frank rolled his eyes. "Enough, already."

We watched some kids play baseball in a park and then headed back into town to grab a snack. We stopped at a restaurant with a green and white awning called the *American Café*. We read the menu posted on the window.

Hot Beef Sandwich/Mashed Potatoes - 25 cents
Hot Turkey Sandwich/ Mashed Potatoes - 25 cents
Meatballs and Beans - 20 cents
Blue Plate Special
Ham w/pineapple w/Vegetable & Bread - 25 cents

The prices looked good so we stepped inside. The smell of grilled hamburgers and fried onions filled the air. Everything seemed modern, from the green linoleum floor to the chrome-edged counter. A Benny Goodman tune played on the jukebox while waitresses hurried by with trays of food. Two men in suits at the counter turned and nodded.

We climbed onto a couple of stools. Above the mirror

behind the counter a sign read, *Serving the Soo, since 1902.* A table with three matronly women checked us out warily. Frank said some of the locals thought we were having a good time at the government's expense. The negative reactions from people bothered me, until a pert redhead set our water glasses out with a friendly smile. Her eyes seemed full of mischief.

"It's my first time here," I told her.

"It won't be your last," she shot back. "So what will you officers have today?" I chuckled. Frank ordered a cheeseburger, but I was undecided.

"Got any brains on the menu?" Frank asked. "He's a moron."

I gave him a dirty look. "Sorry, no brains today," she said. "How 'bout some chicken soup?"

"Yeah...that sounds good," I said.

"Coming right up," she said brightly.

I leaned over the counter to get a better view of her legs. "Nice chassis," I mumbled to Frank.

He craned his neck for a look. "Yeah...a classy chassis."

A minute later, she put out a bowl of hot soup. When I stirred it, something was missing. "Hey, there's no chicken," I said.

She peered into it. "Well I'll be. The noodles are dancing with the vegetables, but the chicken forgot to show up at the party." Frank and I laughed. She leaned over the counter and lowered her voice. "You guys *really* want to know where the chicken is?"

"Yeah," we said and bent forward.

"It's crossing the road to get to the other side." Frank and I busted up. She added meat to the soup and set out coffee.

"And don't complain about the coffee," she said, "it's too weak to fight back." She kept us in stitches. By the time we left, I felt better about wearing my uniform in public. The rest of the afternoon, we explored the downtown and did some shopping. I bought a new pair of dress pants and a short-sleeved shirt.

As we drove out of town, the truck stopped at an intersection. Farmer leaned out and yelled at two cheerleader-type girls on the sidewalk. "What'cha doing tonight, girls?" he yelled. "Lookin' for a little fun? Well, I'm your man!" The girls giggled.

Bricks, the assistant barracks leader, stood up. "You can't talk to women that way," he said. "You disgraced our camp."

"Aw, go fly a kite," Farmer said and waved him off. "I was just having fun."

"We'll let a kangaroo court decide if it was just fun," Bricks said. The boys whooped it up while Farmer showed an ugly scowl. I thought Bricks made a big deal out of nothing, but I looked forward to the trial.

The next afternoon, we gathered at the log circle under the giant oak for the kangaroo court. Boys fought over seats as if John Dillinger was on trial. Even the crows above us cawed with excitement.

Farmer looked like he just got off the farm, dressed in overalls and a red neckerchief. Scruggs came in uniform and acted as judge. He banged a wooden mallet on the lectern.

"Willard Clarence Fields," the judge began, "you are charged with making rude and suggestive remarks to two women on Ashmun Street yesterday afternoon...how do you plead?"

"Not guilty," Farmer said. He stuck out his jaw in defiance. Whistles and catcalls came from the boys.

"Order in the court!" Scruggs shouted and pounded his gavel.

Bricks acted as prosecuting attorney. Well groomed with short-cropped hair, he chose his words carefully. "Every member of this camp must act responsibly when he goes into town. If he doesn't, our good name is lost and all of us lose respect." He proceeded to grill Farmer on his motives for yelling at the girls.

"Can't you take a joke?" scoffed Farmer. "What's wrong with you?"

"This is not about *me*, it's about YOU," Bricks shot back.

Mario was the defense attorney and represented Farmer. He seemed older than his eighteen years and spoke eloquently. "Clarence is an American first and CCC boy second. He did *not* give up his right to free speech when he joined the CCC." Mario paused and let his eyes flow over the audience. "My client did no harm to the girls—in fact they *laughed* at him." There were more whistles, Scruggs slammed the gavel again and called for order.

Bricks stepped up and stared at the audience with his jaw set. He spoke with authority. "Just because the young women laughed, *does not* make it okay." He pointed to an enrollee. "What if one of those women was your sister, how would you feel if Farmer taunted her that way?" The wide-eyed boy shrugged.

Bricks continued, unruffled. "This trial is about how we represent our camp in public—it's *not* about freedom of speech. Farmer made a mistake yesterday, not a big mistake, but *still* a mistake. He needs to be found guilty, so everyone knows this kind of behavior won't be tolerated." The audience murmured.

Mario called up two witnesses for Farmer's defense. A wiry kid with kinky hair said it was common for CCC'ers to whistle at girls from trucks. He claimed that an enrollee met his girlfriend that way. Another boy testified that he yelled at some girls from a truck when he was at another camp, and never got in trouble. The trial seemed like a roller coaster, when one side seemed to have it in the bag, the other side came up with another good argument. Mario rested his case by saying that unless there was outright profanity or vulgarity—the camp could not muzzle an enrollee. "All my client did was ask those girls what they were up to last night. If that's *offensive language*...then many of us has been guilty of saying those very same words at one time or another."

The court went into recess as the eleven boys on the jury walked over to a picnic table to deliberate. After a short break, the jurors returned with serious faces.

"Does the jury have a decision?" Scruggs asked.

"Yes," the foreman said with a poker face.

"Well?" Scruggs leaned forward and waited. "Out with it!"

The foreman glanced around sheepishly. "The jury finds the defendant...guilty!"

Farmer scowled and bared his teeth like a pit bull. The rest of us jumped up and let loose with yells and whistles. When the boys settled down, Scruggs gave out the sentence. Farmer needed to walk backward to Rock River, jump in and return to camp. Then hold a bar of soap in his mouth for one minute. If Farmer embarrassed the camp again, he would have to hold the soap in his mouth for five minutes. Even though I disliked Farmer, it was a bum rap. When a guy couldn't tease a girl in fun, there were too many rules.

The weekend passed much too quickly. Monday morning I was back at work clearing out stumps for a new road. I worked with Sweet Bobby, the orphan boy. Using shovels, we dug down to expose the roots of the stumps and then chopped away with an axe. After we hacked the roots the best we could, a tractor came along to help. With a chain securely wrapped around the stump, the tractor pulled, slowly exposing more roots. We hacked away at the roots some more and then the tractor pulled again until the stump broke loose.

If the stump was too large to cut out, we called in José to bring in the dynamite. He had passed the safety test with flying colors and relished his new job. When I heard a loud KABOOM in the woods, I smiled and thought of José. He had come a long way from blowing up cats. We loaded the stumps onto trucks, and took them to farmers who used them to make fences.

While we worked, Bobby and I talked about his life in the orphanage. He told me that once a week adoptive parents came to choose a child from a line formed in front of the orphanage. Year after year, no one picked him. Once, the orphanage put Bobby and just one other boy out for an adoptive couple to look at. They chose the other boy.

"The other kid said he was sorry he got picked instead of me," Bobby said, "but, I told him to be happy."

I swung my axe. "What a lousy thing to do to you guys."

"Oh, no," Bobby said. "The smaller the line the better...it improved our chances." Bobby joined the CCC at seventeen because the government promised to put the money that normally went to the parents, into a savings account for him.

"Twenty-five bucks a month?" I said. "You're a rich man...what are you going to do with all that dough?"

Bobby jammed his shovel into the ground. His pale cheeks turned crimson from the midday heat. "I'm gonna hit the road. I want to see Chicago and the Grand Canyon."

"Sounds good to me," I said. I asked him how he and Mario became best friends.

Bobby said it happened while they planted trees. "Mario was showing off by working real fast...but he got ahead of the line. I warned him to slow down or he'd get in trouble."

"What happened?" I asked.

"He pulled back just before the forest officer came to check."

"Close call, eh?"

Bobby fitted a chain around a stump. "Yep, we got to be good friends after that."

"Let her rip!" I yelled. Squirt put the CAT into gear and the roots snapped like broken twigs as the stump broke loose.

I heard a voice behind me. "That's what your bones are gonna sound like when I get you into a ring."

I turned. Farmer stood with an axe on his shoulder,

looking like Paul Bunyan Junior. His biceps bulged under his tight shirtsleeves. "You ready for a re-match, Rat Eye?" he snarled.

"Get lost," I said.

"My butt still hurts from that stone your buddy threw at me... it's payback time."

"Take a hike," I said.

"Yeah, get out of here," Bobby said.

"You're just yellow," he said and walked away.

"What's with that guy?" Bobby asked.

I shook my head. "He's a half bubble off plumb."

Later, as I worked, it occurred to me that I didn't know a single thing about Farmer's past. I knew about Bobby, Arky, Frank and others, but *nothing* about Farmer. If the bully ever opened up, maybe I could figure him out and get him off my back.

Camp Raco's boxing team held the best record in the district thanks to the coach, Scruggs. He was also unbeaten in all of his own CCC matches. An hour after supper, I stood nervous with excitement as a boy wrapped my hand with a long strip of cloth before I inserted it into a boxing glove. I signed up for boxing because I knew Farmer and I would have a grudge match someday. I needed all the help I could get. A regulation-size boxing ring sat on the grassy area where I boxed with him back in April. Around the ring, about twenty boys stripped to the waist warmed up by sparring or shadow-boxing.

A short fella with bad breath gave me instructions. "Turn your shoulder on your jab—you'll get a few more inches of reach." The gloves felt uncomfortable as I pounded the heavy bag. It felt like slugging a sack of concrete. After a few minutes, sweat streamed down my forehead into my eye. I pounded away, with each swing a little weaker as my strength gave out. When the bell rang, I collapsed on a bench. After a few rounds, I worked on other things. My coach taught me how to bend side-to-side at the waist to avoid punches. Like a dolt, I usually moved my body *into* the line of the punch instead of *away*.

At the end of the workout, I sat hunched over on a bench. When Scruggs came by, I asked him how to beat a big guy like Farmer. He chugged some water and spoke in low voice. “You got to be smarter and faster,” he said.

I nodded.

“I’ve seen fellas your size take out bigger guys than Farmer.”

“How’d they do it?”

I made space on the bench and he sat down. “You gotta get inside his reach, where he can’t hit you...keep him off balance.”

After he gave me a few more tips, I asked, “How’d *you* get to be a boxer?”

Scruggs took a swill of water and spit. He was such an easygoing fella, it was hard to believe he was a killer in the ring. “When I was a boy, I protected my brothers and sisters from gangs when we walked to school in Detroit.”

“Oh, yeah?”

“One day, when I wasn’t around, someone stole my sister’s lunch pail. I found the guy who did it and beat the hell out of him.”

“What happened the next time you saw him?”

Scruggs grinned wryly. “He and his buddies ran across the street.”

“They were smart,” I said.

Scruggs grinned and nodded.

Dear Mother,

I’ve been planting about a thousand trees a day. I carry a box of pine seedlings and use a spud bar to make the holes. We form long lines and walk across the fields. I plant a tree every three steps. I put the roots in, straighten the tree, and then stomp the dirt. The forest officer tugs the plants to make sure they’re in tight.

The black flies bite something awful. They burrow into my hair—it drives me crazy. All day long, the boys are cussing at the flies. The crew leader let us quit early to go swimming. The water was freezing, but we didn't mind because it numbed the pain from the bites.

There's a bully who wants to fight me. He sneaks up behind me all the time—he really gets on my nerves. The sergeant still thinks I'm guilty every time something gets stolen. If that's not enough, the supply sergeant who everyone likes, hates my guts! I can't figure it out. Other than that, I get along with most of the people in camp. I began training with the boxing team—it might come in handy someday.

I hope everything is OK back home. Say hello to my friends and tell Gabe to sign up for the CCC so you can get an extra $25 a month. You deserve it.

Love,
Nick

As I dug into a corned beef and cabbage supper a couple of nights later, Ollie told us a story from his days in California. He and his friend walked into the mayor's office in San Francisco and told him they were going to steal some food because they were starving.

"The mayor?" I asked and bit into a roll.

Ollie nodded. "Yep...we asked him what he was going to do about it."

"What'd he say?" Arky asked.

"He sent us to his brother who ran a lunchroom at a train station."

"Did he give you a job?" I asked.

"Nope, but he gave us five dimes."

"Five dimes?" A boy echoed.

"Yep. We bought a pig's hock, a sack of potatoes and a couple loaves of stale bread with the money."

I stopped chewing and listened. "We boiled the hock to make a broth and dipped the bread and potatoes in it...it fed us for a whole week."

I rubbed my roll on the plate and soaked up every drop of juice. Ollie's story reminded me how bad it was out in the real world. As I walked across the quad after supper, it occurred to me that the forest around our camp protected us like a big cocoon from the outside world. Inside the camp, there was no hunger, no poverty, and no unemployment. A bad day in camp was better than a good day on the streets of Detroit. *Why can't I keep my mind on the good things?*

A few days later, Ollie volunteered to pick up some rookies at the train depot in Trout Lake. The sergeant allowed him to invite another person so he asked me. We left after supper and rode in a dark green Chevy sedan with nice cloth seats. On our drive through the countryside, we saw farmers bringing in their first hay cutting of the year. Most drove tractors, but a few used horse-drawn reapers. They crept along slowly through the fields making long, straight lines. It reminded me of my days on the farm.

Ollie kept me laughing with stories about his time in San Francisco. He talked about the time he spent on the wharves and going to bawdy vaudeville shows. Just before we arrived at Trout Lake, Ollie pulled off the road and pinned some of his grandfather's war medals on the front of his uniform.

"What are you doing?" I asked.

He smirked, "You'll find out." He straightened his tie. "Keep your mouth shut and play along." I nodded.

When we pulled up to the depot, I ran around and opened his door as instructed. Three fresh-faced recruits came over to greet us. Ollie eyed the boys, his hands behind his back and a strict look on his face.

"My name is Homer Huffington. I'm the captain at Camp Raco." I turned away to suppress my giggles. "You can call me Mr. Huffington, or you can call me captain...or you can call me sir. But, the first time one of you calls me Homer, I'll use your face to clean off the BOTTOM OF MY BOOTS!"

The three recruits stepped back as if they just saw a ghost. Ollie went over some of the rules in camp and then took roll call. We tossed their gunnysacks in the trunk and they crowded into the backseat. No one spoke much on the ride to camp.

We arrived in camp just after curfew. Ollie pulled up to the water tower and then turned in his seat. "Men, the locals have been trying to steal our water tower." He pointed out the window. "If that thing is stolen, we have no water to drink." The boys peered out the window with big eyes. "Can I count on you to put in a few hours of guard duty tonight?"

"Yes, sir," the three said. I struggled to keep from laughing.

"The locals are very tricky," Ollie, said after we stepped out of the car. "Sometimes they'll impersonate an officer and try to fool you into leaving your post, but don't fall for it." We knew the real captain planned to return later that night.

I led the recruits to the water tower and assigned them their posts, two on the ground and one on top. As a boy climbed up the ladder into the dark, he asked. "Don't we need guns?"

"No guns," I said. "Just shout if there's trouble. We'll hear you."

When Captain Bullock later returned into camp, he hit the roof when he found the recruits on sentry duty. The rookies refused to obey his orders and leave their posts. Fuming, the captain woke up all the enrollees, making us get dressed and stand at attention outside the barracks.

"Practical jokes DO NOT have a place in this camp when it involves making recruits miss curfew," he shouted in a high-pitched voice. When he explained how he found the rookies on water tower duty, the guys broke out in laughter.

"Stop it right now." The captain sounded almost comical. "I MEAN IT!" But the laughing continued. When things settled down, he continued. "It's not funny impersonating an officer. I never want to hear of this kind of nonsense again." He turned and marched off in a huff.

The next morning Ollie and I reported to the sergeant for our punishment. Mr. Mulligan spent the night at home with his family and missed all the excitement. He rubbed the sleep from his eyes with his thick index finger. "Okay, tell me what happened and keep it short," he grunted.

Ollie described the prank and made it clear I was not in on it. The sergeant listened carefully with a furrowed brow. I fiddled with my rabbit foot. After a few minutes, Mr. Mulligan held up his hand. "I've heard enough," he said. "First, I want those medals in my office—I'll hold them until your enlistment is up."

"Yes, sir," Ollie said.

He picked up a pencil and began writing. "Second, no more driving privileges. Third, you both have water tower duty for the next two Saturdays."

"Yes, sir," we said.

He rubbed the back of his neck and grimaced. "What's with you, Radzinski? Turn your head sideways," I turned. "That's it...a little more. Just as I thought. I can see through one ear and out the other."

I tried to hold back my giggles.

"You think that's funny? You'd better find your brains or you'll land on your ass outside this camp someday. Dismissed." As I walked out, I noticed a slight grin on the sarge's face.

Ollie stopped outside the office, struck a match on the handrail and lit a cigarette. "We'll have a good time on water tower duty," he said and took a drag on his smoke.

"How's that?" I said and fixed my hat.

"I'll bring my guitar and you bring that thing you're whittling."

"The bear?"

"Yeah, the bear." He laughed and knocked the cap off my head as we headed to the barracks. "Kid, we got off easy...even the sergeant knows a good joke when he sees one." For the first time, it dawned on me that the sergeant might be human after all.

A few days after the water tower prank, I received a letter from my mother. She used the first twenty-five dollar check she received to buy a new wool overcoat on sale for four dollars. She also bought a pair of shoes, some cleaning supplies and lots of food, including ham and eggs.

"My brother doesn't deserve it," I said to Frank who lay on his cot with a comic book in his hand. "That schlep is living high on the hog from my hard work."

"Give the kid a break," Frank mumbled. "Someday, he'll do *you* a favor."

"You don't know my brother."

The mail clerk continued to call out names. Just then, he said, "Bobby LaJoye." I looked up from my letter, because Bobby never got mail. The blond-haired orphan glanced up from his book—he looked like a deer caught in headlights.

The mail clerk grew impatient. "What are you waiting for...an invitation?" The barracks quieted down as Bobby got his letter.

He held it up for all to see with an awkward smile. "It's from my borrowed mom," he said. Someone clapped, followed by another, until the entire barracks reverberated with applause.

Bobby's cheeks flushed pink. He returned to his cot and stared at the letter for a minute.

"Open it," someone urged.

"Aw, leave him alone," another called out.

Bobby looked around the room, self-conscious, and took out his pocketknife. Then, he sliced open the envelope. Most of the boys sat mesmerized, watching him. Bobby unfolded it slowly and began to read.

"Get a load of that," I whispered to Frank.

"Yeah," Frank said, over his shoulder, "his first letter."

When Bobby finished reading, he pressed the letter against his chest, dropped his head and began sobbing. The guys gave each other nervous looks, wondering what to do next. I wanted to get out.

"What's the matter, Bobby?" someone asked.

"Leave him alone," Mario said and sat next to his buddy. He put his arm over Bobby's shoulders.

"I gotta brush my teeth," a guy said.

"Yeah, me too," another piped up. One after another, we made excuses to leave. I never saw the barracks empty so quickly. I grabbed my toothbrush and left, too.

A half-hour or so later, we made our way back to the barracks and found out why Bobby cried. Mario's mother wrote, *"Dear Borrowed Son,"* and signed it *"Love, Your Borrowed Mom."* It shook Bobby up.

"A borrowed mom is *still a mom*," a boy said. Bobby looked up with a half-smile.

"Does that mean Mario is your borrowed brother?" another joked. Bobby grinned and shook his head.

"Hey...you picked up a borrowed sister in the deal," a guy teased. "Are you going to let me take her out?"

"Not *my* sister," Mario said. "She's only fourteen."

Just before lights out, I saw Bobby in bed reading the letter again. He lay propped on an elbow starring at it like a kid with his first baseball card. The letter made *everyone* feel better in our barracks. When something good happened to one of us, we all felt happier. What could be better than finding a mom?

After lights out, I stared up at the ceiling. A lonely hoot owl called out far off in the woods. It occurred to me that for sixteen years, hundreds of mothers passed up the chance to make Bobby their son. Now, in a work camp in the middle of the woods, without a woman in sight, he found a mother! Bobby didn't mind that she was *borrowed,* any more than the baby moose did about its new mother. Good things happened here in camp. Maybe something good will happen to me.

Chapter 4

Hello Betty

It was so dry during the first two weeks in June that cows gave out powdered milk. Our camp received a report of a forest fire about thirty miles northwest of camp, so a hundred of us set out to fight the blaze. They gave us each a stick of salami for lunch and a jug of water to drink. We piled into three stake trucks with axes, rakes, and shovels. I felt jumpy and uncertain about what to expect.

My only experience fighting fires happened when I was about six. I started a fire while playing with matches in a grassy area behind our barn. It slowly spread out into a big circle. My father found me at the water pump filling a bucket and asked what I was doing, but I was too afraid to answer. Dad followed me out to the fire and then ran back to the barn for a shovel and rake. We worked together to put out the fire. My dad never bawled me out, spanked me, or even sent me to my room. He just told me if I ever got in trouble again, I should ask for help.

I stood and watched the passing scenery as we drove out to the fire along a narrow two-track through a thinly wooded area. The road came to a dead end, so we unloaded and searched for the blaze by foot. With shovels and axes on our shoulders, we hiked through an area of cutover pine. Every five minutes or so, Isaac sent a boy up a tree to sniff the air for smoke. Finally, one of them smelled something.

"Over there!" The boy pointed from high in the tree.

We changed direction and picked up the pace.

An enrollee asked Isaac how fires started in the middle

of nowhere. The old lumberjack grinned—he enjoyed the attention. Isaac said a lightning strike, a smoldering campfire, or a piece of broken glass acting like a magnifying glass could have started the fire. He spit tobacco juice. "Some fires are started by fellas dat jus' wanna job fightin' 'em."

"You're joking," someone said.

"Oh no...da county pay men a buck a day to fight dose fires."

We found the fire in an area of dry brush. There was more smoke than fire. Isaac divided us into three groups to build a firebreak. The first group cut down trees, followed by another who cleared brush. Coming up on the rear, a third group raked away leaves and debris. My nerves settled down once I went to work. My job was to put out fires that jumped the firebreaks. The smoke made my eyes water and irritated my nose. It was awful work. I drank water every chance I got to relieve my parched throat.

We brought the fire under control by late afternoon. Then we trudged back to the truck with filthy clothes, smudged faces and greasy hair. Everyone sat on the floor of the truck on the ride home. I felt like a piece of burnt charcoal and smelled like one, too. I looked down at my grubby clothing and smiled to myself. Dog-tired, I also felt exhilarated as if I just returned from a battle. The problems with Farmer and the officers seemed like nothing at all. I stuck a finger through a burn hole in my t-shirt. *Thacker won't dare give me hard time with this shirt!*

A few days after we fought the fire, one of the rookies from my group went over-the-hill. Most of us knew Harold missed his family, but we were surprised when he hitched a train for home. He was a soft-spoken kid who worked hard and followed orders. I figured something must have gotten to him.

I learned the news on the way to supper. I smiled to myself and thought how it could have been me on that train. Trouble was, I was too afraid of my mother and her ironing cord. Besides, she wrote how she spent the money she got and that meant a lot to me. I tried my best to stick it out for her sake, so I was in no hurry to hitch a ride like Harold did.

With July a week away, a nor'easter came through bringing much needed rain. A gentle shower cooled us while we dug wells on the property of the Hiawatha Hunting Club. The club paid the CCC to put in the wells so its members could have drinking water nearby while they were hunting.

"Why can't these people carry their own darn water?" Mario asked from a hole about ten feet deep.

"I bet they carry a hipflask of whiskey," a boy said as he pulled up a bucket of dirt. "Why not water?"

"Quit complaining," the supervising officer said as he came up the trail. "Just do as you're told."

After he left, we began griping again. "This water could use a bucket of kitchen grease," I joked.

Arky laughed. "That'd spice it up it good!"

The rain stopped and the air became thick with black flies. I could swing my shovel and kill a dozen with each swat. "Get away from me you little buggers!" I slapped my head hard.

"I hope them flies git those hunters, too," Arky said.

Later that afternoon, I asked the guys, "Remember that dead porcupine on the road?"

"Yeah?" Arky said.

"Why don't we throw it into the well when we're done?"

"Aw, that makes me sick," Mario said.

"Is that big mouth of yours still yapping?" a voice said.

I turned around. The supervisor came up behind us. "I was just joking, sir." I said, and continued shoveling.

"I warned you fellas to quit your bellyaching," he said and scribbled on his clipboard. "I'm writing you up, Radzinski. You got to learn to keep your trap shut."

When he went out of sight, I smacked my shovel on a

dirt pile. "Crap! I can't even open my damned mouth without getting written up."

"Aw, fuggedaboutit," Mario said.

"Yeah...the sarge ain't gonna do nuthin' to ya," Arky added.

"What do you guys know," I said to myself and went back to shoveling.

That night after supper, I skipped boxing practice and found a quiet spot under a tree behind the mess hall. With a Doc Savage book propped up against a stone, I tried to get my mind off my upcoming meeting with the sarge. The early evening sun warmed my back and songbirds sang overhead.

"Hey, Nick." I turned and saw Elliot coming my way in his mess orderly uniform.

I groaned. "What's up?" I said half-heartedly. A frown crossed his normally cheerful face.

He knelt beside me. "I've had it with the guys teasing me."

A lot of boys called him a "fairy" because he was so neat and polite. "So...what am I supposed to do about it?"

"You *gotta* help me."

I shook my head. "No I don't...I'm not your guardian angel."

"C'mon, can't you think of something," he pleaded.

I thought a moment. "Talk to Scruggs."

"Okay, but only if *you* come." He kept pushing up his glasses. I sighed as I thought it over. Elliot might help me get a mess orderly job someday.

"All right," I said. "I'll talk to him....but no promises."

His face lit up. "Thanks, Nick."

I opened my book. "Now, scram." He hurried back to the kitchen. *He wants me to help him with his problem, but I can't even deal with my own!*

"Reporting as ordered, sir," I said to the sergeant the next morning in his office. I took about three bites of my breakfast because my stomach was in knots. Mr. Mulligan yawned and covered his mouth. He tapped the folder on his desk.

"I've been getting good work reports about you and then you go and *mess up*. What are you...some sort of comedian?"

"No sir," I said.

"Then why'd you say it?"

"It was a joke, sir."

He grimaced and rubbed the back of his neck. "You think it's *funny* to dump a dead animal in a well?"

"Well, at the time..."

He cut me off. "*Work* is not a joke. You don't joke...you don't complain...you don't play...you obey orders, damn it!"

"Yes, sir."

He blew his nose loudly into his handkerchief. "If you get a real job and screw around, what's going to happen?"

"I'll get fired."

"That's right." He folded his handkerchief and slipped it into his hip pocket. "You just bought yourself some latrine duty." He picked up a pen and scribbled something on my folder. "Stop making life hard on yourself. Now get to work and act sharp."

"Yes, sir."

I walked down the steps and cut across the quad. The boys milled around the boarding platform waiting for work trucks. *Son of a bitch!* No one spent more time in the sergeant's office than I did. They were so desperate to nail me, they went after things I *said*, not what I *did*. If any other guy joked about the well, nothing would have happened. *What am I doing in this camp?*

A warm breeze did nothing to take the chill off my attitude. The boys laughed and kidded each other as they boarded the truck. They ignored me when they saw my face. I found a corner to stand in and kept my eyes riveted on the scenery as we drove out to work.

Along the side of the road, I noticed mushrooms growing. It reminded me of how my dad and I collected Fairy Ring mushrooms in the fields on our farm. I wanted to please him so I ran ahead with a pail in my hand and tried to pick more than he did. He rarely complimented me, but once he said, "You're starting to grow a good pair of shoulders."

I looked up and said, "I want to be big like you, Dad."

He patted my shoulder. "No...you can be bigger *and* better." We fried the mushrooms in butter that night for supper and served them over meat. They were delicious.

The truck squeaked to a stop and I snapped back to reality. As I shuffled out with the others, I realized that work duty kept me sane. It took me away from camp...and Mr. Mulligan.

A half-hour before curfew that night, Scruggs met with Elliot and me in the officers' mess hall. Scruggs sat with hands folded on the table. He smiled calmly. "There's nothing to be ashamed of," he said to Elliot. "All I ask is that you level with me, okay?"

Elliot nodded and nervously licked his lips.

"Are you attracted to girls?" Scruggs asked.

Elliot blinked hard. "Yes, sir."

"Relax...call me John." Elliot nodded.

Scruggs pursed his lips. "Do you ever...*think* about girls?"

Elliot fidgeted. "Yeah...I think about a girl I know back home. Her name is Gertrude."

"Good." Scruggs nodded, pleased with himself. "Now...do you ever *dream* about Gertrude?"

Elliot wrung his hands. "Yeah, sometimes I dream that we...cuddle."

"Good," Scruggs said. I gave Elliot a nod of encouragement.

Our barracks leader tapped his pencil and thought for a moment. "Hmmm, how can I say this? Elliot, do girls ever make you, well...you know...aroused?"

Elliot cheeks flushed red—I thought he would burst.

"It's nothing to be ashamed of," Scruggs said.

Elliot fixed his glasses nervously and stammered. "Ah... sometimes when I'm in bed...and I think about what Gertrude looks like naked..."

Scruggs slapped the table. “That’s all I need to hear,” he said. “Sounds to me like you’re a red-blooded American male.” He stood and cracked his knuckles loudly. “The next time someone calls you a fairy, you come see *me* about it.”

Elliot gushed. “Thank you sir…I mean John.” He grabbed Scruggs’ hand and shook it heartily.

As we headed to the door Scruggs said, “By the way…why don’t you go to the dance hall and be seen with some girls.”

Elliot nodded. “Sure, I can try.”

“That’s the spirit,” Scruggs said and gave him a pat on the back. “Thanks for being here, Nick.”

“Sure,” I said and gave him a little wink.

As we walked to the barracks, Elliot thanked me. “Aw, it’s not your fault the rest of us are slobs.” I said and mussed up his hair. “Now you look like the rest of us.” We laughed. It felt good to help the kid.

The next day after supper, I felt restless, so I took a turn around the quad to see what was up. The sky was partly cloudy with a warm breeze. I passed several boys with their mitts heading out to baseball practice and others with books under their arms going to class.

I noticed Mr. Wells building an Indian hut behind the blacksmith shop, so I went over to say hello. He had already constructed three Indian dwellings, which he used to teach Indian history—a long narrow house, a cone-shaped teepee and a simple shack built with slabs of wood. They were one-third their actual size.

Tonight, he erected a hogan, a type of home Navajo Indians lived in. The pyramid-shaped building used forked logs to support the longer logs. There were five sides to the building, and each side represented something in nature. “This side is east and symbolizes morning, the north is for the afternoon,” Mr. Wells explained while he packed mud between the logs.

I leaned against a rail fence. “How long did they live in them?”

"Oh, two or three years. They moved on before they depleted the wildlife."

"Why?"

"They wanted the animals to replenish."

Mr. Wells carefully smoothed over the dark brown paste with his trowel. "Why did the white man kill all the buffalo?" I asked.

"The more a person gets...the more a person wants. The white man is never satisfied."

"Were Indians ever greedy?"

"Indians don't see the land as something to own, it belongs to the Great Spirit. We are visitors, so we treat it with reverence."

I asked him whether the Indians were still bitter at losing the land they once lived on. He stirred the muddy mix with a stick. "When I joined the CCC, I was sent to an Indian camp. I overheard one of the men say that the white man took our land, cut down all the trees, and now they make us plant new trees on the same land."

"Geez..."

Mr. Wells looked serene; his face radiated a deep bronze color in the soft evening light. "I think most Indians feel betrayed, but whether they are bitter or not depends on the individual."

"What do *you* feel?"

A calm smile came to his face. A light breeze caught some of his loose hairs and blew them across his face. "I'm not bitter because I never lost anything. The land still belongs to the Great Spirit...no matter how many fences the white man puts on it."

I felt peaceful when I talked with Mr. Wells. He never showed anger or resentment. He often spoke of me finding my "inner man." I looked forward to talking with him again. Perhaps he could help me understand why I lost so many brothers and sisters.

Two days later, there was a buzz of excitement around camp. It was *the fight of the century*! It seemed like the fight was all anybody talked about. Joe Louis, "The Brown Bomber," had lost to Max Schmelling two years earlier, so we were out for revenge. It was more than a match between two men—it was a contest between two countries. The United States versus Germany—Hitler against Uncle Sam. The first time they fought, I rooted for the German because he was white and Louis was black. Most of my friends also had pulled for Schmelling. But, this time, I wanted Louis, because he was an American and the color of his skin made no difference to me.

Boys crowded around the radio in the barracks, sitting on cots and lockers, filing every empty space on the floor. The announcer's voice crackled over the radio, "Seventy thousand people are here in Yankee Stadium on a hot, sticky night. The sight of this crowd takes your breath away..."

"Clear the way," Elliot yelled as he pushed through the guys. He carried a milk crate filled with peanut butter sandwiches. He received special permission to sell the food, because the money went to the camp party fund.

Suddenly, I heard Farmer yell, "Hey fairy, save one of those sandwiches for me."

Something snapped inside my head. I jumped over a cot to get at the bully. When he turned, I slammed my shoulder into his chest and drove him into the wall so hard he came up off his feet. Two or three boys immediately grabbed me.

"It's the fight of the century!" someone yelled.

Farmer, held back by three boys, taunted me. "Was that your best shot, Rat Eye? I'm gonna kill you in the ring."

The assistant leader, Bricks, escorted me out. "I don't want to miss the match," he said, so we ran to another barracks.

It came on the radio just as we walked in. "A right to the head, a right to the jaw," the announcer said, "Schmelling's back is on the ropes...he's struggling!" The boys listened with open mouths. Then the announcer went into hysterics.

"Max Schmelling is DOWN!" he screamed. "HE CAN NOT GET UP! SCHMELLING CAN… NOT… GET… UP!"

Bricks and I cheered along with the others. I never felt so proud of being an American. Everyone in that room loved Joe Louis that night—he was a hero to all of us.

After the barracks quieted down, some of the boys grumbled because the fight only lasted for two minutes. No one touched his food or drink. It was like going to a picnic where it rained ten minutes after you arrived. Reality sank in when Bricks walked me back to my barracks. "You really pulled a good one tonight," he said. "Scruggs would've dealt with Farmer…you didn't have to."

"I don't know what got into me." I said and slouched along. "I guess I was tired of seeing Elliot picked on."

"That's no excuse for attacking someone."

I said nothing. I plodded up the steps and Bricks opened the door. He patted my shoulder. "You get a chance to use what you learned at boxing."

"He's gonna murder me," I said glumly.

"Hey…it's okay to be afraid, but don't show it."

"Yeah, easier said than done," I muttered. I picked a fight with the biggest bully in camp. *How stupid can I get?*

The next morning after breakfast, I stood next to Farmer in Mr. Mulligan's office. President Roosevelt glared out from his picture frame as if he was mad at me, too. The sergeant rubbed his chin thoughtfully. "So…the Schmelling-Louis fight wasn't enough for you guys. You had to start your own." He leaned back. "Okay, tell me what happened…Nick, you go first."

"I lost my temper, sir." I said.

He opened his mouth with mock astonishment. "Well, *that's* never happened before." I explained how I jumped Farmer.

The sergeant turned to Farmer. "What's your story?"

"I was minding my own business, sir…"

The sergeant cut in. "I heard you were mouthing off."

"Oh...I was just pulling his leg." He rambled on about how he wanted a sandwich and meant no harm to Elliot.

The sergeant held up his hand. "I've heard enough." Then he picked up his calendar. "I'll give you two a choice. I can give you a punishment or you can settle it in the ring. What will it be?"

"Fight." Farmer said with a smug smile.

"Nick?"

My stomach rumbled like a bathtub drain. "I'll fight."

"Do you have anything to say before I schedule it?"

"Sir, I just joined the boxing team a few weeks ago," I said. "I can use another couple months of practice.

The sergeant looked at Farmer. "Got a problem with that?"

"Yeah, I think it stinks...I want to fight now."

The sergeant pointed to Farmer. "Put your right hand up." He put it up. "Nick, put your hand against his." Farmer's fingers were at least an inch longer and twice as thick.

"You got your two months...maybe you'll grow a little by then." He marked his calendar. "We'll do it Labor Day."

He glanced up at Farmer. "Don't taunt, don't tease... don't start anything—or you'll be fighting Scruggs."

Farmer nodded. "Yes, sir."

"Dismissed."

When the door closed behind us, Farmer said, "I'll be counting the days, Rat Eye." He made a guttural laugh and walked off. In an odd way, I felt relieved to get the fight scheduled and over with.

Later that week, I received a letter from home that I wished Mom never sent. She wrote that our neighbors fell behind on their rent and lost their home. My mother put them up for a few days while they prepared for a move to Traverse City. They planned to pick cherries in the summer and apples in the fall. Then, they hoped to drive to California after the harvest. The letter made me think about my living situation. A bed and three square meals a day was a luxury. It sure beat the heck out of living in a shack and picking fruit all day.

After we read our letters, we usually read them aloud to the others, leaving out the personal parts. Everyone craved news from home, even if the news came from someone else's family. Parents typically wrote about how they spent the twenty-five dollars they received from the government. Walt was an orphan who lived with his grandmother. She wrote that she used the money to pay back taxes on her farm.

"I saved my grandma's farm," he said. "I can't believe it...I just can't believe it..."

"Shaddup and believe it," someone yelled.

Scruggs' sister used the money to pay her college tuition. Mario's mother bought a sewing machine and a boy's dad bought some tractor parts. Farmer looked up from a game of checkers. "What kind of tractor?"

"McCormick," the boy said.

"I HATE McCormicks," Farmer spouted. "Tell your dad to get a John Deere, they last longer."

"Shaddup!" a fella shouted.

After a few months, we knew each other's families so well we recognized the names of each other's brothers and sisters. Mario read from his letter. "Now, here's some news about your sister..."

Turk cut him off. "What's new with Maria?"

Mario smiled. "She got a job as a babysitter."

"Some of the guys around here can use a babysitter," Turk quipped.

Frank's mother wrote in Polish like mine, but he never read his letters aloud. He would not even let *me* read them, and I was his best friend. "Same old, same old," he would say and fold the letter.

"Oh yeah?" I said. "Then tell me something old." Frank got under my skin at times.

When my mother wrote that she bought something new

with the money, I felt like the man of the house. At home, my brother and I were equals. Now, Gabe depended on me, from the food he ate, to the clothes on his back. I supported the family the way Dad should have.

A couple days later, as I hauled brush in the woods, I heard someone talking to himself. I came around a clump of cedar bushes and saw Arky dragging a long branch. The bony kid barely filled out his t-shirt. "Who you talking to?" I asked.

"Myself," he said with a grin. "Jus' goin' over my lessons."

"You're joking."

"Nope." He wiped his forehead with the back of his arm. "I can hear my teacher's voice when I work."

I shook my head. "You're nuts." We walked to the burn pile.

"I'm not jokin'...I figured out why I was so lousy in school."

"Why's that?"

"I never paid attention," he said. "I never gave a damn." Arky said he planned to get an eighth-grade diploma. "I'm tired of payin' someone to write my letters for me."

On the way back to the work site, I thought about how I screwed around in school. I dropped out my junior year mainly because other students teased me about my shoes, but it was just an excuse. I would have found another reason to quit, because I got poor grades. I wished I had tried harder.

I picked up my axe and swung the sharp blade into an aspen tree. My swing had improved since my first weeks in camp, I could hit a spot within a quarter inch. I smiled when I realized Arky could lead me out of the woods, but he couldn't even read a letter from home. The CCC seemed to meet the needs of every guy in camp. *I wonder if it can help me?*

When Saturday finally arrived, Frank and I took the early afternoon truck into the Soo. The sun shone brightly and a cool breeze blew in from Lake Superior as we rolled into town. Moms pushed baby strollers and kids flew by on scooters. Frank and I bought a bag of licorice, grabbed a seat on a park bench, and watched people stroll by. When a dad passed us with his two young sons, Frank said it reminded him of his dad. “He used to take me to vaudeville acts on Saturdays,” he said.

I popped a piece of licorice in my mouth. “No kidding?”

“Yep. I saw a guy swallow a light bulb—it lit up his stomach.”

“You’re daffy,” I said.

“No...I’m on the level. The bulb was connected to a wire, and you could even see his ribs.”

“You serious?”

He pointed to his stomach. “It went down to here.”

“Ughh,” I grunted. “So, why’d your dad take off?”

“I told you...I don’t know. Mom wouldn’t talk about it.”

We finished off the candy and went to Woolworths. A green-eyed clerk with auburn hair caught my eye. I stopped and picked up a figurine off the counter.

“What are you doing?” Frank whispered.

I smiled as I fingered the small statue. “Just taking in the scenery.”

Frank glanced at the redhead. “C’mon, we don’t have all day.”

We went to the sports department to look at baseball gloves. A little boy in overalls came by with a loose shoelace. “Hold it kid,” I said and knelt to do it up. His mother, a neatly dressed young woman, smiled down at me.

“What do you do, mister?” the child asked.

“Well, I’m in the CCC, young fella.” He looked to be about five.

He scrunched up his face. “What’s the CCC?”

“Oh...we do things like plant trees.”

He looked at my uniform. “Are you a tree soldier?”

I chuckled. “Yeah, I guess so.”

His mother complimented me on my uniform. If I tried to tie the shoe of a kid a year ago in my beat up clothes, the

Mom would have whacked me on the head with her purse. I found out that nice clothes brought respect from most people. Whatever I did in life, I wanted to be well-dressed.

Frank and I left Woolworths and headed up Main Street. A young boy on a bike almost ran us over. We came to a store called Alpha Sweets where teenagers stood around outside on the sidewalk. The screen door slammed behind us as we stepped inside the ice cream parlor. Well-tanned boys in white shirts flirted with attractive high school girls who sat at tables sipping ice cream sodas and soft drinks.

I followed Frank to the counter. The overhead fans stirred up the air that smelled of freshly made taffy. A Glenn Miller tune played on the jukebox and two couples danced the jitterbug. We hopped onto a couple of stools and ordered chocolate sodas from a long-armed soda jerk. He squirted chocolate syrup into two glasses, added soda water, and stirred it with a long thin spoon. He put a couple scoops of vanilla ice cream in each glass and topped it off with whipped cream. I stuck a straw in mine and sipped. "Hmmm...this is good."

Frank licked his lips. "And how..."

Suddenly Frank's eyes got big. I turned and saw four teenaged girls walking in our direction. Their skirts and blouses were colorful as a rainbow. They sat down at a table only a few feet away. Two of them snickered at us after they sat down. We probably looked like a couple of fish with our open mouths. I ran my hand lightly over my hair to smooth it out. Frank went into action. "What's the matter, girls, never seen a man in uniform before?"

"Oh, we've seen men in uniform," A blonde bookish type said. "But they're usually old enough to shave." The girls snickered.

Frank grinned and nodded. "You're as funny as a barrel of monkeys...I like that."

"You're kinda cute, where are *you* from?" A wavy-haired brunette asked.

"Me...cute?" Frank pointed to his chest and looked around. "You ain't seen nothin' sweetheart—I got a Hawaiian dancing girl tattooed on my chest." They burst into laughter.

"I heard you CCC boys live the life of Riley out there in the woods," one of them said.

"Are you kidding? They're slave drivers..."

"What's with your friend, cat got his tongue?" another asked.

I stopped sipping. "I haven't had a soda in two months."

"I can tell," the girl said. "You're wearing it on your pants." I looked down and saw a chocolate stain the size of a silver dollar next to my crotch. I blushed.

The blonde dipped her napkin in her water glass and handed it to me. "Men in uniform can't look that way," she said with a nice smile. I thanked her.

Frank asked one of the brunettes to dance, and then turned to me. "C'mon, grab a girl."

I decided to sit tight because of the water spot on my pants. Besides, Frank danced so well, he put everyone to shame. The other couples on the dance floor gave him space when he began to dip and weave with his partner. She turned out to be a great dancer and kept up with him. I turned back to the counter and hoped the girls ignored me.

"Gee, I guess he can't make up his mind which one of us he wants to dance with," one of them said.

"Poor fella, should we invite him to join us?"

"Nah, he probably doesn't like girls," another said.

I slowly spun around with a bashful smile. One of them pushed out a chair and I sat down. They sipped their drinks while I told them stories about Detroit and places like Woodward Avenue. "It's so wide you can march three parades side by side." I was telling them about the numbers racket when Frank returned.

"Aw, don't believe what he says," Frank scoffed. "He learned it all from the movies." Before we left, the girls invited us to Gould's Pavilion where they worked on Saturday nights as dancers. I managed to talk a few moments with the blonde and found out her name was Betty. She was a senior at Soo High and played the cornet in the band.

"Hot dawg, we hit the jackpot!" I said after we walked out the door.

Frank slapped my back. "It's our lucky day, pal."

On the ride back to camp, I thought about Betty. She looked like an honor student with her short hair and glasses, but she had a sassy side to her. I loved the shape of her face, the high cheekbones and wide set eyes. I was smitten. As we drove along the road, Frank interrupted my daydream.

"Are you in love with four-eyes?" he asked.

"Aw, mind your potatoes," I snapped.

"Don't get goofy, she's just a dame," he said.

Frank only had one thing on his mind when it came to women. "She's not a dame...she's got more class then you'll ever have."

Frank held his hands up in defense. "Excuse me...sorry I opened my mouth."

On the ride back to camp, I watched farmhouses and barns pass by, but my thoughts stayed with Betty. I overheard her calculate a five percent tip for the girls' drinks—she was the smartest of the bunch, too. Smart, fun and pretty—I was crazy about her!

I woke up with a smile on my face the next morning with Betty still on my mind. After a breakfast of cereal and toast, I joined about a hundred others for chapel under the oak tree. The sun was out and a warm day in the making. A couple of brown squirrels chased each other in the branches above us.

Chaplain Schulz gave a Protestant service. He also did a Catholic service that I planned to check out someday. Mr. Schulz played minor league baseball in his younger days. He still looked fit at fifty with salt-and-pepper hair and a small paunch. He gave pitching and batting tips to the boys after the service.

Our sermon was on the Bible story of the prodigal son, a young man who ran away from home. After a period of "riotous living," the boy returned home, broke. He was so humbled he would have eaten with the pigs. Instead of punishing him, his father killed a calf and made a feast to celebrate his return.

"The boy condemned himself for his actions, but the father didn't," Mr. Schulz said. "Don't blame yourself for past mistakes." He went on to say that today was the day to let go of bad habits. "Whether it's cussing, booze, jealousy, or anger, you can let it go," the chaplain preached. "Love yourself as your Father in heaven loves you—forgive yourself as your Father forgives."

The prodigal son story made me think of my dad. If I ever tracked him down, I would never throw a welcome home party for him. He deserted his family, how can you forgive someone who caused so much misery?

After the service, two mess orderlies brought out pans of warm cinnamon rolls topped with icing. The treats quickly disappeared. Many of us followed the chaplain to the baseball field where he gave pitching lessons. His nickname in his playing days was "Art the Dart." When he kicked back his leg and pitched the ball, batters struggled to connect. Mr. Schulz delivered a great sermon *and* a terrific curve ball.

Later that week, Frank and I swung on the tree ropes whooping it up when Mr. Mulligan appeared out of nowhere. He leaned back and said, "That's quite a set-up you got...where'd you get those ropes?"

A sinking feeling came to me. "I took them from the equipment room, sir," I called down.

"Did you sign them out?"

"No, sir, but I planned to return them in the fall." The sergeant waved for us to come down.

When we hit the ground, he let us have it. "Someone might think you *stole* those ropes," he said with an angry scowl.

"Oh no, sir. I was going to take them back..."

He interrupted. "Ever hear of S.O.P.?"

"Yes, sir."

"Return those ropes to the equipment room and report to my office after breakfast." He turned and left.

I threw my hands in the air. "How'd he know we were here?"

"Someone must've snitched on us," Frank said.

I grabbed a branch and started up the tree. "Let's find the guy who did it and string him up."

"Yeah, we got plenty of rope to do it with, too," Frank said.

We untied the ropes and headed back to camp. My eyes scanned the ground as we walked the trail. I looked for clues from someone who might have spied on us.

"You're screwy," Frank said. "What kind of clue would someone leave?"

"Just keep your eyes open," I said. We shuffled along until we came to an area of ferns. Suddenly, I spotted a brown splotch on a fern leaf. At first, I thought it was a bird dropping but after a second look, I recognized it as tobacco spit.

"Well, *that* really helps," Frank said. "There're only about fifty guys that chew."

"I bet I know who did it," I said.

Frank grinned. "Farmer, right?"

I nodded.

"He goes to woodworking before supper, you idiot," Frank said. "Anyway he's too dumb to track us."

"What do you know?" I muttered. On the walk back to camp, I tried to think of a way to trick Farmer into confessing.

"Why don't you hypnotize him," Frank joked.

"Aw, shaddup." Nothing was worse than a stoolie. Someone was out to get me and I had to find the guy.

The next morning, Frank and I reported to the sergeant. He fiddled with a broken pencil sharpener as we walked in and shot us an ominous look. He quickly tore into us. "I don't care if you said it's borrowed, it's *stealing*," he said and rapped his ruler on the desk. "If you don't sign it out, it's *stealing*...get that into your thick heads!"

He dug into his ear with his finger. "Either of you guys heard of dry rot?" We shook our heads. "That's what happens when you leave ropes out in the rain and sun...they fall apart."

He ordered both of us to scrub the canteen floor on Saturday. Then he sent Frank away and opened my folder. "These infractions are adding up, Radzinski. When's it gonna stop?"

"As soon as possible, sir."

"Cut the crap. It's gonna stop today."

"Yes, sir."

"You don't have the sense that God gave geese." He shook his head and then pointed a finger at me. "Start using your head."

"Yes, sir."

"Dismissed."

The screen door clacked behind me, and I bounded down the steps to catch the truck for work duty. I kicked the ground. The sergeant made another mountain out of a molehill! There was enough rope in the equipment room for all the cowboys in Texas. *Whoever snitched on me better look out!*

My name came up for fire tower duty the next day. The camp staffed three lookout towers in the area and everyone rotated in. The steel ladder on the tower went straight up about eighty feet. I kept my eyes looking ahead the entire climb because it scared the dickens out of me. At the top, I squeezed through a hole on the bottom of the viewing platform.

I felt like an egg on a frying pan when the hot sun came out. With my hat pulled low, I squinted through the binoculars, scanning the horizon for fires. The only thing I saw of interest was a small group of deer feeding in the lowland. Even with the railing protecting me, I felt dizzy looking over the side. When the wind blew, the tower swayed; it was nerve-wracking. A phone line connected me to camp, but I never used it. I brought a mallet and chisel to use on my second bear carving. The first bear I made looked more like a beaver. I spent the morning chipping away at my chunk of basswood.

I tried to figure out who squealed on Frank and me about the ropes; I doubted another enrollee reported us to the sarge. Other than Farmer, Frank and I had no enemies. I concluded it had to be an officer who ratted on us. Maybe a forest officer walked by and saw us swinging on the ropes one night. Regardless, I still planned to grill Farmer when I got a chance.

Just before lunch, I needed to pee. One look down the ladder convinced me to stay put, so I unbuttoned my fly and crawled over to the edge of the platform. I held onto the rail with one hand to steady myself and yelled, "Heads up, look out below!" I gave the ground a good sprinkle.

Two days later, while I brushed my teeth in the bathhouse, Farmer walked behind me and beat his bare chest with his fists. "AAAHHHHH," he roared like Tarzan. "Been swinging from the trees, Rat-Eye?" he teased.

I turned around. "Yeah. The sergeant told me that you saw us on the ropes."

His jaw dropped. "Huh? You're crazy...I'm no stoolie."

I spit out some toothpaste. "You know you squealed on us."

He looked baffled. "I don't even know where you guys went..."

"Who ratted on us then?"

"How should I know?"

"Aw, beat it," I said and went back to brushing my teeth. A lot of guys knew Frank and I got in trouble over the ropes, so Farmer could have picked up the news anywhere. It irked me to no end that there was a snitch somewhere.

After I rinsed, I headed back to the barracks with a couple other boys. It was a warm July evening, and we walked up the sidewalk naked with our towels hung loosely over our shoulders. This was common, since there were no women in camp. As we went around a corner, we almost bumped into the captain and the chaplain.

"Excuse us," I said.

"It's quite all right," he said and they kept walking. Behind our back, we heard the chaplain singing in a low voice, "Swing low, sweet chariot, coming for to carry me home..." We laughed and wrapped our towels around our waists.

A half hour later, I was outside on the barracks steps killing time before supper with my carving, when I heard my name called. "Radzinski, get over here!" The sergeant waved to me from his office steps.

I got up and ran to his office. The whirling fan did little to cool his hot office. Harold, the homesick boy who ran away a few weeks earlier sat across from the desk. He looked forlorn and nervously twitched his foot. The sergeant told me to sit down. "Tell Nick what happened," he said to Harold.

The stoop-shouldered boy spoke softly. "My folks were mad when I showed up...they were using the money I earned to pay the rent."

"Tell him what you did," the sergeant blurted.

"Well...I tried to get a job around town, but no one was hiring. It's still pretty bad out there, Nick."

The sergeant pointed his thumb at the boy. "If you *ever* think about going over-the-hill...talk to Harold first."

"Yes, sir." I said. He dismissed us and we cut across the quad back to the barracks.

"Where'd the sarge get the idea I wanted to run away?"

"Did you ever ask for a transfer?"

"Yeah."

"That's it. The other guys I talked to also tried to transfer."

"What a bunch of baloney." I went back to work on my

bear carving and promptly poked my hand with the business end of a chisel. I ended up going to the infirmary to get it bandaged up and came late to supper.

I stewed that night thinking about the sergeant. He knew I didn't need to ask anyone if I wanted to leave. I *volunteered* for the CCC and could leave whenever I wanted. The way things were going, I might be leaving sooner than later.

The next day I worked with the road crew spreading crushed rock. They loaded the stone in a wheelbarrow and I wheeled it down the road where boys with rakes waited for me. The loaded wheelbarrow weighed a ton, and I struggled to push it over the soft ground. Swarms of mosquitoes came out of the swamp and attacked us. There was no relief, until Mr. Wells found out about the problem. He went into the woods and came back with several strips of tree bark that he boiled in water. We dipped rags in the cooled solution and rubbed it over our skin to keep the bugs away.

During the lunch break, Mr. Wells joined us on a log where we ate salami and cheese sandwiches with pickles. He wore a t-shirt like the rest of us, and a single feather hung at the end of his long ponytail. While we ate our food, he told us about growing up in South Dakota.

"Did you ever hunt buffalo?" I asked.

"No, they were gone when I was a boy, but my grandfather did. He told me that when he was ten years old, some men in his village invited him and some other boys to go on a buffalo hunt. My grandfather wanted to go, but his mother asked him to stay home because it was so dangerous. He stayed home."

"What happened on the hunt?" Arky asked.

"Two of the boys who went never came back," Mr. Wells said in a voice just above a whisper. "Something went wrong and the buffalo turned and charged the hunting party. The boys fell off their horses and were trampled to death." I stopped chewing my food as he spoke, not wanting to miss a single word.

Later, as I thought about the Indian boy who stayed home, I wondered what was so bad about listening to your own mother. What was it about a teenager that made him automatically shut down when his parents talked to him? When Mr. Wells told a story, it made us think about ourselves.

At supper, they served one of my favorite meals, pot roast and boiled potatoes. José usually said a long grace before his meals. He bowed his head and with closed eyes spoke softly to himself.

"When are you going to tell us what you're saying," a boy asked.

Another added, "Yeah, we're your friends...you can tell us."

Arky got in on it. "My dad said it was *his* work that put food on the table, so he didn't have to say a dang thing to God."

José took it all in as he calmly chewed his food. "No kidding?"

"Yeah," Arky said. "We never said grace...not once. Can you teach me?"

José smiled slightly. "There's nothing to it. My folks are poor and we never had enough food in the house. So, when I say grace, I apologize to my mother, my father, my brothers, and everyone else in my family."

"Apologize? For what?" Arky asked.

"That I get to eat all the food I want, when *they* have to go hungry."

The fellas had guilty looks on their faces. "Aw, shucks." Arky said. "Sorry I asked."

José set down his glass. "It's nothing...don't worry about it."

Most of us felt embarrassed for pestering him. Sometimes we got a bit too curious about each other's lives.

On Saturday afternoon, Frank and I reported for our punishment for taking the ropes. The mess sergeant gave us buckets, brushes and a bottle of bleach. They closed off half the rec hall while we worked. We placed a couple fans nearby to speed up the drying. As I mixed the bleach, the bottle slipped from my hand and spilled on my pant leg. I waited too long to clean it and a big white stain appeared on my blue overalls.

"For chrissakes...look at my pants," I said.

Frank turned. "Thacker's gonna make you pay."

"It was in the line of work."

Frank grinned. "Good luck."

Later that afternoon, I hurried to the supply room to find Thacker before he closed up. I caught him just as he was locking up. "What's *your* problem?" he said with a poker face.

I held up the pants. "I spilled bleach on these when I was cleaning the canteen." I tried to sound casual.

He shook his head and undid the lock. He walked behind the counter, pulled out a notepad, and began writing. "It was a careless spill," he said. "You know the rules."

"You can't make me pay," I said.

Thacker raised an eyebrow. "Oh yeah? We'll take it out of your paycheck." Then he grabbed a pair of overalls off a shelf and put them on the counter. I picked them up and headed straight to Mr. Mulligan.

"Not again," the sergeant said after I explained what had happened. He banged his fist on his desk. "What's going on between you two?"

"Nothing. I just got off on a bad start with him."

The sergeant studied me carefully. "You sure there's nothing else is I should know about?"

I shook my head. "No sir...there's nothing else."

He picked up a pencil and began writing. "I'll look into it, but try to be more careful."

"Yes, sir."

"Dismissed."

I hated to ask the sergeant for a break, but a dollar meant a lot to me. My laundry cost seventy-five cents a month and locker rental was fifty cents. Five dollars a month went quickly so I wanted that dollar back, no matter how riled up Thacker might get over it.

After supper, Arky asked me to go fishing. We checked out two fishing rods from the equipment room and walked out the front entrance with our poles in one hand and a bucket of worms in the other. It was a hot, muggy night and we planned to jump in the water to cool down. A woodpecker made a racket in a rotten tree and the black flies were biting.

Five minutes outside of camp, I noticed a little ball of fur on the other side of the dirt road. "What's that?" I said and ran over for a closer look. It was a beautiful brown and white beagle. Blood stains covered part of its back. I put my hand on its chest.

"Still breathing?" Arky asked.

I felt a slight movement. "Yep...you watch him while I get permission to bring him back." I left my pole and ran home.

"Get a milk crate and some rags!" Arky yelled.

I knew we had to act fast to save the dog and hoped the camp doctor could stitch it up. I found Scruggs outside the barracks and asked him if we could bring the dog into camp. "Sure...but have the doc check him out," he said.

"You bet." The boys in the kitchen gave me a milk crate and some clean rags. I hurried back to Arky who had moved the dog off the road onto a bed of grass. We used a wet rag to wipe away the blood on its fur, and then gently lifted the dog into the crate. I carried it while Arky brought the fishing poles. Walking back to camp, we worked on giving the dog a name.

"I got one," Arky said. "Agnes."

"Agnes?"

"Yeah...she reminds me of my ugly sister."

"This dog isn't ugly..."

"Well, she still looks like my sister...."

"Okay. We'll call her Agnes...after your *pretty* sister."

The doc saw Agnes and cleaned a wound near its shoulder. Stitching wasn't necessary. He loaned us an eyedropper that we filled with warm milk sweetened with honey.

We laid her in the shade of the barracks before we put it in her mouth and squeezed. Agnes licked at the milk with eyes barely opened. We took turns feeding her until she conked out. Next, we made a little bed out of a cardboard box and put her in a storage shed. Before I went to sleep, I said a little prayer for her.

Agnes' condition improved quickly. By Saturday afternoon, Arky and I coaxed her into eating some finely chopped meat scraps we got from the cook. She chewed slowly, but got it down. We set her in the shade by the barracks every day where she received loving attention from the boys. Her wound healed up nicely.

Agnes was not the only girl in my life. That evening I planned to see Betty at the dance hall. After supper, I slapped on some Old Spice cologne, slicked down my hair with Brylcreem and gave my shoes a final brush. Frank showed me a couple jitterbug steps out on the sidewalk as we waited to board the truck for the ride into town. The dance steps confused me, at times I felt as clumsy as a cow on ice.

"Back step, side together, push out, spin..." Frank called out in quick succession.

I got dizzy from the spins. "You gotta slow down," I said.

"C'mon, give Ginger a break," one of the boys teased.

"Button it," I said. We practiced until the truck pulled up.

An hour later, a few dozen of us entered Gould's Pavilion. The dance hall was about twice the size of a school gym, with a shiny wood floor. A mirrored ball on the ceiling rotated, sending sparkles of light all over the room. We paid twenty-five cents to enter, plus an extra quarter for a yellow button that let us dance with the girls. We watched as people swayed to the Cole Porter hit *Begin the Beguine*. The male band members looked dapper in their white coats and bow ties. The woman singer shimmered in a purple sequin dress.

We spotted Doris and Betty out on the floor dancing with

two older men. Betty wore a light blue dress that went to her calves. She moved easily to the beat of the music, I was glad Frank gave me some pointers so I could keep up with her. I felt insecure thinking about the good dancers Betty had been with. When the song ended, Frank and I went out to see them.

"Do you gals have a place on your dance cards for a couple of CCC boys?" Frank asked with a wide grin.

"You promise to stay off our toes?" Doris teased.

"Toots, your dogs won't touch the floor when you're dancing with me," he joked.

Betty smiled at me. Her soft blonde hair looked stylish, neatly pinned back off her face. "Hi," she said.

"Hi," I said.

"Ready to cut a rug?"

I nodded. "Can't wait."

She pulled out a dance card from her waistband. "Hmmm, let's see if I can fit you in...it's Nicolas, like Santa Claus?"

"Nah, Nick'll do...like wood tick. That's what they call us."

She gave me a sly grin. "Wood tick, eh? So you want to get under my skin?"

I stammered. "Oh, no...I'll get under the sarge's skin, but not yours."

She smiled and gave me a curious look. Just then, the band started up. Without thinking, I took her hand. Suddenly, a man bumped me from behind. "Quit wolfing in on me buster, get back in the stag line." I looked over my shoulder and saw a husky fella who looked like he broke rocks for a living.

I stepped aside. "Sure..."

"Beat it," he growled.

"Come back in five dances," Betty said over the man's shoulder. I hurried off the floor and joined Frank near the refreshment stand. I nibbled an oatmeal cookie and watched the dancers. A few songs later, Frank got on the dance floor with Doris and went into action. Soon they were jumping around, cutting loose, and going crazy. Doris was a dynamo with short, quick moves. Frank tossed her around like a beanbag...around his back and under his legs. They looked like they had been partners for years. Other dancers backed off and gave them space.

The ceiling fans in the dance hall did little to cool off the steamy room. Sweat dripped down from my underarms like an open faucet and I had not even danced yet! When the fourth song ended, I brought Betty a glass of lemonade. She took a long drink. "Whew, thanks! I sure needed that."

I took the empty cup back to the table and hustled back in time for the next song. They played the pretty melody, *In the Chapel in the Moonlight* at a relaxed tempo. I wiped my palms on my pants and took her hand—we stood eye to eye. She stepped back with her right foot while I followed with my left. Soon, we moved together to the beat of the music. Betty danced with silky smooth moves, Frank's lessons helped.

When I looked at the little beads of sweat above her upper lip, she flashed me a coy smile. "So, what's new at camp?"

"Well...I found a beagle that was hit by a car." I told her how Arky and I nursed her back to health. She listened intently.

When I finished, she broke into a big smile. "That's one of the sweetest stories I've heard in a long time." She pulled out her dance card. "Can I put you down for another?"

I nodded, vigorously.

She looked up and grinned. "Come back in three dances."

"I'll be here," I said and left with a big smile on my face. I got another cookie and watched Ollie and Rosie dance. They made a beautiful couple even though she was a few inches taller than he was. She never stopped laughing. *What I would give to listen in on those two!*

I felt a tap on my shoulder and swung around to see Turk. He looked like a million bucks in his uniform. With his solid body and chiseled good looks, he could easily pass for a soldier in his twenties. "Can I borrow your dance button?" he asked. "I'll give it right back."

I raised my arms in exasperation. "Get your own."

"I don't have twenty-five cents," he said and frowned. Turk looked pitiable. He was probably the toughest guy in camp, but he was always broke. Some of the guys borrowed each other's buttons to save money. They got away with it because most of us looked the same in our uniforms, but Turk looked like a man while the rest of us looked like boys.

"You know it's against the rules." I said.

"C'mon," he said, nervously looking over his shoulder. "Just once...I'm *crazy* about this girl."

I sighed and took off the button. "One dance—that's it."

He glanced both ways before pinning it on. He squeezed my shoulder. "Thanks Nick...I'll get it right back." Then he disappeared.

A few minutes later, I was still near the refreshment table talking with a couple friends, when a short, heavyset man walked up holding Turk by the arm. The man then grabbed *my arm* roughly and escorted us to the front door. "No switching da buttons in my dance hall," he said with a thick accent. "You get out and don't come back!"

The night air felt cool to the skin, but inside, I was steaming mad. "What in blazes happened?" I asked.

"I dunno," Turk said with head bowed. "I guess he saw me. I'm really sorry."

"Aw, forget about it." I gave him a dime to go down the street to buy some pop. I slouched on a bench and mulled over my bad luck. A lone streetcar rattled by. *What will Betty think of me now?*

Suddenly, two pairs of hands grabbed my arms from behind and yanked me off the bench. Two toughs dragged me into a dark alley behind the dance hall while a third followed. A swarthy man with greasy hair grabbed the front of my shirt with both hands and leaned so close to my face I smelled the liquor on his breath. "We don't need CCC boys playin' sweet to our girls," he said.

I struggled to get free, but they held me tight. "I'm not looking for trouble," I said.

"Well, you found it," he said. He let go of my shirt and in one motion slugged me in the gut. "UGHH!" I groaned and doubled over, the wind knocked out of me.

"You guys should stay in the woods where you belong," he said and jerked me up by the shirt. Then he slapped my face three or four times.

Suddenly, I heard a voice. "Is that you, Nick?" Turk walked out of the shadows with his hands behind his back. The streetlight behind him hid his face in darkness. The men let go of me and stepped back.

Turk sounded like John Wayne. "I'm the sergeant around here...what the *hell* are you doing with my man?"

Their leader challenged him. "You ain't no sergeant, where's your stripes?"

"We don't use stripes, we use buckles."

"Oh, we got a clown here, boys," the man taunted.

Turk stuck out his arm and held his fist toward the man's face. Wrapped around his hand was his belt with the buckle facing out. It was the meanest set of brass knuckles I ever saw.

The man stepped back as if he just saw a snake. "Oh... I see what you mean," he stammered. "We weren't doin' nothin' were we boys?" They shuffled backwards.

"Don't mess with my men again or I'm gonna flatten your face." Turk growled. "NOW BEAT IT!"

They took off in a hurry. Turk put his hand on my shoulder, "C'mon kid, your drink's getting warm."

"Thanks for showing up..."

"You okay?"

"Yeah...I always wanted to know what it was like to be a punching bag."

"So what's it like?"

"They knocked the lice clean off me."

Turk chuckled. We sat on a bench under a street lamp and watched the moths flutter overhead. "Here's to you, Nick," Turk said and raised his Pepsi for a toast. "You lost your dance button, you lost your gal...but you didn't lose your sense of humor."

We laughed and swigged our drinks. As we waited for the camp truck, Turk entertained me with voice impersonations and sound effects. It helped get my mind off Betty.

Chapter 5

Framed

Dear Mom,

Our camp is building a state park. Roads need to be cut out of the woods, walking trails made, and bridges built. We put stones on the riverbanks to hold back the soil, and we brought in truckloads of sand for beaches.

An old lumberjack named Isaac is in charge of building a changing cabin for swimmers. He showed us how to strip the bark off logs and then notch them so they fit together. We use rope and pulleys to lift them into place; they fit together tight as a drum. All the work is done by hand just like the lumberjacks did. Isaac is a good boss, we do as much as possible and then he steps in to make sure everything is right.

The cabin we're building is practice for the superintendent's house, a much bigger building. Isaac wants me to help him with some of his carving work.

The weather has been very hot, so after work, we swim in the lake. We tie a rope to a branch and swing out over the water.

I went into town over the weekend and danced with a girl for the first time since I got up here. It was a lot of fun, but I had to leave early because I did something stupid.

Well, I hope it's not too hot in the big city. All my best.

Love,
Nick

I was out on the barracks steps after supper carving my bear, when Mr. Mulligan came up. He asked if I took a c-clamp from the equipment building.

"No sir. I always sign it out," I said.

He gave me a hard look. "You were the last one to take it, so if you know where it is, now's the time to return it."

"I told you, I always return it."

He clenched his jaw. "It didn't grow legs and walk away."

When he left, I took my bear carving and heaved it into the woods. As far as I cared, the sergeant and the camp could go to hell. I was probably the only enrollee who ever checked out the clamp, so of course he accused me. If someone wanted to frame me, he picked the right tool to make disappear. *I bet the same person who ratted on me about the rope ditched the c-clamp!*

I walked into the woods and searched for the carving. When I found it, I sat down on a log. The sound of the wind blowing through the leaves calmed me down. The ground at my feet was soft and sandy. I smoothed over the dirt with my hand and began to doodle. I traced out the word "frame." *Who can be framing me?* There was only one person. I smoothed out the dirt again and moved the "r" so it spelled "Farmer." Proving he did it would be the hard part.

A few days later, I played with Agnes while I waited for supper. I threw an old tennis ball that she eagerly chased down. The beagle recovered quickly with all the love and attention she got from the boys. We gave her a bath in a big tub on Sunday and she loved it. The fur on her back was dark brown. It turned a lighter brown on her sides and then became white on her belly. She spent a lot of time sniffing around for rabbits and other animals. We tried to keep her out of the woods so she wouldn't track down skunks or porcupines. When boxing practice began, I left her to play with another boy.

"On the ground and gimme twenty," Scruggs ordered when I showed up a few minutes late. At times, he acted more like a drill sergeant than a boxing coach. He put me through a leg strengthening drill where I squatted and walked with my rear end close to the ground. I could hardly stand up afterwards.

In another drill, I bounced around the ring while another boy took slow swings at me. Sweat ran down my bare chest as I weaved side-to-side avoiding his hits. The only time to rest was between rounds. During a break, I spoke to the coach. "Something's wrong—I feel stiff."

Scruggs looked up. "You're too wild...make smaller, quicker movements."

I drank a shot of water and went back in the ring for another grueling two minutes. After boxing practice, I threw my shirt over my shoulder and headed back to the barracks. I watched a green delivery truck drive into the camp. The driver backed up to the storage building and began unloading big cartons. They must have been light in weight, because he carried them easily. Then, I noticed something peculiar. The clerk came out and argued with the truck driver, waving his arms around as if he was upset. The driver ignored him and kept unloading the truck.

I decided to check it out and walked over to catch the excitement. I heard the clerk say the camp didn't need so much toilet paper. I chuckled to myself and watched from a nearby bench. The driver wiped his forehead with a handkerchief. "Now listen...I'm under orders to leave this stuff. I'll be back tomorrow and get it if they tell me."

"I'll save you a trip," the clerk argued.

"I have to *follow orders*," the driver said, and picked up another carton.

Suddenly, an orderly stepped out of the building with a c-clamp in his hand. "Hey, look what I found."

My jaw dropped. I jumped off the bench and ran over to him. "Let me see that." I grabbed the missing c-clamp from his hands. He took me into the room and showed me where he found it. "Will you take it to the sarge and tell him where you found it?" I explained how he accused me of stealing it.

"Sure," he said. "Glad to help."

I headed back to the barracks and wondered why someone would throw a c-clamp in the back of a storage building. If the person wanted it to disappear, he would have tossed it into the woods. It made no sense.

The next day I received a letter with a return address from Duluth! I hurried over to the rec hall to find Frank. He was lining up a pool shot when I came in the door. "I hit pay dirt," I said and waved the letter in the air. "It's from Duluth!"

"I don't believe it," Frank said. He handed the cue to his partner. We went outside and sat on the steps. Dark clouds gathered in the sky and gusts of wind kicked up. A few guys gathered around to listen in. It looked like the man wrote on a placemat.

> *Dear Nick,*
>
> *I know where your father is. He's living nearby and works in a sawmill. Please send me $10 and I will tell you where to find him.*
>
> *Sincerely,*
> *Otto Saari*

I smiled at Frank. "I found him...I found my dad! Can you believe it?"

A frown crossed his face. "Let me see it," he said. He took it.

"What's wrong?" I asked after he read it. "Ten bucks is nothing...I'll borrow it somewhere."

"This guy is a con artist—he's out to fleece you."

"What? C'mon...so what if he wants a few bucks."

"Anybody who asks for money to help a kid find his dad is a flake." Frank shook his head. "Sorry to break the news."

Flabbergasted, I grabbed the letter and read it again. "Any of you guys got a match?" I asked. One of the boys tossed me a box. I struck it on the step, lit the letter and held onto it as long I could. The wind carried the ashes away.

"Sorry," Frank said with a glum face.

"Forget about it. I'm just unlucky."

"Sure." He gave me a pat on the shoulder and went inside with the others. Thunder boomed off in the distance. I looked up at the billowy clouds and felt raindrops begin to fall on my face. Lightning lit up the sky in the distance. The world was full of rotten people; I just happened to run into one of them. It was a good thing Frank steered me straight about the letter or I'd be out ten bucks. At least I tried.

A couple days later, I crossed paths with Farmer in the lunch line at the state park. Large brown stains soaked the underarms of his t-shirt. He reeked of sweat. It was a good time to pop the question. "You didn't by chance chuck a c-clamp in the back of the storage room did you?" I watched for his reaction.

He twisted his face into a puzzled look. "What are you talkin' about? I don't know nuthin' about a c-clamp. But if I did...I'd stick it on your nose and turn it *real* tight."

I said nothing. I got the same reaction when I accused him of snitching on me about the rope. Either he was a great liar or innocent; it was probably the latter.

Farmer scooped up some coleslaw. "How are those boxing lessons going?" he asked.

I picked up a roll. "Good," I said. "In a month, I'll be ready to knock your brains loose."

Farmer flashed a leering grin. "Oh yeah? I can't wait to see you try."

I watched two mallard ducks paddle by while I ate my lunch on a log by the lake. Something told me Farmer was not the guy who framed me. He was the type who confronted people. I could not picture him sneaking around and dumping a c-clamp in the back of the storage room. Whoever took it was smart enough to get into the equipment room *and* the storage building without anyone knowing it. A dozen boys worked as orderlies in those two buildings, but I already checked them out and no one had a beef with me.

Off in the distance, a bird made a yodel-like sound. "That's a loon," I heard a fella say. I took a bite of my liverwurst sandwich. *If I don't find out who's out to get me, I might be the one going loony!*

After lunch, I helped one of our local experienced men build a fireplace in the changing cabin. Mr. Koski was a square-faced Finn with slightly slanted eyes. A fine layer of dust covered his clothes from working with cement all day. He grew up in the iron-mining town of Negaunee and spoke with a Finnish accent.

I collected stones on the grounds and separated them by size and grade. The fireplace stood about six feet wide with a twenty-foot high chimney. Mr. Koski talked about his youth. "My dad...he work in da mine, but I say, dat's not fer me." He dipped his trowel in the cement and scooped out a batch.

"Where did you learn English?" I asked.

"I go school, whatch you dink?"

He said they carried skis to school and jumped during recess. "We yumped dirty, forty feet."

I handed Mr. Koski a stone the size of a football, and he studied it for a moment until he found a spot. Then he took his chisel and gave it a hard rap with his mallet. The stone broke in half like an egg. "Every stone has seam," he said.

"How did you learn your trade?" I asked.

"Experience," the old Finn said.

"How did you *get* experience?"

"By doing it."

"But, you had to start somewhere."

"I tell you, I learn by experience." I chuckled at his dry sense of humor.

One of the boys shaped a stone to Mr. Koski's orders and handed it to him. "It's perfect," the boy said.

Mr. Koski gave him a steely look with his clear blue eyes and examined the stone. Then he tapped it very gently with his mallet. "Now it's perfect...it's not perfect 'til I say it's perfect."

At the end of the workday, Mr. Koski handed me his apron. "Give dis to Dacker and bring me new one." I shuddered at the thought of seeing Thacker again.

Back at camp, I debated on giving the apron to another boy to exchange for me, but Thacker asked questions and I didn't want him to think I was afraid of him. I found the back door to the supply building propped open with a brick. I walked in and saw him sweeping the floor.

"So what do you got today," he asked with a grim face. He never smiled at me.

"Mr. Koski needs a new apron," I said and laid the apron on the counter.

Thacker took the apron, tossed it in a bin and took a new one off the shelf. He leaned forward and his eyes narrowed. "Ever since you ran your mouth off to the sergeant about those stained pants, he's been *clamping* down on me." He let out a guttural laugh. "Yep, he's been *clamping* down on me."

I got the heebie-jeebies, picked up the new apron and scooted out as fast as I could. *Did Thacker try to frame me with the clamp? That's crazy!*

As I made my way back to the barracks, I felt flustered. Thacker could have done it because he had the keys to both the equipment room *and* the supply building! On the other hand, maybe he was just teasing me. He may have heard about the missing c-clamp and wanted to goad me. *What a strange man!*

Another thought came to me as I walked across the quad. Thacker might also have been the one who trailed Frank and me out to the climbing trees. It might have been *his* tobacco spit the on the fern leaf! I said nothing about my suspicions, not even to Frank. I needed time to make think it over.

Pay day

Grudge match

The old swimming hole

Blueberry pies

Back from work

Barracks

Woodwork class

Time for hair cut

Canteen

Building a road

Camp and surrounding area

Equipment room

Forest officers

Ready for work

Swing Time

Big Time baseball team

Building changing cabin at state park

Surveying

Recreation Hall

Planting tree seedling

Correspondence Class

Laying limestone

A couple nights later in the rec hall, I overheard a few boys talk about the latest war news. I came over and looked at the newspaper spread out on the table. The headline read, PEACE PLAN DRAFTED IN JAPANESE WAR. Japan had moved troops into China, and a war was brewing. "That's swell. All we need is another war to get sucked into," Elliot said.

"Don't sweat the Japs," Mario said. "It's Germany we got to worry about."

"I'm not fightin' the krauts," Arky said. "I lost two uncles in the last war and for what?"

"Oh yea? Where do you think they'll find their recruits?" Frank asked. "They'll be changing the sign at the front gate from Camp to Fort someday."

"You guys are nuts," Mario countered. "Roosevelt's not going to get us into war—he's for the little guy."

"That's a bunch of hooey." Everyone turned and looked as Ollie walked over with a cue stick in his hand. "It's the *little guy* that fights the rich man's wars."

"Watch what you say about FDR," Mario said. "We wouldn't be here if it weren't for him..."

Ollie cut him off. "*That's* what we'll be saying someday when we're digging foxholes..."

Frank got between them with outstretched arms. "C'mon you guys," Frank said. "Don't work yourself into a lather over it."

I threw in my two cents. "Someone should just cancel the newspaper subscription—it's just full of bad news anyway."

We broke up and went back to reading our books and magazines. Every time I looked at a newspaper—it reminded me that I was born at the wrong time.

I stepped outside the rec hall and saw Mr. Wells walking by in a t-shirt and overalls carrying a saw in his hand. I ran to catch up to him. He asked me to help him saw logs. I was soon working with him, holding down logs on a sawhorse as he sawed. A leather headband held his hair tightly in place. I asked why war seemed to be popping up all over the world right now.

He spoke slowly. "War never ends war, but lays the seed for new wars."

"Why's that?" I asked.

"War doesn't strike at the problem."

"Huh?"

"You may remember the story of Hercules and the Hydra. Each time Hercules knocked off a head, two more appeared."

"So?"

"It was the *beast* that needed to be targeted, not the heads." His saw easily sliced through the cedar log.

I took another log from the pile. "So, who's the beast?"

Beads of sweat dripped from the Indian's long nose. "The *beast* is the belief that man can be a ruler over others, whether he's called a president, king or dictator. Man properly governed is *self-governed* by the Great Spirit."

"But, the world is full of evil people..."

Mr. Wells looked up with his deep brown eyes. "Evil is a quality, not a person," he said. "To call a person evil is to give evil identity—man's identity is derived from the Great Spirit."

"We need more *good* people in the world."

He shook his head. "To say a person is good, *limits* good. All good is the good of the Great Spirit shining through... despite the names we give to it."

I came away from the work refreshed and inspired. He really made me look at things from a different view. If Mr. Wells were born a hundred years earlier, he would have been a wise man in his tribe.

Every new enrollee had a chance to be a heavy equipment operator. When we first arrived in camp, we took a driving test and tried to navigate a tractor out of a tight circle formation. Most of us failed and made a general ruckus by grinding up the gears. Squirt, a country boy who grew up on a potato farm, drove tractors since he was a child.

The pint-size rookie climbed onto a Caterpillar, eased out the clutch and maneuvered the tractor away from the circle of CATS with ease. Now, four months later, he led the charge on our fire fighting team.

Flames flared out of control in tinder-dry forest, and Squirt cleared trees and brush for firebreaks while crews followed behind on foot to clean up. A sudden shift in wind direction caused smoke to blow in our faces, so we retreated about a hundred yards from the fire line. After a head count, we discovered five boys missing. Squirt, who barely filled half the driver's seat of his CAT, yelled at us to hitch a trailer. He stood up and shouted orders like a general. "Put the pea coats in there and water 'em down!"

About thirty of us were milling around when a forest officer yelled, "I need someone to go with Stanley...who can drive?" No one raised his hand, so I did. I figured I could drive as well as anyone.

"Get on the trailer and be careful," he shouted.

"Yes, sir!" I swung my leg over and rolled in.

Squirt tied a red handkerchief around his face like a Mexican bandit. I crawled under a soaking wet pea coat and poked my head out like a turtle. Squirt threw the tractor in gear and we plowed into the thick smoke. I hoped Squirt did not pass out from the smoke or I would be in the driver's seat.

The CAT crashed through small trees bouncing me off the trailer floor like a jumping bean. A couple minutes into the woods, I heard the faint sound of boys yelling. I stuck my head over the edge of the trailer and saw the guys making their way through the smoke. I told Squirt to slow down. The guys climbed in the trailer and crawled under the coats. I passed around canteens of water. Squirt yelled, "We got everyone?"

"Yep...get this bucket moving!" I shouted.

"Hold onto your hats!" he hollered and pulled the handkerchief up over his face. He threw the tractor back in gear and we roared off into a haze of smoke. Under the coats, I came face to face with Turk.

"How you doing?" I asked.

"I could use a cigarette," he wisecracked. The trailer hit something and we bounced about a foot off the floor.

"My teeth fell out," one of the boys quipped.

After a few minutes of a head-banging drive, we heard Squirt say, "We're in the clear." We threw back the coats and saw the smoke billowing up behind us.

"Attaboy, Squirt," Turk yelled.

"What a ride!" another shouted.

We pulled up to the other enrollees who greeted us with a big cheer. Squirt jumped to the ground and fell to his knees coughing and sputtering. An enrollee ran up and splashed water on his face.

"My mouth...not my face," Squirt said.

"So how'd you find them?" a fella asked.

Squirt took a swig of water and spit. "They found me," he said wiping his mouth with the back of his hand. "The smoke was so bad I couldn't see a darn thing...I was knocking down trees right and left."

Everyone took a break while we waited for the wind to shift. About fifteen minutes later, we went back to fight the blaze. By suppertime, the firebreaks did their job and the fire was contained. When raindrops began to fall, the gang let out shouts of joy. I reached with my arms to the sky and let the rain splatter on my face. Rain never tasted so good. I put the rake over my shoulder and headed back to the trucks with the other guys. Nothing in the world seemed important except we got the boys back alive.

Squirt showed us it was not how big you were, but the size of your heart that mattered. Stanley "Squirt'" Rooney was a hero to us on that day. Riding back to camp, we took Squirt's last name and put it in the Battle Hymn of the Republic. So on a warm summer evening—in August of 1937—our voices echoed through the Lake Superior State Forest as our trucks rumbled along the road.

Glory! Glory! All to Rooney...
Glory! Glory! All to Rooney...
Glory! Glory! All to Rooney...
He came and saved the day...

The next morning I turned out to be the goat. When the forest officer discovered I did not have clearance to drive a tractor he reported me to the First Sergeant. I stood at parade rest in Mr. Mulligan's office after breakfast and noticed the chord to the fan hanging over the file cabinet. The sergeant leaned over his desk and rubbed his forehead intensely. He looked up with blood shot eyes.

"What if Stanley couldn't drive that tractor...could you have gotten it moving?" he asked.

"Yes," I said.

"So you get stuck on a stump...what do you do?"

I thought a second. "I'd get some branches to give me some extra traction."

He shook his head. "Why don't you put it in reverse?" he asked.

"I don't think I could."

He slapped his wood ruler on the desk—it sounded like a gunshot. "All you care about is yourself—you put other people at risk yesterday."

"Sir, no one else volunteered..."

He interrupted. "Not everyone was asked...there were two or three drivers out there he could have tracked down."

"Yes, sir."

"You have to make up your mind about what's right and what's wrong," he said. "Dismissed." He nodded his head toward the door.

My hand was on the door handle when I heard my name. I turned. "By the way...that was a brave thing you did yesterday," he said.

"Thank you, sir." As I made my way to the work truck, I felt like I just went through a wringer. One moment I was selfish, the next brave. He threw me out to sea and then tossed me a lifeline. His words left me bewildered, but a smile came to my face when I realized he didn't punish me. Maybe there was hope for me yet.

Three days after the camp celebrated the rescue of the trapped fire fighters, we discovered an enrollee missing. Irving Ivanski, a seventeen-year-old from Hamtramck, missed curfew. Many of the boys knew Irving from the portraits he drew for a dime. His caricatures and portraits were popular gifts to send home to our families. I played checkers with him occasionally, but we never became close friends. Irving didn't have any close friends; he was a loner.

The officers took his absence seriously because he left all his belongings. A boy who went over-the-hill usually took his gunnysack and clothes. The morning after he missed curfew, we organized into search teams and fanned out in all directions from camp. Just before lunch, someone spotted his body floating in a shallow pond. The evidence pointed to suicide. They carried him back in a tarp.

An eerie silence fell over the camp as word spread about the death. There were sullen faces everywhere. At lunchtime, it was unusually quiet in the mess hall. For the first time, I saw a lot of plates taken away with food still left on them. After lunch, we boarded trucks for work duty at the state park. Most of us wanted to get out of camp as soon as possible.

Irving was a moody person, but no one thought he was suicidal. I had tried to get him to talk about his problems, but he never opened up. On the ride to the state park, some of the guys talked about Irving. A few were angry with themselves for not doing more to cheer him up. Others were sad because they lost a friend. I think most of us were just confused. No one could figure out how someone could let down his friends and family by doing something so stupid and cowardly.

That night after supper, I sat out on the steps whittling when Bricks told me Captain Bullock wanted to see me. I promptly stuck myself with a chisel. *Damn it...am I in trouble because of Irving's death?* I took a deep breath and tried to calm down.

I hurried to the captain's office. The screen door squeaked when I opened it and a fan hummed on a shelf. I stood at full attention. "Reporting as ordered, sir."

"At ease," the captain said. He pointed to an empty chair next to Mr. Mulligan. I sat. The office reminded me of the sergeant's, maps covered the walls, with the same portrait of the President.

"Thanks for coming," the captain said somberly. The smoke from his pipe drifted lazily upward and gave the room a rich spicy aroma. "We need your help. Can you tell us what these letters say?" He picked a letter off his desk and handed it to me.

"I'll do my best, sir," I said, and sighed in relief. I studied the letter, which Irving's mother had written in Polish.

For the next twenty minutes, I translated about a dozen letters to the two officers. The letters contained nothing but bad news. One of Irving's brothers landed in jail, his dad sustained a serious injury at work and his family lost their home because of back taxes.

Captain Bullock raised his hand. "Thank you Nick...that's enough," he said. "I want you to forget what you just read. There's no reason to talk about this with anyone else."

"Yes, sir." I returned to the barracks steps, kicked off my shoes and socks, and went back to my carving. The evening sun filtered through the trees and a gentle breeze swirled around me. Shouts from the baseball field and the crack of bats filled the warm August night. I hoped the carving would help me get my mind off the letters I had just read. The duck decoy required a lot of concentration because of the fine detail on the feathers.

Agnes came up and licked my bare feet. I giggled, which

was probably just what I needed right then. Agnes roamed freely over the camp and returned to the shed each night to sleep. She visited me when I sat on the steps after supper.

José came out of the barracks and talked to me about Irving. "I just started to teach him how to use short wave," he said.

"At least you tried to help him, that's more than most of us did." I said and gently scratched away at the duck.

José rubbed the dog's belly. "My mom really liked the drawing he made of me. I asked him once why he didn't just take a picture since it was easier."

"Oh yeah?" I said.

"He said photos didn't show all the things a drawing could."

That surprised me. "No joking?"

"Yeah, Irving said he could show qualities of a person that a photo couldn't...like make a guy look kinder or smarter."

I smiled. "Geez...he could've made me look high class."

"I doubt it, but he could've straightened your nose," he joked.

I looked up. "Thanks...I needed that."

Bricks came by with a clipboard in his hand. "Will you fellas pledge twenty-five cents from your next paycheck for Irving's family?"

"Yeah, sure," I said.

"Me too," José echoed.

Bricks marked his paper. "By the way, we found his self-portrait and hung it in the library."

José and I decided to check it out. We found a few other boys hanging around the little alcove where it hung in a knotty pine frame. A vase of blue and white iris sat underneath it on a table, a nice touch by someone. The pencil drawing showed a sensitive boy with an intelligent face and pensive expression. His hair was tousled and eyes brooding. José and I leaned over the table for a closer look.

"Boy, he was a great artist," José said. "What do you think he added to the picture that a camera couldn't catch?"

"Beats me," I said.

Turk came by. "That boy had a lot of talent," he muttered.

I explained to Turk how Irving enhanced his drawings. "What do you think he added?" I asked.

"What is this...a test?" Turk asked, put off. He lit a cigarette and inspected the portrait closely while José and I stepped back. Turk was smarter than most of us—he spoke German and Polish *and* he knew Morse code.

A grin spread over his wide face. "You fellas got it all wrong. Irving didn't add anything to his picture, he left something out."

José and I crowded up next to him and looked. "What do you see?" I asked.

"He's crying," Turk said softly. "Look at his eyes...that bum left the tears out of his own picture."

"You're right," José said. "Those are the saddest eyes I ever saw."

I nodded. "He saw the good in everyone else, but couldn't see it in himself."

With a heavy heart, I laid my head on my pillow that night. I vowed that if I ever ran into a kid who bottled up his troubles, I would find a way to get him to open up, even if I had to shake it out of him.

The balmy night made it impossible to sleep. The tiny windows hardly let in any air and the fans were too far away to help me. I rolled around in my cot, hot and sticky. The image of Irving's self-portrait haunted me. Suddenly, I felt a tap on my shoulder and heard someone whisper, "You want to go down to Rock River?" It was Frank.

I looked up. "Sure," I said.

Elliot and Ollie joined us and we quietly snuck out. The cloudy night made the path difficult to see so we walked carefully. After about ten minutes, we heard the gurgling sound of water. We splashed around naked in the cool water for a few minutes and then headed back to camp. Halfway home, we heard animals growling. "Uh-oh…" Elliot sounded horrified.

The four of us picked up the pace. The growling sounds got closer so we began to run. "Those are wolves," Ollie shouted. "Up the tree!" We scrambled onto the branches like squirrels, wearing nothing but our shorts. From high up in the tree, we heard snarling and scratching sounds below us.

"This is a fine mess we're in," Elliot whined. "Why do I always end up in a tree when I go into the woods?"

"They smell you," Frank said sharply. "They smell your fat a mile away."

"Lay off," I said.

"Shhhh," Ollie said. The wolves had quieted down. He slowly climbed down to check things out. Suddenly, the wolves barked and howled at us.

"Oh great," Frank said. "Where's Arky and his slingshot when we need him."

When the bugs started to bite, we suffered. Minutes seemed like hours as we waited in the branches for the sun to rise. We told each other stories and sang songs to stay awake. Ollie led us in singing.

Way down upon the Suwannee River,
Far, far away.
There's where my heart is turning ever,
There's where the old folks stay.

Just before sunrise, we saw headlights in the distance and heard a car door slam. Someone headed our way with a flashlight. "Help! Over here!" Elliot hollered. "Watch out for the wolves!"

"What in Sam Hill," a man said waving his flashlight. "Those aren't *wolves*, those are my *huntin' dogs*!" We let out a collective groan. "Git down from that tree, my dogs were jus' bein' friendly." We stumbled back into camp, fell exhausted on our cots and slept through breakfast.

Later that morning, the sergeant met with the four of us. He confined us to camp for two weeks and assigned us to scrubbing and polishing all the garbage cans in camp. He dismissed the others. I waited as he organized his papers.

"What am I going do with you?" Mr. Mulligan said.

"Kick me out?" I said, tentatively.

He rolled his head in exasperation. "That's just what you'd like me to do, but why should your mother suffer? She won't get the twenty-five bucks a month if I send you home."

I ground my teeth.

"No, I'm not going to send you home, but when I'm done with you...you'll wish I did. Dismissed."

A perfect Saturday, ruined.

That afternoon, as I scoured a garbage can with a soapy brush, someone called out, "Ruff, ruff!" I pulled my head out of the can and saw Farmer panting like a dog with his big tongue sticking out. "I'm a big bad wolf, you better climb a tree," he taunted. I picked up the garbage can and threw it at him. He ducked and it went tumbling on the ground.

"Whoa! Easy does it!" Mr. Mulligan yelled from the mess hall steps. He strode over and picked up the garbage can. "What's going on?" he asked.

"I lost my temper," I said.

He showed his least attractive scowl. "You better find it." He glanced over at Farmer who slinked away. "Get over here!"

Farmer hurried back. "Give me twenty push-ups," the sergeant barked. I relished seeing Farmer get in trouble for a change. The sergeant looked at me and pointed at the cans. "I want those so clean the cooks can make soup in 'em."

"Yes, sir." I dipped the brush into the bucket of soapy water and went back to scrubbing.

The camp quieted down that evening because most of the boys were in town. The sun came out from behind the clouds and the wind died down, leaving the camp with a quiet stillness. I sat on the barracks steps with a chisel in my hand and carefully outlined the duck feathers. I debated whether to start over since the duck looked more like a pigeon, with a dinky head and short beak.

Frank came up and asked me to play tennis. We signed out a couple of racquets and walked to the clay courts. It was the first time I ever played, and the leather grip felt good in my hand. I quickly learned the difference between tennis and baseball. In baseball you wanted to hit the ball *over* the fence, in tennis, you wanted to keep it *inside* the fence. The balls flew off my racquet, so I spent more time in the woods looking for balls than I did on the court.

One time, I swung so hard the racquet flew out of my hand into Frank's court. "What are you trying to do?" he yelled. "If I want a lobotomy, I'll see a doctor!"

As I hunted for a tennis ball in the woods, I found a three-foot long milk snake. Rust-colored splotches adorned its creamy brown skin. I pinned the snake down with my racquet and brought it back to the barracks after our game. I put it in Farmer's trunk under his clothes.

Just before lights out, Farmer opened his trunk at the other end of the barracks. I lay in bed and could barely contain my excitement. "Who the hell put a SNAKE in my trunk?" he yelled.

I went to sleep with a smile on my face, but when I woke up, it was a different story. I felt something move against my foot. I jumped out, pulled back the covers and found the snake in *my* bed! *I'll get Farmer back somehow!*

Chapter 6

Grudge Match

Two days later, the forest officers pulled us out of the park to fight a grasshopper infestation. Hordes of grasshoppers ate everything in sight and threatened local farmers' hay fields. They dropped us off near an open field and gave us sacks of arsenic-laced bait, which we hung over our shoulders. About fifty of us walked in a line about fifteen feet apart. I took a handful of bait and threw it with a waving motion as if I was feeding a flock of chickens. My hands turned a rusty brown color from handling the bait.

At lunch, the mess orderlies brought out big pots of lamb stew. So many grasshoppers flew around that some of them fell into the stew. The line moved slowly while the servers tried to pick out the insects. After a while, they gave up and passed the stew out with the grasshoppers in it.

I took my bowl and sat under a tree by Arky. As I picked them out, he said, "Don't worry about the small ones, they ain't so bad."

"Huh?" I mumbled.

He picked one out and put it in his mouth. "Just don't eat the big ones, they're tough to chew."

"Oh yeah?" I was dubious, but I tried it. They crunched like potato sticks and had a slightly nutty taste. "Hey, these aren't so bad after all," I said and picked a leg out of my teeth.

Arky shot me a bucktooth smile. "I think yer ready for my grandma's cookin'...like fried snake and possum stew."

"I don't think so," I said.

That night as I dressed for supper, I slid on my shoes and felt my toes squish against something. I turned the shoe upside down and shook it—three grasshoppers fell out. It had to be Farmer! I cleaned the shoe with tissue paper and wondered if putting a snake in his footlocker was such a good idea after all.

On Saturday, I felt frustrated because I wanted to explain to Betty why I missed my dance with her. She worked weekends as a lifeguard at Sherman Park so I knew where to find her, but I was stuck in camp! I looked up at the partly sunny sky, a perfect day for the beach. With August nearly half over, summer slipped through my hands like sand.

A neat pile of pants lay folded beside me on the barracks step. I picked up a lot of alteration jobs lately because word was getting around about my good work. I listened to a Tiger baseball game while I used the needle. Hank Greenberg knocked in a pair of home runs; he was on track to break Babe Ruth's record.

When I lived in Detroit, I went to the Tigers games and hung out by the dugout afterwards. My buddies and I tried to talk to the players, many of whom ignored us, but not Hank. He chatted with us about everything, from his favorite ballparks to the toughest pitchers in the league. Once I asked him if there was an old scuffed ball he could give me. He went into the dugout and came out with a brand new ball.

"All I wanted was a scuffed ball," I said.

"You want a scuffed ball?" He knelt and rubbed the ball in the dirt. "Now it's scuffed," he said and tossed it to me. What a guy!

I adjusted the radio to get rid of the crackling sound and wondered if my dad listened to the same game. It bothered me that nobody had replied to the letters I wrote asking about his whereabouts. I felt discouraged and wondered if my mom would ever have enough money to move out of her rundown apartment. She deserved real plumbing and new furniture. It made me gloomy just thinking about it. Even Agnes knew something was wrong. She looked up at me with her sad copper-brown eyes and whimpered.

"Hold your horses," I told her. "I'll play with you when I finish these cuffs."

"Nick, get over here," I looked up and saw Turk waving at me.

"Okay, wait a minute," I said and carefully laid down the pants. He took me to the library and we peeked around the corner. A new recruit stood at the flagpole with a watering can.

"What the heck is he doing?" I asked.

"He's watering the flagpole, stupid." Turk said. "He's been at it the last few days."

I felt sorry for the kid. "C'mon, let's straighten him out."

The freckle-faced rookie looked about sixteen. He wore a t-shirt with the sleeves rolled up. "What are you doing?" I asked.

He continued to pour. "What do you *think* I'm doing? I'm just following orders."

"Why?" I said.

"He said it was a dry summer," the boy said. Turk tried to keep from busting up.

"So...you think the roots might be dry?" I asked.

"Nah, flagpoles don't have roots," the rookie said.

"Then why are you watering it? Turk asked.

"I don't wanna get in trouble."

I pushed my cap back a little. "Just between you, me, and the flagpole, you don't have to worry about getting in trouble."

"You think so?" He stopped watering.

"I know so. But, there's another job you can do," I said.

"Oh, yeah?"

I raised my arm and pointed. "The grass in front of the captain's quarters...it needs a fresh coat of paint."

"What? Paint the grass?" he said, baffled.

"That's how we keep it green," Turk said.

"Aw, you're pulling my leg," the boy said with a grin.

I slapped his hat off and laughed. "Don't be a sap," I said. I must have had a soft spot for rookies because of all the grief I went through.

After supper, I visited Isaac to borrow the carving tools. He sat outside behind the equipment building sharpening axes on the grindstone. He wore a t-shirt so tattered it could have been a rag. I asked him about the tattoo on his upper arm with the name *Mabel* under it. It showed the profile of a woman's face with a headband of flowers. Isaac grinned and said Mabel was a girlfriend from Duluth.

My jaw dropped. "Duluth?" Did you ever hear of my dad, Marek...he worked in a sawmill."

Isaac kept his eyes on the axe head and shook his head. "Nah, dat was a long time ago." Isaac gave me the name of three sawmills that I could write for information about my dad. I scratched down the names with a stubby pencil.

"I'll write those letters tonight." I said.

He rolled up his shirtsleeve. "Take a look at dis," he said. A tattoo on his shoulder read *Born to Loose.*

"Didn't you mean to say *Born to Lose*?"

"Yeah...I never could spell dat good." I followed him into the equipment building where he opened a drawer in his workbench. I noticed a set of dentures inside.

"Are those yours?" I asked. "You never wear them."

"Aw, day don't fit so good," he mumbled and handed me the carving knives and chisels.

"You deserve teeth that fit."

"Nobody cares eef I got teeth..."

"Well, I do."

As I walked back to the barracks, the idea came to me to have people in camp chip in and buy him a new pair. If we raised money for Irving's mother, why not do it for someone we know?

Isaac commanded respect with the boys—his word was law. He once told me how lucky he was to get the CCC job because there was so little work for lumberjacks. CCC camps did more than give teenage boys a home; it gave a lot of good men a chance to work and use their skills. Whoever dreamed up the CCC was pretty darn smart.

Just before curfew that night, Bobby kissed Mario's mom good night. Not the person—the picture. Every night just before lights out, he scooted down his cot, and touched his lips with his first two fingers. Then he pressed his fingertips against the photo of his borrowed mom, which he taped inside his trunk.

It made me think about my mother and the way she used to tuck me in at night when I was a little boy. She sat on the edge of the bed and rocked back and forth singing me the Lord's Prayer. When I was asleep, my dad often came in and gave me a little kiss on the forehead. I knew he did, because if I was awake, I pretended to be asleep. Once, when he leaned over to kiss me, I said, "Boo!" Boy, did he jump. He cussed me out good. Sometimes, the thought still nagged me that I was the reason my dad ran off. Who could stand living with me?

We started our workweek by cutting tall grass to reduce fire hazards. A dry spell had turned the grass tinder-dry. About twenty of us walked lengthwise across a field and made long sweeping motions back and forth with our scythes. Suddenly, I heard a boy cry out in pain.

Our conservation officer hollered for everybody to kneel while he ran to where the boy lay in the grass. It turned out that another boy clipped him with the scythe. The blade sliced through his pants and gashed his calf. They cut off his pants, wrapped the wound with a white bandage, and then sent him to the dispensary for stitches.

During the lunch break, I walked by some officers eating under a tree and overheard them discuss ways to prevent accidents. I listened for a moment until one of them motioned with his hand for me to sit down. "I think we should cut the tips off the blades," a conservation officer suggested.

"How about putting a little ball on the tip?" another said. The conversation went on and on with the men unable to agree on a course of action. As I chewed my bologna sandwich, an idea came to me. I timidly raised my arm.

"Go ahead, Nick," one of them said.

"Why not file down the ends of the blades to make them dull." Most of them smiled and nodded.

"That's the best idea yet," the chief officer said.

"Way to use your old noggin," Mr. Rushford said.

I smiled and bit into my pickle. *Imagine a high school dropout like me solving their problem!* I wished Mr. Mulligan were here to see me.

That night before supper, I sat on the barracks steps and worked on my latest carving, a box turtle about half the size of a football. I gave up on the duck decoy after I had hacked away at it for a month. I figured the turtle might be easier. Isaac drew an outline of it on a piece of basswood to get me started. He suggested I mount it on a log when I finished it.

Using a mallet and a chisel, I gently chipped away at the wood to form the outline of the shell. Agnes sprawled out on a lower step and watched me with her long tongue hanging out. She had just finished a big meal of meat scraps.

Over the past week, I gave a lot of thought to Thacker and the missing c-clamp. I figured the chances were small that he was behind it. If he wanted me in trouble, the clamp would have disappeared. As an officer, he was privy to items stolen in camp and the boys who were under suspicion. They probably talked about me at one of their officers' meetings and he figured he could rub it in by teasing me. I decided not to let it bother me.

Mario stopped by with his baseball glove and looked at my carving. We talked about Agnes and her tracking ability.

I bet him a nickel that she could pick out my shoe from any other boy's. "You're on," he said and went inside the barracks to borrow some shoes. He wrote the names of each boy on the sole, placing them a couple feet from one another.

I held my other shoe up to Agnes' nose, so she caught my scent. "C'mon Agnes, find my other shoe," I said. She hopped up the stairs and sniffed a few shoes until she came to mine. She barked and picked up my shoe with her mouth. Mario paid up.

Ten minutes later, a shadow fell across my turtle. I looked up and saw Farmer standing with a towel around his waist and soap dish in his hand. Pimples and red splotches covered his broad chest and shoulders.

"What cha' carving Rat Eye, a cow pie?" he joked.

"Yeah, you should know," I said.

"Let me see." He snatched the turtle from my hands.

"Give it back," I said and reached for it. We both fell to the ground and it turned into a tug of war. We rolled around in the dust trying to pry it from each other's hands.

"What the HELL is going on here?" Scruggs yelled. He pushed the screen door open and looked down at us with his mouth half open. In the scuffle, Farmer had lost his towel so he was buck-naked in the dirt with his arms wrapped around me.

"We was just wrastlin'," Farmer said and crawled to his towel.

"Yeah, just wrastlin'," I said and got up on my feet.

Scruggs shook his head with a wry grin. "You fellas better clean up fast, supper's in ten minutes." He went inside.

Farmer glared at me. "Futz," he uttered and lumbered off to the bathhouse.

"You made a mess of my uniform, you big oaf!" I shouted. I brushed the dirt off my clothes and sat back down on the step. Agnes still slept. "Where were you when I needed you?" I asked. She opened one eye and gave me a puzzled look. "Aw, go back to sleep."

The next day when I returned to camp from work duty, Scruggs met me at the truck. "Better leave your work clothes on, you're going blueberry picking," he said.

"For wrestling with Farmer?" I asked.

He nodded grimly. "Sarge's orders." He pointed to a pick-up truck. "Be there in five minutes."

When Scruggs turned the corner, I threw my hat on the ground. "Son of a bitch," I swore.

A few minutes later, I sat slumped in the truck with a half-dozen other unlucky fellas. I loved picking wild blue-berries, but not for punishment. Why? Because they took us to a patch next to a mosquito infested swamp! With our glum faces, you would have thought they were taking us to a firing squad.

I looked across at Farmer. "Why can't you keep your hands to yourself?" I asked.

"Aw...shaddup," he muttered.

Each of us carried two pails to fill. The moment we set foot in the blueberry patch, the mosquitoes attacked us. We slapped and cussed as we hurried out to the bushes. Even with long-sleeved shirts and hats, they bit our skin. Nothing could stop them. "Hells bells," I said and slapped my neck.

I normally ate half the blueberries I picked, but not that day. I wanted to fill my pails as soon as possible and get back into the truck. Farmer stared angrily at me whenever our paths crossed, which annoyed me because *he* was the one who started it.

"Quick, someone give me a transfusion," one of the boys said as he climbed into the truck. "I lost a gallon of blood out there."

Back at camp, we took the berries to the bakery. Curly the baker thanked us as we dumped them into a big tub for washing. "These will make some fine pies, boys," he said. He gave us each a molasses cookie.

As I undressed for the shower, Farmer walked by with his towel in hand. "Sorry, Rat Eye," he said in a low voice and continued walking. *Did I hear that right? He apologized to me!* I brushed it off and figured the mosquitoes got to him.

A half-hour after supper, we had mail call outside the barracks. Most of us lounged on the bench or sat on the grass and listened to the mail clerk call out our names in a nasally voice. "Dagenais, Dodge, Gasperich." One by one, we went up and collected our letters.

Agnes sprawled out next to me on the grass as I read my letter. I noticed that Bobby got another letter from his borrowed mom. Suddenly, his smile disappeared, he looked like he was about to cry.

Someone else saw the same thing, "What gives, Bobby?"

Bobby got up from the bench fighting back tears and quickly hopped up the steps to the barracks. Mario followed him in. A few minutes later, Mario returned and told us what happened. "It's all right, guys," he said quietly. "My mom crossed out the word *borrowed* in the letter so it read, *Dear Son*, instead of *Dear Borrowed Son.* It shook him up a little."

Our worried faces turned to smiles. I scratched behind Agnes' ears. "Did you hear that girl? She called Bobby *her son.*"

Elliot excitedly rubbed his hands together. "Oh, boy," he said, "I can't wait to tell my mom."

Mario held up his hands for quiet. "That's not all. My mom always ended the letters, *Love, Your Borrowed Mom...* but this time she crossed off the word, *Borrowed.*"

The guys faces froze with looks of amazement.

I rolled Agnes around on her back. "Can you believe it?" She yelped when I rocked her a little too hard.

Some of the boys slapped Mario on the shoulder and kidded him that Bobby was now his brother. Mario put a finger to his lips. "Shhhh! Don't say anything...let him get used to the idea."

It dawned on me why none of the adoptive parents ever chose Bobby at the orphanage—it was not his time. If there was a God, he must have had a plan because the parents always chose the other kids. It was not by chance that Mario and Bobby became best friends. It happened because Mario would lead him to his new mother. Mario's mom probably needed Bobby as much as he needed her for some reason. Fate worked in mysterious ways.

A boy began throwing a tennis ball to Agnes, so I headed off to boxing practice. Since I was early, I swung by to see Mr. Wells at the Indian huts. He rocked back and forth over a cedar log as he stripped off bark with a wood shaver. Sweat soaked through his t-shirt as he worked in the late afternoon sun. I told him about the letter Bobby got from his borrowed mom.

"Was that the *good* of the Great Spirit shining through Mario's mom?" I asked.

He smiled. "You're a good listener."

I held the log steady as he made long smooth strokes. "If the Great Spirit makes good things happen, who makes bad things happen?" I told him about my brother and three sisters. "Mom said it was the will of God that they died. Is that true?"

The Indian picked up his canteen and drank. He looked at me with soulful eyes. "I'm saddened by your family's loss. It should never have been. It is never the will of the Great Spirit to punish or destroy. The Great Spirit is Life...how can Life bring death?"

"But why did they die so young?"

He spoke as he shaved the bark. "Above the door to many Hindu temples in India are inscribed the words, *Know thyself.* To know ourselves...we must first know the Father."

"My dad?"

Mr. Wells smiled. "In the Hebrew, the arrow is called the *son* of the bow, a month the *son* of a year, the week the *son* of the month and so on. If the Great Spirit is your Father, what does that make you?"

"I'm...a little spirit?"

He grinned. "Close...it means you are *spiritual.*"

"Huh?"

"You are spirit in *quality*, not *quantity*. The sun sends out light, not suns. So if the Great Spirit is light...*you* are His shining."

"So my brothers and sisters...never really died?"

"They are *still* shining, from the viewpoint of the Great Spirit, which in reality...is the *only* viewpoint."

He stumped me. "Yeah, but my view is human, I saw them buried."

Mr. Wells laid down the wood shaver and took out his tobacco pouch. "Nick, this may seem difficult to understand, but in reality there is no human perspective. What we called a human view is really the upside-down view of a spiritual fact."

Now, he *really* lost me. "Huh?"

He took a pinch of tobacco from his leather pouch and began rolling a cigarette. "The only correct view of anything, from a rainstorm to a wildflower, is the view of the Great Spirit and this view can be ours if we allow it."

"I still don't get it."

"When a surveyor looks through his instrument, is he alarmed at the upside-down view?"

"No."

"When a photographer develops a photograph, is he worried that the photo is reversed?"

"Of course not."

"These people are not taken in by the false picture because they *know the truth*."

"So, what does that have to do with my brother and sisters?"

"The human picture of mortals living and dying in the flesh never takes place in the light of truth. Their true being has always resided in Spirit, not matter." He struck a match and lit his cigarette.

"So, I'm not here?"

"Oh...you're here all right. But all that's true of you is what the Great Spirit knows of you."

I scratched my head. "I still don't get it. Why didn't they teach us that in catechism?"

He exhaled slowly. "The Jesuits teach *demon est Deus inversus*—the devil is God upside-down."

"Do I have to go to college to understand this stuff?"

He chuckled and gazed off toward the woods. "Wisdom is *not* the accumulation of human knowledge...it's giving up false beliefs for the spiritual reality of things." He turned toward me. "No...you don't need to go to college. But, it's good to ask questions and search for your inner man."

I nodded.

He looked over my shoulder. "Now...if you're smart, you'll hurry to boxing practice."

I turned around and saw a group of boys gathering around the ring. "Thanks for talking to me!" I took off running. Mr. Wells was the wisest man I ever met. *How wonderful it must be to see things as the Great Spirit sees!*

As a boy tied up my boxing gloves, I looked across the quad to where Mr. Wells worked. A break in the clouds caused the sunlight to shine on his Indian dwellings giving them a golden glow.

When Saturday arrived, I rolled out of bed with a smile on my face and a lump in my throat. *I get to see Betty today!* My two-week confinement finally ended. I did up my shoes and thought about what I would say to her. She would probably laugh at me. Morning clean up and inspection seemed to last forever. I swept cobwebs off the eaves of buildings and found two hornet nests. My lucky rabbit foot saved me from stings.

In the afternoon, I boarded one of the trucks for the Soo with a couple dozen other boys. I carried a canvas bag with a swimsuit, towel, and a Doc Savage book. Mom always taught me to take a book wherever I went. The two-and-a-half weeks that had slipped by since we danced at Gould's did little to dampen my affection for Betty. The memory of her smiling face remained fresh in my mind. I felt as anxious as a kid on the first day of school. *Why are you so nervous? You're a man. You fight forest fires!*

Sherman Park beach overflowed with people. Mother Nature delivered an ideal day with sunshine and temperatures in the eighties. The St. Mary's River ran dark blue, with children floating by on inner tubes and adults paddling canoes. Mothers waded into the water with children, teenagers tossed balls on the sand, while dads read books on benches. I plodded along in the soft sand wearing Frank's baggy swim trunks.

I spotted Betty on a lifeguard seat dressed in a red suit, straw hat, and sunglasses. She had the figure of a swimmer, long and lean. I adjusted my trunks and walked with a jaunty swagger. She recognized me and smiled. "Are you here for that dance?"

"Aw, shucks," I said and kicked the sand, "I didn't mean to stand you up."

"I know. I heard you got kicked out for sharing your button."

"Yeah, it was stupid..."

"It's nothing—happens all the time." She lifted up her glasses and stared at my trunks. "Nice suit, did you lose some weight lately?" I looked down at my loose trunks and shrugged.

She laughed. "I'm just kidding!"

Another lifeguard came to replace Betty, so she invited me to join her at her next post on the raft. We swam out together in the cold water. She swam with long, smooth strokes like Tarzan, and I struggled with short choppy ones, like Jane. Betty climbed up on the high seat while I sat on the edge of the raft with my legs dangling in the water. We talked about the Tigers.

"Think Greenberg will break the Babe's record?" she asked.

I gently splashed my feet. "Are you kidding?" I said. "It's a cinch—they'd have to break his legs to stop him."

Betty listened to the ball games with her dad. "What's the best part of the going to the park?" she asked.

I thought a moment. "The smell of food—the hot dogs and roasted peanuts."

"Mmmm, sounds wonderful," she said.

Some of her friends from school climbed up on the raft and began chatting with her, so I decided to take a little snooze. I stretched out on the warm planks and soaked up the sun. The gentle rocking of the raft and splashing sounds lulled me to sleep.

The next thing I knew, cold water drenched my face. I sat up and saw Betty smiling down at me. "Hey, sleepyhead, you better cover up or you'll get burned." I looked down at my belly, it glowed beet red. I needed to cool off so I got in line for the diving board. Most of the kids ahead of me jumped in feet first. No one did my specialty—the jackknife.

When my turn came, I glanced over at Betty who waved to me. The board was at least ten feet high and my trunks flapped in the wind like a loose sail as I gathered myself for my big jump. I took three long smooth steps, jumped, touched my toes and opened up into a perfect jackknife. I nailed it! The cold water turned me into an icicle. I popped up to the surface and swam back to the raft with quick strokes.

Betty clapped. "Nice dive!" Suddenly, she began laughing and pointed behind me. I turned and saw a teenaged girl floating on an inner tube with my trunks in her hand!

"Did you lose something?" She asked and tossed them in my direction.

I looked like a drowning man the way I sank every time I tried to get my feet inside those trunks. When I finally got them on, I swam back to the raft. A dozen children stood on the raft and teased me. "Jaybird, jaybird, he's naked as a jaybird." Humiliated, I turned and swam back to shore.

"Where are you going? C'mon back!" Betty called. I found my towel on the beach and headed for the changing room. Then, I rode the next streetcar back into town. My day in paradise turned to hell. Just when I patched things up with Betty, I made a complete fool of myself. I wondered if I was just stupid or cursed—probably a bit of both. The ride back to camp took forever. I looked down at the little rabbit's foot dangling from my belt loop—I should have stuck it on my trunks. I would need more than luck to bring Betty back into my life.

My day went from bad to worse. When I returned to camp, I got a letter from my mother that included a newspaper clipping about a couple of friends I went to school with. I flopped down on my cot and read how they had robbed a mutual man, the person who collected money for the numbers racket. Mutual men were easy targets because they carried big sacks of coins.

The police caught my friends the next day and put them in jail. While they waited in jail for their hearing, someone slit their throats. I went to grade school with these guys. The clipping depressed me; I wished my mother had never sent it.

Bad news from the outside always spoiled the peaceful feeling I felt in camp. I knew I would have to go home someday, but until then I couldn't have cared less about all the problems they had. I knew how Irving felt when he got those awful letters from his mother. I planned to write my mom and tell her not to send any more bad news. If she couldn't write about anything nice, she shouldn't write at all.

Most of my life I avoided work, now I looked forward to it. Isaac assigned me the job of roughing out the carving he planned for the mantle in the new superintendent's house. He intended to carve the head of a deer in a block of wood and attach a rack of antlers to it. A pattern of oak leaves would line the border.

Little did I know how tedious the work was. I stood for hours hunched over a large block of maple set on two sawhorses. I chipped away with a mallet and chisel following his outline. Isaac stopped by periodically to check my work. "Here...try dis one," he would say and hand me a different-size chisel. He told me to stay alert and not chisel off too much.

The state park came together quickly in the two months since we began work on it. A new log bridge crossed over a stream. Fresh sand covered the beach and the boys built a swim raft out of oil drums and wood. We used cinder on the walking trails and crushed limestone on the parking lots. I felt proud to be part of the project.

It was the last week in August on a peaceful Sunday morning when I overslept and missed breakfast. I attended chapel so I could get the free cinnamon rolls they passed out. The sun peeked out from behind the clouds and birds chirped overhead while I sat outside under the oak tree for the service.

"If you don't know where you're going," Chaplain Schultz said, "any road will get you there." He asked us how we knew which road to take in life. "How do you choose the right friends, the right job and the right thing to do?" Then, he read from the story of King Solomon. When God offered Solomon power and riches, the king asked only for an understanding heart.

"When you don't know what direction to go in life, pray for an understanding heart," he said. "When your motives are pure and desires holy, you will be led to the right decision when you have tough choices." I smiled smugly to myself. He talked about good motives and I came to chapel for the cinnamon rolls!

"The captain informed me that there is a language problem around here." The chaplain stepped away from the lectern and put his foot up on one of the log benches. "He says there are too many four-letter words coming out of your mouths." Some of the fellas chuckled. The chaplain then told us a story about how he got into the ministry. "I couldn't afford it, but I found out if I joined the army for six years, they would send me to college and seminary. That's why I'm here now."

He stepped up on top of the bench and looked down on us. "We had rough language in the army, believe me...you wouldn't understand half the words they used." He said when they ordained him as a minister, he was finally able to go home. “There I was, wearing my best uniform and sitting at the dinner table with my wife next to me and my parents across the table. Even my in-laws were there, so I say to my wife’s mother, pass the *damned* butter.”

All the guys cracked up. The chaplain raised his arms for quiet. “Let me tell you,” he said, “it was not very funny when it happened.” He warned us to begin improving our language *before* we went home or we might say something we regret.

Later, that afternoon someone reported Frank for stealing gas from the camp pump. He would gladly have paid for it, but the camp did not sell fuel to enrollees, who were not supposed to have motorbikes in the first place. Frank took only a pint, just enough to ride into town to buy more, but that didn’t matter.

For punishment, Mr. Mulligan sent him up the water tower to repaint the words *Camp Raco 667th Company* on the side of the tank. With the letters several feet high and only a tiny paintbrush to work with, the sergeant made sure he would be busy all day. After the sergeant left, I saw Frank perched on the edge of the tank about thirty feet high. I teased him. “You missed a spot,” I yelled. “C’mon, you can do better than that!”

Frank ignored me, but I continued to razz him. Just as I was about to leave, he looked over my head as if someone stood behind me. I turned and there stood Mr. Mulligan with a little paintbrush in his hand, pointed straight at me! I took the paintbrush and climbed up the water tank. The sergeant didn’t say a word, not a *single* word. I slid over next to Frank. “Wipe that smile off your face,” I said.

“Sure, big mouth...”

“Shaddup.” I muttered and dipped the brush into the can of paint. I never learned my lesson at the water well. *When are you going to keep your big mouth shut!*

Frank and I talked about my upcoming fight with Farmer. “So what’s your strategy?” he asked.

"Strategy? I don't know…maybe I'll drop a piano on his head."

"C'mon…the fight's a week away…"

"Okay, I'm gonna hit him low and stay away from his swings."

"Why don't you just take a dive when he hits you? Nobody expects you to win."

I carefully traced the letter "A" with my brush. "No dive… all he has to do is connect once and I'm down anyway."

As the fight grew nearer, I discovered I became less afraid. Nothing happened to cause this, except that I felt Farmer was vulnerable. When I pinned him against the wall during the Schmelling – Louis boxing match, his feet came off the floor for a split second, and he was powerless to do anything. I made my point. I also figured if he busted my nose, maybe the docs could set it right this time.

Four days before Labor Day weekend, just before supper, I got a note from Scruggs. The sergeant delayed the boxing match a week because of a meeting he had to attend.

"That gives you another week to practice," Frank said as he fixed his tie.

I crunched up the note and tossed it in a waste can. "I'd rather get it over with," I said.

A more important letter came after supper during mail call. Doris wrote Frank, that she and Betty planned to go to the Chippewa County Fair. They invited us to join them!

"Are you on the level?" I asked as I fixed my belt.

"Plumb level," Frank said.

"Geez, she likes me," I said, "she *really* likes me."

"She probably feels sorry for you…"

"Aw, get lost."

Maybe there's hope for Betty and me yet!

Saturday morning I woke up with a twinge of excitement. Even the overcast day could do nothing to spoil the fun in store for me at the fair. I breezed through morning clean-up and inspection and then relaxed after lunch out on the barracks steps. I was chiseling away at my box turtle when Bobby sat down beside me. He told me about a monarch butterfly that landed on his knee during a lunch break a few days earlier. He said the butterfly perched on his knee for a couple minutes, giving him a close-up look.

"Did you try to catch it?" I asked.

"Heck no, I might've hurt it."

I carefully scratched along the inside of the turtle shell and formed the outline of a leg.

"You should have seen it," Bobby said. "The edge of the wings looked like they were lined with fur and the silver markings were as pretty as a necklace." He talked about the insect like a guy would talk about a girl. I shook my head in wonder; Bobby was a one-of-a-kind.

After he left, I wondered why he looked at things so differently from the rest of us. I figured it had to do with being an orphan. *Why didn't I appreciate the little things in life?* All I ever cared about were my clothes and the way I looked. Bobby seemed sensitive to everything around him, whether it was another guy in camp or an insect in the woods. In a camp of hard-boiled men, he looked at everything through the eyes of a child.

I scratched away at my carving and smiled to myself. The thought came to me that Bobby was just like the butterfly he talked about. He went from being a sixteen-year rookie with nothing but the shirt on his back, to a confident eighteen-year-old with lots of friends, money in the bank and a new mom to boot. The kid had earned his wings, and when his enlistment ended in a couple months, he would be ready for the real world.

That night, Frank and I waited for the girls by the ticket booth at the fairgrounds. We wore overalls and t-shirts. Frank shared his Old Spice cologne with me. He said it made girls want to neck. Music blared from the calliope, and the smell of cotton candy filled the air.

"Hey, fellas," Doris called as she and Betty walked up in blue denim skirts. Betty looked adorable in a red western shirt, while Doris wore a leather vest and cowboy boots.

Betty put her hands on her hips and gave me the once over. "I forgot what you looked like with your clothes on." We laughed. "What's with you...people lose their suits all the time in the water," she said. I felt like a heel.

"He's just shy around girls," Frank said and pinched my cheek. I pushed him off.

"Next time, you'll know better," Betty said.

I grinned. "Yeah, next time I'll climb up on the raft naked."

The girls laughed. "You're silly," Betty said.

"Step right up and knock the pins down," a carnie yelled as we passed by his booth. "For one thin dime you can win this teddy bear for your sweetheart!"

"Save your money," Betty said. "There are better things to spend it on."

"Yes, mother," I teased.

Our first stop was a lumberjack show where two men put on a logrolling demonstration. We also watched sawing and axe-throwing demonstrations. After that, we took in a show of a husband-and-wife acrobat team, Nadia and Perez. They looked like they just stepped out of a Halloween party, dressed in skintight suits and hoods with little cat ears sticking out. They jumped through rings of fire and performed balancing acts.

"Jimmy Lynch and the Death Dodgers" were the best show of the night. Jimmy drove a car balanced on two wheels a couple hundred feet, and later jumped over six parked cars. Betty put her hands over her eyes in mock fright. "Can I look yet?"

"Better wait," I said. "They're trying to pry him out of the car." She gave me a sharp elbow.

Next, we headed to the pavilion where "Skip Dean and his Nebraska Sand Hill Billies" played square-dance tunes. All types of people filled the dance floor, from rough-looking backwoods characters to stylish couples from the city.

"Swing your partner round and round," the caller sang as I locked arms with Betty. She skipped around with a playful grin on her face. Her honey blonde hair bounced with each step and her cheeks turned a rosy pink from the heat of the room. I noticed how her nose wrinkled whenever she laughed, and she laughed often.

Frank and I bought the girls lemonade before we boarded the Ferris wheel. Soon we sat high atop the fair taking in the sights. With each turn of the Ferris wheel, I snuggled up closer to Betty.

"You smell nice," she said. "Old Spice...right?"

"Yeah, how'd you know?"

"My dad wears it."

Great, now she's going to think of her dad when she smells me!

I glanced down and saw Frank and Doris necking in the car below us. His hands were all over her! I looked timidly at Betty. She bit her lower lip as she straightened her glasses. Then she nervously ran her hands across her thighs to smooth out her skirt. *She's waiting for me to kiss her, but I've only seen her three times!* Feeling like a riverboat gambler, I leaned over and gave her a little peck on the cheek. She gave me a coy smile.

I licked my lips and turned to give her a real kiss. Just then, Frank yelled, "No smooching!"

I jerked and my teeth banged against her lips. "Ow..." she said and pulled back.

"Geez...I'm sorry," I said and rubbed my lip. "HEY, SHADDUP DOWN THERE!" I yelled at Frank.

"Do you guys *always yell* at each other?" she asked.

"I'm sorry...it's not very polite." I felt like a moron.

We sat in silence for the next minute. I glanced over, she gave me a sly smile. I grinned and leaned toward her. Our lips came together, tenderly this time, for a long, gentle kiss. A light breeze kicked up and blew her hair into my face. I brushed it back and gazed into her brown almond shaped eyes. I found it hard to look away.

Finally, I sat back and just held her hand. We waited as the Ferris wheel stopped occasionally while people unloaded. The setting sun cast a bright, golden haze over the fairgrounds. The colored lights from the amusement rides glimmered in the dusk, creating a marvelous sense of excitement for the night ahead. We sat in silence casting shy glances at each other. I was still in shock from kissing my first girl since the eighth grade.

We left the fair and rode the streetcar back into town. From there, Frank and I walked the girls to their homes to get them in by nine o'clock. When Betty and I got to her house, the street lamps were just turning on. The neighbor's kids were running around in their yard. Betty playfully climbed up on the swinging gate in front of her house. She began to swing back and forth, bringing her face within inches of mine before swinging away.

"I did this a lot as a little girl," she said.

"I bet you were a *very pretty* little girl," I said.

She frowned. "So, I'm not pretty anymore?"

"No, no...you're still pretty, but now you're a woman... well, at least a teenager."

She flashed me a sly smile. "Close your eyes and I'll give you a big surprise."

I closed my eyes and raised my lips. Just then, I heard the squeak of the gate and the sound of footsteps. I opened my eyes and saw her running up to her house. She bounded up the steps to the porch, and then turned to wave. "Good night, Nick!"

I waved back. *What a gal!* Frank and I met at a corner and headed back to the truck. We talked and joked about our big night out as we walked through the neighborhood. Then we began singing, *"Jimmy crack corn and I don't care, Jimmy crack corn and I don't care, Jimmy crack corn and I don't care...my master's gone away!"*

Dear Mom,

I'm writing this outside the barracks on a bench. Agnes our beagle lies at my feet with her belly full of supper. It's warm outside, but fall is in the air. A few yellow leaves are showing up on the trees.

I still work at the superintendent's house at the state park. I finished roughing out the mantle. Now Isaac has me putting up molding around the house. I like woodworking. Isaac thinks I could be a carpenter or wood-carver someday.

Hamtramck seems like a different world to me now. I don't think about it as much as I used to. Did you know that things aren't half as bad in the Soo as they are back home? Maybe things will get better for you, too.

The First Sergeant still watches me like a hawk. Next week I have a grudge match with that bully, Farmer. Maybe my boxing lessons will help me. Tell Gabe to take boxing lessons with Skip—he'll need them if he joins the CCC.

I sent letters to three sawmills in Duluth asking about Dad. I know it's a shot in the dark, but it's worth a try. Let me know right away if you hear anything from your letters.

Tomorrow is Labor Day so I'm going fishing with Arky and some other guys. Maybe I'll catch a big one. Hope you're doing fine.

Love,
Nick

I went up to the canteen to buy a stamp. Some fellas stood around the newspaper rack in the rec hall. I leaned over the table and read the headline. HITLER WARNED NOT TO START WAR.

"Hitler warned?" Turk said with a cue stick in his hand. "You can't *warn* a lunatic."

"If enough countries stand up to him, he might listen," José said.

"There's gonna be a war and we're gonna be in it." Elliot said, fretfully.

"Oh yeah?" Mario said and put down his *Life* magazine. "What makes *you* such an authority?"

"My mother." Elliot said. "She won't let me re-enlist because she's afraid they'll turn our camp into a boot camp."

"She's nuts..." Mario said.

"Your mom's off her rocker," another said.

"She *must* be daffy," someone quipped. "She had *you* as a baby." The guys laughed.

Elliot pouted. "My mother's never wrong."

"Give the kid a break," I said. "His mom's right, they could turn this place into an army camp overnight."

"Yeah, but we're a long way from war," Turk said.

Mario put his hand on Elliot's shoulder. "We'll write your mother a note and ask her to let you re-enlist."

"Yeah, someone has to serve us food or we'll go hungry," José joked. Even Elliot laughed at that one.

I headed back to the barracks and thought about the trouble in Europe. America was safe for now, but if war broke out, who knew what would happen? There was one bright spot. If there was a war and America got in it, I didn't have to worry about a job.

The next day was Labor Day so they gave us the whole day off. At least we thought so. After breakfast, the sergeant called a camp meeting and announced we had some business to take care of in the Soo. He wanted us to bust up a communist rally.

"The Young Communist League is behind it," he said in an ominous tone. "We don't know where they're from or what they're planning to do...but I'm counting on you to let them know they are not welcome in our community. I don't want anyone hurt...just rough 'em up a little."

Mr. Mulligan said to stick close to our buddies and warned us to get back on the trucks immediately after we broke up the rally. "I don't want any stragglers getting their mug shots in the newspaper...is that clear?" he asked.

"Yes, sir!" we shouted back.

I teamed up with Frank and we made our way to the truck. Some of the guys griped about the assignment as we climbed into the trucks.

"Fighting's only for defending yourself," Mario said, "I never started a fight in my life."

"Yeah," Ollie added. "What ever happened to free speech?"

"This ain't about free speech," Turk said. "It's shutting up people who wanna destroy our country." He threw a couple punches in the air.

"He's right," Arky said as he climbed into the truck. "Communists don't let people own guns—we can't let that happen here."

As we drove off, it felt like going off to battle. The only thing missing were army clothes and guns. We dressed in civilian clothes to blend in with the crowd. Most of us wore t-shirts and overalls. I stared out the back of the truck as we drove along the dirt road and thought about the communist friends my brother had. Most of them were decent guys—it turned my stomach thinking about what I had to do. I'd rather be fishing, not fighting.

The trucks split up when we entered the Soo and dropped us off at different points around the city. We paired up and entered the rally from different directions. A few hundred people congregated at Sherman Park, most of them sat on blankets or folding chairs. Frank and I worked our way into the crowd and ended up next to a group of union guys who worked at the local tannery. If those fellas wanted to fight, I was in trouble. I knew why the sergeant delayed my fight with Farmer. He wanted us to sacrifice our bodies at the rally.

A clean-cut man in his early twenties stood on stage and spoke into a microphone. He wore a white shirt and tie with sleeves rolled up. Speaking in short outbursts, he jabbed his fists into the air for effect. Four of his comrades sat in chairs behind him with arms folded and somber looks on their faces.

"The rich are getting richer while the poor are getting poorer," the speaker shouted. "We need to tax the rich and give the money to the poor!"

"Look at those college boys—the biggest wimps I ever saw," Frank muttered under his breath.

"Yeah, they probably go to University of Michigan," I said.

"Workers of the world must unite to fight the bankers of the world," the speaker railed. "No more exploitation of workers!" The audience politely clapped.

In the middle of his speech a CCC enrollee yelled, "If you don't like it here, why don't you move to Russia?" Then, he threw a rotten tomato, hitting the shoulder of the speaker. A few other boys took their cue and soon apples and tomatoes flew from all directions, pelting the speaker and his friends. They jumped off the stage as if it was a sinking ship.

When someone tried to stop a tomato thrower, two other CCC guys jumped on him immediately. Frank took off for the stage to find someone to get his hands on so I ran off after him. When I caught up, Frank held one of the communists in an arm lock. "Go back to school, college boy," he snarled. I never saw Frank so vicious.

"Sock him," Frank said.

The lanky college boy looked petrified. "Aw, he ain't worth messing with." I slapped his face a couple times. "Hit the road, jack," I said.

Frank gave him a shove and he stumbled to his knees. "Don't show your mug in this town again," he said.

The rally ended and people scurried away. "Let's get out of here," I said. We headed back to the truck.

"Why didn't you slug him?" Frank asked.

"I don't hit sitting ducks," I said.

"You could've taught him a lesson."

Out of the corner of my eye, I saw Betty walking with three other people. I broke into a big smile. "I'll be right back," I said and raced to see her.

"Get back here!" Frank yelled.

I caught up to Betty after she crossed the street. The man next to her held a handkerchief to his nose—it was red with blood. The moment I saw him I knew I was in trouble. Betty scowled at me. "You and your friends should stay in the woods where you belong," she snapped.

I stepped back. "Geez...I'm sorry," I said. "We had our orders..."

"Orders?" she said, with rage in her eyes. "Look what your friends did to my brother—you're just a bunch of hoodlums."

It was useless to argue so I turned and ran back to Frank. I was crestfallen.

"What's the matter with you?" Frank asked.

"I'll tell you later," I said.

Back on the truck, I sat with my face in my hands. Frank tried to cheer me up, but I was heartbroken. I lacked the guts to stand up for the right, and I paid a price. It was a quiet ride back to camp. Many of us regretted coming. I shook my head in disbelief. *Why did I bother to come!*

Back in the barracks, I lay on my cot and wrote a letter to Betty. I tore it up five times before I came up with something short and simple.

Dear Betty,

I'm very sorry for the way things turned out at the rally. You were right. It should never have happened and it made our camp look bad. I hope your brother heals up soon.

There's nothing I can do to change the past, but

I learned a good lesson—not to do things you don't believe in. I hope you accept my apology and we can stay friends.

Yours truly,
Nick

I folded the letter and put it in an envelope. It was a good thing there wasn't a cliff nearby, because I would have jumped off it. If there ever was a jinxed romance, I was in one.

There was a nip in the air the next day when Mr. Wells led a group of us through a cedar swamp after supper. I hoped the hike with my arts and crafts class cheered me up. Mr. Wells explained that deer came together in the swamp during the winter and pointed out the plant damage from overgrazing.

On the walk back to camp, we asked all sorts of questions. There was no such thing as a short answer with Mr. Wells. Sometimes he gave ten minutes of background information before he answered a question, but nobody ever complained.

Arky asked him how Cherokee men chose their wives. Mr. Wells first spoke about the problem of tribal inbreeding, which caused babies to be born with physical problems. He said it threatened the future of the tribes.

"Indian chiefs from different tribes held secret meetings where they agreed to share each other's women. They kept it secret from their own people because some of the tribes quarreled with each other. The chiefs came up with plans to steal women from one another and do it in a way that no one suspected it was deliberate, *and* in a way no one got hurt."

We trudged through a dense swamp and made our way up a gentle hill into a pine growth. "When my grandmother was a young woman, she and six other women were taken blueberry picking by an elder woman who was in on the scheme. An elder man from another tribe led a dozen young men to the very same patch. When the men saw the single young women, they kidnapped them and carried them back to their village over their shoulders, kicking and screaming."

"Did your grandma put up a fight?" I asked.

"Are you kidding?" Mr. Wells said with an ironic smile. "She bit and scratched her future husband so bad he was covered with blood by the time he returned to his tribe."

"What happened when they got back?" Mario asked.

"His mother ignored him and comforted the young woman he kidnapped."

"That's not fair," Elliot said. "You're granddad was the one who was scratched up."

Mr. Wells crossed his hands over his chest. "My grandfather's mother wanted to bond with the young woman. Remember, they kidnapped her from her own family so she had *no friends*. By fussing over her, my great-grandmother made her future daughter-in-law feel loved." I smiled. What a story!

"Did they ever let the kidnapped women go back and visit their families?" Elliot asked.

"Yes, but only after they were married and settled into their new life." It took Mr. Wells half an hour to answer the question and we loved every minute of it. Mr. Wells didn't just talk about history—he lived it. He wore it like the vest on his back. Our class returned from the woods with several branches of cherry wood to make our bows. The hike got my mind off Betty for a little while and made me feel better.

When I returned from work duty a few days later, I found a note from Scruggs on my cot. The sergeant cancelled Saturday's grudge match with Farmer again. Mr. Mulligan planned to be out of town so he delayed the fight another week.

"What's going on?" I said to Frank. "This is the *second time*."

"Don't complain," Frank said and pulled off his t-shirt. "What would you rather do...go fishing or get your face punched in?"

I was tempted to ask Scruggs to hold the match, just to get it over. I sat on the edge of my cot and yanked off my overalls. The sergeant was a cagey fella, he probably had something up his sleeve. "Okay, we'll go fishing," I said.

"Good," Frank said. "You can get the worms." Frank always looked out for himself.

The next day as Frank and I checked out fishing poles from the equipment room, Arky came in with his buck knife hanging from his belt. "I've been lookin' all over for ya," he said. "You wanna go on meat patrol?"

I grimaced. "Oh geez...not again."

"Pays fifty cents," he said.

I dreaded seeing more blood and guts. "What's it this time?"

"A wild pig, I'll do all the work."

"Is this another bloody mess like those sheep?"

"Heck no, this is *one* pig, not *twelve* sheep."

I turned to Frank who was busy tying a hook on his line. "What do you think?"

Frank nodded. "Have him drop you off at my bike on the way home so you can pick up some worms in town. We'll fish after supper."

"All right," I said to Arky.

If meat patrol bought some favor with the mess sergeant, it was worth it. We met up with Elliot behind the mess hall and loaded the pickup with knives, pots of water, rags, and buckets. The boy who shot the pig climbed in the front seat with Arky to give us directions. I sat with Elliot in back on the truck bed. We turned off the camp road into the woods and Arky drove carefully, winding around trees and stumps. Branches scratched against the truck as we passed through dense thickets.

"So...have you've been teased much lately?" I asked.

Elliot lazily munched a peanut butter sandwich. "Not since I started going to the Gould's," he said.

"Oh, yeah?"

He smirked. "I met a nice girl there."

"What about Gertrude back home?"

He shot me a naughty smile. "She'll never know."

"You rascal."

We drove down into a ravine and found the pig lying on its side on a layer of pine needles.

I looked out from the truck. "My God, it's as big as a Buick!"

Arky walked around the beast and gave it a kick with his boot. "That ain't no wild pig. That there's a farmer's hog."

The boy who shot it slapped his forehead and moaned. "I'm in trouble now."

Arky sharpened his buck knife on a stone while I collected dead branches for firewood. I built a fire and used rocks to set the water pot on. Arky went to work on the hog. He sliced into the jugular vein to drain the blood. Then he cut around the base of the head through the throat and twisted the head off like the lid off a jar. I felt green about the gills as I watched him make a long deep incision from the crotch to the chin. The belly opened up letting the guts spill out. Arky dug into that pig like a kid who just cracked open a watermelon on a summer day.

I looked away as much as possible. With the water boiling, Elliot and I carefully poured it over some rags we had spread over on the hide. Arky guided us every step. After the rags soaked for a few minutes, we removed them. Using dull knives, we scraped away the fur—it smelled worse than rotten eggs.

Arky saved the intestines for sausage and fat for lard. His pails filled quickly. "When my pa rendered a hog...the only thing left was the oink," Arky joked while he scraped the inside of the carcass. He sliced off the ears and threw them into the pail. "We can smoke those and give 'em to Agnes, she'll love 'em."

When Arky finished gutting the pig, we tied it by its legs to a pole and carried it to the truck. On the drive back to camp, Arky dropped me off near Frank's motorbike. I pulled it out from under the lean-to and gave it a kick-start. Ten minutes later, I rode into the little village of Raco to get some worms. I found out the town got its name from Richard Anderson & Company, the original settlers.

There was a risk of being seen driving on the road, but Frank said camp officers looked the other way if they saw an enrollee driving a car or bike. I pulled up to Olav's General Store. Olav was a tall, blonde Swede with a cheerful smile. "Vat can I do for you?" he asked with a thick accent.

"Worms, please," I said.

"Comin' right up." He ambled over to the wooden icebox and took out a coffee can full of worms. He counted out a dozen and wrapped them in an old newspaper with some soil. They cost a penny a piece. I put a dime's worth of gas in Frank's motorcycle and headed back to camp.

While driving down a dusty road, a hawk flew over my head. I looked up, and at that moment, I ran over a sharp stone. POP! The tire blew! I brought the bike under control and pulled off to the side of the road. The tire had little tread—it was ready to go. I pushed the bike along the dirt road hoping someone might give me a lift.

About ten minutes later, I heard the sound of a vehicle. I turned to see a forest green truck slowing down beside me. It was a CCC truck. I groaned when I recognized Thacker at the wheel.

"Flat tire, eh? Too bad," he said with his elbow hanging out the window. He stuck his thumb out. "Throw it in the back and jump on in."

I studied his face—he showed no emotion. "No thanks," I said. "I'd just as soon walk."

He frowned and spit tobacco juice. "Whatever suits ya." He shifted the truck into gear and rumbled off. I noticed big wood barrels in the back of his truck, he probably just returned from Newberry on his corned beef run. An hour later, I arrived back at camp and found a note on my cot. Thacker squealed on me! The note said to report to the sergeant on Monday.

"That stool pigeon," I said and crunched up the note. "I knew he'd report me."

"Don't blame him...I should've replaced that tire a long time ago." Frank said.

I handed him the package of worms. "Take 'em," I said. "I don't wanna go."

"You sure?" Frank asked. I nodded.

"Okay," he said and headed out with his fishing pole. "Keep your chin up, kid."

I lay down on my cot and stewed. I felt lousy about Betty and now I was in trouble with the sergeant. He would confine me to camp again, so there was no way to see Betty and make up. *I'm sick of all the rules in this damn camp!*

That evening after supper, I went to the rec hall to see the Saturday night movie. Two big fans whirled away in the back of the room, spreading the smell of freshly made popcorn. About fifty boys sat waiting for the cartoons to begin. I saw an empty seat next to Turk and sat next to him.

"Why aren't you in town?" I asked.

He smiled and stuck out his bag of popcorn. "I'm broke, what do you think?" Turk not only spent his money loosely, he was an easy touch for anyone who wanted to borrow some.

When the lights went down, the projector lit up. They played a couple *Betty Boop* cartoons followed by a *Little Rascals* short. Turk almost fell off his chair in hysterics. Watching him laugh made *me* laugh.

The feature film was *Bad Man of Brimstone* and starred one of my favorite actors, Wallace Beery. Beery played "Trigger Bill," an outlaw with a soft spot for a young man that rode into town. Trigger discovered that the young man was his long-lost son and began doing kind acts for him behind his back. At the end of the movie, the sheriff arrested Beery for killing another man. As the sheriff walked him by a church in handcuffs, the outlaw saw his son's wedding and asked the sheriff if he could stop for a minute to watch it. When Trigger Bill peered through the church window and saw his son at the altar with his new bride, he started to cry. I felt tears well up in my own eyes and pulled out a handkerchief.

"Hey, are you all right?" Turk whispered.

"Yeah, it's nothing," I sniffled.

When the movie finished I went back to the barracks and lay on my cot. Curfew was an hour away, but the lights dimmed for the boys who wanted to go to bed early. As I gazed up at the ceiling, I wondered what made me cry at the movie. I never cried at movies. The thought came to me that Trigger Bill might have reminded me of my dad. Perhaps Dad wanted to contact our family, but something prevented him from doing it.

My imagination went wild. What if my dad watched Gabe and me from a distance, like Trigger Bill watched his son. Maybe he even sneaked into our neighborhood and watched us walking to school or spied on us at night. I shivered just thinking about it.

Why did I have to be so harsh in judging my father? It must be hard to be a dad when everything went wrong in your life. Why could I not forgive him as my mother did? I rolled over on my side and thought about the last weeks Dad lived at home. I remembered how despondent he was over the baby's death and how he fell apart. I could see his face like it was yesterday, the unkempt hair, the worry lines on his forehead and his permanent frown.

It dawned on me that I was angry with Dad because I was angry with myself. I was irate at being poor, tired of being in trouble, and bitter that I was born at the wrong time. I needed someone to blame for my troubles, so I picked Dad. My dad did nothing *against* me—he wanted the best for me. In fact, the last thing he did before he walked out the door was give me one of his most prized possessions, his baseball glove. Tears filled my eyes again. How could I be so blind? A huge wave of remorse crashed over me. I felt pathetic, like a little beetle that needed to be stomped.

I fluffed my pillow and turned away from the light. In the movie, Trigger's son never knew the identity of his father, so he couldn't show his appreciation. But, I *knew* the identity of my dad so I *could* show my gratitude for all he did for me. I needed to stop being angry with him and stop condemning him for what he did. As I rolled over on my side, a big chip slid off my shoulders. After seven years of anger and bitterness, it was time to make things right. The next thing I needed to get rid of was the guilt I felt for judging him all those years.

Monday morning after breakfast, I reported to the sergeant's office to discuss the motorbike issue. I waited outside his door on the steps while he finished a meeting with an educational advisor. I overheard her talk about her students through the screen door.

"When I speak to your boys, they lay down their pencils and listen," she said. "They show such respect. And when I turn my back to write on the blackboard, I hear the scratching sounds of their pencils as they take notes."

I heard the squeak of the sergeant's chair. "That's very kind of you to say that," he said. "I'll be sure to pass your comments on to the captain."

"You've got some fine young men here. You can be *very* proud of them."

"Thank you, ma'am."

I heard footsteps and then the screen door opened. A thin, gray-haired woman holding a little dachshund in her arms appeared in the doorway. I took my hat off and nodded. She gave me a loving smile and stepped sprightly down the steps.

I knocked and went inside. "Reporting as ordered, sir."

"Nick, what's going on...why did Thacker report you?"

"Ever since day one, I've been on his bad side, sir."

Mr. Mulligan rubbed his forehead deep in thought. "I don't like grudges between officers and enrollees," he said. Then he told me what kind of person Thacker was. Orphaned at twelve, his older brothers kicked him out of the house. "He may be a little rough around the edges, but he's a good man and gets along well with the enrollees." The sergeant asked me to try to patch things up.

"I'll do my best, sir," I said.

The sergeant looked down at the report on his desk. "Now about that motorbike...replace *both tires* before someone kills himself."

"Yes, sir."

"And, you're confined to camp for two weeks."

"Yes, sir."

"And I want you to roll the tennis courts tomorrow after supper... and don't forget to bury the hatchet with Thacker."

"Yes, sir."

"Dismissed."

I walked out and headed for the work truck. Why should I patch things up with Thacker? The burden should not be on *me,* but the old goat himself! He started it all by giving me a small shirt. What am I supposed to do, bring him a bouquet of flowers every day? I knew the sergeant would side with his buddy. I picked up a rock and flung it into the woods. *I'm stuck in this joint for two more weeks!*

While we waited for the work trucks to come in, a farmer drove into camp in a rusty pickup. He stuck his ruddy face out the window. "I lost one of my hogs," he said. "Any of you fellas heard or seen anything?" We directed him to the mess sergeant. Ten minutes later, the farmer walked out with five dollars in his pocket and a blueberry pie in his hand. He gave us a friendly wave good-bye and drove off.

For supper, Mr. Kiefer cooked up the farmer's hog Arky had rendered. The ham tasted delicious and was so tender I could cut it with a fork. The camp treated its neighbors fairly and was quick to pay the locals if they incurred any losses because of the actions of the enrollees. I just wished the camp would treat its own enrollees as fair.

The superintendent's house we constructed at the state park looked more like a home every day. The two-story log building included stone masonry, walnut banisters, and the beautiful carved mantle I worked on. I also helped Isaac build cabinets for the kitchen. One day while we worked, I told him about a letter I received from a sawmill in Duluth.

"No, kiddin'," he said as he took a nail from his pouch. "What dey say?"

"They put the word out for a few weeks, but no one got back."

"Well, dey tried...eh?"

"Yeah...I'm still waiting to hear from two more mills."

He hammered. "If he's up dere, dose boys will find 'im."

The camp planned a grand opening for the park the second week in October. Isaac suggested that I be a host in the super's house. "You know der house better den any of da boys," he said.

"*You're the one* who should be the host," I said.

He flashed a toothless smile. "Me? Oh, no...I don't talk so good." He gently tapped a nail. "Dose high-class people, dey don't listen to ol' lumberjacks like me. You can do it."

It bothered me that a guy with Isaac's talents had so little confidence. People judged you on appearance, so I figured if he wore a new set of clothes and a pair of teeth, it might improve his chances of getting a job in the outside world.

After supper that night, some boys set up a gag behind the supply building called, "Kissing the Blarney Stone." A boy, who lay on his back with a towel folded over his eyes, played the shill. Another guy placed his knees on either side of the boy's head on top of the towel, pinning his head down.

When an unsuspecting rookie stopped to watch, the boy on top pulled off the towel and the fella on the ground attempted to sit up, but he couldn't budge. It was a set-up—he only *pretended* to be stuck in the prone position. He groaned as he tried to sit up.

When the unsuspecting rookie found out there was a can of money to win for the boy who could do a sit-up, he couldn't resist taking a shot at it. It cost a nickel to try to do the sit-up. I watched the shenanigans as Farmer strode up with his buddy, Inky.

"Hey, what's going on?" Farmer asked and watched a boy try to do a sit-up without success. "What's the matter with him?" It surprised me that he was in camp for so long and never caught on to the prank.

The boy who failed to do the sit-up got up dejected. "What a waste of money," he grumbled.

"What money?" Farmer asked.

"This money," a boy picked up the can and shook it. "It's all yours if you can do a sit-up, but you got to put in a nickel first."

"I want to try," Inky said and reached in his pocket.

Farmer shoved him away. "Me first, runt."

The rest of us held back our laughter as the two argued over who went first.

Farmer scowled. "Who can borrow me three cents?" No one offered him money, probably because he was afraid of what Farmer would do to him afterwards.

"I can help," I said and waved him over to the side. While I fumbled in my pockets I whispered, "If you know what's good for you, you'll let Inky go first."

Farmer scrunched up his nose, "Huh?" he said. He turned and looked at Inky who already lay down. "C'mon, hurry up, give me the money."

"Let him go first," I repeated. "You won't regret it."

He narrowed his eyes. "You better be on the level."

I held my finger to my lips and then pointed to Inky. He turned and watched with me.

"Ha, ha...I'm gonna win *all* the money," Inky said just before they put the towel over his face.

Mario put his knees over the towel and pinned Inky down tight. "On the count of three I'll let go of the towel," he said. "Good luck."

Turk came over, dropped his pants and squatted over Inky's face. Farmer's eyes almost popped out when he saw what he just missed.

Mario counted, "One...two...three!" He pulled the towel off

and Inky's head shot right into the crack of Turk's bare ass. He immediately pulled his head back, and fell back on the ground stunned. His body convulsed like a fish on land.

"Ohhhh, I'm dying..." he moaned, and covered his face with his hands. Turk pulled up his pants, as the boys burst into fits of laughter.

Even Farmer laughed over it. "I owe you one," he said. Then he scowled. "But...I'm *still* gonna murder you in the ring."

"I'm ready," I said and smiled. With our fight four days away, I wanted to get it over. It occurred to me that he hadn't called me Rat Eye for over a month. Maybe he was softening up.

Two days later the sergeant approached me out on the barracks steps as I hemmed some pants. "Didn't I tell you to roll the tennis courts?" he said angrily.

I set down the pants, "Yes, sir."

"Why didn't you do it?"

I stammered. "I...ah...didn't think you were serious."

"WHAT? I'm always serious when I give orders. Get your butt to the equipment room and get that roller."

I put away the clothes and took off. When he first asked me, I thought it was another wild goose chase! Who ever heard of a tennis court roller? When I saw the roller, I groaned. It was the size of an oil drum and filled with concrete! I struggled to pull it up the slope to the tennis court. Halfway there, I lost my footing and it slid sideways off the path. It finally came to a rest against a tree. I sat down on it, befuddled. All I could do was wait for someone to come along to help me. I watched a couple squirrels chase each other in a tree.

A couple minutes later, I heard a familiar voice. "What's the matter...too weak to move the roller?" I looked up and saw Farmer coming up the trail with a bat in his hand and Inky by his side. "I can use your head for batting practice." He swung the bat near my head.

I backed off. "Scram."

Then he swung the bat like a golf club and scuffed dirt on me. "Get up, futz. We gotta move this thing," he said. "C'mon...I don't have all day."

"You're full of hooey," I waved him off.

"I'm serious!" The three of us hauled the roller out of the brush and up the path. Inky, a pint-size guy with a bad complexion moaned the loudest and pulled the least.

"So how'd you end up in the CCC?" I asked as we hauled the roller slowly up the cinder trail.

He shot me a skeptical look. "My brothers and I ran our farm after my dad died...we figured out our profits and found out we each earned about a dime a day."

"Geez, that's nothin'," I said.

"Yeah, and I worked...sunrise to sundown," he said. "I was the grunt, *they* drove the tractors...I did the heavy lifting."

"So, did you ever sell the farm?"

He grimaced. "Yeah, they sold it behind my back for eight hundred bucks. I didn't see a lousy dollar. I'll beat the crap out of 'em if I ever see their faces again."

"How about your mom?"

"Mom?" he said with a puzzled look. "She died when I was four...I don't even remember her."

We finally got to the tennis court. "Thanks for your help fellas," I said.

Farmer pointed to the roller. "Someday, I'm gonna use that to turn you into a pancake." He let out a guttural laugh.

I smiled. "You're all talk."

Farmer punched his hand with his first. "Two days 'til you get a one-way ride to the hospital...I heard they already built you a coffin."

"I hope they made it extra large," I said.

"Why's that?"

"Because *you* might be the one using it."

"That's so funny, I forgot to laugh." He and Inky took off. I swept the courts with a long push broom and then I rolled it.

While I worked, I thought about what Farmer told me

about his life on the farm. My hunch was right—Farmer was not a bully like the ones I knew in Detroit. He was just a guy who got the short end of the stick in life and took it out on everyone. What impressed me was he never complained about it. Now, I knew why he never got any letters from home.

I finished up by sweeping the white lines with a regular size broom. I wondered what I would have been like if I lived the life Farmer did. I never put in a hard day of work in my life before I came into the CCC, no wonder his arms were so huge. They called our fight a grudge match, but *massacre* was more like it. Maybe, I was more afraid than I wanted to admit.

The next day I stopped by the Indian huts after supper to see Mr. Wells. The evening was warm and the dusty smell of fall filled the air. I noticed his vest and coat hanging on a fence post. I pointed to them. "Can I try those on?"

He looked up from a log he was sawing. "Go ahead."

The vest looked small on Mr. Wells, but on me, it hung well below my waist. The soft leather felt supple and I ran my hands over the beads sewn into the material. When I tried on his leather coat, the sleeves hung six inches longer then my arms. Finger length tassels hung from the bottom of the coat.

"What are the tassels for?" I asked.

"They help the rainwater run off, so it doesn't spoil the leather," he said.

Mr. Wells invited me to walk with him to Goose Lake to get some muck he used for fill. I took two steps for every one of his as I tried to keep up. We filled a few buckets and then went out on the camp dock to check his crayfish traps. They were empty, probably raided by locals looking for bait. We sat on the dock and dangled our bare feet in the warm water. He pulled out his tobacco pouch as I told him about my upcoming fight with Farmer.

"How do you feel about it?" he asked and rolled a smoke.

"I don't know. Sometimes I'm not afraid and other times I think he's going to murder me," I said.

Mr. Wells made a knowing smile as he rolled a smoke. He told me about a lake he visited as a boy that the Indians called *Smile of the Great Spirit.* "What do you *feel* when you look at this lake?" he asked.

I looked out at the calm water. Short gusts of wind created little ripples on the surface that glistened in the evening sun. "I feel peaceful," I said.

"The peace you feel, is the peace of your *own being.* It never was in the lake."

"How can that be...I'm here and the lake is over there?"

"Remember how I said the good in our life—is the *good* of the Great Spirit?"

"Yeah..."

"The Great Spirit is *universal* which comes from the Latin and means "turned into one." Since you *reflect* the universal nature of His being...you *include* all of His qualities as part of *your* own being."

"So...when I'm getting my brains bashed in by Farmer, I can still have the peace of the lake in my head?"

Mr. Wells smiled gently and nodded. "When you stand in the ring, you can feel the *peace* of the lake, the *bend* in the willow, and the *strength* of the wind. You don't have to try to be any of these things—they *already* are part of who you are."

"I'll remember that when he knocks me out..."

"You can go into the ring unafraid..."

"With *that* gorilla?"

Mr. Wells smiled gently. "You are never alone, but always one with the Great Spirit. Remember Jesus said, 'I and my Father are one.'"

"I thought that meant he was God."

Mr. Wells shook his head. "One in nature and that nature is Spirit."

"Am I a spirit?"

"You are not *a spirit,* you *are* spirit," he said.

"What's the difference?"

He gazed out over the lake. "It's the difference between

rays of light and pure light. Dust in the atmosphere causes rays, but in pure light, there are no rays." He turned to me. "You are light, Nick, not a ray."

He lost me. "Is the Great Spirit *in* me?"

Mr. Wells took a slow breath and turned his gaze upward. "The Great Spirit is not in us, just as an artist is not in his painting, but we include all that He is...as part of our own being."

I nodded and tried to make sense of his words. The setting sun illuminated the shoreline—making the early fall colors soft, yet vibrant. It was a scene worth painting. I wished Irving were still around, Mr. Wells lifted his feet out of the water. "Time to go?" I asked. He nodded.

As we walked back to camp, he talked about his grandfather's life and his experiences before he moved to a reservation. When we stopped near the barracks, Mr. Wells put his arm across my shoulders and squeezed my arm. "Good luck with your match against Clarence," he said quietly. "Try not to hurt him." Then he winked.

I grinned. "Okay...I'll try."

When we parted, I felt rejuvenated, even though much of what he said remained a mystery. I liked the part about the peace of the lake being inside me, I could use a lot of that peace, especially with the fight coming up.

The next day, mail call came after we returned from work duty. We were reading our letters outside the barracks on the long bench when Bobby suddenly jumped up from his seat. "Hey, fellas...my new mom invited me to live with her!" He grinned from ear to ear.

A boy looked up. "Forever?" he asked.

"Nah, just until I find a job or a place to move to," Bobby said.

The boys congratulated him. "She's going to make him a bowl of spaghetti so big—he'll need a shovel to eat it." Mario joked.

"You're going to find out what it's like to share a bathroom with a sister," another said.

Elliot sputtered. "Are you going to get your own bedroom?"

Bobby blinked, surprised at the question. "I dunno... who cares?"

"Yeah...he'll get his own room," Mario said. "We'll give him the attic." The boys laughed.

Turk busied himself rolling cigarettes. "How does it feel to have a real home to go to?" he asked.

Bobby ran his fingers through his blond locks. "I think it's about the best thing that ever happened to me."

I felt happy for Bobby—he not only found a mom, but a real family to go home to.

My mother wrote that they accepted Gabe into the CCC. They changed the rules so two boys from the same family could enroll. That meant my mother received another twenty-five dollars a month. She wrote that she would earn more than the fireman next door who received vouchers from the city instead of money. With Gabe accepted in the CCC, I could now go home at the end of my first term. Six months was enough. When I told Frank about it after supper, he thought I was nuts.

"Why would you do a stupid thing like that?" he asked and tossed me a baseball.

"I'm tired of the same routine...I want a change."

"Aw c'mon...there must be more than that."

"You want a reason? How's this, I'm in the sarge's office every darn week."

He threw me a fastball. "So you're gonna stiff your mom twenty-five bucks a month because you get latrine duty once in a while...gimme a break."

"She's getting dough from my brother...nothing changes."

"It's Betty, isn't it...you're all busted up over a skirt."

Frank got on my nerves. "That's a bunch of baloney, and you know it."

"Farmer's leaving so it must be Thacker...he's getting to you, right?"

I kept the ball and walked over to Frank. "I didn't decide this yesterday. I put in for a transfer two months ago."

He took the ball. "So what are you going to do back home...walk the streets?"

"I got a dad to find and it's worth a lot of money if I can do it." I explained how I planned to knock on doors and talk to people face-to-face.

Frank nodded. "Okay, but I still think you should stay another term."

"If I stay here and finish my term, that leaves me only two months to find him. That's not enough time."

Frank slapped his hand in his mitt and made a cynical smile. "I know what's bothering you...you don't want to work in the woods in the winter."

"That's it...I just hate the cold," I said in jest. We headed back to the barracks. He agreed to keep his mouth shut about my decision to leave camp early.

That night, sleep eluded me. My head told me it was time to go, but my heart wanted to stick it out. I didn't want to leave my friends, the good food, and the money, but I had a feeling in my gut it was time to move on.

With the superintendent's house finished in the state park, they sent me to work with the surveying team. Five of us drove out in a pickup to state land about ten minutes north of camp. We hiked through a logged-over hardwood forest, until we found the marker they had left the day before. It was a warm fall day with the trees vibrant in color. We left our coats in the truck and worked in our shirts. I was the tail end of the surveyor's chain. The guy ahead of me stuck a metal stake into the ground and my job was to follow him up, pull it out, and keep count.

Mr. Dalton headed up the surveying team; he worked as slow as cold molasses. There were times I waited fifteen minutes or more before they moved forward. I killed time by looking for Petoskey stones, the state stone with petrified fossils embedded in it.

In the afternoon, we worked near a stream. During one of my breaks, I decided to take off my shoes and dip my feet in the cool water. I rolled up my pants and waded in the knee-deep water. When I saw a turtle sunning itself on a log further up the stream, I decided to catch him. He saw me coming, slid into the water, and tried to hide under some fallen logs. "C'mon on out little buddy...I know you're down there," I said.

Suddenly, I heard Mr. Dalton's voice. "Radzinski, get over here!" The wiry technical officer stood on a small bluff with the three other boys in the surveying crew.

"Oh brother, I'm in for it now," I said to myself. I quickly slid my wet feet into my socks and laced up my boots. "I'll be right there!" I yelled.

When we returned to camp that afternoon, he sent me to the sergeant. Mr. Mulligan leaned back in his seat with his arms folded as I explained why I took a break. When I finished, he rubbed his chin, deep in thought. "What am I'm going to do with you?"

I said nothing.

"Meet me at the woodpile tomorrow after work duty."

"Yes, sir."

Temperatures dropped overnight, and by the following afternoon a chilly rain had begun falling. I headed out to the woodpile after work duty and saw Mr. Mulligan standing in his long raincoat and round rain hat. I shivered in the cold. "See that piece of wood over there?" he asked, and pointed to a spot about fifty feet away.

"Yes, sir," I said.

"Move this pile over there, one log at a time."

"Yes, sir." I groaned inside, the pile stood ten feet high and would take forever to move. I picked up the logs one by one and slogged across the muddy grounds while the sergeant stood with arms crossed watching me. *Why doesn't he go home?* The skies opened up and water dripped off the brim of my hat like rain off a roof. I watched the guys head up to the mess hall for their supper. Then, half an hour later, I watched them come out. The dusk turned to darkness, and still the sergeant stood like a statue, watching me in silence.

Just after eight o'clock, I dropped off the last log. It took me over three hours to move the logs and I was soaked to the bone. As I slogged up to the barracks, the sergeant called out, "Hey, let's get some chow." I turned and walked stoop shouldered to the mess hall. He caught up with me on the sidewalk.

"Why do you punish me?" he asked. "I should have been at home with my wife and kids, but instead I had to stand out in the rain watching *you*."

I said nothing.

"I could have asked someone else to take my place, but then I would have punished them. Understand?"

"Yes, sir," I mumbled.

"Every time you get in trouble you punish someone, do you know that?"

"Yes, sir."

"You're a thief...you steal other people's free time. It's all because of your screw-ups."

"Yes, sir."

The tone of his voice became more forceful. "Why do you do it? Why do you *punish me*?"

I hung my head in shame as we neared the mess hall. The sergeant persisted. "C'mon...tell me. Why do you *punish me*?"

I felt tears run down my cheek and I sniffled. He was right. I made his life miserable just as I did my Mom and Dad's, my schoolteachers, the beat cop, the judge and everyone else who tried to tell me what to do. I stammered, "I guess...it's because I only think of myself."

I felt his arm across my shoulders. "That might be part of it. You just got to buck up...be a man about these things."

"Yes, sir."

We trudged up the stairs to the officers' mess hall where the cooks had set aside two plates piled high with pot roast, boiled potatoes and carrots. As we dug into our food, he talked about his job as a guard at the Marquette State Prison. He told me stories about breakouts and the things the men smuggled into the prison. By the end of the meal, he had me laughing. The memory of moving the log pile vanished. Mr. Mulligan seemed less like a sergeant and more like a friend.

The day of my boxing match with Farmer finally arrived. During Saturday morning cleanup, I noticed how the fellas treated me differently. They seemed more cheerful and said kind words to me, as if they were never going to see me again. I felt fine, for a guy about to get his face pounded by the son of King Kong. The few boxing skills I picked up did little to bolster my confidence. I needed a miracle to survive. Maybe Arky would show up with a rifle and shoot Farmer in the back.

Farmer and I reported to the sergeant's office after lunch to discuss the fight. Mr. Mulligan asked us to sit down, which was unusual. He appeared in a jovial mood. They served a delicious meal of pork chops and hash browns for lunch, with blueberry pie for dessert. The sergeant poked at his teeth with a toothpick.

"Well, fellas, today is the day," he said. He burped noisily and covered his mouth. "Excuse me." Then he opened a folder and took out a few papers. "I have a little paperwork to fill out. What was that grudge match back in April fought over?"

"He took my pie," I said.

The sergeant nodded and began to write. "Okay, that's a start. What kind of pie?"

"I think it was apple," I said. Farmer and I looked at each other, puzzled.

"Yeah, it was apple," Farmer said.

He scribbled some more, then looked up. "Was there *ice cream* on the pie?"

Farmer shook his head. "No, I don't think so."

I shook my head.

He licked the tip of the pencil, "No ice cream...got it. Clarence took the apple pie...now what happened?"

"When he took a bite, I pushed it in his face," I said.

"Okay, apple pie in...the...face," the sergeant spoke as he wrote. Farmer shot me a curious look.

The sergeant looked up with raised eyebrows. "What next?"

"I took a swat at him," Farmer said.

The sergeant went back to writing. "Oh...an apple pie brawl, this is serious stuff. Okay, what happened next?"

I giggled. "The guys pulled us off of each other."

The sergeant frowned. "You think this is a joke? This is apple pie we're talking about and that's no joke."

Farmer tried to hold back his laughter, but his face turned red.

The sergeant slapped his pencil down and stared at us. "Do you guys *really* want to go into that boxing ring?"

Farmer and I glanced at each other. I shrugged and then Farmer shrugged.

"C'mon...I don't have all day," the sergeant said.

Farmer spoke first. "We don't need to fight."

"Yeah, we don't need to," I echoed.

"Good, because I want to go home and take my daughters fishing." He stood. "Get up and shake hands." We shook. "Now, get outta here and have some fun, it's Saturday."

The screen door slammed behind us as we stepped out. "You owe me one," Farmer said as we walked down the steps.

"What are you talking about?" I said. "I busted my ass at boxing practice getting ready for you."

"Oh, yeah?"

"Yeah..." Suddenly the screen door opened and the sergeant came down the steps. He brushed by us.

"Okay," I said. "I'll buy you a Coke, but I want the bottle when you're finished."

We walked off to the canteen. "Bottle?" Farmer asked. "What do you want the bottle for?"

"I wanna clunk you on the head with it."

"Funny...you belong in a circus."

"Oh, yeah? You belong in an insane asylum."

We continued our banter up to the rec hall. I pulled a couple bottles out of the red cooler by the canteen. Farmer reached into his pocket and pulled out a dime. "Here, let me buy one," he offered.

"Thanks, you can afford it," I said.

"How's that?" He asked.

"You made a dime a day on the farm...remember?"

He sneered. "How can I forget?" We went outside and sipped our drinks on the steps in the warm afternoon sun. I learned a lot from Farmer out on those steps. He told why John Deere tractors ran so well and why farmers rotated crops. I also found out that even a buffoon like Farmer had an interesting side to him. He collected arrowheads and old water faucets. And at sixteen, he won a corn-shucking contest in his county.

The sergeant always seemed to find a way to make things turn out the way he wanted them to. Some days, that meant he could be a real pain in the ass, but not that day. The fight that I dreaded so much fizzled out. I felt the peace of the Great Spirit when I hit the sack that night.

Chapter 7

Re-united

On Saturday afternoon, the Camp Mackinac baseball team visited our camp for the district league championship. Two mascots attended the game, a bear and our beagle. Agnes sat near first base while the black bear cub, attached to a leash, watched from third. Agnes spent most of her time on her back getting her belly rubbed by the boys.

It turned into a breezy day with leaves blowing across the field, reminding us that winter was around the corner. The game started slow, with no runs until the fourth inning. Ollie hit a two-run double, which gave us the lead in the sixth.

Rosie, the cobbler's daughter, watched from the stands. She wore a dark burgundy dress and a sun hat. She stood out like a rose in a potato patch. When Ollie connected with a hit or made a great play, the curvy brunette bounced up and down cheering her boyfriend on while the fellas in the stands ogled her with silly grins.

Camp Mackinac tied it up in the seventh, but Frank hit a double in the eighth with one on, and put us ahead for good. Camp Raco won the game 7-6. The real surprise came when Squirt relieved Mario as pitcher in the seventh. The half-pint kept the other team hitless with his dipping curve balls.

After the game, Agnes ran around the infield like a puppy in spring while the other team walked the bear around on his leash. Although the two mascots stayed apart, the teams came together at a picnic table for cookies and lemonade. I grabbed a couple of sugar cookies and found a bench to sit on. I watched the players laugh and joke around; everyone seemed content and happy. I wondered if I really wanted to go home. *Why can't life be more black and white when it comes to making decisions?*

I looked around at some of my friends. Frank ran a chin-up competition, while Ollie played his guitar along with a banjo and fiddle player. I headed back to the barracks feeling melancholy. Agnes ran after me. So many good things happened to me in camp that it tore me up inside thinking about leaving.

Out of the corner of my eye, I saw Thacker carrying a load of clothes to the supply building. I wondered why he was in camp on a Saturday afternoon, since most officers went home after lunch. *Does he have special duties that keep him in camp?*

We worked at full steam to get the state park ready for the October 16 grand opening. They named the park, "Lone Pine State Park," after our camp's nickname. On the big day, dark clouds blanketed the sky and a chilly wind blew, but by late morning the sun broke through and the wind quieted down. The leaves on the trees peaked in color with blazing reds, bright yellows, and brilliant oranges. The grounds looked immaculate with nicely edged walking paths, neatly trimmed bushes and newly planted grass.

"Ladies and gentleman...thank you for joining us today." The head of the Michigan Department of Conservation spoke from a small stage to a crowd of several hundred people. The tall, distinguished-looking man wore a long coat with hat and tie. "We owe this camp to the work and dedication of the men of Camp Raco. This includes the hardworking enrollees who provided the muscle, the talented Local Experienced Men, and the seasoned forestry officers." Everyone applauded respectfully.

The camp officers, politicians, conservation officers, and other V.I.P.s, sat up front. The public sat behind them, with the enrollees standing in the rear. Mothers with children gathered around picnic tables on either side of the audience. Most of the men were dressed in gray, while their wives wore earth-tone dress coats and stylish hats.

Half a dozen people made remarks, including a state senator and a congressman. Captain Bullock received the loudest round of applause. "I have great faith in the potential of our youth. This park is a testimony to what young people can do with proper guidance and supervision. The CCC slogan is *we can do it,* and by God...we did it!" A big cheer went up from the guys in back.

He continued. "This state park will bring joy and happiness to the people of Michigan for generations to come. I hope they remember that it was created with the sweat and toil of young men who asked for only one thing—an opportunity to work." Another loud round of applause went up in the rear. I felt proud as I listened to the speakers and wished my mother were there. Someday I wanted to bring her for a visit.

After the speeches, I hustled to the superintendent's house to greet visitors. I stoked up the fire, straightened cushions on the sofas, and then checked my hair in the mirror. Soon, people streamed in the door. They peppered me with questions, asking everything from the building process to the materials we used. They made many compliments about the deer head carving on the mantle.

At one o'clock, another boy relieved me so I could grab a bite to eat. I hurried over to the grill where the tantalizing smell of hamburgers filled the air. I waited in line for about ten minutes before I filled my plate with baked beans, potato salad and a couple of burgers. I wolfed down my food at a picnic table with some other enrollees and then went looking for Frank. I found him standing on some large boulders at the river's edge where he addressed a dozen people. He looked dapper in his uniform and played up to a couple of cute teenage girls in the group.

"These river banks were destroyed by the log rolls of the lumberjacks," he said. "When we began work...the bank was nothing but dirt with a few patches of grass. The stones we put here will prevent further soil erosion. The myrtle and grass we planted will help keep the soil from washing away."

Frank presented himself well and people listened carefully. If they only knew! He was an egomaniac, hell-bent on making big muscles. I glanced at my watch and saw it was time to return to the super's house. As I cut across the grounds, I saw children darting down hiking trails, couples resting on park benches, and mothers feeding babies—the park seemed to come alive with all the happy faces.

By late afternoon, the number of people visiting the super's house dwindled, so I relaxed on an easy chair by the fireplace. The warmth of the blaze caused me to doze off. Suddenly, I heard a familiar voice—I thought I was dreaming.

"Hey sleepyhead, I want you to meet my family." I turned around and blinked. It was Betty!

I gathered my wits and shook hands with her parents. Her father was tall and refined-looking in his long overcoat. He gave me a firm handshake and I noticed the smell of Old Spice. She also brought her younger sister and brother. Her little sister was the spitting image of Betty and playfully hid behind her mother's legs. "Have you seen much of the park?" I asked them.

"We were all over, it's wonderful," Betty said. She pointed to the mantle, "So that's what you've been up to."

"Isaac did most of the carving." I explained how I roughed it out. Betty looked all grown up in her brown tweed jacket and matching cap. Her summer tan had faded, but she still looked radiant with a healthy glow on her cheeks.

"Let's check out the upstairs," her dad said.

"I'll stay and talk to Nick." Betty said. I nervously picked up the poker and moved the logs in the fire. With her parents out of hearing range, she said, "I'm sorry for what I said at the rally...you were only doing your job."

I set the poker down and turned around. She looked rueful. "Come here," I said and held out my arms. With tentative steps, she came to me and I wrapped my arms around her. "You don't need to apologize. I would have said the same thing if it happened to me."

She pulled back misty-eyed. A smile slowly spread across her face. "You're not mad?"

"Oh, yes...mad at myself for doing something I shouldn't have done. But mad at you? Never."

A little tear rolled down her cheek. I pulled a handkerchief from my pocket and wiped it away. "I bet you could win a crying contest for being the prettiest crier." She fought back her tears.

We sat together on the hearth by the fire and chatted about how school was going for her. Soon we heard footsteps on the stairs. "Can I see you again?" I asked quickly.

She nodded. "Yes, I'd like that."

"Nice workmanship," her dad said from the stairs.

"Yeah, I like the bathroom," her sister chimed in.

Her father studied Betty's face carefully. "Everything okay, sweetheart?" he asked.

"I'm fine," Betty said as she adjusted her glasses. "I just got a little smoke in my eyes."

He gave her a knowing grin. Then he gripped my hand. "Keep up the good work, son."

"Thanks for coming out," I said and walked her family to the door. I felt on top of the world. *Maybe my love life isn't jinxed!*

A week after the state park grand opening, our camp put on a farewell party for departing enrollees. The event happened twice a year with locals from the surrounding area invited to bring their daughters along for an evening of fun, food, and dancing. The camp also sent a truck into the Soo to pick up teenage girls for the party. The visitors toured the grounds and buildings. The party drew a big crowd because of the lack of social life out in the sticks.

Just after six o'clock on a Saturday night, cars and trucks began rolling in the front gate. The camp soon took on a new look with teenage girls wearing their prettiest dresses. We cleared out the rec room to make space for a dance floor. Colored crepe paper hung from the walls and yellow light bulbs gave the room a warm, festive look. "A hearty welcome to all our friends and neighbors," Captain Bullock said into the microphone. He wore his brown uniform and knee-high boots.

"We are honored to be part of your community and proud to have you as our neighbors. Enjoy the punch and cookies...let the music begin." People applauded.

Mario took the mike. He looked sharp with his wavy hair neatly slicked back. Ollie played his guitar and another boy his accordion as Mario sang, *"Che bella cosa 'na jurnata 'e sole, 'N aria serena doppo 'na tempesta"* Starry-eyed thirteen and fourteen-year-old girls crowded up front and fawned over him. Then he picked up the tempo with a Bing Crosby tune. The dance floor quickly filled with enrollees snatching up any free girl they could find. Parents and officers joined the dancing.

After three songs, Mario turned the stage over to a five-piece band that played western-style songs using washboards, banjos, fiddle and guitar. Their foot-stomping music brought the backwoods people out on the floor, especially the old lumberjacks. Isaac flapped his arms around like a chicken when he danced. His partner, a rough-looking woman who walked like a man, bumped the others with her wild hip moves.

Mess orderlies brought out punch and cookies, while the Drum and Bugle Corps set up. The dance floor emptied while the band played a few marching tunes. The next act was a trio who sang *Sweet Adeline.* Then, a boy played the song, *Over the Waves,* with a mouth organ. When he finished, Mario returned to the stage and took the mike.

"May I have your attention, please," he said. "While the main entertainment sets up, I have some awards to give out. The neatest enrollee award goes to...Elliot!" The chunky orderly sauntered up and blushed when he took the ribbon.

"For the hardest worker, let's hear it for Squirt!" The half-pint made a salute as he took the ribbon. "Squirt was driving CATS when most of us were still on three-wheelers." Mario joked.

"The biggest Sheik award goes to the man with extra starch in his shirts and grease in his hair. Butch Harrigan—c'mon up!"

"Next is the Goldbricker award. This is a tie between Fred, Hap and Inky. They all deserve it because they're lazy bums!"

"Hold onto your cookies, the next award goes to the biggest chow hound in camp. This fella can be found wherever there is food. Turk...c'mon up!"

He strutted up and said, "I hope I get a big steak for this." The audience laughed.

Mario raised his hand for quiet. "For the best dancer award, there is only one 'Slip and Slide,' the Polish dancing machine!"

Frank tap-danced up to the front and leaned over the mike, "I owe it all to my mother."

Mario pointed to the band. "Give me a drum roll please... the most popular enrollee award goes to...are you ready?"

"Yes," the crowd yelled back.

"Will the one and only Sweet Bobby come on up." The fair-skinned orphan turned red-faced as he worked his way through the crowd. The hall echoed with applause as he accepted his ribbon.

Mario then introduced the band. "Join me in welcoming... Corky Corrigan and his Tune Twisters!" The band struck up an Artie Shaw tune and the floor quickly filled with dancers. I glanced at my watch and saw it was time for my shift for parking lot duty. I grabbed my coat and hat before heading out the door into the night. A nippy breeze blew and I fixed my scarf. Outside, a dozen boys with Coleman lamps directed traffic in the parking lot and guided visitors along the sidewalk.

I took a spot in the parking lot and pointed the way for a few latecomers. Things quieted down so I sat on one of the loading platforms with my legs over the side. The wind whistled through the trees. I shivered—a touch of sadness enveloped me.

In four days, about thirty boys planned to go home, including Ollie, Mario and Bobby. My turn would come in a few weeks after I received word that Gabe had settled into his new camp. I dreaded saying good-bye to all my friends. My lamp shone a dim light on the parking lot and I watched the wind scatter leaves into the darkness. A haunting feeling came over me. *My friends are like those leaves, I'll never see them again!*

A melody came to my head and my feet bobbed to the beat of the music. I wished Betty had come, but it was too far for her to drive at night. Ever since she visited me at the state park, I felt like a new man. I was tempted to stay in camp just so I could keep seeing her. As much as I liked Betty, I knew that we could never be serious. She planned to attend college in a year and I was a high school drop out. She was going places and I would just hold her back. The arrival of winter told me it was time to move on.

Four days later, a group of boys went home. The sky turned gray and a brisk wind blew, taking down the few leaves that remained on the trees. The officers gave most of us the day off, so we could say good-bye to our friends. I helped carry some of their lockers out to the loading platform. The departing boys hurried around camp to get everything in order before the trucks took them to the train station.

They filled out paperwork in the rec hall where an educational advisor handed out proficiency certificates. The company clerk gave certificates of commendation, while an orderly sold camp mementos such as pennants, belt buckles and coat patches. Discharge papers came in the mail after the boys got home. I ran into Bobby outside the rec hall and he showed me his certificate for machine operation.

"I bet that'll get you a job," I said.

"Hope so...I want to build car engines," he said.

"Maybe they can use you at the Dodge plant in Hamtramck." I scratched down my address. "Write me if you're in the neighborhood."

"I sure will," he said.

I gave him a pat on the back. "Good luck with Mario's family."

He smiled. "I can't wait to meet them."

I found Mario packing his gunnysack. "Hey, watch out for Bobby...he never lived in a big city," I said.

Mario looked up. "He'll do okay. He's loaded and when you got dough there's lots to do."

"You guys better write us," I said, "or we'll send the sarge to track you down."

"Hey Rat-Eye!" Farmer yelled from the loading dock. I walked over. The smart uniform he wore took away his country bumpkin look. "I wanted to flatten your nose before I left," he said, "but it looks so ugly, I figured I'd leave it the way it is."

"Thanks," I said. "I'm going to miss your mug."

"Really?" he said and smiled.

"Yeah...I'm glad we didn't have that grudge match."

"Why's that?"

"My dad told me never fight a guy uglier than myself, because he's got nothing to lose."

He punched my shoulder. "Ha, ha...very funny."

"I heard you got a job selling McCormicks," I teased.

"Wise guy," he said and threw his gunnysack over his shoulder. "Don't let me ever catch you eating apple pie."

We shook hands. "Stay out of trouble, you," I said. "Drop us a line sometime."

He nodded and walked off. "See ya around..."

I heard a guitar and followed the sound. On the steps of the mess hall, I saw Ollie. I sat down a couple steps below him. "So, what are you going to do?" I asked.

He played a Jimmy Rogers tune. "There's a guitar factory in Kalamazoo...maybe I can get work there making guitars."

"I got a brother who lives there." I said. "Next time I'm down there I'll stop by the factory and ask for you." He nodded. We chatted about some of his favorite pranks.

He reached into his breast pocket and pulled out a couple war medals. "Remember these?"

"How can I forget?" I said, and looked at them. "You should have gotten a ribbon for best jokester."

He took out a smoke and struck a match on the step. "You have to carry the ball after I leave..."

"Sure, Ollie...what's with Rosie?"

He shook his head and gave me a sad grin. "She's got her life...I got mine."

We walked back to the loading dock together. I said goodbye to half a dozen others before they stepped up on the loading platform. "They're getting out of Dodge at the right time," Frank said to me as he looked up at the threatening sky.

"You're right." I said and pulled my collar up. The guys bunched up around the back of the truck and stuck their faces out from the canvas top. "So long...see ya around... been good to know ya!" they shouted. The engines turned over and the trucks slowly drove off.

We stood and waved until the last truck went out of sight. One by one, we walked off in different directions, not a happy face among us. I wondered who felt worse, the boys who left or the ones who stayed behind. I needed to cheer up, so I went to the canteen for a candy bar. I picked up a Snickers bar and gave the orderly a nickel. As I tore off the wrapper, I said, "What are we supposed to do now that our buddies are gone?"

He gave me a funny look. "What we always do...we give the rookies hell and make them pay for taking the place of our friends." I smiled to myself and bit into the candy bar. *I'm not a rookie anymore, I'm a veteran.*

Chapter 8

Veteran

November 7, 1937

Dear Nick,

I just got a letter from Gabe, he arrived safely at Camp Newaygo, northwest of Grand Rapids. He has a good barracks leader and already made some friends. He loves the food and said that on his first night in camp, someone put Grape Nuts in his bed as a joke and it scratched him.

Now that Gabe is in camp, I can tell you about a trip I have been planning for a while. Next spring, I will go to Chicago to visit my mother and sister. I haven't seen them for ten years and they can really use some company. I'll spend a few weeks there and take them shopping and help them out.

I've saved over twelve dollars from the money you earned. Now that I'm getting money from both of you boys, I'll have enough to make the trip. It will be my first vacation since we moved to Detroit. You can't imagine how happy this makes me.

Things are picking up at the restaurant since the Dodge plant re-hired some workers. My tips have improved by fifty cents a day in the last couple months.

You make me very proud, son. I wish I could give you a big hug for all the good work you've been doing. I was so happy to hear that things went well at the park opening. I look forward to hearing more good news from you.

Love,
Mother

I grabbed my coat off the hook. "Hey, where are *you* going? What happened to our game?" Frank asked, looking up from the checkerboard.

"I need some air," I said and headed for the door. My plan to return home early just went up in flames—stuck for another six months!

Snow flurries swirled around me, as I made long strides around the quad. Winter arrived like a beast and I had to make the best of it. My plan to knock on doors to find Dad would have to wait. Everything changed because of the letter.

I thought of the stories Mom told us about her mother and growing up in Kwiechen, a small village in Poland. Each year at Christmas, she made our family eat out of a common soup pot called a tureen, just as she did as a little girl. She placed the bowl of cabbage stew in the middle of our kitchen table and everyone reached over with a spoon to eat from it. We did it so we knew how she ate as a child. They couldn't afford tableware.

Her father drove a horse-and-carriage taxi for a living. When the royalty in his village went on hunting trips, they brought back game the peasants cleaned. Her dad managed to get his hands on some of the leftover scraps and brought them home to my grandmother, who made meat pies out of it. They called it humble pie.

The letter I received from my mother was like a big piece of humble pie. I pushed my wishes aside, so she could take her dream trip. She and Dad never took a trip that I ever knew about. It was only from the movies that I knew that people took vacations. No one in my neighborhood ever went anywhere.

The sergeant and Thacker owned me for another six months, but I would survive. Any inconvenience I bore was nothing compared to the joy the trip would bring Mom. When I returned from the walk, I quietly told Frank of my plans to stay. "You're what?" he said.

I held a finger to my lips. "You heard me," I said and hung up my coat.

He grinned broadly. "That's great," he said and set up the checkerboard again.

"Don't tell anyone I was going to leave..."

"My lips are sealed," he said. I stretched out on the cot and laid the checkers on the board. Six more months as a veteran. Life could be worse. I figured there was a reason for everything.

That weekend, the new recruits rolled into camp. Some of them were tough-talking city kids with attitudes, while others looked like they just walked off the farm, raised on milk and honey. A couple days after they arrived, Frank was clipping my hair in an empty classroom, when a pimply faced rookie stuck his head in the door. "Either of you guys know where I can find a tree squeak?" he asked.

Frank shook his head. "Sorry, why don't you check the garage," he said with a straight face.

"Thanks a lot," the boy said. He left and we chuckled. I felt a little sorry for the kid, but everybody went through it. Another rookie came by looking for a left-handed monkey wrench.

I smiled. Six months earlier, I scurried around camp looking for a skyhook. Now, I was the one giving it out. It felt better being the windshield than the bug squashed on it. The last six months were not easy and there were times I wanted to throw in the towel, but I stuck it out. *Maybe it isn't such a bad idea that I'm staying around this place.*

That night just before supper, the sergeant came into our barracks. "If you haven't noticed, most of the leaves are down," he said. "If you need to move anything out there in the woods, now's the time to do it." He left as abruptly as he came.

"What was *that* all about?" I asked Frank.

He looked up from fixing his tie. "Aw, he's just giving the guys notice to move their motorcycles and cars deeper in the woods."

"Huh?"

"So they won't be seen, numbskull."

I buttoned my shirt. "Why does he warn us?"

Frank shrugged. "I guess he doesn't want us to get caught." I straightened up my tie and went out the door to supper. There was a good side to the sergeant and I hoped I saw more of it now that I was a veteran.

The bow and arrow I began making back in May was finished. Every part we made from scratch, from the cherry wood used for the bow, red tail hawk feathers on the arrow, to the sharpened ham bone for the arrow tip. Mr. Wells even made strings from the rawhide of a ground hog. We decorated the bows with little feathers that hung from the bottom of the bow. We hand-sewed leather arrow quivers.

During class, a couple dozen of us stood around a table and admired each other's work. "Why did we have to spend so much time making them?" A boy asked.

Mr. Wells flexed a bow into a large C-shape. "I wanted you to learn patience," he said. "We could have made them in half the time, but there were other lessons for you to learn."

Then he surprised us by asking that we donate our bows

to Camp Marquette, a CCC camp for Indians. He explained that they needed new items to sell in their gift shop. "The money they earn will be given to the men when they leave camp."

Every face showed disappointment, not a smile in the room. It was the nicest thing I ever made in my life. Why would I want to give it away? In spite of our feelings, we laid our bows and arrows on the back table as we filed out the door. "I don't really want to do this," I said to Mr. Wells as I set it down. "Are you sure it's good enough to sell in a store?"

He nodded. "Yes, it is. Trust me when I say the lessons you learned are more valuable than the bow and arrow."

I nodded, grim-faced.

He placed a hand on my shoulder and squeezed. "Thank you, Nick. I knew you'd understand."

I walked out of the classroom feeling as if I left a part of me behind. I went straight to Isaac to borrow some carving tools. There was still work to do on the turtle and I needed to do something to take my mind off the bow and arrow.

The following week we found out that a group of hunters was lost in the woods not far from camp. The sheriff called and said some men did not return as planned. The sergeant pulled us off tree-planting work and organized us into search parties.

We loaded up on trucks after breakfast and drove to an area about ten miles south of camp. We formed a long line with each of us about a hundred feet apart. Then, we fanned out through the woods in search of the lost men. Flurries started falling and I adjusted the new scarf I had just bought. A fella in my barracks cut a blanket into narrow strips, and sold the pieces for a nickel each.

I hiked through thickets and pushed through the brush with a staff made out of a dead branch. The sergeant told us to hit the ground if we heard gunfire since it was hunting season. The leaders carried whistles to communicate with us. I figured the lost men built a fire and stayed up all night. I remembered how I got lost in the woods with Arky and Elliot when I first came to camp. The sergeant blew his top, and now I understood why. The search disrupted our work in camp—we could have been planting trees.

Just before noon, I heard the distant sound of a whistle followed by another. Cheers went up from the boys. I turned and saw Turk cutting across the woods toward me.

"I bet some kids are happy we found their dads," I said. "Your dad ever take you hunting?"

"Nah, we went on hikes...long hikes," he said.

I used the staff to push back some branches. "Hey, I haven't heard any good stories lately about you blowing your top...what gives?" Turk destroyed things when he lost his temper.

"I got over it," he said coolly.

"What?" I asked. "What happened?"

"I couldn't sleep when I came to camp...it made me ornery."

"So?"

"So...I got over it. Now I sleep like a rock."

"You mean like a log?"

"You know what I mean...hey, why does Thacker have it in for you?"

We spotted cars through the trees. "Why do you ask?"

"I heard him say he wished you shipped out last week with the others."

I jabbed at a rotten stump with my staff. "That old goat can go to hell."

Turk shot me a sideways glance. "That old goat can make your life hell if you don't watch it."

"Why do you think he hangs around camp on Saturdays?"

Turk looked puzzled. "Beats me...never thought about it."

"The officers with homes go home...but he stays."

Turk shook his head. "Who knows?"

We climbed up from the ditch to the road. The hunters

huddled around a blazing fire with cups of coffee in their hands. Brown wool blankets covered their shoulders and their wives hovered around them. They laughed and carried on as if it was a big party. I wondered if they realized they made our camp lose a day of planting trees. *I sound like the sergeant!*

The camp put on the Ritz for Thanksgiving. We invited people from the community for the dinner and a tour of the camp. They served us on linen-covered tables and each place setting had its own engraved menu. They served turkey with sage dressing as the main dish along with several side dishes, including sliced cucumbers, celery, fresh cranberry sauce, oyster soup, mashed potatoes, buttered peas and hot bread. For dessert, we could choose among plum pudding, pumpkin pie, and ice cream.

After the meal, many of us wandered over to the rec hall and listened to the Lions and Bears football game on the radio. Frank gave me a hard time because the Bears were winning. A bunch of us went outside to the quad for a game of touch football during halftime. It was just above freezing with light flurries in the air. Frank held his palm up and used his finger to trace a passing pattern. "Ten steps, then button hook to the left, on five."

I squatted over the ball, as Frank called out the signal. "Mash potatoes, rutabaga, three, two...five!" he yelled. I hiked the ball and took off. I made a left on cue and circled around. I held my hands out for the ball, but Arky jumped in from the sidelines and snatched it right in front of me. "Hey!" I yelled.

He lobbed the ball back to me. "Sorry...couldn't help it," he said. "Ya wanna go on meat patrol with us?"

"Gimme me a break...it's Thanksgiving," I said.

"It pays fifty cents and you earn some brownie points with you know who..."

I tossed the ball back to the others and stepped off the field to think about it. A mess orderly job sounded good with winter setting in. I could use the money, too. "Okay, let's get it over with," I mumbled.

Ten minutes later, we barreled down the road in a pick-up with me driving and Elliot wedged between us. I almost drove off the road when they told me what we were getting. "A dead cow? You got to be kidding."

"It's a piece a cake," Arky said.

"If I barf, I'm never doing this again," I said. "That was a good turkey dinner."

"Ah...you won't loose it," Arky said.

"The cook said we can have first dibs on the cuts," Elliot said. "I'm getting the tenderloin."

I shook my head. "I don't eat road kill."

"Some of the best food I ever hung a lip over was road kill," Arky said.

"Yeah...I believe it," I muttered.

Twenty minutes later, we found the cow on the road just beyond a farmhouse. A farmer called and said a truck hit it the night before. We chased away a few crows and unloaded a couple wood crates. I expected the cow to be in one piece, but it looked like it swallowed a stick of dynamite. Pieces were scattered everywhere.

"It must'a been one big truck," Arky said.

I felt a bit nauseous at first, but I got over it. My tolerance for blood and guts improved since I first came to camp. Elliot and I shoveled up the smaller chunks into a crate while Arky slipped on an apron. He sharpened his buck knife and began cleaning off the meat. Later, I watched as he took a saw from the truck that was almost as big as he was.

"You really like doing that, don't you?" I asked him.

He looked up with a grin while he lined up the saw on the cow's hip bone. "I'm feeling finer'n frog hair and twice as fluffy," he said.

I turned away just before I heard the grinding sound of the saw cutting through bone. My stomach felt queasy and I hurried away.

When Elliot and I finished collecting the smaller chunks of meat, he asked, “Where’s the head? It’s got to be somewhere.”

I looked around. “I dunno.”

When Arky finished, we filled up the second crate and loaded it into the truck. We walked down to a stream along the road to wash up. Climbing back up the slope, Elliot pointed. “Hey, there it is!” Sure enough, the head of the cow had rolled down the slope into a ditch.

“Way to go, Elliot,” I said.

The captain had made a special request for the cow brains. Before we put the head into the crate, I popped an eyeball out of the skull with a spoon and wrapped it in wet paper. “What’s that for?” Elliot asked.

I grinned. “Oh, it’s a little promise I made to Ollie.”

He looked puzzled.

Back at camp, the cooks waited eagerly for the meat and quickly dumped it into a sink to wash it. With Mr. Kiefer away with his family, the assistant cooks decided earlier to make a stew out of it that night for the late meal. They told Elliot, Arky and me to keep our mouths shut about where the meat came from. “What’s wrong with telling the guys?” I asked.

“What they don’t know won’t hurt them,” one said.

“Yeah, they’ll never know the difference,” another added.

I carried out the empty crate stained with blood. “Well, I’m sure not eating it.”

That night at supper, I ate peanut butter sandwiches and watched the others devour their bowls of stew. For dessert, the orderlies served vanilla pudding. I asked Elliot to slip the cow eye into Turk’s pudding just for fun.

“Yecch!” Turk said. “Who did this?” He held up the eyeball while the boys sitting near him burst out laughing. He stared up and down the tables with a scowl. “Whoever did it, better watch out.” I got a little thrill from it. Ollie would be proud.

The next morning, most of the boys suffered bowel problems. The latrine quickly filled, so the guys ran into the woods with toilet paper in their hands. When Mr. Wells found out about it, he sliced strips of inner bark from a red oak tree and gave it to the boys to chew. It seemed to help their stomachs.

The next time I saw something wrong going on, I planned to do something about it, no matter how much trouble it brought me. It annoyed me to see so many guys suffer when I could have prevented it.

On the first Saturday in December, we woke up to find about three inches of fresh snow on the ground. Mail call came in shortly after lunch. I lay sprawled out on my cot with a Popular Mechanics magazine and asked Frank to get my letter when the clerk called my name.

"Lazy bones," Frank muttered. He dropped it on the bed and said nothing. When I finally got around to looking at it, the return address nearly took my breath away. "Why didn't you say something?" I asked.

"I wanted to see your face," Frank said with a smirk.

The letter came from Duluth! I read it carefully, twice. The manager at Sorenson Brothers Sawmill wrote that my dad had worked at their mill for several years, but they had laid him off three years earlier. The manager found out that Dad left with three friends for Jefferson County, Pennsylvania to work in the coalmines. No one had heard from Dad since he left. I put the letter down and collected my thoughts. I felt like I was riding a hot air balloon and someone shot an arrow in it. I found Dad, but then I lost him!

"Damn!" I crumpled the letter and threw it to the floor.

When I told Frank he rallied me. "C'mon, you're on his trail...you just got to track him down."

"He left three years ago...he could be anywhere now," I sat dejected with my face in my hands.

"Put an ad in the newspapers, write the coal companies, the hospitals...everybody," Frank said.

I looked up. "You're right. If he ever got there, someone's got to know where he is." I reached for my coat and stepped out in the cold for a walk. The thought of my father digging coal with his face covered with soot gave me a sinking feeling. *What a lousy way to end up!*

Two weeks before Christmas, I got a note to report to the sergeant after work duty. I stayed out of trouble for weeks and had no idea what he wanted with me. *Maybe the job came up for mess orderly!* I spent the day clearing trees under power lines, so I was ready for a job inside where it was nice and warm. I hurried through my shower and dressed as fast as I could.

"Reporting as ordered, sir." I stood at parade rest in his office.

He studied my face in earnest. "Someone's been stealing field jackets in camp," he said with a dour face. "We've lost five in the past week." Boys often stole coats and sold them to a fence to make a few bucks. Since it only cost a dollar to replace it, a guy could sell his *own* coat and report it as stolen.

The sergeant leaned forward. "Two coats were stolen last Saturday. You were one of the three boys on probation who were in camp that afternoon." My jaw dropped.

I stammered. "Sir...I wouldn't steal a jacket...and I wouldn't even know who to sell it to."

The sergeant pursed his lips and gave me a long hard look. "There are plenty of people to sell it to. You know what they fetch outside of camp."

"I know...but I didn't take any."

He drummed his fingers on the desktop. "Keep your nose clean...and your eyes open," he said.

"Yes, sir."

"There are other things disappearing that I don't want to

talk about right now. So if you hear anything, come see me."

"Yes, sir."

"Dismissed."

As I trudged up to the mess hall, I pondered the sergeant's words. He accused me of stealing, but he also asked for my help. He asked indirectly, but he asked, nonetheless. Maybe something serious was happening in our camp. *Maybe he thinks it takes a thief to catch a thief!*

The next day, while Frank and I tossed a football in the quad before supper, Arky showed up with a jar of live fingerlings. He worked at the Sullivan Creek Trout Rearing Pond, where they raised baby trout. The fish were only a few inches long with brown markings.

"Who are those for?" I asked.

"For you and Frank," he said.

I watched through the glass as the little fish swam around. "What are we supposed to do with 'em?" I asked.

"Bite their heads off, stupid," Arky said. "We do it all the time at the fish hatchery...they're as cute as a bug's ear." He pulled one out, bit the head off and chewed.

I felt my jaw drop. "Huh?"

Frank shrugged his shoulders. "I'll try it...but just one," he slid his fingers in the jar and grabbed one. "Down the hatch," he said and bit the head off.

Arky held the jar out to me. I looked at both of them as they chewed. Something seemed funny, but I took off my glove and grabbed a slippery fish. I bit the head off with a loud crunch and chewed. Arky and Frank scrunched their faces when they swallowed. I got up the nerve and swallowed, too. It scratched my throat going down—it tasted awful. Just then, Arky and Frank spit their fish heads out and broke out laughing,

"Agghh...water!" I gasped and ran into the rec hall.

Frank came in with a grin on his face. "I thought you knew about that one," he said.

I leaned against the cooler with a glass of water in my hand. "I thought you were my friend," I said and took a swig.

"Hey, can't you take a joke?" he asked.

Arky followed in with a silly face. "If your brains were gunpowder, you wouldn't have enough to blow your own hat off." They both cracked up.

"Out of my way." I gave Arky a shove.

"Whoa," he said as water splashed out of the fish jar. I stomped out the door. Their joke rubbed me the wrong way.

While walking back to the barracks, I noticed an old rusty pickup slowly pull into camp. The driver waved me over. "Can you tell me where I can find the mess sergeant?" a leather-faced man with a week-long growth of whiskers asked. I peered in the window and saw a teenaged girl beside him.

I pointed. "Pull up behind that building," I said. "I'll track him down."

"Hop in," he said. I climbed in the front seat next to his daughter who smiled and batted her eyelashes.

"I'm Delores," she said. "But you can call me Dotty."

She was a pathetic sight with a smudged face and filthy coat. "Uh...nice to meet you," I said.

"Pardon her filth, she jus' got done feeding the pigs," her dad said. She pushed back her stringy hair and looked up at me with a playful grin. We pulled up behind the kitchen and I jumped out to find the mess orderly. The man had a deer in the back of his truck he wanted to sell. The camp bought deer from the locals outside of hunting season if it was road kill.

"Nice buck," the mess sergeant said as he examined the animal, "a ten pointer."

"Yep, it ran right in front of me," the farmer said scratching his whiskers.

I noticed a bullet hole just below the shoulder of the animal. There were no dents on the front of his truck, either.

Maybe the farmer backed into it and then shot it to put it out of its misery.

"C'mon in," the mess sergeant said. "I'll do the paperwork and get you some money." The two walked off and left me alone with his daughter.

She got out of the truck and approached me slowly. "Can you get me some sugar?" she asked with a puckish grin.

"You want *me* to steal you some sugar?" I asked.

She licked her lips. "Well, maybe not steal...just borrow."

"Uh, uh...I don't steal."

"Aw c'mon...just a little, maybe a cup or two."

I backed off as she stalked me around the truck like a bad comedy routine. I raised my hand, "Stop...stay right there." I reached in my pocket, pulled out a nickel and put it in her hand. "That'll buy you some sugar."

She rushed me and gave me a bear hug. I tried to pry her arms off, but she clung to me like an octopus. Just then, I heard a voice. "Git your hands off my little girl!"

She jumped back. Her father walked gimp-legged toward us with the mess sergeant and two orderlies following behind. The farmer stuck his face inches from mine and glowered "We may be poor young man...but we're proud." He pointed to his daughter. "My little girl's like a nice white linen cloth...if you touch her...you'll soil her." Actually, the opposite was true, but I was not going to argue the point.

"It's not what you think..." I said.

He cut me off. "I saw you groping her with my own eyes...yer not the first to git friendly with her." He looked back at the others. "Go on...take the deer." The mess sergeant motioned his head for me to go. I quietly walked off and headed for the quad.

I chuckled as I thought about the antics of the girl. The idea came to me that the person who stole the coats in camp might be doing it for reasons *other* than to make money. A desperate woman could easily compromise a man into stealing something more than sugar. Maybe the trick to finding the thief was to find a guy who was dating a hard-up woman. That would not be tough, since most of the gals who lived in the back woods were flat broke.

A couple nights later, Mr. Mulligan stopped by our barracks with a letter from Bobby. The boys crowded in close around him, sitting on cots and lockers. The sergeant took out a pair of wire rim glasses from his front shirt pocket and glanced up self-consciously as he slowly unfolded them.

He cleared his throat and read tentatively. "Many greetings. Thank you for giving me the best two years of my life. I miss all of you. It's been swell living with Mario. He has a nice two-story house here in Dearborn. I have a wonderful new family. I met my mother, my dad, grandparents, two brothers and a sister named Maria.

The sergeant coughed nervously and continued reading. "Mario's family really makes me feel welcome here and they treat me like family even though I have blond hair and everyone else has dark hair." A few of the boys chuckled.

"Mario's mom is a great cook—she makes lots of Italian dishes like spaghetti and lasagna. His dad is a brick mason, so Mario and I work as apprentices at his job site. The economy is getting better and there are more building projects going on, so we hope to find a job someday. Keep up the good work. I'll stay in touch. I hope to hear from some of you. Your friend, Bobby."

The sergeant took off his glasses and put them back in his pocket. He held up the letter and sniffled. "If any of you want to read this, it'll be in my office." Then he walked out.

A hushed silence fell over the barracks. The guys got up and went back to their cots—no one said a word. I noticed some wet eyes among the fellas. Suddenly, someone broke the ice. "He's one lucky fella, that Bobby."

"Nah...that's one lucky family to get such a nice guy," another said.

"I love lasagna," Elliot said, "I wish the cooks made it here." We looked at him as if he was screwy. He shrugged. "What'd I say?"

I decided to write a letter to my mom, so I walked over to the canteen to buy some stationery. When I got there, the orderly said he just sold out. "Everyone's buying paper tonight," he said.

"I'm not surprised." I noticed Turk at a table so I went over. "Who you writing?" I asked.

He gave me a bashful look. "My mom."

"You *never* write your mom."

"Now, I do."

"Son of a gun...can you spot me some paper?"

He handed me a sheet. "It's on me."

It occurred to me that most of us loved our moms, but we took them for granted a lot of the time. I wondered why teenagers could be nice to friends and strangers and be mean to their own mothers. Bobby's letter reminded me how important a mom was, especially with Christmas coming up soon.

The spirit of Christmas swept over our camp. A spruce tree brightened up our rec hall with its colorful ornaments. Christmas wreaths hung next to the barracks doors and paper cutouts of candles and snowflakes adorned the walls of the mess hall.

With pent up anticipation, I rode the truck into the Soo on Saturday afternoon to meet up with Betty and do some Christmas shopping. On the ride into town, I looked out at the fresh blanket of snow that covered the forests and fields. We stomped our feet and rubbed our hands to keep warm on the cold ride. Holiday shoppers filled Main Street as we pulled into town. Christmas lights lit up trees that lined the street and large wreaths hung from the lamp posts.

I needed to do some research at the library to find my

dad before I met with Betty. Gusts of wind blew as I walked down Ashmun Street so I tied a knot in the string to hold my cap. The librarian beamed when I told her about the letter I received about my dad. She wore a red sweater with little Christmas trees sewn on it. "Pennsylvania? Why that's not far at all," she said as she led me to the reference section. She pulled out a thick leather bound book and ran a finger down the index page. "Here we are," she said and flipped the pages.

"Wow," I said. She found a section about Jefferson County. I scanned the pages for useful information and discovered that Johnston and Indiana City were the two biggest towns in the county. I jotted down the names of their newspapers and several mining companies. When I walked out of the library, I had a dozen places to send letters.

I headed off to Malta's Drugstore to join Betty for a cup of coffee. The wind had died down and big fluffy snowflakes fell like feathers. The colorful window displays of Christmas scenes put me in a happy mood. I kicked the snow off my boots and stepped inside the warm drugstore. Red and green candy canes decorated the walls and ceiling. The sweet aroma of taffy and peppermint candy created a holiday atmosphere. Betty sat at a corner table dressed in a navy pea coat with a cream-color scarf draped over her shoulders. I snuck up from behind. "Ho, ho, ho...have you been a good little girl?"

She turned and smiled, her cheeks still rosy from the cold. "Oh, Santa Claus, I've been a *very* good girl."

We ordered coffee and shared a piece of cherry pie. When I told her about my research at the library, she smiled. "Oh, that's swell, Nick. You'll find him...I know you will."

When we finished our pie, she laid down her fork. "Did you bring a shopping list?"

"Yep, it's four pages long," I teased.

She grinned. "Were you always a joker?"

I shook my head, "No...just since I could talk." She

laughed easily at my dumb jokes. We bundled up, paid the cashier and stepped out into the cold. Christmas songs played over loud speakers and the sound of children filled the air. We stopped at a store window where children gathered to watch a train set.

Fluffy snowflakes collected on Betty's cap. "Did you have trains when you were young?" she asked.

"No, but I used to hang out with the hobos down by the tracks...does that count?" She giggled.

I stuck out my tongue and caught a snowflake. "Hey, you try it," I said. She tilted her head back and poked out her tongue. When two older women walked by, I pointed at Betty. "Her tongue is frozen..." The two ladies chuckled.

Betty punched me in the arm. "You big clown."

We entered Leader Department Store, where a large circular counter filled the front lobby. A conveyer belt sent packages up to the second floor for gift-wrapping. "Gee, I can ride that up and they can gift wrap me for *your* present."

Betty shook her head. "I'd return it for something I need."

I played along. "Like a new pair of shoes?"

"Yeah...but I'd let you polish 'em."

"Thanks a lot..."

We went around the corner and came to ladies' accessories. "This is perfect for my mom," I said and picked up a red beaded purse. It cost $2.50.

Betty chose a vase for her mother and a pigskin wallet for her dad. Later, I bought a buck knife for my brother Gabe and some perfume for Betty when I was alone. We dropped our packages off for gift-wrapping and caught the streetcar to Brady Park. When we arrived, snow was falling heavily and people stood in line for the toboggan slide.

"Ready for some excitement?" I asked, wide-eyed.

"I've been riding this since I was three," she deadpanned.

I grabbed her hand. "I'll make it exciting for you...all over again—c'mon."

She rolled her eyes. "Oh, brother."

People yelled as they whooshed down the icy slide. Then they slowly hauled the toboggans back up the hill. When our turn came, we climbed the steps of the take-off platform and paid a nickel each to the operator. Wooden rails on the side of the run kept the sled from sliding off. We sat down at the end of the eight-foot-long toboggan and three kids climbed in front of us. Betty wedged herself between my knees and I wrapped my arms around her.

"If you squeeze any tighter I might pop," she joked.

Suddenly, the ramp tipped down and off we went. "Aaaahh!" we screamed and shot down the track. Everything turned into a white blur as we raced down the hill. When we came to a stop a few seconds later, the kids jumped off, leaving us alone.

I leaned forward and rubbed my cold cheek next to hers. "Hmmm," she moaned.

"You're like a cuddly teddy bear," I whispered.

A young boy ran up. "You better get off quick or someone's gonna crash into you." Betty and I jumped up and pulled the sled off. We took a couple more runs and then walked back to the streetcar for the ride into town. We picked up our wrapped gifts at the department store and went back to the streetcar stop. I led Betty to a small recess between two shops. We stood face to face in the little niche. I set my bag down and put my arms around her. Her glasses fogged. "You got me all steamed up," she said.

I smiled. "I was gonna say the same thing."

I rubbed my nose against hers. "You're so cute," she said.

"Anything but handsome..."

"You're screwy..."

"Yeah...screwy enough to give you this." I reached in my coat pocket and gave her the perfume. "Merry Christmas."

She dropped it into one of her bags. Then, she took a gift from her bag and slipped it into mine. "Merry Christmas *to you.*"

I looked over my shoulder to see if anyone was watching. "Ready for your Christmas kiss?" I said and tightened my arms around her. The downy snowflakes collected on her eyelids.

She nodded. I closed my eyes and pressed my lips against hers for a short kiss.

I smiled. "When you warm up, you really sizzle."

"Oh, really?" she said. She glanced over my shoulder. "Hey, look at that man." I turned around and when I looked back, "SPLAT!" she rubbed a handful of snow in my face. "You need to cool off, Santa," she said, giggling.

"Ahhhh..." I pulled off my gloves and began wiping the snow from my face. We heard the clang of a streetcar.

"Gotta run," Betty said and grabbed her bags. "Merry Christmas," she said and gave me a little peck on my wet cheek. "See you New Year's." She dashed off leaving me with snow on my face. I saw the ledge where she scooped it up. *I still say the dumbest things!*

I headed back to the drop-off spot for the camp truck. In five days, she would open her gift and find the bottle of *Blue Topaz* perfume! On the ride back to camp, I imagined living in the Soo to be near Betty. I liked the people, the downtown, the parks—the town had everything. But, there was a little problem. Betty planned to go to a teacher's college in Marquette in the fall.

"Bad News" Bonovich came into camp five days before Christmas. The no-nonsense camp inspector visited several times a year and came up with maintenance jobs for us. They sent José and me to the icehouse to scrub the shelves. The icehouse was built into the side of a hill to use for food storage. A solitary light bulb lit a damp room that was big enough to park several trucks. Floorboards lay over ice blocks stacked ten feet deep, which kept the room a constant forty degrees year round. Bushel baskets filled with vegetables covered the floor. Jars of canned goods crowded the shelves and slabs of pork, lamb and beef hung on hooks from the ceiling.

Mr. Bonovich stopped by to check up on our work. A short man who always had a cigar in his hand, he constantly found more work for us when he showed up. I asked him why we had to do so many things.

"If it breaks down, you'll get in trouble," he said chomping on his cigar. "Things need to stay clean to keep you fellas healthy."

"But we have inspections every week," José said.

"The officers don't notice how bad things get," he said. "They live with it every day. I come in from the outside and spot things they miss."

In the early afternoon, the door creaked, and we saw Mr. Thacker wheel in a barrel of corned beef. He just returned from his monthly run into Newberry dressed in overalls and a heavy camp jacket. Thacker ignored us until he spotted me.

"Well, if it ain't the boy with the big shoulders," he said before he stepped out the door.

"What's wrong with that guy?" José asked.

"He's got a grudge because I embarrassed him," I said. We went back to wiping the shelf.

Thacker and his helper rolled in five more barrels with the name *Maloney Meats* stamped on the sides. After his last barrel, Thacker waved. "Merry Christmas, fellas."

"Merry Christmas," José and I mumbled back.

"Why does he pick up the meat, anyway?" I asked.

José lifted an earthen jar of cabbage off the shelf. "His sister lives out there...he visits her."

"Makes sense..."

Around two o'clock, Bad News came inside, grabbed a pickle from a barrel and inspected our work. Mr. Bonovich acted as if he owned the place. "Nice job, men. Go ahead and help yourself to a pickle and don't forget to kill the light." José and I carried the wash buckets outside before returning for our treat. My eyes took a moment to adjust to the dim room.

We popped the barrel lid off and reached in for a pickle. When I stepped outside, José looked at me and did a double take.

"Spit it out," he said waving his hands. "Spit it out!"

Something was not right about that pickle. I felt something dangle over my chin, like a string. I leaned forward and coughed it out. "Yeeeuuuch!" I shouted, when I saw what it was.

José's eyes turned white. "A rat!"

"Auuggggghhh!" I upchucked right there and fell to my hands and knees coughing. "Don't say *anything* about this *to anybody*," I croaked.

He patted my shoulder. "It's our secret," he said. "It must've fallen in and drowned." I ran to the bathhouse and rinsed my mouth. If the other boys found out, I would never hear the end of it. And God forbid if Betty learned about it, she would never kiss me again. *No more pickles for me!*

When Elliot's mom found out at Thanksgiving that I planned to stay in camp for Christmas, she invited me to their home in Newberry, about an hour west of camp. They lived in the same town where Thacker picked up the corned beef. Elliot's father came by the camp two days before Christmas to get us. He looked and sounded like an older Elliot, with a round face and infectious laugh. He spent most of the drive telling us lumberjack stories.

The next day, Elliot's older brother Tom drove us to Tahquamenon Falls, the highest waterfall in the Upper Peninsula at fifty feet. We strapped on snowshoes and set off in two-foot-deep snow. The sun shone brightly and newly fallen snow caused tree branches to sag. The snow muffled our sounds so it was eerily quiet, except for the groans of Elliot who struggled to keep up with us.

About twenty minutes into our hike, we saw the falls in the distance. Gigantic, rust-colored icicles five feet thick reached upward with water rushing over the top. Tom explained that the water got its golden brown color from the cedar, spruce and hemlock trees that grew upstream in the wetlands. Behind the icicles loomed dark spaces that looked like underground caves. As we approached, we saw four men about our age walking under the icicles. "Hey, is it very wet in there?" I yelled.

"Dry as a bone," one of them quipped. I cringed.

We removed our snowshoes and inched our way into the ice caves with our backs against the wall. A fine mist covered us as we stared up at the icicles. I noticed two of the boys wore purple CCC field jackets. I had heard that fences often dyed stolen coats different colors. "Where'd you get your jackets?" I asked.

"Don't tell him," one of the guys said.

Elliot's brother cut in. "I bet it was Hot Harry's."

"Yeah...you been there?" the boy said.

"Everyone's been there," Tom said. "It's no big secret." Later, while we plodded through the snow back to the car I asked Tom about Hot Harry's.

"He's a fence that works out of his garage," he said.

"Those coats might be from our camp," I said.

"I doubt it," he said. "Camps Rexton and Strongs are much closer than Raco."

"It's still possible," I said.

He shrugged. "Maybe."

I came back from our snowshoe trek with bruises on my legs from slipping down a ravine and banging into a tree. Elliot's mom suggested I take a sauna to make the bruises go away. I stripped down to a towel and followed Elliot and his Uncle Otto into the garage. We walked down a narrow hall to the sauna. When I stepped in, the heat from the cedar-paneled room scorched my lungs. "Can you make it a little cooler?" I asked. It was my first sauna.

"Sure," Otto said with a goofy grin. "Pour some water on the rocks." He handed me a tin cup. I reached into the bucket, and splashed water over the red-hot rocks. A cloud of steam filled the air and made the sauna even hotter.

I gasped. "I can't breathe."

"Why don't you climb up here?" Otto said and patted the bench. I climbed up and it was even hotter. I felt like a boiled lobster! Pink faced, Elliot grinned. I knew a gag when I saw one.

"I'm getting outta here," I said and wrapped the towel around my waist. I went out the door and Otto followed me down the hall. When I opened the door to the outside, I felt a hand grab my towel. He ripped it off and pushed me through the door into a pile of snow. The pile was not there when I first came in! I lay in the snow a few moments and cooled off. Just as I stood up, the porch light went on. I saw Elliot's family, including his sisters, standing on their porch looking down at me!

I covered my crotch with one hand and grabbed the door handle with the other, but Otto held the door tight from the inside. "Let me in!" I yelled and banged on it. I heard him laughing his head off. "C'mon...let me in!" I pounded away.

"My, that boy has a cute butt," Elliot's sister said. I turned and ran up the steps to the house with my hands covering myself the best I could. His family howled with laughter. I found out later that the gag was a family tradition; they did it to many of their guests, even women. I slept well that night, a little embarrassed, but refreshed.

Christmas day began with the opening of presents in Elliot's house. We visited two of his uncles' homes in the afternoon and did some sledding on a nearby hill. The day flew by so quickly I hardly had time to think about my mother back in Detroit. It was my first Christmas away from her, and I hoped she wasn't too lonely with Gabe and me gone.

The next day, Elliot and I played ice hockey at a neighborhood rink. I spent most of the time standing on my ankles, so they let me play goalie. By the afternoon, I looked forward to the drive back to camp and a chance to rest my sore feet. Elliot's brother drove us in his dad's Chrysler sedan.

"Can we swing by Hot Harry's?" I asked as we pulled out of their driveway.

"Sure," Tom said. We made a few turns in the neighborhood until we came to a run down house with crooked shutters and a yard filled with junk cars. I eyed the green garage door and imagined all the stolen goods behind it.

"Let's go," I said. We drove in silence along M-28 while the darkness closed in. The song *Silent Night* crackled over the radio as I watched the darkened landscape pass by. I rested my chin on the cool window ledge and thought about Hot Harry's. For some reason, the idea hit me that Thacker might be the guy supplying the CCC goods to the fence.

It made perfect sense. Thacker hung around camp on Saturdays when the camp was half-empty so he had the opportunity to steal. Plus, he went into Newberry once a month for the meat pick-up. It was the perfect cover for visiting Hot Harry's! Ever since he teased me about the c-clamp, I thought he might be up to something, and now I knew what it was. With keys to the equipment room and storage room, he could steal the camp blind and get away with it. Fencing goods in Newberry also made sense, because there was less chance they could trace the hot items back to our camp.

I struggled with a reason why Thacker would steal. Perhaps gambling debts drove him to do it or a girlfriend with fancy tastes. Who knew? I planned to tell Frank of my suspicions. I needed to tell someone or it would drive me crazy.

The next morning we cleared trees under power lines. During our lunch break, I told Frank about the boys wearing purple CCC jackets and my theory about Thacker as the culprit. We slurped our ham and bean soup outside, sitting on a log. It was just what we needed to warm up. Frank listened intently to my story. When I finished, he looked at me as if I came from Mars. "Don't tell *anyone* what you just told me," he said.

I chewed my roll. "What's wrong?" I asked.

"Everything. Thacker's an officer...you don't accuse an officer because you got a grudge against him."

"I don't have a grudge..."

Frank interrupted me. "You accuse him of taking the c-clamp, then you tell the sarge he's overcharging you on clothes. Now you say he's pinching coats..."

"But..."

"The sarge won't buy it. He already told you to patch things up with him."

I thought about it. "Okay, I'll drop it...sorry I said anything."

Frank wiped his mouth. "Thacker and the sarge are friends, they share rides into camp...don't mess with his friend."

I nodded. "But, the more stuff gets stolen, the more the sarge thinks I'm the guy."

"Show, don't tell. Get some evidence...*then* go to the sarge."

"I'm not Sherlock..."

"And I'm not Doctor Watson. Leave me out of this." Frank stood and went back to the warming fire. I took a bite of my soup. Frank was right about one thing—the sarge would give me hell if I accused Thacker of anything else.

That night in bed, I tossed and turned trying to think of a way to prove Thacker was the thief. If I trailed him to Hot Harry's, he might catch me and that would get *me* in trouble. Maybe I could sneak into his home when he was in camp and case it for stolen goods. Or, I could set a trap by leaving a coat somewhere he was sure to steal and mark it with something to identify it later.

As I dozed off, I heard someone yelling outside. I rolled out of bed, hustled to the door and saw Curly the baker running into the officers' barracks with a frying pan in his hand. *That's odd!* I climbed back into bed.

At breakfast, we found out that someone was stealing pies from the bakery cooling-shed. Curly stayed up and waited behind the door hoping to catch the thief. When a big black bear came inside the door, Curly tackled it and they tumbled on the floor. They only scuffled for a second and then both ran out the door dashing off in different directions. Curly showed us a handful of brown hair he pulled off the bear. We got a good laugh out of it. As I rode out to work duty, I thought about how Curly's plan backfired. Maybe it was a *sign.* If I designed a trap to catch Thacker and it backfired, he might have more bite than a bear!

All week long, I chopped trees and cleared brush for truck trails. I suffered from cold feet even with two pairs of wool socks on. With a scarf around my neck and earflaps tied tight, I made it through the bitter cold. I wondered if I would ever get a job in the mess hall, especially when I found out that over a dozen boys had signed up for the next job opening. With all the trouble I had been in, the sergeant would probably skip over my name when a position finally came up.

After we chopped down the trees under the power lines, Isaac instructed us to trim the tree limbs flush to the trunk so they dragged smoothly over the ground. However, he told us to leave the top limb about six inches long, so there was a handle to grab. We loaded the logs on hitches and brought them back to camp to cut up as firewood. Branches went to the burn piles, which gave us a chance to warm up.

The work in the woods gave me plenty of time to think about Thacker. The day before, the sergeant addressed the enrollees about the stealing problem in camp, so I knew something big was happening. He asked everyone to keep his eyes peeled for anything that looked suspicious.

"Don't be afraid to snitch," he said. 'If this stealing continues, there could be some unpleasant changes around here." My ears perked up. What did he mean by *unpleasant changes?*

The sarge's comments motivated me to find a way of trapping Thacker. I was a man possessed, on a mission to expose the scoundrel. At times, I thought it was crazy that no one else suspected the supply sergeant, but Thacker showed a side to me that he had not shown to anyone else. Also, no one else connected his trips to Newberry with the fence who sold CCC stuff.

I finally came up with a strategy to trap Thacker and decided to tell Frank when we went out for a stroll around the quad after supper. Someone had spread sand across the icy sidewalks so our feet scratched along the surface. It was very dark with the only light coming from the lamps on the barracks.

"It's too hard to catch him stealing," I said. "But what if I caught him fencing?"

"How do you do that?" Frank asked.

"He makes a monthly run into Newberry, right?"

"Right."

"We post a lookout by Hot Harry's and catch him going in."

"Did you say *we*? I'm not in on this..."

"Okay...but you get my point."

"Yeah, I get your point, but that's not evidence."

"What do you mean?"

"When the sergeant asks Thacker about it, he'll say he was shopping for a gun or something."

I pondered his words. "You're right."

Frank scooped up a handful of snow off a bench and packed a snowball. "You need *hard* evidence."

"Maybe I could wear a disguise and walk into Hot Harry's when Thacker's inside."

Frank threw the snowball at the library. SPLAT! "Yeah, you could dress up like Groucho Marx....they'd never guess."

"Aw shaddup..."

"You've been reading too many Doc Savage books. If Thacker and Hot Harry catch you, you're dead."

"They'd never catch me. I'd outrun 'em. "

Frank groaned. "C'mon...."

"I'm serious about catching him."

We walked up the barracks steps. Frank turned. "If you're serious...you got to catch him red-handed."

"Okay, okay..." I muttered. We went inside. For the rest of the night, I read my Doc Savage book. After lights out, I stared up at the ceiling and wondered what Doc would do.

Old man winter turned our camp into an icebox two days before New Year. With the temperature at fifteen degrees below zero, they excused us from work duty. To keep everyone busy, the camp scheduled classes and other activities. Mr. Wells gave a talk on animals. We met in the rec hall where about fifty of us crowded around as he held up a large book with pictures. "An owl has excellent night vision," he said. "That's why people think owls are wise. It also walks like an old man," He pointed to a photo. "See how its eyes are on the front of the head like a human?"

Mr. Wells spoke in a mysterious tone. "The cougar is a very special creature because it was awake during the seven nights of creation; that's how it got its night vision. It screams like a woman and its habits are secret and unpredictable...also like a woman." The guys laughed.

Then he picked up another book and flipped the pages until he found some pictures of trees. "Trees have spiritual origins," he said. "The cedar, pine, and spruce trees keep their leaves all year long because they stayed awake during the seven days of creation."

I glanced out the frost-covered window and noticed Thacker walking hunched over through the wind. It seemed odd that he was busy at work since most of the officers went home because of the cold. *Why can't I get him out of my mind?*

When Mr. Wells finished his talk, Isaac entertained us with lumberjack stories. "You dink dis is cold...you don't *know* cold." He held up a rusty lantern in his hand. "Why... one winter it was so cold, it froze da flames in our kerosene lamps when we walked to work in da morning. At night, we couldn't sleep from da light. So's we break off da flame and drow it out in da snow!"

"Aw...you're pulling our leg," one of the boys yelled.

"Oh, no...in da spring when da snow melt...dat ol' flame dawed out and start burnin' an make forest fire."

We busted up laughing. "Tell us another one," someone said.

"Well...some days was so cold we couldn't talk to each udder. Our words froze in din air...but in da spring when it warms up, you walk in da woods when no one's dere and you can hear da sound of men talking and laughing!" The guys went into hysterics.

Isaac taught us a few games that lumberjacks played in their bunkhouse. He picked two strong fellas to hold a peavey a few feet off the floor. "Who dink dey can ride da mule?" A dozen hands shot up and each boy climbed up and tried to balance himself on the peavey handle as long as possible.

Squirt was on the peavey when Mr. Mulligan appeared in the doorway. He pointed at me. "Nick, can I see you for a minute?" *Oh, for chrissakes, what's it this time?* I followed him to his office and stood at parade rest. The sergeant wore a poker face.

He leaned back and folded his arms. "Did you hear about Gilbert leaving?"

"No, sir," I said. My heart skipped a beat. Gilbert worked as a mess orderly in the officers' barracks!

"He got a job offer back home so his position is open. The mess sergeant recommended you for it...you still want it?"

"Yes, sir," I said.

"There's a two-week trial period and then you'll get a review. If you pass, it's permanent."

"Yes, sir."

He relaxed and smiled. "Congratulations, you report to work tomorrow. Follow Gilbert the next couple days."

"Thank you, sir. I'll do my very best."

"And go see Thacker...he'll issue you a couple uniforms."

"Yes, sir," I said and reached for my coat.

"By the way...you're no longer on probation."

I turned. "Sir?"

"You stayed out of trouble the last couple months, and I want you to start the New Year with a clean slate."

"Yes, sir...that's A-okay with me." I rushed out into the frigid cold and almost tripped over my feet running back to the rec hall. I shook my fist at the overcast sky. "You're not getting me old man winter!" I yelled. It felt like I won a vacation to Florida.

The sergeant surprised me when he took me off probation, but other boys said that after they paid their dues, the sergeant forgot about their past.

"Mess orderly?" Frank said when I told him the news. He laid his pool cue down and slapped my shoulder, a little too hard. "You lucky dog," he said. Then he lowered his voice. "You better bring me some snacks once in a while."

I picked up his cue and shot a ball into the side pocket. "I'll think about it. Why do you think the sarge approved me?"

Frank shrugged. "Probably wants to keep a close eye on you."

"Aw...dry up."

I went to Thacker with a bounce in my step. He sat behind the counter with a magazine in his hands "I need two mess orderly uniforms—large, please."

Thacker raised an eyebrow and grunted. "Which mess hall you workin'?" he asked.

"Officers'," I said casually.

His face twitched when I said it. "Good for you," he said feebly and laid out the clothes.

"I guess I'll be seeing you," I said.

He gave me a long look and nodded.

"Thanks," I said, and headed for the door. *He's not going to mess with me anymore!*

When New Year's Eve finally arrived, I was in the mood to celebrate. The smell of starch and shoe wax filled the barracks as the guys got ready for the big night. I slapped on some Old Spice before stepping out into the cold to join Frank at the loading deck. We planned to meet the girls at Gould's Pavilion.

The dance hall was already crowded with revelers when we arrived. Most of the men dressed smartly in suits, while their dates wore formal dresses. Betty looked stylish in a blue chiffon dress and a bow tied at the waist. She pinned her hair neatly back and wore a corsage on her near her shoulder.

Balloons floated from tables and streamers hung from the walls. A swing band played a Benny Goodman number as we entered the hall. The four of us found a table and then we hit the dance floor. I took Betty's warm hand and led her to a spot near the middle of the floor. She turned to face me and slid her hand up on my shoulder. I stepped forward and we glided easily together to the song, *Moon over Miami.* The scent of her perfume put thoughts of romance in my head.

I smiled to myself. Nine months earlier, I stood in front of a judge for stealing a pair of shoes. Now, I was dressed in a new uniform, dancing with a beautiful young woman. What a year! Betty looked dazzling. "You look like the wrapping around the neck of a champagne bottle," I said in her ear.

She playfully grabbed the back of my neck. "So you're the bottle, eh?"

I smiled. "You know it."

"I bet you're ready to pop your cork..."

"It popped the moment I laid eyes on you."

She flashed a warm smile. "You're sweet." The band picked up the tempo with Irving's Berlin's, *A Fine Romance.* Betty sang along, "A fine romance...without kisses."

"I can do something about that," I joked.

She squeezed my hand. "I bet you can."

I glanced over at Frank and Doris. His subtle head movements and precise steps made the rest of us look like amateurs.

The night passed quickly as we danced, chatted with CCC pals, and talked with Betty's schoolmates. As midnight neared, we sat at our table with glasses of sparkling cider. Frank lifted his glass and made a toast. "The Lord gives us relatives...thank God we can choose our friends." We laughed and raised our glasses with his.

"C'mon Nick, your turn." Betty said.

I gave a sheepish grin and raised my glass. "Here's to our friends," I looked at Frank, "and the strength to put up with them." They chuckled as we clinked glasses.

We returned to the packed dance floor just before midnight. It seemed with every step we bumped into the person next to us. Suddenly, the music went down, and the bandleader led us in a count down to New Years. "Nine, eight, seven, six..." we shouted. At zero, people erupted into wild cheering with the blowing of horns and shaking of rattles. In spite of the racket, I felt as if Betty and I were alone. Nothing in the world could wipe the smile off my face at that moment.

"Happy New Year, Nick."

"Happy New Year, Betty."

The lights went down. I put my hands on her waist and kissed her. Her soft lips welcomed mine and she gave me a sensual hug. The band played *Auld Lang Syne*. We danced slowly and sang the words together. *"Should old acquaintance be forgot... and never brought to mind? Should old acquaintance be forgot...and auld lang syne?"*

As I held her in my arms, I wondered what the New Year would bring. Would I find my dad? Would Betty still be in my life? Would I move back to Hamtramck after my second term was up? Would I catch Thacker stealing stuff in camp? So many questions, but they could wait. Tonight, I held my sweetheart in my arms and nothing else mattered.

Chapter 9

January 1938

My new job as an officers' mess orderly required that I get up at five in the morning, half an hour before the men did. I didn't mind getting up so early, because I looked forward to the work. After I set the tables and prepared my station, I went into the officers' quarters to wake up the lower-ranking forestry and conservation officers. The captain, sergeant and supply sergeant slept in their own quarters or at home.

At five-thirty, I shook their shoulders and said, "First call sir, first call." They usually rolled over and went back to sleep. Fifteen minutes later, I returned and did the same thing again. "Second call sir, second call," but this time I spoke louder. Most of the men sat up and thanked me. At six, I came into the room and announced loudly, "Gentlemen, breakfast...is...served."

For the next thirty minutes, I ran back and forth between the mess hall and kitchen carrying plates of eggs, bacon, and hash browns. I quickly learned how each man liked his coffee and eggs. By six thirty, most of the men were out the door. Mr. Dalton was always the last to leave. After he left, it was my turn to sit down and relax. One of the cooks usually joined me at the table for breakfast.

One day during my first week, Curly the baker came in with his plate piled high with ham and eggs. A garrulous fella who loved the Yankees, I often wondered if his shirt buttons would pop off when he sat down because of his rolls of fat. He explained why he made such a variety of pies and puddings. “Everyone has different tastes, so I give them choices,” he said. “If the dessert is good, the meal is good.”

“Why do the orderlies hold off serving the main course until the soup bowls are cleared away?” I asked.

He grinned. “Don’t tell anyone, but that’s how Mr. Kiefer makes sure the boys eat all their vegetables.”

“No wonder it’s loaded with veggies,” I said. The cooks were no dummies. The longer I stayed in camp, the more it seemed like there was a reason for everything. Smart men ran the camp, whether it was for planting trees, building a state park or running a kitchen. They hired men ripe with experience. Most of the cooks had worked in lumberjack camps, the reserve officers had seen action in the First World War, the Local Experienced Men were former lumberjacks, and Educational Advisors were unemployed teachers. What the younger officers lacked in experience, they made up with their energy. It took fit, young men to keep up with all the enrollees in the field.

I gained a new perspective of the camp because Mr. Mulligan filled me in on the latest news during his morning snack visits. The leftover pancakes turned tough as leather after a couple hours. To make them tasty, I spread jam on top, rolled them up so the jam was on the inside, and stuck a toothpick in. The sergeant loved to come in for a snack around nine o’clock and knock down a few. He’d stick his head in the mess hall and ask, “Any leftovers today?”

“Yes, sir,” I called back. I brought out a few pancake rolls with a pot of coffee and he usually invited me to sit with him. During my second week on the job, he talked about the “stupid orders” he got from his superiors.

“Was clearing snow from the fire trails a stupid order?” I asked.

The sergeant nodded as he chewed. “The only people using those trails are poachers.”

“Where do the orders come from?” I asked.

He slurped his coffee. “Don’t repeat this, but sometimes the captain gets his orders from the district superintendent ...who gets *his orders* all the way from Washington.”

“No wonder they’re stupid,” I said. After the sergeant left, I couldn’t’ believe he confided to me about his problems. He treated me more like a friend then an enrollee. I liked that.

A week later as I polished silver in the mess hall, I glanced up at a calendar. It read, January 17, exactly one month since I sent letters to Pennsylvania asking about the whereabouts of my dad. I received no word even though I put missing person ads in two newspapers, sent letters to coal companies and wrote to three hospitals. If no one responded, I planned to go there in person after my second six-month term ended in April. I needed to save at least thirty dollars to make the trip. All I could do in the meantime was hope that someone wrote me about his whereabouts.

On a frigid Friday night in late January, the cook sent me to the officers’ quarters with a plate of cold cuts along with mustard, pickle relish, onions and bread. It was a regular treat for the younger officers who stayed in camp over the weekend. They played card games into the night and loved the snack.

I normally dropped off the food and came back later to pick it up, but it was so cold outside I decided to bring a book and read while the men polished off the food. Thacker was there because he was spending the night to avoid driving in the cold. I was minding my own business reading a book, when Thacker looked up from his card game and said, “This is the officers’ quarters, not a kid’s quarters.”

I glanced up—everyone looked over at me. No one challenged the supply sergeant, since he was the highest-ranking officer in the room. "Ah...I guess I should leave," I mumbled and stood. I put on my coat and returned to the mess hall. The next day several officers pulled me aside and apologized for Thacker's comment.

"He was just in a bad mood," Mr. Rushford told me. "His rheumatism makes him grumpy."

"Yeah...don't let it bother you," Mr. Dalton said.

In a way, I felt sorry for Thacker. The winter cold penetrated the thin walls of the buildings in camp. He must have suffered from the ailments he picked up in his lumberjack days. In time, my theory about Thacker as the camp thief began to fade away. The sergeant never brought up the stealing issue again, so I assumed the problem had gone away.

One of the nice things about working in the mess hall was that I saw things that other boys missed. In late January, a car drove into camp with two matronly women. Bundled up in heavy coats, they entered the captain's office as I watched through the mess hall window. A few minutes later, I received word to bring them tea and cookies. While I served their tea, I listened to the woman berate the captain for not informing them about their son's drill class.

"Perhaps we can change the rules so parents will be notified of their son's participation," Captain Bullock said.

"That's not good enough," one of the women said. "You should ask our permission *before* they enroll."

"That's right," the second woman added. "We don't want our boys being trained for the army—that's not what the CCC is about."

I left before I heard the captain's response. Elliot's mother was not alone in fearing that the army might take over the camp someday. The cold wind whipped up as I traversed across the quad. I wondered what I would do if they drafted me. Maybe I could be a mess orderly.

The wind caught the door and slammed it behind me when I entered the kitchen. It felt good to be back inside. The delicious aroma of baked ham whetted my appetite. I went back to work separating silverware. The two women visitors reminded me that people outside the camp feared for the future. I was in no hurry to go home.

On a Saturday afternoon in early February, mail call came in after lunch. I sat on my cot and listened as one of the boys read his letter aloud. When he was done, we looked around to see if anyone else wanted to read. Arky surprised us by standing up. “Fellas, I wanna try to read this dang letter from my sister. Don’t none of you laugh.”

Heads turned and we smiled because Arky never read a letter in his life. We listened as he stuttered and stammered. “Pa bought some new…fence wire…with the money we got from the…ah, ah, government. We’ve been… losing chickens to the foxes…”

When Arky finally finished reading, the boys gave him a big round of applause and cheered. His freckled face turned crimson. It dawned on me, that Arky was not dumb—he just never tried before. His educational advisor helped change his attitude.

I sat on my cot and hemmed a pair of slacks for a boy. I thought back to all the time I wasted in school fooling around. If only I could go back and do it over again, but I was too old. Someday I wanted to go to a trade school. When I did, I planned to be the hardest-working student in the school.

On a frigid morning in early February, the sergeant came into the mess hall for his usual morning snack. I was about to sprinkle powdered sugar on his pancake rolls when he raised his hand. “Hold it Nick,” he said. “I wanna try something new.”

“Sure,” I said and gave him the plate.

He spooned some cane sugar onto his plate. Then, he took a rolled up pancake, dipped it in the coarse sugar and bit into it. After he finished chewing he smiled, "My girls eat it this way at home...I always wanted to see how it tasted."

I chuckled. "So...is it better than powdered sugar?"

He shook his head. "Nah, I like it your way."

I went back to polishing silverware. "Thank you, sir."

He stopped chewing. "When we're sitting around like this, just you and me...you don't need to say yes, sir or no, sir."

"What should I call you?"

"Well...I'll tell you what. Why don't you just call me by my name, John."

"Oh, no sir...I could never call you that."

He wiped his mouth. "Then, you come up with a name."

I thought a moment. "How about...Pops?"

He gave me a quizzical look and thought a moment. "Sure, why not? Call me Pops."

Later, he unbuttoned his front pocket, and pulled out a newspaper clipping. The headline read *SENATE VOTES TO SLASH CCC FUND.* My eyeballs almost popped out when I read it. The article stated that Congress decided to reduce CCC funding because of an improved economy. They planned to close six camps in the Upper Peninsula before year's end.

"Geez, that's terrible," I said. "Have they picked the camps yet?"

The sergeant cradled his cup and shook his head. "No, but we're in trouble because of our inventory problem."

"Inventory problem?" I asked.

"We're still losing inventory and the brass is fed up with it."

"Geez, you haven't talked about it lately...is it still the coats?"

"It's more than coats...someone's stealing from the equipment room. Hell, a generator walked off."

"A generator?"

He placed his cup on the saucer and stood. "Yep. They have to shut six camps so they're looking for reasons to do it. We have the second-worst record for stealing."

"Who's first?"

"The sergeant slipped on his coat. "Camp Escanaba. They caught someone shipping out a truck engine, piece by piece."

I felt my jaw drop. "No...I don't believe it."

He nodded and held up the newspaper clipping. "Don't talk about it, or repeat what I said about our camp closing."

"Yes, sir...I mean Pops." A gust of cold air blew in as he left the building. I cleaned the table and picked up the broom. *Did I really call him Pops?* I shook my head and smiled. Why not? The name jumped to the tip of my tongue. Ever since he began coming in for his morning snacks, he seemed more like a dad than a sergeant. He gave me advice and even trusted me with camp news. Beneath his gruff exterior, there was a gentle man.

As I swept under the table, I thought about his comments on stealing. An enrollee could not easily steal a generator—it had to be someone who had a key to the room... someone like Thacker! It annoyed me that I couldn't tell the sergeant about my suspicions. Frank was probably right—Mr. Mulligan would just say I held a grudge against Thacker. The thought came to me that Thacker might have stolen the coats as a diversion, to make it look like the work of an enrollee.

My early suspicions were right. Thacker *was* the thief—he had to be! I wanted to climb on top of the water tower and shout to the whole camp, "Mr. Thacker is your man! He stole the generator; he'll steal the shirt off your back!" I remembered the promise I made to myself after I saw the cooks poison the boys with bad meat. This was a way to make things right and a chance to save the camp from closing.

When I served supper that night, I noticed how the supply sergeant showed little emotion when he spoke with the other officers. He seemed distant, aloof. I felt so jittery being around him that I dropped a plate while clearing the table, something I never did before. When it crashed to the floor, everyone turned and looked, except for him. He continued eating as if nothing ever happened. His blood ran cold as ice.

That night I felt frustrated trying to come up with a way to nail Thacker. I could have punched a hole in the wall—I was *that* discouraged. I confronted the mail clerk about some money I gave him back in the fall. Sears & Roebuck came out with a new product called *thermal underwear* and I gave Butch Harrigan $2.38 to order a pair and send in the money. Winter was half over and I still waited for my thermal underwear!

"Let's go outside and talk," he said when I found him at a pool table. Butch drank like a fish and ran after the ladies.

"Why can't we talk here?" I asked. "It's freezing out there."

"Aw, c'mon." he said so we slipped on our coats and stepped outside in front of the building.

"Make it snappy," I said.

"You're not gonna like this...but I spent the money on my girlfriend."

I got in his face. "The whole two bucks? What'd you do, buy her a new dress?"

"I promise to pay you back next payday," he said and backed off.

I came after him. "You dumb cluck." I grabbed him by his jacket and slammed him against the stair railing. "I *need* that long underwear."

"I'm sorry, really..."

"Aw...shaddup," I socked him hard in the face and then pushed him down in the snow. I gave him a kick in the butt for good measure.

"I want that money," I said and headed back to the barracks. *Why did I hit him in the face!* If I made any marks, I was in big trouble.

I hung up my coat and sprawled out on my cot. Some guys played card games on the other side of the room. The Doc Savage book in my hand did little to take my mind off what I did to Butch. There was no denying it—Thacker had gotten to me. It annoyed me to no end that I couldn't come up with a plan to catch him in the act.

The next morning, Mr. Mulligan stuck his head in the door of the mess hall a couple hours after breakfast.

"Any leftovers?" he asked.

"You bet, Pops." I said.

He unbuttoned his coat. "What flavor today?"

"Blueberry."

"Oh boy, let me at 'em."

While he ate, I laid out table settings. The sergeant talked about his days in the First World War where he fought in France. A few days before the war was officially over, he saw a German soldier walking alone on a street. The sergeant picked up his gun and aimed it at the man. "I had him in the cross hairs and my finger was on the trigger," he said.

"Did you shoot him?"

He shook his head slowly. "Nope...I let him go home to his mother." He rubbed his pancake in some loose jam and took a bite.

"Wow...what a story." I said.

When the sergeant finished chewing, he turned to me. "Who split the mail clerk's lip last night?"

I took a quick breath. "I socked him." Then I explained how he spent my underwear money on his girlfriend.

The sergeant grinned. "A man can't go through winter without his long johns."

I said nothing.

The sergeant stood up. "Harrigan probably got what was coming to him, but you still have to be punished."

"I understand," I said.

He fixed his scarf. "During your afternoon break, I want you to go around camp and dust the snow off all the outside lights."

"Yes, sir."

"Let me know tomorrow how it went." Then he stepped out into the cold.

I let out a big breath. The sarge let me off easy.

When I returned to the barracks after work that night, I noticed a car pull up. A boy and his father got out and went into the captain's quarters. Fifteen minutes later, that same boy walked into the barracks with Scruggs. "Listen up," Scruggs said. "This is Harry. He's a new enrollee just in from Brimley."

The red-haired, round-faced boy removed his hat and gave us a friendly wave. "Hi ya, fellas," he said with zest.

Scruggs led him to his cot and spent a few minutes going over the rules of the barracks. Then, he stepped out of the building and left the rookie to unpack. The moment Scruggs walked out the door, Harry took two bottles of beer from his suitcase and held them up. "I brought you boys a little drink," he said. "Help yourself...I got plenty more, too."

I looked up from my sewing work and saw Squirt square his shoulders and stand up to him. "You can't bring beer in here—it'll get us *all* in trouble."

"Aw, clam up...it's my first night, no one's got anything to worry about." He popped the cap off. "Who wants the first one?" No one spoke. "You guys aren't any fun," he said and took a swig.

We turned our backs on him as he unpacked. "He's going to get it," I said under my breath to Frank.

Frank began dealing cards. "Yeah...and how."

Ten minutes later, Mr. Mulligan stomped into the barracks. He went straight to Harry. "You know the rules—no alcohol in camp."

"Aw, it's my first night...cut me a little slack will ya?"

"Pack your bags—you're going home," the sergeant snapped. "I want you out front in five minutes." He left in a fury.

The exchange left my jaw hanging. "That was the shortest enlistment I ever saw," I whispered to Frank. Harry pulled out two more beers. "Who wants these...they shouldn't go to waste."

"Didn't you learn your lesson moron? Get out!" a guy yelled.

Another shouted, "We don't need your kind around here."

"Oh yeah? Well, I won't miss this place," he said, and stuffed his clothes back in the suitcase.

When he walked out the door, Arky yelled, "That boy don't know his ass from apple butter." We cracked up.

My new job as a mess orderly kept me from seeing Frank as often as I used to. It seemed like the only time we talked was before curfew. While playing a game of checkers a few days after Harry got kicked out, I asked, "What do you think happened to that fella who brought in the beer?"

Frank looked over his shoulder to see if anyone was listening. "You don't know?" He asked in a voice just above a whisper.

"Know what?" I asked.

"Don't tell anyone I told you...it was a set-up."

I looked up from the board. "What?"

"Sarge does it twice a year—he gets actors to play the part."

"I don't believe it...why does he do it?"

"So the rookies know he won't put up with any nonsense."

I shook my head in amazement. *Mr. Mulligan must be the smartest man in camp.*

When food went stale in the kitchen, we tossed it into the garbage pit. One day in early February, the mess sergeant asked me to dump a dozen boxes of stale breakfast cereal. As I walked through the quad with a big cardboard box in my arms, I passed Elmer. He worked as an orderly in the infirmary.

"Hey, where are you going with those?" he asked.

"Garbage pit...they're bad," I said.

His eyes lit up. "I want 'em."

I shrugged. "Okay with me." We went to his barracks and stuffed the boxes in his gunnysack.

"I'll hitch a ride home this weekend," he said.

"Isn't it too cold?" I asked.

The Croatian shook his blonde head. "My family's hungry...they need food."

Elmer made me feel like a coward. He was willing to freeze in a freight car to take cereal to his family and I hesitated in trying to catch Thacker stealing. *Find a way to catch Thacker...now!*

The late hours I worked as a mess orderly prevented me from attending arts and crafts class, so Mr. Wells offered me voice lessons during my afternoon work break. When I walked into the music room, I often found him at the keyboards singing his favorite song. *"Love walked right in and drove the shadows away. Love walked right in and brought my sunniest day..."*

He sang in a beautiful tenor voice, it gave me goose bumps every time I heard him sing.

"Ready for your lesson?" he asked when he saw me.

"Ready as I'll ever be," I said. On earlier lessons, he made me lie on the floor to learn how to breathe through my diaphragm. He said I needed to maintain air pressure to keep my notes from going flat, but the exercise didn't help.

I took several deep breaths as I prepared to sing.

"Relax," he said.

"How can I relax and keep up the pressure at the same time?"

"Breathe deeply, down here," he said as he placed his hands on his lower stomach.

His long fingers danced across the keyboard and I began to sing. *"My grandfather's clock was too big for the shelf, so it stood ninety years on the floor..."*

After I finished the song, he looked up with a doleful look. "Patience," he said. I sounded awful, but he was too kind to tell me.

I placed the sheet music on the table. "Mr. Wells, I've been thinking about quitting, I don't think I'm cut out to be a singer."

Mr. Wells nodded slowly. "Thanks, Nick. Thank you very much." He looked relieved.

He showed me a photo of his wife in a small walnut frame. She was as beautiful as he was handsome, with large brown eyes and a kind face. He visited her on weekends in the Soo.

"She's the reason you sing?" I asked.

He smiled and nodded.

"I got a girlfriend, but all I do is squeak..."

"You have many talents...don't be so hard on yourself."

"Mr. Wells, did you ever have to decide on doing something you thought was right, but might get you into trouble?"

He looked up from his sheet music. "History is filled with stories of people who took a stand for what they believed in and suffered for it."

"How about you?" I asked.

"Yes, even me," he said.

I buttoned up my coat. "What'd *you* do?"

Mr. Wells crossed his arms as he leaned back on the edge of a table—he made the table look small because of his height. "I was punished for challenging the church's authority."

"Was it worth it?"

"It's always right, to do right. Remember the good we do is the good of the Great Spirit...this gives us strength and courage."

"So, I shouldn't be afraid of what happens?"

"What if Abraham Lincoln was afraid of saving the union?"

"Well...it would be a different country."

"Rightly said. If you can make the world a better place by taking a stand for the right, do it and don't fear the consequences."

"Thanks...that helps," I said and stepped out into the cold. His words lifted my spirits and gave me confidence. I walked out convinced I needed a plan to catch Thacker, whatever the risk. The mess sergeant said Thacker planned to make a meat run into Newberry over the weekend, but it was too cold to try a stakeout. With temperatures in the low teens, I could freeze to death sitting outside. He still had meat runs in March and April, so I had more time to come up with a plan. There was another reason I didn't want to go into Newberry that weekend—the girls invited Frank and me to the Soo Winter Carnival!

On Saturday afternoon, Frank and I met Betty and Doris at Brady Park in the Soo. A brisk wind blew smoke from the mills across the St. Mary's river. The snow-covered park buzzed with activity. Children charged through the snow with scarves flying while dads pulled little ones in wooden sleighs.

We stopped and watched a broom-hockey game played on the ice-covered river. I smiled at the crazy antics as the men knocked around a big ball trying to get it into a net. "So *this* is what people do for fun in the winter."

Betty grinned. "Beats shoveling snow."

We walked by some people putting on skis, and a woman invited us to sign up for the one-foot ski race. "C'mon..." Frank said. "Let's try it."

I gave him a skeptical look. "I never skied before."

"Go on," Betty said. "You'll have fun."

I grimaced. "I gotta a bad feeling about this."

After we slipped one of our feet into a bear-trap binding, we lined up with a dozen others for the start of the race. BAMM! A pistol fired and we pushed off. I lost my balance on the first step and tumbled sideways onto the snow. Betty grabbed my arm and helped me up. Once up, she shoved me from behind. "Hurry…you have to catch up!"

I pushed with smaller steps kicking up snow along the way. Fifty yards into the race, I came to a four-foot-high hurdle made from a log attached to two trees. I straddled it and then flipped over on my back with the ski up in the air. People in the crowd cheered me on, but it didn't help. I finished last.

Betty dusted snow off my back after I crossed the line. "I'm proud of you," she said. "You made it."

I pouted. "Barely…"

She held my face in her warm hands. "You know what they say…unlucky in sports, lucky in love."

"Hmmm…maybe last place isn't so bad after all."

She gave my scarf a playful tug. "Don't make a habit of it, Buster."

We headed off to City Hall to see the ice throne. People stood in line waiting to sit on a ten-foot-high throne carved out of blocks of ice. The girls each posed while a newspaper photographer snapped shots.

Afterwards, we got some cups of hot cocoa and watched the parade. People carried skis on their shoulders, a car towed a long toboggan packed with riders, and ice sculpture floats drove by. I marveled how people celebrated their winter.

"I can't figure it out," I said as I watched children dressed as snowflakes ride by.

"What's that?" Betty asked.

"People complain about the cold and then they make a big festival."

"So? People complain about their lives, and then they want to live to be a hundred."

I pulled her close—she flashed a playful grin. "God gave you an extra helping of brains."

"Oh yeah? Then why am I hanging out with you?" She pulled my hat down over my eyes and ran off. I caught up with her outside the train station with Frank and Doris.

"Let's go inside and warm up," Frank said and winked at me. An older couple sat on one of the pews and some children ran around, but the depot was largely empty. Our voices echoed off the wood floors and high ceiling as we made our way to the drinking fountain. I noticed there were little niches to go into for some privacy.

"Let's rest our legs," I said and led Betty around a corner to a short wooden pew. Frank and Doris headed off to the opposite side. Soon, Betty and I snuggled up in a little alcove without a soul in sight. She unbuttoned her coat.

"A penny for your thoughts," I asked quietly.

"You first," she said as she laid her glasses off to the side.

I unbuttoned my coat. "Well, I was thinking how cold my hands are."

"I think I can help that." She took my hands in hers and rubbed then briskly.

"My lips are cold, too," I teased.

"Poor boy," she said and planted a soft kiss on my lips. I slid a hand inside her coat. She giggled. "Don't tickle me." But it was too late—my hand was under her arm.

"Stop it ...c'mon Nick," she pleaded and tried to pull away.

"Okay," I said and gently turned her face toward mine. Her smile melted into mine as our lips came together. I cradled her in my arms. I felt like the luckiest guy on earth.

Just then, I heard the sound of children whispering. I turned around and saw three children duck behind a pew.

"Uh, oh...we've been caught," I said. Betty picked up her glasses.

"Party's over, kids," I said. We heard the sound of boots hitting the floor and saw them scamper off.

We gathered our hats and gloves and then went looking

for Frank and Doris. We found them in a little cubbyhole, necking passionately, so we sat by the door and waited. After a few minutes, Betty yelled, "All aboard...train's leaving!"

Frank and Doris soon emerged from their love nest with flushed faces.

"You two look like you just ran a hundred-yard dash," I said.

"I did...but he caught up to me," Doris said.

"She put up a fight, didn't you, Sweetheart?" Frank teased.

"I bet," Betty said and took Doris' arm.

After a long drink at the water fountain, we stepped out into the cold. Frank and I said good-bye to the girls at the streetcar stop and walked up to our drop-off spot. We squeezed into the truck with the other boys and were soon cruising along snow-covered roads.

I turned to Frank. "I decided to RE-UP."

He smiled. "For another year?"

I nodded.

"I thought you were gonna look for your dad?"

"I want to be with Betty...I'm crazy about her."

Frank rolled his eyes. "You're goofy."

"Finding my dad is a long shot; Betty is a sure thing..."

"I thought she's going to college?"

"So...I'll follow her. I'd go to Siberia to be with her."

Frank shook his head. "You've lost your marbles."

I grinned. "I hope I never find 'em."

"Better get used to the long winters..."

"Betty will keep me warm."

"You're a goner."

I nodded. "I know...I'm crazy about her."

On February 15, a day before my eighteenth birthday, I signed up for re-enlistment at the clerk's office. I figured my chances were fifty-fifty. When I returned from supper, I found a letter on my cot from my mom. I kicked off my shoes and stretched out on the wool blanket. She wrote about Gabe's new life at Camp Newaygo and said some of my pals stopped by the house to say hi. Mom ended the letter by wishing me a happy birthday. I opened up a second letter folded up inside the first. When I read it, my heart stood still. It came from the *Western Pennsylvania Asylum.* I had used my Detroit address in the letters that I sent out inquiring about my dad.

February 3, 1938

Dear Mr. Radzinski,

We are happy to inform you that your father is alive. He has been living here at the asylum since November of last year. Marek was trapped in a coalmine for four days, along with five others, and was rescued unharmed. However, he incurred psychological damage and suffers from delusions and memory loss.

We are pleased to report that your father is in relatively good health; however, he is incapable of caring for himself so he is staying here indefinitely.

You and your family are welcome to visit him, however please be aware that there is a chance he may not recognize family members. Please let us know if you plan to visit so we can make arrangements.

Sincerely,
Gerald Parkhurst, M.D.
Asylum Superintendent

I felt overwhelmed and lay on my cot with the back of my arm over my eyes. I tried to blank out the sound of guys talking a few cots down. It was difficult picturing my father in an insane asylum. Did he wander around in a bathrobe and slippers? Was he able to hold a conversation with people or to feed himself? I imagined the worst. *Oh, Dad, what's happened to you!*

It was heartrending to discover my father in such a pitiful state. This once strong, independent man was a shell of his former self and reduced to a life of dependency. What did he do to deserve it? Was it not enough that he lost his farm? Was it not enough he lost nine children? What did he do to justify four days trapped underground? I felt remorse for the years I condemned him for deserting our family.

How do you make sense out of his life? I remembered what Mr. Wells said that evil was only the upside-down picture of some pre-existing truth. He told me not to be taken in by the outward, but to stay with the inward, which was the real. If that was true, then the picture of my dad as a mentally ill patient was false. What was true? Mr. Wells said the only correct view of something was from the perspective of the Great Spirit and that seemed impossible to figure out.

A troubling thought came to me. Because of Dad's mental state, I would never have a real father again. I felt sorry for myself, it seemed like Dad's bad luck was now my misfortune. Everything in my world seemed dark and gloomy. I wondered what Mr. Wells would say. I kept thinking of his statement that, "All good is the good of the Great Spirit, although it may appear as friends, family, jobs or even food." I pondered this and how it related to my father.

Then, like a burst of sunlight that broke through the clouds after a storm, I understood what he meant. My father was never in person, but remained in the Great Spirit. What appeared as people helping me through my life was always the Great Spirit shining *through* them. Whether that person went by the name of my mom, Lefty the cop, Skip the waffle man, Mrs. Rosenberg or the judge—there was always someone to help and guide me when I needed it!

In the CCC, the Great Spirit shone through people like Isaac, Scruggs, the First Sergeant and Mr. Wells. The good that these people brought into my life was really the Great Spirit, shining through in their words and deeds. At every stage of my life, the Great Spirit placed people in my path who steered me in the right direction. I saw that my anger and resentment toward my father was unfounded because he never was my real father in the first place. The *grudge* I held against him had disappeared after I viewed the Wallace Beery movie. Now, I felt the pangs of *guilt* and *remorse* vanish...like the mist before the morning sun.

I heard a familiar voice. "Nick, hey Nick...you okay?"

I slid my arm off my eyes. "Huh?"

"It's me Frank...remember me, your buddy?"

I sat up. "What time is it?"

"Lights out in ten minutes."

"Oh my gosh." I got up and grabbed my toilet kit. "By the way, I found my dad."

Frank's eyes widened. "What?"

I grabbed my coat. "I'll tell you about it tomorrow."

The next morning in the mess hall, Mr. Kiefer was at the table with me when Mr. Mulligan stopped in. I got up and brought him some coffee and pancake rolls. "Nick, you can stay," the sergeant said, "but not a word about this to anyone."

I organized my workstation and listened in as the sergeant spoke to the head cook. "A general is coming by tomorrow for a surprise inspection," he said. "Make the kitchen a little neater than usual, but not too neat...and don't let anyone in on it."

Mr. Kiefer nodded. Then they discussed other business. I felt privileged that the sergeant let me hear inside information. Officers rarely confided camp business to enrollees, so the sergeant showed a lot of trust in me. I found out the next day just how much faith he had in me.

I had just finished stacking some dishes, when a clerk came and told me to report to the captain as soon as possible. My pulse quickened. *What the heck is this about?* I threw on my coat and ran to the captain's office where he, the sergeant, and a general sat around a table.

"Reporting as ordered, sir," I said standing at attention. Cigar smoke filled the room like a blue fog.

At ease," the captain said. "Thanks for joining us. I'd like you to accompany the general on his inspection. Answer any questions he may have."

"Yes, sir," I said. I knew that visiting brass invited enrollees to accompany them so they could get straight answers to their questions. I glanced at the sergeant—he gave me a little nod of encouragement. *I hope I say the right thing!*

March arrived like a lamb and the mild weather created a hazy mist over the snow-covered grounds in camp. The four of us cut across the quad to the equipment building. The general asked me when it was last painted.

"I think last week, general." The sergeant grimaced. I said the wrong thing!

"Interesting," the general said holding back a little smile. "How's the food, Nick?"

"I put on about fifteen pounds in the past ten months, general."

"It *must* be good," he said nodding. The sergeant and captain looked happier with that answer.

For the next hour, we toured almost every building in camp, from the icehouse to the blacksmith shop. The general asked the sergeant technical questions while he queried me about work routines, camp morale and maintenance. At the end of the tour, the general turned to the captain. "You've got a damn good camp here."

The captain smiled broadly. "That's because I got a *damn good* First Sergeant."

Mr. Mulligan kept a stiff upper lip as the general gripped his hand. "Keep up the good work."

Then the general turned to me. "Thank you for your time."

"You're welcome, General," I said and nodded. I hustled back to the mess hall to prepare for supper. *I wish Lefty the beat cop could have seen me on that tour!*

Mr. Mulligan came to work the next morning with bags under his eyes. I set out a plate of three neatly rolled pancakes filled with raspberry jam for his mid-morning snack. "What's wrong, Pops? You don't look so good," I said.

He rubbed the back of his neck. "The general gave us the word yesterday that we're still on the list for camp closings."

I poured him a cup of coffee. "That's terrible...how soon?"

He gave me a sharp eye. "You don't know about this... got it?"

"Yes, sir."

He took a large bite and chewed slowly. "Let me put it this way...if you're approved for re-enlistment, you might have to finish up at another camp." It dawned on me the sergeant was out of a job if they closed the camp.

"Any luck in finding the thief?" I asked.

The sergeant slurped his coffee. "Nothing...but it's probably more than one," he said. "They're even hitting the canteen at night." He said the general grilled him about the stealing problem. "Don't breathe a word of this to anyone... there are enough rumors already."

"I understand."

"I need you to be my eyes and ears, but don't ask too many questions...people know you and I see each other here."

"I'll keep my eyes peeled, Pops."

He wrapped his scarf around his neck in front of the door. "I'm counting on you, Nick," he said and stepped out. Suddenly, I remembered that last week someone tailed me after work on my way back to the barracks. I wondered if they suspected I was stealing from the canteen. *What the hell is happening to this camp?*

Over the next few days, I asked a few of my closest friends if they had heard of anyone working with a fence. I got blank looks. Even if someone knew something, it was doubtful he would snitch. It confirmed my suspicion that the thief was *not* an enrollee.

Later that week, the kitchen clerk gave me a few dollars and told me to pick up some eggs from a local farmer. When the clerk handed me the car keys, I asked him if Thacker was picking up the corned beef this month.

He gave me a funny look. "Yeah, he does every month... are you gunning for his job?"

I shook my head. "No, but if he can't do it...I can fill in."

"We'll see. Drive carefully with those eggs."

"Yes, sir." Fifteen minutes later, a farmer with a wind-burned face dressed in a heavy overcoat greeted me as I drove up his muddy drive. He led me past the chicken coop to his barn. "I suppose you wanna taste one to see if they're any good," he said.

"Oh no, I trust you," I said.

"Aw, fiddlesticks...don't be ashamed. These are fresh this week." He took out his pocketknife and sliced off the top of an egg. Then, he tilted his head and poured it down his throat. "It's good," he said and smacked his lips.

He picked up a second egg, cut off the top and offered it to me. I hesitated. "Go on...don't be afraid," he said.

I looked at the raw egg and then up at him. He gave me a menacing look. "What's the matter, not good enough for ya?"

I took the egg, poured it in my mouth and swallowed. I heaved a couple of times and almost spit up. The old man patted me on the back. "That wasn't so bad was it?"

We loaded four boxes of eggs in the trunk, and I paid him six cents a dozen, a penny above market. The camp thought higher prices helped neighbor relations.

As I drove through the village of Raco on my way back to camp, I noticed Mr. Thacker walking out of the post office! I pulled off Main Street and backtracked to the old caboose, which served as the post office. They had taken off the wheels and painted the old train car green instead of red. I stomped the dirt off my boots and stepped in. A strong-looking woman with a wide face stood behind the counter doing paperwork. "What can I do for you, young man?"

"I need five postcards please," I said. "I noticed our supply sergeant was just here."

She counted out the cards. "Yep...Ned's a regular."

I laid a nickel and five pennies on the counter. "How often does he come?"

She took the coins. "Oh...every other week."

"Why doesn't he use the camp post office?"

She shrugged. "Maybe the packages are too heavy."

"That makes sense," I said. "Thank you ma'am." I tipped my hat and turned to the door.

I stepped out into the cold. *I hit pay dirt!* Thacker used the post office in town because he was hiding something! But, it created another riddle. Why would he mail a package to Hot Harry's if he drove to Newberry every month? Maybe he never stopped at Hot Harry's, or he sent the packages somewhere else. All I knew was Thacker had no business shipping packages from a local post office when he could mail them from camp.

A few days later I heard the door open in the officers' mess hall. "Any pancakes that need a home?" It was the sergeant.

"You bet, Pops. I've been waitin' for you," I said and picked up the coffee pot.

He unbuttoned his coat. "Oh...it's a cold one today," he said. I put out three pancakes rolled up with strawberry jam and sprinkled powdered sugar on them. He took a quick bite and washed it down with coffee. "Nick, I gotta talk to you about Agnes."

"What's wrong?"

"She can't sleep in your barracks anymore."

"Do we have to get rid of her?"

"Oh, no...she can stay in my office. I'll let her out when the fellas get back from work duty."

"That's great...she'll keep you company."

The door opened and an equipment room orderly stepped

in and removed his cap. Earl planned to go home because his parents found him a job. The bushy-haired boy with big ears slammed the door behind him. "Sorry to disturb you..."

"That's all right—what's up?" the sergeant said.

He stammered. "Well...I just want to see if I could stay a few extra days to say good-bye to all my friends."

The sergeant turned to me and winked. "Well, I got a lot of paperwork...and I could use a few more days to finish it."

"Oh, thank you very much, sir," the boy said.

"We'll miss you, Earl. Good luck with your new job."

"Thank you, sir." He turned and left.

Mr. Mulligan chuckled.

"That's a nice thing you did, Pops," I said.

He frowned. "I didn't do anything, so don't tell anyone I did...understand?"

"I won't," I said and grinned. I decided it was a good time to ask him something on my mind. "Pops, I want to buy Isaac a new set of teeth for his birthday." The sergeant's eyebrows shot up. "Can I sit by the clerk on pay day and ask the fellas to donate a dime?"

The sergeant sipped his coffee. "How much do you need?"

"There's a dentist in the Soo that'll make a plate for fourteen bucks."

"It's a good idea...I'll run it by the captain and get back."

"Thanks..."

"Oh, and if I get the okay, don't forget to hit up the officers."

"Good idea."

He wiped some jam from his lips with a napkin. "How do I look?"

"Clean as a whistle, Pops." The sergeant smiled whenever I called him Pops. He bundled up and stepped out into the cold. I stood at the window and watched him lean into the driving wind as he made his way across the quad. I loved working inside. The meat patrols were the best thing I ever did.

Strong winds buffeted the camp over the next few days. With Thacker's run into Newberry coming up on Saturday, I asked Frank again if he would help me on the stakeout. The cold weather made it dangerous to go alone.

I quietly brought up the subject while we played cribbage in the rec hall. "If I can help, I will," he said. "But don't ask me to put my butt on the line. I got six more months here, and I don't want to get kicked out."

I nodded and said nothing.

When Saturday rolled around, it turned out to be a blustery day, too cold to sit outside and wait. I decided to postpone the stakeout until April when the weather was warmer.

The captain approved my request to collect money for Isaac's teeth so that afternoon I sat with a donation jar while the boys were paid. The captain told me not to beg, so I made a little sign that read, *PLEASE GIVE TEN CENTS FOR ISAAC'S NEW TEETH.* I found a guy to draw a caricature of Isaac in suspenders and holding a giant toothbrush up to a toothy grin.

The second lieutenant counted the money for each enrollee and handed it to the clerk who then recounted it. Then, the clerk gave it to the boy receiving the money and *he* had to count it. They counted the money three times to make sure it was correct. While I sat at the table, I reached down and stroked the back of Agnes' head. She stared up at me with sad copper-brown eyes and tongue hanging out half a foot. One of the boys had spanked her for putting teeth marks in a ping-pong ball, so she needed some loving attention.

About four out of five boys put a dime in the jar. Some begged off and said their money went to pay off debts or they sent it home to their parents. When payroll ended, I emptied the jar and counted the coins. It added up to $16.30! I also planned to ask the officers for donations. Any extra money would go to buy Isaac a gift certificate at a department store so he could get fitted with some new clothes.

That night I walked over to the captain's quarters to check the bulletin board for re-enlistment announcements. The wind died down and it was quiet except for the sound of my boots scraping across the sandy sidewalk. A dim light bulb barely lit up the typed list of names posted on the board. I put my nose up to the glass and read. Then, I saw it...Radzinski, Nicolas! They approved my RE-UP! The sergeant must have put in a good word for me.

I flew back to the barracks to tell Frank and the others, but when I reached the steps, I pulled up. I decided to keep quiet about it. If I botched my stakeout with Thacker, they would boot me out of camp. Even if I succeeded, they might *still* kick me out. I took a turn around the quad to clear my thoughts. My approval for re-enlistment put everything in a new light regarding Thacker.

Frank convinced me it was a big deal to go after the supply sergeant. If things went wrong, everything I worked so hard to get could be lost. My job, my friendships, and income would all go down the tube if they sent me home. Then, there was Betty. How could I risk losing those smiles and kisses!

The bitter cold wind gave me shivers. By the time I took a second turn past the captain's quarters, I made up my mind. I couldn't let the guys down. I owed it to my buddies, no matter what the risk. I owed it to the First Sergeant, to the L.E.M.s, the forest officers and everyone else in camp, to give it my best shot. Besides, how could things go wrong? If Thacker showed, I would report him and let the sergeant do the investigating. If he *didn't* show up, I would keep my mouth shut and no one would know what I did. Frank blew it all out of proportion; it really wasn't such a big deal.

A warm breeze blew in from the south as I walked across the quad a few days later. It was mid-morning and I heard the birds chirping while I carried some jam-filled pancakes and thermos of coffee to Isaac. I heard he had a touch of the melancholy, so I thought a little treat might cheer him up. I found him sitting on a stool by a window, sharpening a crosscut saw. Even with an overcast sky, the window provided plenty of light for him to work with. He carefully slid the thin file between the saw teeth.

"Oh...dat's a nice surprise," Isaac said when he saw me. He wore about four layers of shirts and underwear, each one a different color.

"Only the best for Isaac," I said and poured some coffee into a dented tin cup. He showed me my turtle carving which he had coated with shellac until it glowed to a nice sepia color. "It's beautiful," I said, turning it over in my hands.

He sat down to eat, and we talked about my latest carving of Agnes. Isaac tore into the rolled pancakes, chewing with his gums. It took him about three times longer to chew than the sergeant. "What's been bothering you?" I asked.

"Aw...you know what's goin' on. Dem dieves are stealin' me blind. Saws, axes, peaveys—and dey go fer da new stuff." He gulped his coffee.

"Don't let it get you down...who do you think it is?"

He swallowed hard. "If I knew, I'd string him up myself."

"Someone will find him, you just wait and see," I said.

He wiped blueberry jam off his big mustache with a filthy handkerchief. "Yeah, but it's too late....dey close six camps dis fall and maybe we get da axe."

I poured more coffee. "Don't worry, they'll find a new place for you if they do."

"I dunno," he said and looked out the window. "Der be so many jacks—ain't enough camps to hire us all."

"I heard the economy's getting better...there might be more jobs out there."

Isaac looked glum and set the cup down. "People don't hire ol' jacks, dere's only da poor house fer me."

The mid-morning light from the window gave his face a soft glow and erased many of his wrinkles. He showed a gentleness that belied his hard life. We chatted a bit about his days in the lumber camps and then I put the cap on the thermos. "Well, I gotta go," I said. "Keep your chin up. Good things are happening."

He smiled a toothless grin. "Danks fer dinkin' of me."

It amazed me that Isaac was worried about finding a job when he had so many skills. Walking back to the mess hall, I thought about what he had said about tools disappearing. The thief had easy access to the equipment room. *It must be one of the staff, so it has to be Thacker!*

If the camp operated another year or two, the economy might improve enough for Isaac and the others to get good jobs. They deserved another year of work, and I was the person to make sure it happened. Every day seemed to give me new reasons to pursue a stakeout at Hot Harry's!

The following Saturday, I rode the truck to the Soo for a date with Betty. A warm spell turned the landscape brown and barren. A gentle mist fell as the truck roared over wet country roads lined with dirt and gravel left over from the winter road crews. I reflected on my life, which seemed caught in an awkward balance. On one hand, there was the peace and stability of life in the camp. On the other, I was prepared to lose everything to catch a thief. I figured it was a good time to level with her about my future in case things didn't work out the way I planned.

I bought a carnation from a woman outside the Gould's dance hall before I stepped inside. Betty stood talking with her friends near the ticket window when I entered. She looked dazzling and carried herself with self-confidence. I approached slowly and relished her beauty. She was dressed with flair in a rose-colored dress that went just below her knees. Her soft blond hair curled around her ear and fell almost to her shoulders. She caught me staring and broke into a smile.

"Hi," I said.

"Hi…oh, how sweet." She took the white carnation from my hand and pinned it on her dress. "Thanks, Nick." We paid the door charge and were soon dancing to a Johnny Mercer tune. I must have been stiff. "Is anything wrong?" she asked.

"Well…a lot of my friends are going home soon," I said.

She grinned. "Well, this one isn't." She squeezed my hand. "C'mon, cheer up."

I swallowed hard. The thought of losing Betty tore me up inside. "I'm so lucky to know you," I said softly in her ear.

"Me, too," she said.

We left the dance hall early and took the streetcar to the locks. The cold water of Lake Superior kept the city in a damp chill. The street lamps glowed in a misty fog, casting mysterious shadows into the night. Betty held my arm as we approached the water. The lights of a freighter blinked in the darkness as it passed through the channel. Betty talked about her family's upcoming Easter vacation to Colonial Williamsburg.

"Maybe we'll be on the same train when I visit my dad in Pennsylvania," I said.

She tightened her grip on my arm. "Wouldn't that be neat?"

We walked along the edge of the locks where the air smelled of diesel fuel and the low rumble from the engines filled our ears. After a while, we found a bench. I wiped it dry with my handkerchief before we sat down. We watched the freighter float by at a snail's pace

Without thinking, I asked, "Ever wonder when your ship will come in?"

She turned and smiled softly. "No…it already has."

I gave her a mock look of surprise. "Don't look at me… I'm as free as a bird."

She gave me a playful grin with wide eyes. "That's what *you* think."

A foghorn sounded a warning off in the distance. *Now I'm in trouble, but it's the kind of trouble I like!* I leaned forward and found her warm lips willing. After a few gentle kisses, she reached for her glasses. "Let's get rid of these," she said.

I playfully rubbed my nose against hers. "I like it when there's nothing between us." She giggled, and I kissed her forehead. "The closer you are the more beautiful you look," I whispered.

She stroked the side of my face with the back of her hand. "The closer you are...the more interesting *you* look."

"Interesting?"

She traced my lips with her finger and gave me a sly grin. "Your smile is a little crooked..."

"Thanks a lot..."

She ran her finger down my nose. "Your nose is...how can I say it?"

"It's bent...just say it."

"No...it's got character."

Then she ran her fingers in my hair. "Now, you're going to say my hair is like a mop."

She tugged at it playfully. "It's...it's like fur."

I growled in her ear. "Grrrr...*now* you're in trouble, Little Red Riding Hood.

"Please don't eat me Mr. Wolf."

I pulled back a little. "You're lucky...I forgot my salt and pepper."

She giggled. I pressed my lips to hers. Her mouth was watery and inviting. Her tongue darted lightly into my mouth, I felt my passion rising.

"Oh, Nick," she moaned and peppered the side of my face with kisses. "I care about you." Her body trembled as I kissed the nape of her neck. The scent of her perfume was intoxicating.

Just then, we heard the footsteps of people approaching. We pulled apart while a man and a woman walked by. "Whew," she said. "Are you warm, too?"

"Boiling," I said.

She cuddled up to me and asked, "Wouldn't it be nice to take a cruise to Hawaii someday?"

I toyed with her hand. "I better start going to the race track."

An older couple walked by. "Why?" she asked

"To bet...that's the only way I could ever afford to take you anywhere nice."

"Oh, Nick...you're going to do great things with your life. Why do you talk like that?"

I sighed. "I'm a high school drop-out."

"But, can't you go back?"

"I got lousy grades...they'll just tell me to go to trade school."

She stroked my hand. Even in the faint light, I saw the frown on her face. "You have to reach for the stars..."

"I'll do okay...but, I'll probably work in a factory. I'll be a guy who comes home with dirty fingernails."

"You have to shoot higher..."

"Just because I'll never be in your class doesn't mean we can't be friends now."

She sat up straight. "What do you mean...in *my class*?"

"You're high-class, you're going to college..."

"So?"

"So...you're going to meet a guy who's gonna be a professor or a banker...someone who'll buy you a nice house and fill it with Grand Rapids furniture."

"How do you know?"

I took her hand. "I just know." Her eyes welled up with tears. "You deserve the best, Betty. The best right now won't be the best a year or two from now."

I took out my handkerchief and she wiped her eyes. "What you're saying is...you're like that ship. One day you'll be sailing out."

I bit my lower lip and nodded. "It's for the best..."

She sniffled. "Let's not talk about it anymore."

I lifted her chin up with my finger and smiled. "Hey...as long as I'm in this town, you're my girl. Don't *ever* forget that."

"Thanks...for helping me see things better."

"Sure...but don't stop wearing your glasses." It was a lame joke, but it worked.

She smiled and picked them up. We stood and walked off into the foggy night. "For a guy with a crooked nose...you're a straight shooter, Nick."

"Betty, you got it all wrong. My *smile* is crooked...the *nose* is bent."

She clung to my arm and laughed. "Oh, Nick...how I love you."

Thacker's next meat run into Newberry was Saturday. As I went about my duties during the week, I considered all the possible things that could happen during a stakeout. I debated whether to take a knife to protect myself and wear sneakers so I could outrun any trouble. I decided to tell Frank my plans and to give him instructions on what to do in case I didn't return as planned. We strolled around the quad after supper on Tuesday night trying to avoid patches of ice that formed from melted snow.

"You're walking into a hornets' nest," Frank warned. "Hot Harry could rough you up if he catches you."

"He's *not* even gonna to see me..."

"You still better be careful." Frank suggested I take food and dress extra-warm in case I got stuck on an empty road.

"If you're so concerned, why don't you come with me?"

"If we were off-duty, I'd do it. But, I'm not skipping clean-up...that's pretty damn serious."

"That's when he goes...I got no choice."

Frank shook his head. "You better have a good excuse when you come back."

The following afternoon, an announcement came over

the loudspeaker as enrollees unloaded from their trucks. I stood on the mess hall steps with a broom in my hand and listened to the company clerk.

"May I have your attention...for all of those enrollees leaving next week, today is your chance to drag your commanding officers through the mud." A cheer went up across the camp. "The fun begins in ten minutes at the mud pit."

The mess sergeant gave me permission to run down and watch the shenanigans for a little while. The warm weather and rainy spring produced ideal mud conditions. When I arrived, I saw two enrollees dragging Mr. Mulligan on his back by the legs. Mud covered him from head to toe. He egged them on as they slipped in the slick mud. "C'mon... can't you do better than that!"

I smiled to myself. I could hardly believe the sergeant let the guys do that to him. Was he really the same man, who sent me to mosquito-infested blueberry patches and made me empty the grease pit? It dawned on me that while his job required him to be tough, he never lost his sense of humor. Today was payback, and he enjoyed the fun as much as the boys did.

It also occurred to me that the officers and enrollees were not much different when covered with mud. In fact, we were not much different without the mud. We both came to the CCC to find work. The older men with experience became officers, while the younger ones enlisted as enrollees. Other than our age difference, we were in the same boat. The guy who dreamed up the CCC must have been a genius.

I walked back to the mess hall while other boys hurried by on their way to the mud pit. When I saw Agnes bounding along with the guys, I decided to put a stop to it. "Agnes... come here, girl," I yelled and clapped my hands. She ran over panting with her tongue out. I rubbed her head. "I'm not going to let you get all muddy." I threw a stick to divert her from the boys and walked her back to the mess hall. The thought came to me that if Camp Raco was not here—I never would have found Agnes on the roadside.

Chapter 10

Stakeout

The big day finally arrived for the stakeout. The early morning sun and southwest breeze promised a warm day, a good sign. After I served the officers their breakfast, I sat down for my own, but I hardly touched my food. I felt like an athlete with a big race ahead. I wanted to get moving.

The most difficult part of the day would be hitching a ride in the back of Thacker's truck. It was the only way to get into town, since no one wanted to loan me a car during morning cleanup. The fellas who owned cars figured if they helped me skip out of work duty, they could get into big trouble and lose their car.

The crew leader put me to work with five other boys raking grass in the quad. I kept an eye on the officers' quarters to see when Thacker came out of his officers' meeting. It usually ended around nine-thirty, sometimes later. From there I knew he walked to the garage, checked out a truck and drove it to the icehouse to pick up the empty barrels. If things went according to plan, I would catch a ride in the back of his pickup truck.

At nine forty-two, the officers came out. I took a deep breath. "Hey, guys," I said to a couple other boys, "I got something important to do. Can you cover for me?"

"Sure," one said. "You comin' back?"

I grinned. "I sure hope so." I dropped the rake and made a beeline for the icehouse. I knew Thacker would back the pickup close to the icehouse, so I hid around the corner and waited. Sure enough, within ten minutes I saw him heading my way in a dark green Chevy pickup. My heart pounded. This was it!

Crouched behind the icehouse, I listened as he put the truck in reverse and backed up. I heard the truck door open and the sound of feet crunch along the gravel path. He unlatched the back gate. One by one, he rolled the empty barrels out of the icehouse and hoisted them into the truck. After the sixth, he latched the gate and climbed into the truck. I waited until I heard some yelling. It was Frank acting as a distraction.

I peeked around the corner and saw him run up with a jar in his hands. "Mr. Thacker," he said, short of breath, "can you get me some gas when you're in town?" That was my cue. I ran bent at the waist straight for the truck. It took me about ten steps to get there. I knelt behind the back gate and listened.

"You know the rules about motor bikes..." Thacker said.

"Just this once," Frank pleaded. I put my hand on the bumper and waited to feel any movement. Frank stood on the sideboard and gently rocked the truck. That was my cue. I quickly straddled the rear gate, slid down on my belly, and crawled over the cold, grimy floor. I needed to be directly under Thacker's rear window or else he could see me.

"Well...just this once," Thacker said. The engine turned over.

As we drove off, I saw the top of Frank's head. If Thacker stopped on his way out, someone might see me so I laid low and hoped the barrels blocked me from sight. Thacker drove slowly through camp to keep the barrels from tipping over. Finally, we passed under the log beam over the camp entrance. I made it out of camp!

The ride into Newberry gave me time to think about my strategy. I sat with my back against the cab, only inches from Thacker, and toyed with my buck knife. The layers of clothes I wore kept me warm against the chilly wind that blew in. I guessed Thacker would visit his sister, the meat-packing house, and Hot Harry's, but not in that particular order. I planned to jump off the truck when we came to the second stop sign in town and walk directly to Hot Harry's. Elliot had drawn me a layout of the city streets and marked where the stop signs were. I needed to walk quickly, in case Thacker stopped at the fence's house first.

Once I located Hot Harry's, I needed to find a hiding place. If that wasn't possible, I planned to walk through the neighborhood and keep a safe distance away. All I needed to do was see Thacker's pickup, and then my work was over. Even Frank thought the plan made sense. He promised to stay in camp in case I phoned. He could borrow a car and pick me up if needed.

After an hour or so, I felt the pickup slow down as we came to the first stop sign. We were still outside of Newberry, with few buildings in sight. I kept my eye out for the high school Elliot said to watch for. When the large brick school came into view on our left, I prepared to bail, but a sedan full of kids pulled right up behind us at the stop sign. I ducked out of sight and lay on the floor. Thacker continued driving into the downtown.

I became anxious because there was a greater chance of someone seeing me jump out in town. I crawled to the rear of the truck bed and put my back against one of the barrels to block Thacker's view. We drove by an insurance agency, a gas station, and a restaurant. Finally, we came to a stop sign—the coast was clear! I swung my leg over the gate using the barrels to shield me from Thacker's view and lowered myself carefully to avoid rocking the truck. A rush of excitement swept over me as I casually walked off in Thacker's blind side.

When I stepped up on the sidewalk, I noticed a barber standing near his window sharpening a razor on a leather strap. He gave me a curious look. I nodded and continued walking. With a map in hand, I turned down a neighborhood street. I was on my way!

A few blocks into the neighborhood, I heard a vehicle pull up beside me. I looked over my shoulder and saw a black police car! A gray-haired officer with heavy jowls rolled down his window. "What brings you into town, young man?" He asked in a skeptical tone.

I became tongue-tied. "Oh...ah...doing some shopping."

"The town's back there." He said and stuck his thumb out.

"Oh, I know...I just wanted to see what the neighborhoods are like." It was a weak excuse.

He looked me over and frowned. "We don't like strangers in our neighborhoods. Why don't you jump in my car, I'll give you a lift back to town."

I opened the door and slid onto the red cloth seat. The car reeked of cigar smoke.

He glanced over. "So tell me...why'd you jump out of that CCC truck?"

My stomach dropped like an elevator. The barber called him! "Oh that?" I said nonchalantly. "I got a lift from the supply sergeant. He'll pick me up after he takes care of some business."

The cop's eyes narrowed. "Oh, yeah? I'd like to meet your supply sergeant," he put the car in gear. "Where can we find him?"

My jaw clenched. "Maloney Meats," I replied.

A few minutes later, we pulled up to a gray plank building the size of a barn. I breathed easier—Thacker's truck was nowhere in sight! Out on the loading dock a short, wiry man dressed in overalls was rolling barrels around. The cop got out and asked about Thacker.

"You just missed him," the man shouted. "He's on his way to see his sister."

"Really?" the cop asked. "Who's that?"

The man grinned. "Thelma Thacker."

"You don't say," the cop snickered and pushed back his hat. The man came down and the two talked a few minutes about a bear reported in the neighborhood. After a few minutes, the cop returned.

"You belong with your supply sergeant, but I'm not taking you to Pine Stump Junction." He drove me into town and stopped in front of a movie theater. "Now, get out and stay in town. Don't go wandering around in our neighborhoods."

"Yes, sir," I said.

"And keep out of our bars."

"Yes, sir," I said, relieved. I had dodged a bullet. The early afternoon sun felt warm on my back as I made my way up the sidewalk. I took off my heavy field jacket. The local people I passed on the street lacked the style of those in the Soo. Women wore boots more often than high heels and overalls instead of dresses. I studied my map and tried to figure a way to find Hot Harry's without walking in the neighborhood. I could take a cab to get there, but how could I get out afterward?

I decided to find out how far it was to Pine Stump Junction. Then I could calculate when Thacker might return. I folded the map and walked across the street to a drugstore. A couple guys who looked like salesmen with rolled up shirtsleeves, sat at the end of the lunch counter. I hopped onto a stool and ordered lemonade from a curvy tart in her thirties. She went a bit heavy on the pancake makeup.

"How long is it to Pine Stump Junction?" I asked her.

"A half-hour or so. What takes you up there?"

"There's someone I might visit."

"Oh, yeah? Who's that?"

I hesitated.

She gave me a playful grin. "C'mon…no secrets in this town."

"Thelma Thacker."

"Thelma?" Her mouth opened. "No kidding?"

I stuttered. "Well, ah…maybe."

"Hey, Otis," she said in nearly a shout. "This fella wants to go up to Pine Stump and see Thelma."

The man smiled. "What for?"

She turned to me. "Looking for work at her lumber camp?"

I lied. "Yeah…thinking about it."

"So, how'd you hear about Thelma?"

"I know her brother at a CCC camp."

"Ned?" She asked. I nodded and sipped my drink. "Thelma's one tough cookie. You know she killed her husband don't you?" I gagged, spitting out lemonade all over her counter. "Easy does it." She picked up a cloth and wiped up the spill. As she leaned over, she exposed the top part of her breasts. She caught me looking, smiled and winked.

I blushed. "Sorry for the mess I made," I mumbled. "So what happened?"

"He used to beat her up when he got drunk."

"Terrible…"

"He went after her in the kitchen with a belt, but she grabbed a knife and got to him first."

"Geez…"

The waitress glanced over her shoulder and lowered her voice. "They say another man was in the house at the time…some people think *he* had something to do with the killing."

"Son of a gun." She picked up a pitcher and refilled my glass. "Did Thelma go to jail?" I asked.

"Nope, she got off because of all the bruises on her body…the jury felt sorry for her."

"How 'bout the guy in the house..."

"Never proved."

I said nothing, shaking my head in disbelief.

She smacked her lips and grinned. "So...*still* want to go out there?"

I looked away. "Well, I don't know..."

"If you go...be careful."

I nodded and fingered my glass. "Did Thelma get the camp when her husband died?"

"Yep, she runs it with her boyfriend, Rusty. He takes care of the logging part while she cooks and runs the store."

I winced. *Thelma runs a lumber camp store? That's where the stolen goods are going!*

The woman noticed my reaction. "Something wrong?"

"Oh, no. I just thought of something."

"If you're a friend of Ned's that'll help get you a job. But don't cross her."

I shook my head. "Oh, no...believe me, I wouldn't *dream* of crossing her.

She chuckled and went off to wait on a couple that sat down a few seats away. It gave me time to think. *Do I really want to go up there?* With my enlistment ending in a few days, I wanted to get it over with.

When she returned, I asked, "Is the camp hard to find?"

She flipped over a place mat. "I'll draw you a map." She picked up a pencil and sketched out roads and landmarks. "If you go by the schoolhouse, you've gone too far. You thumbing it?"

I nodded.

The woman turned to the men. "Either of you fellas headed north? This CCC boy can use a lift to Pine Stump."

"Yeah," one of them said. "I'll take him part-way."

Five minutes later, I opened the rusty door to the man's Ford Woody and climbed up onto a patched seat. Vacuum cleaner parts lay scattered across the floor. I found out he sold vacuums door-to-door with the eastern U.P. as his territory. He asked about my work in camp, so I talked about planting trees and clearing roads. The man said no timber was coming out of the woods lately because of the spring thaw, but loggers still cut trees. "Don't tangle with anybody up there," he said when he dropped me off. "Some of those men work out there for more than one reason."

"I'll remember that," I said. "Thanks for the lift." It took about ten minutes before a farmer picked me up in a rickety Model A. He dropped me off at the two-track that led back to the lumber camp. I stepped carefully on the muddy trail that went through a sparsely wooded area. The warm sun made it feel like it was fifty degrees. I only saw a couple patches of snow in the woods.

After I walked a mile or so, second thoughts filled my head about what I was doing. The waitress' story about Thelma and her boyfriend knocking off her husband gave me goose bumps. Nobody knew where I was except the vacuum cleaner salesman and the waitress! I should have called the camp and left a message, but everything happened too fast.

I planned to check out the store and get out of the camp as fast as I could. If Thacker visited his sister directly after the meat house, he probably arrived a good hour ahead of me. That gave him plenty of time to unload his goods, have a cup of coffee, and hit the road. If I spotted his truck, I would hide in the woods until he left. With any luck, the loggers would be off working in the woods. Suddenly, I heard a car approach. I jumped off the trail and knelt behind a big stump. A gray sedan drove by, so I waited until the coast was clear. Further down the road, I came around a bend and saw chimney smoke rise above the trees. I found the lumber camp!

Lumberjack camps were a thing of the past, since most men lived at home and drove to work—but a few camps remained that housed single men. A dozen beat-up cars and trucks stretched along the road leading up to the camp, so I knew some of the loggers drove in to work. Thacker's pickup was nowhere in sight, so I kept walking.

Half a dozen ramshackle, cedar-sided buildings, arranged in no special order, made up the camp. Red long johns and overalls hung from a clothesline. Neatly stacked piles of stove wood stood next to each building. I stayed clear of the kitchen where smoke poured out its chimney. Instead, I made my way past a blacksmith shop and equipment building full of lumber tools. I stuck my head in one of the bunkhouses and saw messy beds covered with nightclothes and old magazines. Then, I came to a small, dark-stained wood building with a board nailed over the door with the word "Wanigan" painted on it. It was the camp store, but the door was padlocked! I circled around the building, but found no windows.

I needed to find someone to let me in the store, so I went to the kitchen. The warped door scratched the floor as I shoved it open. I stepped cautiously into the mess hall where two rows of picnic-like tables were already set for lunch. The room smelled like liver and onions, but I was in no mood to eat. I heard the sound of pot lids clinking.

"Hello?" I shouted and walked through the swinging doors. I saw a stout woman chopping a side of beef at a butcher block. Her eyebrows shot up when she saw me. She raised her cleaver shoulder height and bared her teeth. "Don't take another step if you know what's good for ya!" she bellowed.

I stepped back and threw my hands up. "I don't mean any harm."

She lowered the cleaver. Thelma was a handsome woman with ruddy skin and thick gray streaked hair tied back off her face. She gave me an intimidating look. "So, what's your business?" She snapped.

"I'm a CCC boy and I'm looking for work."

"You running from trouble?"

"I'm always in trouble—too many rules in camp."

"You look kind of young."

"I'm eighteen, ma'am."

"Call me Thelma...so why should I hire you?"

"I can handle an axe and saw...and I'm a hard worker."

She set down the cleaver. "How soon can you work?"

"I can be back in a couple days—just need to get my clothes."

Thelma pulled a pan of rolls from the oven. "You can stay for lunch and talk to the foreman about work."

"Thank you ma'am...the food smells good."

"Thanks..."

"Do you have any hats in your store? I said casually. I lost mine when I was thumbing out here."

She shot me a sideways glance. "How'd you know we had a store?"

"I saw it coming over here."

"Took a little tour of my camp, eh?"

"I was looking for people..."

She slapped a lid on a pot. "I can take you there for a few minutes...no more." She untied her apron.

She moved briskly toward the door and I followed her outside to the store. She took a key ring off her belt loop and opened the padlock. Then she stepped inside and pulled a string to a light bulb. My eyes adjusted slowly to the dimly lit room, I could barely contain my excitement. The room overflowed with clothes and tools from our camp! I recognized the pants piled on the shelves and half a dozen field jackets hanging on hooks. Axes, peaveys, and saws stood neatly organized in racks. She probably made a good side income selling the tools and clothes to the loggers.

"The hats are over here," Thelma said and pulled open a drawer. I tried on a couple of caps with a medium-wide brim.

"This fits just right," I said and reached in my pocket for money.

"Fifty cents," she said. "So what camp did you come from?"

I lied. "Ah...Camp Rexton."

"Is Captain Bradley still running your camp?"

"Yes, ma'am."

"We had a fella from there last year...good worker." She locked up the door and we headed back to the kitchen. "I need to get something from my house...c'mon, I'll show you around."

I followed her down a cinder path that led to a tarpaper-sided house set back from the lumber camp by fifty yards. She pointed to a fenced-in area. "That's where I plant my vegetables." She nudged the door open with her shoulder.

I felt a little nervous. "I can wait out here," I said.

"I'll be right back," she said and stepped inside. I settled onto a bench on the porch. The warm sunshine filtered in through the cleared-out area. Things worked out better than I thought. After lunch, I would thumb it back to camp and tell the sergeant what I found. After a few minutes, I heard the door open. I looked up over my shoulder—she held a rifle and it was pointed at me!

"Stay right there," she ordered. "Give me your wallet." My heart raced as I reached into my back pocket. "Throw it over here," she barked. I tossed it to where she stood about ten feet away. She kept the rifle trained on me as she picked it up. Then, she pulled out my camp I.D. and examined it.

"Camp Rexton, eh? This says Raco. You got some explaining to do." She had tricked me when she asked about Captain Bradley!

I stammered. "I didn't want you to know what camp I came from, in case you reported me. I skipped clean-up duty and could get in big trouble."

She stuck the card in the wallet and tossed it back to me. "I don't buy that...you were in an awful hurry to get in my store."

"I needed a hat..."

"Cut the baloney. You trailed my brother out here today. Get in the house...now." She waved the gun at me. The dusky room smelled of moldy furniture and dirty clothes. She pointed her gun to a ladder that led up to the attic. "Get up there," she snapped. My hands trembled as I gripped the ladder.

I climbed up and stuck my head through the opening. It was dusty and dark. "Where do I go?"

"Just crawl to the center, next to the post."

"You can't lock me up here," I protested.

She knocked the rifle against the ladder. "Get moving." Then, she slid the attic door closed and fastened the latch from below.

When my eyes adjusted to the dark, I made out a couple footlockers and boxes. I crawled to the attic door and slid the blade of my knife in the crack between the door and the floor, but the latch refused to budge. Then I crept to the side and hid my knife behind a crate in case they frisked me.

A while later—it could have been a half hour—I heard voices below me. Soon, the attic door opened. "C'mon down," a man said. I carefully stepped down the ladder. A broad-shouldered man wearing a green cap with shaggy red hair poking out from under it, stood at the bottom. Thelma sat at the kitchen table with the rifle lying in front of her.

"Sit down," he said and pointed to a wooden stool. "Who knows you're here?" I noticed he was missing a couple of teeth.

"No one except the two men who gave me rides..."

"I don't believe you."

"I'm just out here looking for work..."

He cut me off. "...so why'd you pick our camp? You're pretty far from home aren't you?"

I said nothing.

"He's a liar, Rusty," Thelma said. "He trailed Ned out here. Why else would he ask about the store?"

Rusty scratched his unshaven face. "Where's your home?"

"Detroit."

"When's your enlistment up?"

"This week."

Rusty thought a moment and then looked over at Thelma. "This boy's got to go back to camp or they'll be all over us."

Thelma shook her head. "Shouldn't we talk to Ned first?"

"Aw, hell, it'll take days to reach him."

"He's gonna squeal when he gets back." she said.

Rusty walked over to a spittoon in the corner and let loose some juice. "It don't matter...you and I'll be long gone."

Thelma made a pained expression. "For God's sake, I don't want to..."

"...it's that or the jailhouse."

She groaned, "Oh, I don't want to hit the road..."

Rusty thought a moment. "We'll sign the camp over to Marcos and Detlef. Marcos is the best timber man and Detlef can do the books."

Thelma raised her hands in exasperation. "For chrissakes, you just told the boy our plan."

Rusty slapped his forehead. "Aw, crap...sorry, Thelma." He walked back over and hit the spittoon from five feet out.

Thelma toyed with the gun and gave me a look to kill. "God-damned nosey kid..."

Rusty glowered at me. "You should've minded your own business."

"How long do we keep the boy?" Thelma asked.

"As soon as we're packed, we send him back."

"Where do we put him?"

Rusty scratched his neck and looked up at the attic. "I don't like him up there...I want him where I can see him."

"So?" she asked.

He thumped his hand on a support pole in the room. "I'll chain him to this."

Thelma stood up. "I'll get a lock." She handed Rusty the gun and went into the kitchen.

Rusty sized me up. "Can you do anything with your hands to keep busy?"

I nodded. “I can whittle and sew.”

“Good, you can patch up clothes.”

Thelma returned with a lock.

Rusty got up and moved to the door. “You watch him while I get some chain.”

My fingers grasped the edge of my stool while he was gone. Part of me wanted to pick it up and throw it at Thelma, but I figured Rusty would catch up to me if I escaped.

Rusty returned a short while later and wrapped a chain tightly around my ankle. He slipped a finger between the chain and my skin to give it a little slack. Then he fastened it with the lock and attached the chain to the pole with a second lock he brought. The chain, with inch-long links, stretched about five feet. Thelma laid a pile of pants and shirts by my side. Then she brought over a crude sewing basket. “Start working. I'll fetch you some grub,” she said. With that, they walked out the door and left me alone.

I tried to thread the needle, but it was impossible. My hands shook like the devil. All the excitement had left me shaken. In one way, I was relieved they planned to send me back to camp, but I wondered if I could believe them. The last person who got in their way was Thelma's husband. And the thought of what they did to him made the hair stand up on the back of my neck.

Thelma was good to her word and brought me a plate of liver and onions, which I only nibbled on. I spent the rest of the afternoon patching up shirts, dungarees, coats, and underwear that belonged to the loggers. I put the unwashed clothing at the top of the pile because it smelled so bad.

For supper, she brought me a plate of corned beef and cabbage. Thacker must have skimmed the CCC camp out of corned beef, too. After I ate, Rusty connected the chain to both of my feet to make leg irons and then he took me for a short walk to the outhouse. I carried the loose chain in my hands. Rusty brought his gun on the hike, he said we might run into a wolf. He must have thought I was an idiot.

That night, I read old issues of *Life* until it was time to go to bed. Rusty slid the couch over next to the support pole for me to sleep on. When they went off to their bedroom, the house became ghostly silent. The only sound came from the crackle of wood burning in the stove. I stretched out on the hard sofa and thought of Frank and the others. If they visited Hot Harry's like I told him to do, they would come up empty and probably go to the police. When the cop told them about Thacker, they should have the common sense to look for me in the camp. I hoped they acted fast.

The next day was Sunday. I spent the morning sewing clothes and took a short walk with Rusty. That afternoon, I was quietly working on a pair of dungarees, when he burst into the room. "Time for your afternoon walk," Rusty announced. It surprised me because he had just taken me to the outhouse a half hour earlier. He fumbled with the lock and undid the chain from the supporting pole.

He then made me push the couch back against the wall while he watched with the gun in hand. "Thelma's expecting visitors later today," he said. He led me out the kitchen door. For the next hour, we looked for porcupines to shoot. Rusty hated them. "They kill trees," he muttered as we paced through the young forest. The walk felt good, and it was warm enough to unbutton my coat.

I wondered who might be visiting on a Sunday afternoon. Then it dawned on me, the camp must have sent someone out to look for me! That would explain why he was in such a hurry and why he made the house look normal. I felt like a moron. I should have shouted for help when I had the chance! Rusty would not have dared shoot me in broad daylight with camp officers nearby. I hung my head as I stepped over the damp leaves in the woods. I blew a golden opportunity to escape. I consoled myself with the fact that they were on my trail.

That night after supper, Thelma and Rusty were strangely quiet, something was wrong. I was on the sofa reading magazines when Rusty came out of the bedroom. He undid the lock that held the chain to the support pole. I noticed Thelma at the supper table fingering the rifle.

"Put your other leg up," Rusty said from his crouched position. I raised my free leg up onto the sofa. He looped the free end of the chain around the other ankle to make leg irons.

"What's goin' on?" I asked.

He stood. "I'm taking you back to the camp tonight. Thelma and I are ready to hit the road." Rusty walked over to the closet, grabbed my coat and tossed it over to me.

My eyes darted around the living room. They had not moved a single thing since I arrived! The chest of drawers, the books on the shelves, the antlers on the wall, nothing had been touched. *He's lying, they're not leaving!*

Rusty put on a heavy coat and took the gun from his girlfriend. Then he picked up a box of bullets off the desk.

I felt anxious. "Why do you need a gun for if you're taking me back to camp," I said nearly shouting. "I'm in leg irons...I can't run away."

Rusty creased his brow. "I always carry one in case I hit a deer...I can put it out of its misery." He nodded to the door. I hobbled along holding the extra chain in my hands. I glanced over at Thelma, who followed my moves with no expression on her face. She said nothing as we walked out the door.

We stepped outside into the damp cold night. Rusty's lamp cast a soft glow as he led me through the woods to a woodpile where he parked his pickup. In the back of the truck, a large buzz saw stood out. He probably made a few bucks on the side cutting stove wood for people.

I climbed into the dank, musty-smelling cab and dropped the chains on the floor with a clank. Rusty drove slowly down a two-track keeping his distance from the camp buildings. We circled around and finally came to the trail that led out to the main road. A full moon stared down at us and lit up the woods and fields. We drove in silence.

I glanced over at Rusty. His arms were three times the size of mine. He would break me like a toothpick if I tried anything. The chain scraped across the floor, reminding me there was no chance of running away. My only option was to get my hands on his gun, which he stuck next to the buzz saw.

Rusty made a left turn onto the road that led back to Newberry. Soon, we were motoring along at forty miles an hour down the hard-packed dirt road.

"Why're you taking me back to camp so late?"

He curled his lip into a nasty sneer. "Shaddup."

Taking me back to camp made no sense. Something told me he had other plans for me. My throat dried out and I coughed nervously. I was ready to open the door and jump out of the truck the moment a car came our direction. But, the road was desolate, not a single car passed us in over ten minutes. Suddenly, Rusty slowed down and pulled onto the shoulder of the road. He turned off the engine and killed the lights. I took short quick breaths. *He's going to kill me...I know it!*

He stepped outside, grabbed the rifle and walked around to my side of the truck. He opened the door. "Get out," he barked.

I reached for my chains and slowly stepped out. When I saw what he held in his other hand, my knees went wobbly. He carried a shovel! *He's going to make me dig my own grave!*

Rusty pointed the rifle at me. "Now start walking," he said and motioned to the woods. I picked my feet up carefully through the brush holding the chain with one of my hands. With every step, the chains rattled. It would be suicide for me to run with the leg irons. I limped along with Rusty in silence. After about twenty minutes, he told me to stop. He pointed to a spot in a clearing and handed me the shovel. "Start digging," he said. Then he sat down on a nearby fallen log with the rifle across his knees.

I felt a hollow pit in my stomach as I stuck the shovel in the dirt. "Faster!" Rusty squawked. One after another, I scooped out shovelfuls of sandy soil and tossed them onto a pile. I glanced over and saw his bulky figure silhouetted in the light of the lamp.

"C'mon...keep it moving," he said. After an hour, the hole was a foot deep and about seven feet long. I stalled by making it longer and wider than necessary. Every time I came across a loose rock, I casually kicked it into the corner. The stones and the shovel were my only weapons.

Maybe I could soften him up. "So why'd Thacker do it?" I asked.

"Do what?"

"Steal stuff from camp..."

"None of your damn business."

I shoveled. "Why mess with me? Heck, you'd probably only get a few weeks in jail..."

"Shaddup and dig!"

I persisted. "They'll figure out that you..."

He cut me off. "SHADDUP!"

Rusty struck a match and lit a pipe. Over the next hour or so, I took the hole down another foot. The rock pile grew to a dozen fist-size stones. Rusty walked over with the lantern and gun. He peered into the hole and pointed the rifle at me. "Back up," he said. "Get out..." He jumped into the hole and tossed the rocks out, one by one keeping an eye on me the whole time.

After he climbed out, he motioned with his rifle. "Start diggin'—and no more funny business." Then he returned to the log.

A few minutes later, I heard a strange cracking noise in the woods. I stopped and listened. It sounded like a tree branch snapped. Rusty heard it too and stood up. CRACK!

It was a stone hitting a tree! Arky must be near! BAMM, BAMM, BAMM! Rusty fired blindly in the direction where the stone came from.

I dropped down on my knees in the grave. I thought of running for it, but the leg-irons would slow me down too much. I slid a finger under the chain and tried to slide it over my ankle. *If I could only get these damn leg-irons off!* Another stone slammed into a tree. Rusty knelt behind a large stump about thirty feet away from me and took aim at Arky. BAMM, BAMM! *He's got Arky pinned behind a tree!*

"Don't even think of running," Rusty shouted over at me.

Who needed to run? Maybe I could crawl. I slowly crept out of the hole on my stomach and waited for him to start firing again.

Just then, I saw what looked like a sparkler flying through the air. *Jesus Christ, it's dynamite!* The stick fell between Rusty and me. I rolled back into the hole and landed with a thud.

"Hit the dirt, Nick!" *It's Frank!* I covered my ears and turned my back toward the dynamite.

A few seconds later...KABOOM! I felt the shock of the blast through the ground and flinched. A terrific explosion sent up a cloud of dirt and debris that fell like rain. My ears rang. A cloud of dust settled over the grave. I got up on my hands and knees, hacking. *Now's my chance!* I began crawling out of the hole and was about fifteen feet away, when I heard a voice. "Where do you think you're going?" I froze. "Stand up." I felt a hand on my coat yank me up. Rusty positioned me between himself and Arky. *He's using me as a shield!* "Start walkin'," he said.

I grabbed my chains and shuffled slowly toward Arky. "Run, Arky!" I yelled.

"Shaddup," he jammed the butt of his gun into my shoulder, causing me to stumble to the ground. He pulled me up by the arm. "Get up," he growled.

I continued hobbling with the chain in my hand when,

out of the corner of my eye, I saw a blurry movement close to the ground. ARF, ARF! Agnes ran straight for Rusty and latched onto his leg. Thacker raised the gun and took aim at the pint-sized dog. I shuffled quickly, jumped and collided with Rusty square in the chest. BAMM! The gun went off and we both tumbled down to the ground.

The gun landed a few feet away and Rusty made a move for it. I crawled onto his back and grabbed his right arm to slow him down. He was too strong, it felt like I was riding the back of a giant turtle. I needed help. "WHERE ARE YOU GUYS!" I screamed. Agnes tugged at his pant leg, but it did little to slow him down.

Rusty had his left hand on the gun and was shaking me off with his other arm when I heard Frank yell, "We're coming!" I held onto Rusty's arm with all of my might and kept my head on his back so he couldn't punch me. I breathed in the dust from the back of his coat and gagged. Just then, I felt another body thump down next to me. Rusty grunted.

"You bastard," Frank growled. He put Rusty in a headlock and squeezed so hard the logger squeaked.

I saw some legs running by. Somebody scooped up the rifle.

"I got the gun!" José yelled.

Frank pinned Rusty to the ground and I rolled off gasping for air. "It's all over, pal," Frank muttered. Rusty met his match with Frank.

Arky ran up and took the gun from José. He cocked it. "I got 'im, Frank," he said. "You can get up."

Frank held Rusty by the arm and pulled him up. "Gimme your belt," he told me. He took it and tied Rusty's arms behind his back.

Agnes jumped up on my leg. "Easy girl, I should have known you'd find me." She wagged her tail like crazy.

I limped back to get my coat and Rusty's lantern while the others waited. I turned. "Hey, I need the key for these locks," I told Rusty.

Frank twisted Rusty's arm. "Don't try anything funny."

I came back, stuck my hand in Rusty's coat pocket and groped around until I felt a metal ring with keys. The fellas waited while I undid the chains.

"Better bring 'em," Frank said. "That's evidence."

Then the five of us headed back to the road with the aid of Arky's compass. The moon was higher in the sky and lit up the woods.

Frank walked by Rusty's side while Arky followed behind us with the gun. Rusty scowled so mean he would have scared a bear away if one crossed our path.

"Geez, I couldn't hit the side of a barn with a bag of rice if I tried," Arky joked.

"That's okay—you did your job," I said. "How'd you guys find me?"

"Agnes," José said. "We brought one of your shoes to give her the scent."

"The cop told us about Thacker," Frank said. "We came up this afternoon with the sergeant, but couldn't find you."

"He took me out in the woods when you came." I said. "So why'd you come back tonight?"

"We knew you were out there…" Frank said.

"…but the sarge told us to wait until tomorrow," José added.

I smiled. "No kidding…"

"Yeah, we figured you were in hot water." José said.

I smiled. "You guessed that right…"

"We got Turk to hot wire a car," José said.

"How'd you know it was a camp truck?" I asked.

"I remembered seeing the truck with the buzz saw by the wood pile," Frank said.

"That saved me," I said.

"When I saw it, I figured he was gonna slice you up like salami," Frank joked. The guys laughed.

"Thanks a lot," I said. "Where's Turk, anyway?"

"We sent him to get the police after he dropped us off," José said.

I walked lamely through the woods, my ankles still sore from the chain. "I can't believe all the trouble you guys went to."

"Yeah, what ever happened to your *simple* plan?" Frank said.

I ignored him. "What took you guys so long to help me after the dynamite went off?

"We heard the gun and thought he shot you...so we hid." José said.

"Yeah, we figured we were next," Frank added.

We walked up a gentle slope. I breathed in deeply. The fresh tangy scent of pine trees filled the air.

"What made you think you could get away with it?" Arky asked Rusty.

Rusty said nothing as he plodded along with slouched shoulders. "Leave him alone," Frank said. "He'll have plenty of time to stew about it in jail."

"How'd you get Agnes out of the sarge's office?" I asked.

"We had Squirt crawl through his window and grab her," José said. "We held him by the legs...we almost dropped him."

I leaned over and patted the beagle. "I'm going to find you a nice meaty bone when we get back."

We walked another five minutes and then saw the lights of a police car through the trees. "The cops are here!" José said.

"First time I ever wanted to see a cop," Arky said.

"Hey, you never told us...why'd they hold onto you?" Frank asked. "Their store didn't have a darn thing from our camp."

"It was *full* of CCC stuff...they must've emptied it," I said. "Thacker even cut them in on the corned beef."

"You're as crooked as a bedspring," Arky taunted Rusty.

"Aw shaddup," he growled. The rest of us laughed as we walked up the slope to the road.

"Here's your man, officer," Frank said, and gave him a quick rundown on what happened. I recognized the cop. He handcuffed Rusty and then put him in his car.

After they drove off, the five of us climbed into the Dodge sedan the guys came in, and headed back to camp. It was almost one o'clock. I sat in the back with Agnes resting her head on my lap. Turk drove. "Damn...I missed all the fun!" he said.

After we filled Turk in with the details, things quieted down in the car. I stared out at the passing woods as we drove along the desolate road. I wondered what went wrong with Rusty and Thelma's plan to go on the lam. I figured their plan to turn the camp over to the two fellas didn't work out for some reason. I gave up trying to make sense of it all and soon fell asleep.

When we arrived in camp, I heard a voice. "Time to get up, Nick, we're here." I slowly opened my eyes and saw Frank in the dim light of the car. Agnes still slept with her head on my lap.

"Let's go, girl," I said and gave her a gentle push. We got out of the car, and I dragged myself wearily up to the barracks. Soon, I was under my sheets and fell asleep, exhausted.

When I opened my eyes in the morning, I thought I was dreaming. *I'm back in camp!* I never knew the inside of the barracks could look so good. Another boy covered for me in the officers' mess hall so I ate breakfast with the other guys. Word spread quickly about what happened and I took a lot of razzing.

After breakfast, I reported to the captain's office, where he and Mr. Mulligan grilled me on the chain of events that followed after I skipped clean-up duty. A clerk took notes in the corner.

The captain shook his head again and again, as I recounted my story in detail for an hour or so. "I thought I'd heard it all," he said when I finished. "So tell me...why'd you do it? You took a terrible risk going out like that all by yourself."

I looked him in eye. "I didn't want the camp to close, sir. The guys can get transferred, but the cooks, L.E.M.s and others would lose your jobs."

He pursed his lips and nodded slowly.

I looked over at the sergeant. "Do you think the camp will stay open?"

He spoke tight-lipped. "If the captain and I have anything to say about it, it will."

"That'd be great," I said.

"So why didn't you just come to me when you suspected Thacker?" the sergeant asked.

"I had no evidence. I'd already accused him of stealing that c-clamp and overcharging me on clothes and got nowhere...I figured you'd think it was just a case of sour grapes."

The sergeant spoke softly. "You're right...that's probably what I would have thought."

"I'm sorry for all the trouble I caused."

The captain closed my folder and reached for his pipe. "I'm not going to waste your time with a lecture. What you did was dangerous. You took matters into your own hands. Right or wrong, the camp can't excuse your actions."

"I understand, sir."

"You put me in a difficult position," the captain said and leaned forward. "You did a great service to the camp, and it might even keep us open for another year or two, but you'll have to be discharged."

I nodded.

He studied me for a moment. "The best I can do is try to get you an honorable discharge, but I can't promise anything."

"Thank you, sir."

Mr. Mulligan spoke. "You were very brave...we're just glad you came back in one piece."

"Thank you, sir."

He gave me a wry smile. "I've seen a lot of boys come and go, but I've never had anyone cause as much trouble as you."

I bit my lower lip.

The sergeant continued, "But then again, I can't remember anyone I've more enjoyed working with. We'll all miss you and wish you success in life."

"Thank you, sir. Can I ask a question?"

The captain nodded.

"The guys who helped me escape...can they stay?"

The captain nodded. "Yes, but they'll be punished for breaking camp rules."

"And Thacker?"

"He's going to jail for a while." The captain pushed his chair back and stood. "Have a safe trip home."

I got up. "Sir, I'm not going home. *This* is my home. I'm just going back to the place where I came from."

The captain tightened his jaw and nodded.

"Good luck, Nick," Mr. Mulligan said. "I hope things go well with the visit to your father."

"Thank you, sir." I turned and stepped out the door. The gray overcast day reminded me of my first day in camp. After a quick stop in the barracks, I hurried to the mess hall to help train the new boy who had taken over my position. It was my last day in camp and I had many friends to say good-bye to.

Chapter 11

Farewell

The next morning I awoke at five to serve the officers their breakfast. The new mess orderly let me go through my normal routine one more time. After I set the table, I went into the officers' quarters and gently shook each of their shoulders to let them know it was first call. Then, I returned fifteen minutes later and quietly said, "Second call, sir, second call." When I returned the third time, I departed from my usual announcement. Getting up my courage, I yelled, "Come and get it...or I'm throwing the stuff out!" The officers laughed at my joke.

After I served their breakfast, the captain tapped his glass for silence. "Most of you know that Nick is leaving today. This is a good time to let him know what a fine job he's done for us."

For the next few minutes, each officer complimented me on my work. Some thanked me for knowing just when to refill their coffee and remembering how they liked their food served. One of them brought up the story of the scythe, and another commended my work on the mantle carving.

I stood and listened, embarrassed by all the praise. I never received so much attention in my life. They all knew I broke the camp rules, yet they still praised me. Their words choked me up.

"Well, Nick, do you have anything to say?" the captain asked when the men finished.

I cleared my throat and looked out at the twenty or so forest and conservation officers dressed in green uniforms. Half of them were just out of college for a few years. "You're the finest group of men I ever worked for. You taught me a lot of things. You were patient when I screwed up...you gave me lots of second chances...and I made a lot of friends. I'll miss all you guys, but I'm sure not going to miss getting up at five in the morning." The officers chuckled. It felt good leaving on a happy note.

I turned the mess hall back over to the new orderly and headed to the barracks. The quad was a beehive of activity with boys scurrying around. Everyone needed to pack, take care of paperwork and turn in his bedding. When I dropped off a couple of carving tools in the equipment room, I found a group boys crowded around Isaac. I smiled when I saw him. He wore a new pair of dungarees with a green plaid shirt. Isaac's hair looked neatly trimmed and he was clean-shaven, but the biggest change was the smile on his face. Isaacs's new teeth shone like pearls.

He saw me. "I've been looking fer ya, Nick!" He pulled an object out of a canvas bag and handed it to me—it was a small wooden owl, the size of a baseball. He had carved the bird in fine detail, showing off the layered feathers.

I rolled it around in my hands and passed it to the others to look at. "This is beautiful...I love it," I said.

"You be like da wise owl," he said.

"Heck...no one's smarter than you," I said. I gave him a pat on the back. "Now, don't go breaking a lot of hearts with that new smile of yours."

"Oh, no...not me," he said. The boys laughed. I hurried back to the barracks, where the guys quizzed me about my adventure in Pine Stump Junction. After I put on my winter uniform, I folded up my bedding and mess uniforms and returned them to the supply room. Then I packed my locker and carried it to the loading platform. The area was crowded with guys saying good-bye to their friends.

I felt a hand on my shoulder—it was Frank. "Be sure to write about your dad."

"Sure...hey, you need to find *your* dad."

"Aw, I don't have a chance."

I reached down and undid the chain to my rabbit's foot. "Take this...it'll help."

Frank looked surprised. "I can't take that."

"Just take it," I said and put the rabbit's foot in his hand. "It didn't help me find my father...Mr. Wells did."

He looked puzzled. "Huh?"

"Ask him about the Great Spirit sometime...."

"Sure...the Great Spirit. Whatever you say."

Arky walked up looking gloomy. "Who am I gonna rescue when you go, dang it?"

"Keep that slingshot handy," I said, "you'll find someone."

Turk pushed his way through the boys. "Hey Nick, can you spot me a dime for some smokes?"

"You're kidding, right?"

He grinned, "Yeah..."

"If you're looking for work when you get out of camp, look me up. A guy with your talents can easily find a job."

"Huh? What kinda job?"

"Hot wiring cars...I know some gangs that can use you."

"Funny, very funny," he said.

A few minutes later, Elliot showed up with a paper sack. "Here's something for your trip," he said and gave it to me.

"Let me guess...peanut butter sandwiches?" I asked. He nodded. "Stay away from the moose, Elliot."

He grinned and pushed his glasses up his nose. "We're gonna miss you...don't forget those meat patrols we did."

I smiled. "Are you joking? I *get sick* every time I think of those meat runs."

I heard a dog barking and saw Agnes and José work their way through the guys. I knelt and stroked her head.

"Did you come to say good-bye, too?" I looked up at José. "Take good care of her when I'm gone."

"Sure, Nick," he said with a sad face.

"And be safe with that dynamite...don't go throwing it around at people, someone might get hurt."

He smiled and nodded.

It felt awkward saying good-bye to the best friends I ever made. We worked together, ate together, slept in the same room and suffered the same punishments. I made more friends in a year than in all the other years of my life.

As I stepped up onto the loading platform, a curly haired boy I didn't recognize came up and said, "I'm really sorry you're leaving, Nick."

"Hey, thanks," I said. It seemed like everybody in the camp was your friend, even if you didn't know his name.

Scruggs checked us in as we stepped onto the truck. "Don't go picking fights now that I turned you into a first-rate boxer," he joked.

I gave him a half smile. "Thanks for everything, coach." We shook hands. Then I squeezed between a couple boys on the long seat in the truck. A minute later, the truck started up. I looked out the back and watched the fellas who were staying behind cheer and wave good-bye. I never felt sadder in my life.

The truck passed through the gate and I watched the buildings fade from sight. I leaned back and reflected on the people I had met in camp. I learned that little guys like Squirt were big enough to be a hero in times of danger and that bullies were not always what they seemed to be. I discovered how far people would go to help the ones they loved, like the boy who took stale cereal to his family. And I learned that when people were depressed, they needed extra attention.

I thought about the staff, like Mr. Kiefer, Curly, and Isaac. They were all the best at what they did, and made my time special in camp. Chaplain Schultz inspired me with his stories, and Mr. Wells helped me look at the world in a new light. Mr. Mulligan surprised me the most. He punished me harshly during my first months at camp, but still promoted me to mess orderly. By the end of my enlistment, he was like a father to me.

The long faces I saw on the truck said it all. The CCC was more to all of us than just a paycheck. It gave us an escape from The Great Depression. It was "a new deal." Just as boxers needed a rest between rounds to catch their breath, the CCC gave us a break from a harsh world. Along with hard work, we learned responsibility, discipline, and self-reliance.

About twenty minutes into the ride, a few of the boys in the rear of the truck started rocking up and down. After a minute of this mischief, I felt the truck slow to a stop. We heard the front door open and waited for the driver to chew us out. Squirt came around the rear and gave us a hard look, with his hands on his hips. In his thin voice, he let us have it. "If you guys want to get out and walk to Trout Lake...just keep on rocking." He returned to the cab.

Someone yelled, "That's telling 'em, Stanley!"

The guys cracked up. Most of us were old enough to go into the army, but we were still boys at heart. I unwrapped one of the sandwiches that Elliot gave me. I chewed it slowly, savoring my last camp food. I found a pickle in the bag. I looked at it and smiled to myself. "Hey, who wants my pickle?" I gave it to the boy next to me.

After I ate, I took out a bear carving from my gunnysack. It was a gift for Mr. Mulligan. I turned the bear over in my hand and studied it. The head was a bit too small for the body and one leg was longer then the other, but it didn't matter. I would remember the First Sergeant as a bear of a man, a gentle giant.

The truck pulled up to the little brick depot and we unloaded. With some time to kill, I took out my dad's old baseball mitt and tossed a ball with a couple of guys. Suddenly, I realized my hand had grown large enough to fit snugly into the glove. For years, my hand slipped around loosely inside, but the hard work in camp made them stronger and bigger. I smiled to myself as I tossed the ball. *I've got Dad's hands—I've got the hands of a man!*

"Clang, clang, clang." I looked up and saw a train slowly approaching. When it stopped, the porter slid open the doors to the luggage car, and the fellas lifted the footlockers up to him.

I stood in line to board, with my gunnysack slung over my shoulder. Mr. Mulligan checked off the names on his clipboard as the company clerk called the names aloud. The clerk told me that he got the job because he could pronounce all the Polish names.

"Radzinski," he called when my turn came. I handed the clerk the bear carving and told him to give it to the sergeant after we pulled out. He nodded and set it on a ledge.

I took a deep breath and walked up to the train car. The sergeant pressed his lips tightly together; his face seemed full of emotion.

"Sorry for the trouble I caused you, sir," I said.

He gave me a look of disbelief. "Trouble? What are you talking about?

"Well..."

"Forget it. And what's this *sir* stuff?"

I smiled. "Thanks for everything, Pops."

He forced a smile. "That's more like it." He put his hand on my shoulder and gently squeezed. "It's time to go, son."

I felt my eyes get misty as I stepped up into the train. I threw my gunnysack onto the rack and found a seat. With my face up close to the window, I watched the sergeant check off the rest of the guys. A few minutes later, the ticket master walked along the train, checking the doors.

The train car jerked and we slowly pulled out of the station. Mr. Mulligan leaned against a support pole and watched us. He took a handkerchief out of his back pocket as if to blow his nose, but instead, he wiped his eyes. I felt my own tears flow as I watched him. I wondered why he was so special...why he was like a father to so many boys. Then it came to me. Mr. Mulligan was like the father in the story of the prodigal son. When a boy paid his dues, the sergeant forgot about it and moved on. He was *hard*, but he was *fair*. It took me six months to see that, but I did, just as the others in camp did. I thought about how many guys came into the CCC without a dad and how the sergeant and other officers filled that spot in their lives.

The station disappeared from view, and I turned away from the window. I did not want to leave, but maybe it was my time to go. Perhaps I had learned all that I needed to learn from the experience, and it was time for another boy to take my place. In a couple days, a mother would bring her son to a train station for his first big trip away from home. The boy would be a bundle of nerves when he first arrived at camp, but in time, he would settle in.

I took out a piece of stationery. Betty deserved a letter as soon as possible. We never had the chance to say good-bye. I thought about what to say as I gazed out the window. The logged-over forest that had once looked so ominous and strange, now gave me warm feelings and happy memories.

Dear Betty,

I am writing to you from a train. From my window, I look over rivers, forests, and fields...but I see only you. I'm leaving camp and will not be coming back. Something happened that I don't want to talk about. I made a choice to do something I believed in and it got me in trouble. I regret that I had to leave in such a hurry.

You will always have a little piece of my heart.

Sometimes I think about living in the Soo, but I know it's best that I help out my mom for now and live at home. You'll be going to college soon, and I know you'll be the prettiest girl on campus. You will be a wonderful teacher someday.

If I ever get back up in these parts, I will try to look you up. If you are ever in Detroit and want to see a Tigers game, I know where the best seats are. Maybe I can introduce you to Hank Greenberg. I will always remember our happy times together.

Love,
Nick

I folded the letter and slipped it into an envelope. The train hugged the shoreline of a small lake. I watched a swan fly in for a soft landing. It reminded me of Betty, so graceful and beautiful. From my worn leather wallet, I pulled out a small photo she gave me. I traced her face with my finger and smiled. How I loved her laugh. Nothing in the world mattered when she was beside me.

I put the photo away and pulled out my baseball mitt. The leather felt soft and pliable in my hands. The smell took me back to my childhood days. I wondered if my dad could toss a ball with me went I visited him in Pennsylvania. I bet he would love to put the old glove on one more time. Seeing my dad was the best thing I could do to get my mind off Betty and the camp.

Dad might not recognize me, but it hardly mattered. I just wanted to give him a pat on the back and tell him I loved him. The insurance money was a bonus, but incidental. It would let my mother move into a better home and buy some new furniture that she deserved, but it would not change my life. I still needed to find a job.

I leaned back in my seat and closed my eyes. The gentle rocking of the train relaxed me. In my mind's eye, I saw myself swinging in the trees with Frank, hanging on a rope from a pulley, flying through the air from tree to tree like two kids. I smiled. The future was unpredictable, but one thing I knew for sure, my days of stealing shoes were over. I always was a lousy crook, and I had no plans on changing that.

THE END